KISSING THE MARQUIS

"My lord?" queried Constance, her eyelids drifting open to reveal eyes dark and vulnerable with yearning. "What is it? Why have you stopped?"

Indeed, thought Vere, why *was* he vacillating—he, who had never before denied himself of a woman's proffered pleasures? She wanted him as much as he did her. Who the bloody hell was he to disappoint her?

"The devil, Miss Landford," he rasped, "you tempt me too far." Clasping his hands about her willowy waist, he lifted her without warning to the writing table. Spreading her knees apart, he inserted himself between them. "And now I think I must have you."

"An excellent notion, my lord," gasped Constance, who, despite the fact that she could not but think it long past time that he came to precisely that conclusion, was nevertheless more than a trifle startled to find herself perched on the edge of an oak desk with the marquis between her thighs.

It was not quite the way she had envisioned events when she had imagined herself in the role of Vere's in-amorata. But then he pressed his lips to the side of her neck as his fingers busied themselves with undoing the tiny pearl buttons at the back of her bodice, one after the other, and suddenly it came to her with a thrill of anticipation that things were precisely the way she should have imagined them . . .

Books by Sara Blayne

Published by Zebra Books

MARRYING THE MARQUIS

Sara Blayne

ZEBRA BOOKS
KENSINGTON PUBLISHING CORP.
http://www.kensingtonbooks.com

ZEBRA BOOKS are published by

Kensington Publishing Corp.
850 Third Avenue
New York, NY 10022

All Kensington titles, imprints and distributed lines are
available at special quantity discounts for bulk purchases
for sales promotion, premiums, fund-raising, educational or
institutional use.

Special book excerpts or customized printings can also be
created to fit specific needs. For details, write or phone the
office of the Kensington Special Sales Manager: Kensington
Publishing Corp., 850 Third Avenue, New York, NY 10022.
Attn. Special Sales Department. Phone: 1-800-221-2647.

Zebra and the Z logo Reg. U.S. Pat. & TM Off.

First Printing: October 2004
10 9 8 7 6 5 4 3 2 1

Printed in the United States of America

To Mike and Arnie Holder,
with my thanks and good wishes.
And a special thanks to Kathryn, my dearly loved friend
and daughter, without whose help I could not
have finished this manuscript.

Prologue

England had had her fair share of brigands, smugglers, and thieves long before Mr. Royce Wilmet laid his plans in Wells to make off with Miss Letitia Chadmore, the daughter of an East Indian nabob. There were recorded, for example, the colorful exploits of John "Nicks" Nevison, who was a well-known highwayman in the time of Charles II. He was, in fact, reputed to have ridden from Gad's Hill to York, a distance of one hundred ninety miles, in a mere fifteen hours in order to provide himself with an alibi. And there was Dick Turpin, of course, a deer-thief and smuggler who joined the infamous Tom King in robbing coaches until Turpin gallantly shot and killed his partner to prevent King's capture. Turpin himself was nabbed some little time later for the crime of horse stealing and met his demise on the gibbet in 1739. Perhaps most notorious of all, however, was Jack Sheppard, who not only bragged that he robbed nearly everyone who had the misfortune to cross his path, but had the dubious distinction as well of having escaped Newgate Prison, not once but twice, to evade execution. Aided in the first escape by his accomplice, Edgeworth Bess, he accomplished the second on his own and in spite of being chained to the floor of his cell. No doubt he might have gone on to achieve ever greater notoriety in the pursuit of his chosen profession in crime had he not had the temerity to return to his old haunts in Drury Lane. There he was reapprehended while three sheets to the wind and summarily hanged at Tyburn on November 16, 1724, just short of his twenty-second birthday. The latest scion of that long line of highwaymen, however, promised fair to outstrip all the others in sheer audacity, not to mention the originality of his *modus operandi*.

Perhaps it was only happenstance and not the work of the devil, as some were fond of theorizing, that ordained that Mr. Royce Wilmet should choose to take one particular road out of Wells on one particularly fateful night. Certainly, when he brought Miss Chadmore foolishly to agree to steal out for a moonlight tryst, only to bundle her unceremoniously onto the seat of his curricle, the farthest thing from Wilmet's mind was to discover his way blocked at the crossroads less than a mile from town by a sinister figure obscured in black garb and astride an ebony steed. Miss Chadmore herself was later moved to assert that Mr. Wilmet, far from looking forward to the possibility of being waylaid by a highwayman, had been rather more preoccupied with what might be approaching from behind him—as well he might. Miss Chadmore, after all, was not only her doting father's only daughter, but she was in possession as well of four exceedingly fond older brothers. Mr. Wilmet, taken by surprise, had little recourse but to hold to, precisely as he was ordered to do.

"Take my purse and be damned, you thieving bastard," growled Wilmet, flinging the aforementioned article at the highwayman's head.

The masked man's left hand flashed up and with unerring accuracy plucked the purse out of the air. "You may be sure I sold my soul to the devil long ago," drawled the bandit, kneeing his mount closer to the carriage. "You, however, are proving an embarrassment to your lady. I suggest you watch your language in her presence."

"I am *not* his lady!" exclaimed Miss Chadmore with every manifestation of unadulterated loathing. "Mr. Wilmet has abducted me against my will."

"You two-faced little baggage," snarled Wilmet, his expression exceedingly ugly. "You will hold your tongue if you know what is good for you."

"*Enough!*" Wilmet went deathly still, his face singularly ashen, as he found himself staring down the bore of a pistol aimed with unswerving precision at a point midway between his eyebrows. "I warned you to mind your tongue in front of the lady. Obviously, however, you are undeserving of further consideration. What would you have me do with him, miss?" he inquired of Miss Chadmore. "I shall summarily dispose of him if you but give me the word."

"No, dear me, no. As much as I have come to despise him, I should not wish his—his demise on my conscience," Miss Chadmore breathed, a hand pressed to her throat around which sparkled a magnificent diamond-and-ruby necklace. "Mr. Jonas Chadmore, my father, will reward you handsomely if you will but return me to him, sir."

"Then so be it," declared the highwayman, bringing his mount alongside the carriage. "Your wish is naturally my command."

"I shall see you in hell for this," declared Wilmet, red-faced, as, helplessly, he beheld the female whom he so recently had seen as the means of his attaining a more than comfortable existence allow herself to be pulled to a seat across the front of the bandit's saddle.

"I should not be at all surprised," murmured the highwayman with chilling deliberation. "You, however, will undoubtedly be there before me. I suggest you do not return to Wells. If you dare so much as to accost this lady again, I shall find you. Further, you may be certain

I shall not be inclined to treat you with mercy a second time."

Wilmet, meeting the pale gleam of the masked man's eyes in the moonlight, blanched to a sickly hue.

"Quite so," agreed the highwayman and fired his pistol into the air.

Wilmet's pair bolted in fright. Upon which, Wilmet, borne with precarious haste around the bend in the road, found himself relieved, not only of his purse, but of his prospective bride as well.

Miss Letitia Chadmore, nestled in the arms of the highwayman, on the other hand, strangely did not entertain the least fear that she might have leapt from the frying pan into the fire. To the contrary, she found that she liked it very well where she was. Nor did it once, during that gentle ride back to the house in Wells to which her father had recently retired, come to her to think that she had made a poor bargain. Lost in the unfamiliar sensations engendered by the security of having a firm arm about her shoulders and her cheek nestled against a hard, masculine chest, she felt rather as if she had fallen into the grandest, most romantical adventure of her entire life. Indeed, it was to occur to her some little time later, as her rescuer pulled his mount to a halt in the mews at the back of her father's house, that her midnight ride in the arms of a captain moonlight had come far too soon to an end.

She was to report later to her eager feminine confidantes that a distinct thrill positively shot through her as, dismounting, the highwayman reached up to close strong hands about her waist. Indeed, she had felt most peculiarly mesmerized by his manly strength as he lifted her from the saddle and lowered her to the ground as easily as if she were a mere child. She was wont ever afterwards to say with a singularly dreamy expression on her lovely face that she had had the strangest sensation of having been transported to some enchanted place all silvery with moonglow as, tucking her hand in the crook of his arm, her captain moonlight escorted her through the iron gate into the rose garden and thence to the French doors through which she had stolen only two hours earlier.

"You are safe now, child," observed her rescuer, halting in the deep shadows beneath an arched trellis teeming with roses in full bloom. "I trust in future you will think twice before allowing yourself to fall victim to the wiles of an adventurer. You may not be so fortunate to escape unscathed a second time."

"You may be certain that I have learned my lesson," replied Miss Chadmore, her heart behaving in a most ridiculous manner beneath her breast as she gazed up into eyes that held her spellbound. "Your gallantry has placed me in your debt, sir. My father will wish to reward you for saving his only daughter from scandal and a fate worse than death. How shall we find you?"

"You will not," replied the captain, reaching behind Miss Chadmore's ear and bringing forth a perfect red rose seemingly out of thin air. "Nor is it necessary," he added, presenting the flower to the startled young beauty. "You may be certain I have already been well paid." Bending over her hand with a flourish, he gallantly saluted her knuckles. "I bid you farewell, Miss Chadmore. Pray go inside before you are missed."

Before Miss Chadmore could voice the protest that rose to her lips, her mysterious highwayman had turned with a swirl of his black cloak and melted into the shadows back the way they had come.

As the sound of hoofbeats receded into the night, Miss Chadmore was left staring into the darkness into which her captain moonlight had vanished. With a sigh, she raised the flower to her nose to inhale its sweet scent, then, turning, she entered the house.

It was not until she reached her room and stood before the ormolu looking glass that she realized her diamond-and-ruby necklace was gone from about her throat.

"The sly devil!" she exclaimed, a smile of enlightenment breaking across her lovely face. She had never felt a thing when he released the clasp and slipped the necklace from her! Then, hugging the rose to her breast, she twirled gaily about the bedchamber before flinging herself, laughing, across her bed. Never had she had a more splendid adventure. Indeed, she could not wait to share all the delectable details with Miss Mary Inglethorpe, her bosom bow.

First, however, she sternly reminded herself, she must tell her mama and papa everything. They must not blame her gallant captain moonlight for the loss of her necklace. That, she told herself, was his just reward for having saved her from the machinations of a fortune hunter.

It was to develop in the following weeks, as the highwayman garbed all in black continued to add to his growing reputation, that more than one romantically inclined young woman of fashion was to share Miss Chadmore's sentiment. A bauble or two was but a small price to pay, after all, for the privilege of being robbed by a highwayman who had the distinction of being rendered thrillingly attractive by the mystique that had come to surround him. There was little doubt that he had the manner of a gentleman of breeding, and certainly he was a man of magnetic charm and sinister fascination, who made it a practice to treat his feminine victims with a deference that they could not but find irresistible. His habit of dressing impeccably all in black, in addition to his custom of leaving a single, perfect rose in his wake, had made him a figure of interest as far away as the fashionable salons of London. He was the Black Rose, and speculation was running rife as to his true identity.

It was little wonder, then, that Lady Constance Landford, upon being stopped en route from Wells to her

family estate outside of Bridgwater one December afternoon, stared with no little bestartlement into eyes which
were not only a most peculiarly mesmerizing blue, but
were also distinctly and unmistakably familiar to her.
They were, after all, the eyes of the Marquis of Vere, her
father's sworn enemy!

Constance's heart leapt beneath her breast. But then,
even though she had only a passing acquaintance with
his lordship—indeed, had had occasion to view him up
close only once before—she was all too aware of the bad
blood between their fathers. In truth, she could not but
think that Blaidsdale had behaved in a less than admirable
manner when he presented gambling markers to a be-
reaved son only days after the loss of his father, especially
as the debt had apparently taken a goodly portion of
Vere's inheritance from him.

"How dare you stop my coach, sir," declared Constance,
choosing not to betray that she knew his identity out of
some vague impulse that she did not fully understand.
"Indeed, it is most ungentlemanly of you."

"Then naturally I must beg your pardon, my lady,"
drawled the highwayman, leaving little doubt that he
recognized her as well, the devil! Very likely he took
special pleasure in robbing the Earl of Blaidsdale's daughter. "I promise I shall require no more of your time than
it takes you to hand over your purse and the brooch you
are wearing."

Constance, who until that moment had been enjoying her unlooked-for adventure, could not quite stifle a
gasp of dismay at that final pronouncement.

"Then I fear, sir, that you are going to be disappointed.
This brooch is all that I have left by which to remember
my mother. She gave it to me shortly before she died."

"And now you will give it to me, fair lady, that *I* may
have something by which to remember *you*," said the
highwayman, odiously smiling. Clearly, he did not believe her, the rogue, thought Constance, marveling that

his previous victims had thought him in the least gallant.

"No doubt you will remember me well enough as one who refused to do your bidding, sir," retorted Constance, her eyes flashing dangerously. "You may take my purse if you will, but you will not have my mother's brooch."

"As a gentleman, I should naturally prefer not to dispute the word of a lady," declared the devil. Slipping his pistol into his belt, he dismounted with supple grace. "If not the brooch, then I really must have something else."

Constance's breath caught in her throat as, with a single, swift stride forward, the villain reached out and pulled the coach door open. Faith, things were not proceeding at all as she might have been led to expect from the tales going the rounds of the ladies' salons. But then the Black Rose, as it turned out, had little cause to feel generosity toward one connected to the house of Landford.

"I beg your pardon," gasped Constance, confused by the sudden racing of her pulse at sight of his long, lithe form at exceedingly close range. Faith, but he was a magnificent specimen of manhood. It was little wonder that his earlier victims had nearly swooned at the sight of him!

Constance Landford, however, was made of sterner stuff. She would rather die than let the arrogant marquis see that he had so much as rattled her composure.

Hardly had that thought crossed her mind than the Black Rose, clasping powerful hands about her waist, lifted her bodily out of the coach.

"How dare you lay hands on me!" Constance exclaimed, as he set her on her feet. She would have pointed out that he was no gentleman and that, further, if he did not unhand her at once, she would not hesitate to publicize that the mysterious Black Rose was far from being a mystery to her.

No doubt she *would* have done, that was, had not the villain chosen that moment to cover her mouth with his.

It was a curiously gentle kiss, which, though stolen, was neither an assault on her innocence nor an insult to her womanhood. Nevertheless, she was hardly prepared to experience a melting pang pierce her through in the vicinity of her midsection and spread to her lower extremities, which immediately threatened to buckle beneath her.

When he released her lips, she was left feeling somewhat dazed and not a little bemused. Indeed, she could only regret exceedingly that the purloined kiss had had so soon to end. Breathing a sigh, she dreamily opened her eyes to find the Black Rose staring down at her with a strange, fixed intensity.

"You kissed me," she said, moved somehow to state the obvious.

She was rewarded for her absurdity with the faintest of smiles, which had the curiously devastating effect of softening the hard glitter of his eyes.

"Yes, that is more like it," he said, lightly flicking the tip of her nose with the side of his index finger. "Now, away home with you." The next instant, he was lifting her back onto her seat in the coach.

"But, wait," exclaimed Constance, as he closed the door then turned away. Lightly, he swung astride the big black.

"You may keep your brooch and your purse." Kneeing the stallion close, the rogue leaned down to proffer her a single, perfect red rose. "With my compliments, *enfant.*"

A rueful gleam of laughter sprang to Constance's eyes. "You, sir, are a terrible rogue," she declared, accepting the blossom. "We are not finished yet, I promise you. We shall meet again."

"I think not, my lady," said the Black Rose, touching the brim of his hat to her. "You are a beautiful woman.

The next time I might not be able to resist temptation. Go home, *enfant*, and do not look back." Drawing his pistol from his belt, he waved it at the driver. "Coachman, drive on before I change my mind."

The coachman, all too pleased to do as he was bid, lashed the team into motion. Constance, flung back in her seat, clutched the rose, neatly trimmed of its thorns, tightly in her fist. And when she had got herself set to rights again enough to look back the way she had come, the Black Rose had gone.

Chapter 1

It was the thirteenth of February, a most significant date to those who made up the festive company in the Queen's Salon. It was also a singular gathering, not only because it included the illustrious presence of a duke, a marquis, two earls, and a newly appointed rear admiral, but also, and more importantly, because there had never before been that particular assemblage in the Queen's Salon. But then, the Duke of Albermarle had never before come so close to death's door as he had done that autumn—only to defy the grim reaper in time to celebrate his eighty-second birthday with every appearance of being fully restored to his normally impeccable health. It had taken that auspicious event to bring his entire family all at the same time to Albermarle Castle in the south of Devon.

No doubt it would have been noteworthy enough that the duke's one remaining son and his six grandchildren were at last all together beneath the ducal roof. The addition, however, of four great grandchildren, one but newly arrived into the world (and all of them bundled away with their nannies to the nursery at present), made for a particularly momentous occasion.

Gideon Rochelle, who had the distinction of being the Marquis of Vere and the duke's heir apparent, could not but view the domestic scene before him with a keen sense of irony. It was not that he did not rejoice with the others in his grandsire's having reached an advanced age of maturity or that, having done so and looked death in the eye, the duke appeared in phenomenal good health, because he did rejoice in it. Vere, at thirty, was in no hurry to inherit the title, especially at the cost of the present duke's well-being. Though Vere's sisters were wont to claim that he was at great pains to hide his emotions behind a façade of worldly indifference and though he took no pains at all to remain in Albermarle's good graces, the truth was that he entertained a deep regard for his ducal grandparent.

It was not, then, the nature of the celebration that occasioned the marquis's cynical outlook. But then, neither did it stem from any lack of pleasure in the signs of domestic bliss displayed by his sisters and their noble spouses. No one could have been more gratified than he when his older sister Elfrida had at last presented her dearest Shields with the son and heir that she had once foreseen in a vision before ever they were wed—or when, little more than a year following that auspicious occasion, she had given birth to yet another boy. Not to be outdone, Vere's younger sister Violet had produced a son to carry on in the tradition of his father, who, before he was the Earl of Blackthorn, had been Captain Trevor Dane of his majesty's navy and the hero of countless naval battles. And now Violet had additionally given birth to a girl, who even at three months gave every manifestation of having inherited her mama's extraordinary beauty.

Vere, who held his brothers-in-law in the greatest esteem, could not but be glad for their happiness. Being

Vere, however, he was given to see with keen perspicuity the vast gulf that separated their existence from his, which was far less than exemplary. More to the point, he knew that Albermarle was aware of it. What he did not know was of how *much* information Albermarle might be in possession concerning his heir's most recent plunge into the depths of iniquity.

The devil! He took no pride in the fact that he seemed fated ever to incur his grandsire's displeasure. On the contrary, he was all too cynically aware that he had failed abominably to measure up to the example set by his father, James Rochelle. Worse, he knew that his mama, the gentle, loving Clarice, would have been greatly disappointed in him had she lived. Perhaps if there had not been a cloud over the tragic demise of the former Marquis and Marchioness of Vere, Gideon might have felt some compulsion to resist the dark impulses that led him to live his life with a reckless disregard for the consequences. Perhaps if there had not been a worm of discontent gnawing at his vitals, he would not have sought solace in every sort of vice imaginable.

Perhaps, he thought, ironically amused at himself. Or perhaps none of it would have made a whit of difference. He was far too much a realist to try and fool himself into believing that he did not derive a perverse sort of gratification in being the black sheep of the family. He was Vere, a man with a reputation for being exceedingly dangerous, and he knew better than anyone how well deserved was his notoriety. More than that, he had no illusions as to the depths of depravity of which he was capable.

He had come long since to believe that his excesses would in time bring him to a bad end. Being Vere, however, he entertained a morbid curiosity to discover how far his jaded taste for the meanest planes of life experience might take him before he was made finally to fall a victim to them, as fall he surely must if he continued on his present course.

But then, what did it really matter? Vere cynically mused. Aside from achieving the single goal he had set for himself, it was not as if his existence really counted for anything. There was always his uncle, Sir Richard, to inherit the title should Gideon Rochelle succumb to his excesses. Sir Richard Rochelle had proven himself to be a man of courage and honor. He was a far worthier candidate to succeed the duke than was the dissolute heir apparent. And should the rear admiral fall, his son Valentine stood ready to take up the cudgel. At fifteen, the boy had already served two years as a midshipman aboard a man-of-war and now demonstrated a maturity far beyond his meager years. No doubt he would grow to be a man whom the duke would be proud to have follow in his footsteps.

As for Vere himself, he was perfectly aware of his precarious standing with the duke. Albermarle, he did not doubt, had long since given up all hope that the only male scion of his beloved elder son would mend his ways. It was equally certain to Vere that the duke's birthday celebration must inevitably prove ill-fated for Vere himself. He knew his grandsire far too well to suppose that the numerous examples of domestic bliss surrounding him would not serve to arouse Albermarle from his customary detachment from the world at large to take note of the one glaring fly in the ointment of his present contentedness.

Even then, Vere was made uncannily aware that the duke's chill, flat gaze had lifted to impale him from across the room where he sat enthroned between Sir Richard and Roanna Rochelle's daughters—the lovely Alexandra, who, a slender replica of her fair-haired mama, was just turned seventeen, and the dainty, raven-haired Chloe, who was a precocious thirteen.

"As it happens," Albermarle was saying in reply to some comment of Violet's regarding her dearest Trevor's most recent address before the House of Lords, "I have been following Blackthorn's career with keen interest these past four years. It would appear that the Earl of Blackthorn has become a man of no little influence, a man who commands the respect of others. Unlike this rogue who has become the idol of the ladies' salons. The Black Rose, indeed. He is naught but a common thief."

"A thief, most certainly," commented Roanna Rochelle, indolently waving her ivory stick folding fan before her lovely face. "But hardly a common one. From all accounts he is exceedingly charming in his manners and never fails to treat his victims with a gentlemanly gallantry."

"I daresay he *is* a gentleman," growled the duke, clearly less than impressed with his daughter-in-law's description of the intriguing Captain Moonlight. "A gentleman of breeding and the scion of a noble house. He would not be the *first* scapegrace to be born of nobility."

Vere, sardonically aware that the duke was thinking of the black sheep who stood ready to inherit the ducal title, could not but wonder what the duke would say if he knew the truth of the matter. What had begun as a mere escapade born out of ennui had not only proven to be a lucrative enterprise, but also was fast assuming all the bizarre aspects of a romantic farce. Vere could not but find ironic amusement in the fact that the rather overblown captain moonlight had generated a host of would-be imitators. Nevertheless, there was only one Black Rose, and he preferred that Albermarle remain in ignorance of his identity. His thoughts unreadable behind the bored mask of the Corinthian, Vere returned his grandsire's pointed stare with an unblinking dispassion, all of which was not lost on the others present.

"No, not the first," quietly interjected the Earl of Blackthorn, deliberately drawing attention to himself. "Nor would our illustrious Captain Moonlight be the first to be condemned without the benefit of a hearing. As one who has borne the stigma of being thought a traitor to king and country, I find that I am become less prone to judge a man on the basis of speculation and hearsay. There may be more to this rogue than meets the eye."

"And more to the lining of his pockets, if he continues to relieve honest people of their purses," Albermarle said in tones heavily laced with irony. "Which I doubt not will be the case so long as he has a lot of silly females mooning over him and a gentleman of reason, who should know better, willing to play the devil's advocate."

"Really, your grace," spoke up Elfrida, clearly desirous of spreading oil over troubled waters, "I cannot think that you are being quite fair. As one who was born under the Sun Sign of Libra, Blackthorn must naturally be desirous of upholding the principles of justice. I daresay he meant his comments to be taken as a defense in general of a man's right to trial by jury rather than as an advocacy of a lawless individual."

"Do you, indeed," drawled Albermarle, manifestly unamused at his eldest granddaughter's efforts to provide an astrological motivation for Blackthorn's ill-advised commentary.

"Certainly, the navy has found itself an advocate who is both well informed and relentless in his determination to better the existence of the common sailor," hastily interposed Rear Admiral Sir Richard Rochelle, who, at eight-and-thirty, might easily have been mistaken for Vere's older brother rather than his uncle.

Undeniably, the family resemblance was unmistakable. Tall and slender like the duke himself, both the rear admiral and the marquis were broad-shouldered and honed to a muscled hardness which lent each the easy, supple grace of the born athlete. Both also possessed the Rochelle propensity for raven-black hair and startlingly blue eyes. Only, Sir Richard's eyes were the azure of the sea on a clear day, while Gideon's were the mesmerizing hue of lapis lazuli. Further, where the rear admiral's features were honed by his years of command at sea to a stern cast that might give way without a moment's notice to a flashing grin, the marquis's wore an arrogant façade of utter impenetrability to which his infinitely gentle smile could lend a distinctly chilling aspect, if he were of a mind to have done.

At the present, Vere, lounging on the arm of a sofa with one long leg stretched out before him and his elbow propped negligently on the sofa's back behind his sister Violet, was at his most inscrutable, as his Uncle Richard went on to add: "We may all be grateful that, thanks to Vere's timely intervention, Blackthorn was spared a most demmed inconvenient, early demise. The navy may have lost one of its most promising captains when he resigned his commission, but it gained a much-needed voice in Parliament."

"More importantly, Philippe did *not* lose a father," appended Violet, her gaze going fondly to her eleven-year-old stepson, who, standing next to Blackthorn, was a boyish replica of his tall father. "Or I a husband. And just look what has come of it—little Gideon and now our sweet Meredith Clarice."

"Who has already demonstrated she is possessed of a formidable will of her own," observed Blackthorn, a gleam in his dark eyes for his countess. "Not unlike her mama."

"No doubt we may all be grateful that Vere's talent for marksmanship was, in this case, of benefit to someone—unlike his other, less highly motivated meetings at gunpoint," said Albermarle in tones heavily laced with irony.

"You are right, of course, your grace," agreed Vere, smiling ever so gently at his grandsire. "Putting a period to the French spy before *Le Corbeau* could shoot Blackthorn in the back might possibly be seen as a single ray of light in an otherwise distinctly unilluminated career.

But that noteworthy event, alas, is already obscured in the rapidly receding past. Indeed, I cannot think why it should have been dredged up again after four years."

"Because, my dearest, best loved brother," said Violet, awarding Vere a knowing glance, "you are far too prone to forget how important you are to all of us."

"Softly, sweet Violet," murmured Vere at his most maddeningly inscrutable. "You are in grave peril of putting a pall on the festivities. The truth is, I am important to no one, save perhaps my man, Gresham, who prides himself on dressing a marquis, and my tailor, who lives in anticipation of the day upon which I shall settle my account with him."

"Really, Gideon," spoke up Elfrida, who had never ceased to entertain the hope that Vere might at last find something to lure him back from the brink of ruin, "you are utterly impossible. It is Albermarle's birthday, and we are all together. Pray do acknowledge that we should miss you exceedingly if you were not here to celebrate with us."

"I shall acknowledge that I should be exceedingly sorry not to have been here," Vere smoothly riposted. "What is far more important is that Albermarle is here to celebrate it."

"Here, here," applauded the Earl of Shields, lifting his brandy in salute to the duke.

"Many happy returns of the day," chorused through the room, and the momentary undercurrent of unease that was like to attend any coming together of the duke with his heir apparent receded beneath a swell of merriment.

Vere, however, was not lulled into believing he had weathered the storm that had long been building inevitably toward some potentially cataclysmic event. Despite the fact that Albermarle had let fly only that single brace of darts, Vere was far too observant not to note the duke's long, measured glance before his grace turned away. Nor was Vere impervious to the altruistic motives behind his sisters' pointed remarks.

He was sardonically aware that Elfrida and Violet had plotted more than a few times in the past to try and shield him from Albermarle's wrath. The little meddlers, he thought. It was something that he had neither asked for nor wanted from them. It was bad enough, after all, that they had foolishly risked bringing the duke's displeasure down upon themselves, but the very notion that he was somehow in need of hiding behind a woman's petticoats he could not but find rather amusing. He might be a dissolute rake, an inveterate gambler, and a ne'er-do-well, but he was hardly a milksop.

He was and always had been fully prepared to accept the consequences of his own actions, something that Albermarle must know and expect of him, but something that neither Elfrida nor Violet had ever understood. It was, after all, a matter involving a gentleman's honor.

He loved and respected his grandsire, the duke. He had even been dependent upon Albermarle for longer than he cared to remember to maintain him in the manner to which he had grown accustomed, but he was demmed if he would live in dread of him. Certainly, he would not pretend an unctuousness that was not in his nature. Nor, he was convinced, would the duke want that from him. The duke might not approve of his heir's dissolute lifestyle, but he knew his grandson. Whatever else Vere might be, he could be depended upon not to be less than a man.

Not that Vere could ever bring Elfrida and Violet, who were motivated by womanly love, to accept the unwritten code that governed the conduct of men, he reflected dryly, as no little time later he made his way along the winding passages to the duke's private study to which some ten minutes earlier he had been summoned. He knew his sisters far too well not to recognize when they were up to their feminine tricks again. Patently, something had occurred to arouse their old protective instincts. Though he could think of any number of things that might have given birth to what he perceived to be their present concern had they but known of them, he was fairly certain that they did not. The Countess of Shields and the Countess of Blackthorn, after all, would hardly have had concourse with the circles in which he moved.

Of course, there were always Elfrida's uncommon intuitive powers to be considered, mused Vere, smiling reminiscently to himself at the memory of his brief exchange with Shields only an hour earlier.

"I daresay you already know the answer to that," declared the earl in reply to Vere's gentle query regarding Elfrida and Violet's too obvious leap to his defense in the withdrawing room. "Elfrida says she has had glimpses of you in her Grandmama Lucasta's shew stone. And she has been disturbed by dreams of late that have set her to fretting over you. She fears you are slipping into one of your black moods, my friend."

"No, does she?" murmured Vere, little amused to hear that he had somehow begun to figure in his elder sister's prophetic dreams and visions. While Vere himself placed little credence in Elfrida's self-proclaimed powers of prognostication, he knew from past experience where *her* unshakable belief in them was likely to lead. Hellfire! He little relished the distinct possibility that she might be motivated to concoct one of her irresistible schemes for his salvation. "And what, if I may be so bold as to inquire, does she intend to do about it?"

Shields, who was a deal too perceptive to mistake the meaning in that gentle query, had not bothered to evade the obvious. "Elfrida will be far too occupied with domestic pursuits to do anything. I have decided to renovate Clavering's west wing, a project that will require Elfrida's constant supervision for some little time to come."

"How very farsighted of you," applauded Vere, well aware that the earl's plans for renovation must be of exceedingly recent origin. Shields knew better than anyone, after all, to what extremes his countess was capable of going in an effort to preserve one whom she apprehended to be in dire straits. Eight years had elapsed since Elfrida had dashed off to London with Violet in tow in order to save Shields from the pall of danger that she had perceived hanging over him in her Grandmama Lucasta's shew stone. And, while Shields had come to bless the fates that had dropped her into his previously well-ordered existence, he could hardly wish to see his countess embarked on another audacious undertaking, this time for her brother's sake. More than that, he would be equally certain that Vere would not welcome any interference in his life from Elfrida, or anyone else, for that matter. "I daresay I am in your debt."

"I was only too glad to oblige," said Shields, studying his brother-in-law with penetrating eyes. "On the other hand, I should not like to see Elfrida's peace cut up. If you should feel the urge to sink yourself into a slough of despond, come to us at Clavering for diversion. You must know our door is always open to you."

Indeed, thought Vere with a wry twist of the lips. And the earl's purse as well, he did not doubt. Either one or both of his brothers-in-law would freely have plumped his pockets, which were habitually to let. As fate would have it, Shields and Blackthorn entertained an overblown notion of some small services that he had rendered them. The truth was, however, that he had helped to rescue Shields from a murderous abductor purely for Elfrida's sake. And as for saving Violet's dearest Trevor, Vere would have put a period to the French spy even if *Le Corbeau* had not been on the point of shooting Blackthorn in the back. The Frenchman had been a cravenly brute who, besides serving as a spy for the enemy, had preyed on helpless women and children purely for his own amusement. Killing him had meant less than quashing some particularly vile and loathsome sort of vermin beneath his heel.

The slate, then, so far as Vere was concerned, was clean, and his brothers-in-law owed him nothing. Therefore, while he was not averse to paying Shields a visit for the sake of diversion, he would undoubtedly abstain from doing so in order to avoid the disagreeable eventuality of Shields offering to advance him a sum to alleviate any financial embarrassment he might be suffering.

Thought of what everyone knew to be his habitual impecunious state brought a cold, hard gleam to his eyes. It served, after all, not only as a constant reminder that he was, to all intents and purposes, dependent upon the duke, but worse, *why* he was kept in that untenable position.

Reminder? reflected Vere, clenching strong, slender fingers into a fist at his side. Hellfire! It was a canker devouring his soul! It had been ten years since the former Marquis and Marchioness of Vere had perished in what had been officially termed a yachting accident. Even at twenty, Gideon had known it was no such thing. The marquis had been a superb sailor, and he had had his marchioness on board. It was inconceivable that he would have allowed the swift, agile *Swallow* to sail onto the rocks and then, foundering, be swept out to sea. How much more certain had Gideon been when he learned that it was rumored the *Swallow* had been carrying a fortune in gold, the fortune his parents had left behind in France when they fled the Reign of Terror!

Someone had known what the marquis was about. *Someone* had betrayed that knowledge to the marquis's enemies. Hell and the devil confound it! It was the only explanation possible. The *Swallow,* along with its cargo and all those aboard, had fallen prey to James Rochelle's enemies. And still those terrible losses had not been enough.

A cold, searing flame burned through Vere's belly at the hated memory. Called home from a walking tour in Scotland to be made privy to the terrible news, he had hardly been prepared to receive the one man who had long nurtured an overweening hatred for James Rochelle.

The Earl of Blaidsdale, damn his black soul to perdition, had come bearing a gambling marker against the deceased marquis's estate for a sum that had served to deplete a once-sizeable fortune to little more than a pittance. Gideon, forced to sell out of the Funds in order to satisfy his father's debt of honor, had known with bitter certainty that the whole had been contrived to ruin him along with his father.

Hellfire! Blaidsdale had never seen the day that he could prevail over the former marquis at any game of chance, let alone faro, a game at which James Rochelle had excelled. Blaidsdale, who was noted for being clutch-fisted, was no bloody gambler. And even if he had so far forgotten himself as to engage Vere in a game, it was exceedingly doubtful that Blaidsdale himself would have risked so great a sum. Certainly, Vere, a man who had known where his duty lay, would not have imperiled his family's future well-being by rashly wagering the greater part of his fortune at the gaming table. And how very convenient it was that the only witnesses to such an unlikely event had been Rear Admiral Sir Oliver Landford, who happened to be the earl's brother, and Lord Ridgley Sinclair, who was wed to the earl's sister, the formidable Lady Clarissa!

The gambling markers were forgeries. Vere was certain of it. Just as he was certain that Blaidsdale was behind the ill fortunes that had befallen his house.

There was not a moment that he allowed himself to forget that his mother and father had died under exceedingly questionable circumstances and that he, as their only son and heir, had failed in his duty to find and wreak vengeance on those who were responsible for their loss.

It did not help that he knew in his heart that Blaidsdale and Landford had plotted his father's ruin, even going so far as to lend themselves to acts of piracy and murder to attain it. The earl and his brother were men of wealth and influence. Without a shred of tangible proof against them, Vere was powerless to bring them to justice.

It did not mean, however, that he would not have his revenge, vowed Gideon, turning down the corridor that led to the duke's study. Had he been a less patient man, he might long since have called them out on some pretext or other and put a period to their miserable existences. To kill them on the field of honor, however, and subsequently find himself forced into exile would hardly have served his purposes. He required a deal more than the mere deaths of his enemies to satisfy the demands of vengeance.

Blaidsdale and Landford would indeed be brought to forfeit their lives, Vere coldly reflected. Not, however, before they were utterly ruined and their crimes exposed to the public in such a manner as to give him free rein to dispose of them with impunity. Only *then* would vengeance be satisfied.

Vere smiled ever so gently to himself. And perhaps that time was not so very far away, he mused, thinking of the message that had arrived for him immediately before he departed London. Caleb Roth had proven an exceedingly valuable investment, just as Vere had known that he would. The young firebrand had quite possibly stumbled across one who knew the truth of the events surrounding the loss of the *Swallow*. And if Roth's find did indeed prove to be all that it would seem to promise, the waiting would finally be brought to an end. By the devil, he thought, a fierce gleam in his eyes. All the long years of preparation were about to bear fruit.

He had not been quite so idle over the past ten years as everyone had presumed him to be. But then, he had taken great pains to ensure that no one would realize how very carefully he was formulating his plans. And now, after having painstakingly laid the foundations, he was very nearly ready to set matters in motion. There remained only one last detail to which he must attend, one final safeguard to be put in place.

Ironically, Vere was aware of a hard knot drawing tight in the pit of his stomach. It was not a step that he relished taking. Hellfire! He would rather endure torture than to cause his grandsire the final disillusionment. Unfortunately, he would seem to have little choice in the matter. If he were to have free rein to do as he must, it was necessary to distance himself from Albermarle and all those who would otherwise be endangered by his actions. He must bring Albermarle to cast him off.

Vere stopped before the door to the study.

The devil, he thought, it would be simple enough to bring Albermarle to sever all ties with his heir apparent. Vere had ever been on the thin edge of the duke's displeasure. The thing that tormented Gideon and filled him with reluctance was whether, when it was all over one way or the other, Albermarle could ever bring himself to pardon Vere's transgressions.

A blur of pain crossed the normally impassive features, then as quickly passed.

Hellfire! If he achieved his purposes, his grandsire would surely be brought to see the necessity of his actions. And if he failed, it would hardly matter. He, Vere, after all, would be dead.

Smiling mirthlessly, he rapped the back of his knuckles lightly against the oaken barrier.

"Yes, yes, come in," issued from the other side of the door.

Vere entered the duke's private sanctum to find Albermarle standing with his back to the room, his hands clasped behind him, as he stared meditatively out the window over the Channel, which lapped against the base of the cliffs upon which the castle perched. Vere, well used to his grandsire's moods of abstraction, softly closed the door and crossed the room to stand quietly waiting before the great mahogany desk for Albermarle to acknowledge his presence.

The moments ticking away on the ormolu mantel clock elicited memories of other times that he had been summoned to this room. Upon the first occasion, he had been six years of age and newly given into the care of Mr. Elias Beck, who had been engaged to serve in the capacity of tutor, a circumstance to which Gideon had found no little objection. Egad, the man's hair, what little he had had left of it, was grey, and he had walked with a cane. Clearly, he was doddering with one foot in the grave. Oh, no doubt he would do well enough for Latin, mathematics, and logic, but he was hardly the sort to be relied upon to instruct a budding young gentleman in the really important things, like the manly art of pugilism or the finer points of cricket. Certainly, if Papa had been there and not called away to the East Indies on one of his diplomatic missions, *he* should never have picked such a one to tutor his only son.

"And that is what you, in all your worldly wisdom, have determined, is it, sir?" had demanded Albermarle, peering down at the boy with singularly chill blue eyes. "No doubt I should be moved to dismiss Mr. Beck solely on the grounds that he does not measure up to your expectations."

"Indeed, your grace, I should be ever so pleased if you would," Gideon had replied promptly, gratified that his grace had been brought so easily to the crux of the matter. Even as the boy's mood had brightened, however, his grandsire had proceeded to nip his hopes in the bud.

"Yes, no doubt," Albermarle had drawled in exceedingly dry tones. "As fate would have it, however, I am of the opinion that the man has a great deal more to offer than that for which you, in your exceedingly brief acquaintanceship, give him credit."

"But, Grandfather," Gideon had begun to protest, only to be instantly silenced by the dreaded lift of a single ducal eyebrow.

"Quite so," had murmured the duke chillingly. Then, gravely, he had added, "You stand second in line to inherit a dukedom, Gideon. It is a position that carries great responsibilities, not the least of which is the ability to judge men. Henceforth, I suggest that you refrain from doing so either in haste or based solely on appearances, which can be deceiving. You will return now to your tutor and put that tidbit of advice into practice. Is that understood, my boy?"

As young as he was, Gideon *had* understood that it would have been fruitless to offer any further protest, and as fate would have it, the event had proven to be a life lesson, one that Gideon never forgot. Elias Beck had in short time manifested himself to be a man of many parts. Possessed of a droll humor and a unique understanding of the foibles of the young, he had opened the youthful Gideon's eyes to the marvels of science, history, literature, art, and music; but, more than that, he had inculcated in him a love of books. It was little wonder that Albermarle had chosen Beck to tutor his grandson. Having led the life of a traveling scholar, the man had been everywhere and done everything, it seemed. And that which he had not experienced in actuality, he had lived vicariously through the medium of books. In the six years of his tutelage, Beck did more than broaden the intellectual horizons of his pupil. He molded the boy's thought processes.

Unfortunately, the thirst for knowledge that had been Beck's legacy to his young charge, and that Gideon had taken with him to Eton, had taken a decidedly dark turn in the years following the death of his parents. Strangely, Vere did not doubt that Beck, who had known him better than anyone else ever had, rather than holding him in reproach, would somehow have understood what he was about. The same, however, could hardly have been said of Albermarle.

Gideon's visits to this room in the years since he had grown to manhood could not have been described either as amicable or as conducive to a mutual accord between the duke and his heir. This one promised to be even less so, decided Vere, studying the uncompromising set of his grandsire's shoulders.

Not for the first time since his arrival at the castle, Vere suffered a distinct pang at sight of the lingering signs of havoc that the duke's recent bout with illness had wrought. Though Albermarle held himself as erect as ever, there was about the slender figure a new aura of fragility, a sense of brittleness, perhaps, that had never been there before. The hands clasped behind his back were no longer the strong, supple members that had once seemed possessed of a peculiar grace all of their own. They were fleshless now and claw-like, the paper-thin skin mottled and writhing with blue, bulging veins. How Albermarle must hate that, thought Vere, hating it himself. It was wrong somehow to think of Albermarle succumbing at last to the susceptibilities of mortal flesh. He had ever exuded a sense of ageless indestructibility.

Altered though he might be by illness and brought at last to feel the brunt of his years, Albermarle, coming about to face Vere, was yet a formidable presence. Certainly, the duke's glance had lost nothing of its keenness, Vere noted, acutely aware of the powerful intellect behind that level gaze. The countenance, too, despite the pallor of its complexion, not to mention the deep lines etched about the corners of the eyes and the mouth, was yet expressive of a forceful will unimpaired by the years. He was still the duke, weathered perhaps, but a power with which to be reckoned nonetheless, thought Vere, experiencing a soft thrill of pride at the realization.

"So, my word still has the power to summon you to my presence," pronounced Albermarle, studying his heir apparent with sardonic appreciation of the elegant figure poised with sublime ease before him. "I suppose I should be pleased at that much at least."

"But you are not pleased, are you, your grace?" Vere countered softly. "And who can blame you? Not I, certainly."

"No, not you," agreed Albermarle with a sudden tinge of weariness. "You take pride in being a thorn in my side. No doubt it is pointless to inquire where you have been keeping yourself these past six months."

Vere's eyes narrowed sharply on the duke's countenance.

"Pointless, indeed, your grace," he said, "since the answer would hardly be to your satisfaction. You look worn to the nub, if I may say so, your grace. Perhaps we should postpone this interview until you have rested."

"You may not. And we shall do no such thing," snapped Albermarle. "I shall thank you not to patronize me, Vere. I may have one foot in the grave, but I am far from requiring you to play nursemaid to me."

"A circumstance for which I can only be grateful, your grace," murmured Vere, the faintest of smiles twitching at the corners of his lips. "Perhaps a brandy, then, purely for my own stimulation."

"Yes, yes, if you must," Albermarle consented, lowering himself into the high-backed armchair ranged behind the mahogany desk. "Though do not think you can pull the wool over my eyes. You intend the restorative for me."

"You are mistaken, surely, your grace," demurred Vere, pouring two brandies from a decanter set out on a silver grog tray. "What can I have possibly done to make you believe I should wish to earn my way into your good graces?"

"I never said your intention was to woo my favor,"

growled the duke, accepting the libation Vere held out to him. "It will take a deal more than a glass of brandy to do that."

"Of that, I have not a single doubt." Vere, settling easily into a chair across from the duke, lifted his glass in salutation. "Health and long life, your grace. Whatever else you might think of me, you may be certain that I wish you that."

"The devil, you do." A bleak hardness touched Albermarle's features and as quickly passed, leaving the duke's face peculiarly devoid of expression. "Enough of your blasted parlor games, Vere. I have watched you grow from a boy to a man. Do you think I do not know you?"

"I should never presume to think any such thing, your grace," answered Vere, who could not but wonder where, exactly, the duke was leading. Given to a quirkiness which manifested itself in esoteric projects of a scientific nature, the duke was predictable only in his unpredictability. One could never be certain what Albermarle might be thinking at any given moment. On the other hand, those who were most intimately acquainted with him never made the mistake of assuming that Albermarle ever said or did anything for no particular reason. "On the contrary, I should be exceedingly surprised if anything escaped your understanding, your grace."

"So you say," Albermarle uttered, awarding Vere a piercing glance. "And yet you continue in the misguided belief that I know nothing of what goes on inside your head."

"Do I, your grace?" queried Vere, little demonstrating by his casual sip from his glass the sudden wariness with which he had received that singular pronouncement from the duke. "I was not aware that you considered there was anything worth your consideration going on inside my head."

"Do not play the fool with me, Vere!" thundered the duke, slamming a hand down hard on the desktop. "You are not the man you pretend to be. Pray do not try and deny it. Or have you forgot that I was there when you made your vow of vengeance? I told you then, and I tell you now, it will little avail you to squander your life on revenge."

Deliberately, Vere unclenched the hard fist of his misapprehension. "You are right, of course," he said easily. "But then, having failed to wreak vengeance on my father's enemies, it would seem I have still managed to squander my life. There is a certain irony in that, do you not think?"

"Harrumph," snorted Albermarle, eyeing Vere with sardonic disfavor. "If there is any irony in it, it bloody well escapes me. I have found that looking death in the eye serves to give one a whole new perspective on life. The truth is that, in allowing myself to believe that time would heal all hurts, I failed you. But that is all going to change from this moment hence. I have decided it is time you were married."

"Yes, of course you have," murmured Vere, caught suddenly off guard. Egad, things had taken a decidedly unexpected turn. Married? He would sooner cast himself to the devil than submit to being legshackled. Especially now, when the last thing he could wish for was a wife to further complicate his existence. "Why, I wonder, did I not think of it myself?"

"No doubt because you have misled yourself into believing I should be satisfied to look to your uncle to inherit the title," Albermarle stated flatly. "As it happens, I am not in the least sanguine at such a prospect. My son was taken from me. I will not allow *his* son to dishonor the memory of his father by abnegating his responsibilities. You will marry before the end of summer, Vere, or I shall bloody well wash my hands of you."

So the moment had arrived, thought Vere, his face revealing nothing of the hard fist of regret that had tightened on his vitals. The one remaining obstacle was removed, and there was nothing left to prevent him from his chosen path to perdition. It occurred to him that he should have felt relieved at least that the waiting was finally over. Strange that he did not.

"No doubt I shall regret that exceedingly, your grace," he said gently. Then rising to his feet, he lifted his glass to the duke. "Many happy returns of the day, your grace. May all good things come your way."

Downing the drink, he set the glass on the desk. "Will there be anything else, your grace?"

Albermarle stared across the desk into cool, impenetrable eyes. His lips thinned to a grim line. "It would appear that everything has been said that needs to be said. Pray get you out of my sight."

"Quite so, your grace." Bowing, Vere made his exit.

An hour later, settling back against the squabs of his travel coach, Vere rode out of the castle gates.

He was conscious of feeling vaguely unsettled, an emotion that hitherto had been wholly unfamiliar to him. But then, he had never before been quite so unfettered of familial obligations, he reflected cynically. Desiring solitude in which to ponder this new turn of events, he had even sent Gresham, his valet, on to London to wait for him in the Town House. Still, no doubt he would feel himself again once he had reached his hunting lodge tucked away in the Mendip Hills.

His mood, however, was only a little improved when a good deal later, having traveled the fifty-odd miles to Wells in record time, the coach pulled into a post inn to breathe the horses. He allowed himself to be momentarily diverted to discover a young woman scrutinizing him from the window of a carriage. Indeed, despite the fact that her features were obscured behind a veil, he had the distinct impression that the lady was as fetching as was the gay Gypsy bonnet she wore, tied with a blue riband beneath her chin. Unfortunately, his attention was diverted just then by the hostler, who informed him that the lead black had a loose shoe that had ought to be attended to before the animal were permanently lamed by it. Instructing the man to see to the matter at once, Vere looked back to find the intriguing miss had gone.

Resigned to the necessity of having to endure an hour or more in the rather unprepossessing surrounds of a private sitting room at the inn, Vere disembarked from the coach. It was to prove, however, due to the unforeseen circumstance that the smithy had been partially incapacitated in a donnybrook fair the night before, that three hours were to transpire before Vere's coach pulled out of the yards.

In an ill humor from the unforeseen delay and impatient to reach his destination, Vere sat, tapping the silver head of his walking stick idly against the toe of his boot propped on the seat facing him. At least he could be grateful that with the onset of night, a gibbous moon had come out to light the way. John Vickers, his coachman, would make short work of the few remaining miles to the hunting lodge. Once there, Vere would take a day or two to put his affairs in order before he departed for London for the long awaited meeting with Caleb Roth. The devil keep him from any further delays.

Hardly had that thought crossed his mind than the coach gave a sudden lurch that nearly flung him from the seat and lumbered to a precipitous halt. A shot rang out, followed by a shout.

"*Hold to!*"

Vere, straightening himself, glanced out the window and into the bore of a pistol.

"Good evening, my lord," commented a masked figure, dressed all in black. "No doubt I should apologize for causing you this delay. However, I promise I shall require no more of your time than it takes for you to hand over your purse and the diamond solitaire you are wearing."

Chapter 2

Lady Constance Landford awakened with a start to the realization that not only was the morning well advanced, but she had been dreaming again of the highwayman who had stolen a kiss and then gallantly had not taken either her purse or her mama's brooch. The rogue. Really, he was every whit as disarming as his reputation had painted him. More than that, he was an irresistible enigma that would seem to defy resolution.

Even now she had difficulty accepting that the elusive Black Rose was in actuality the notorious Marquis of Vere, who had, by the time he was two-and-twenty, fought three duels and in each hit his man. He had the dubious distinction of being a womanizer, a hardened rakeshame, and a gamester—a man noted for being as arrogant as he was coldbloodedly dangerous. More than that, however, he was the Duke of Albermarle's heir apparent.

Good God. What in heaven's name had possessed him to take up robbing coaches?

The reckless devil! she thought, sustaining a helpless thrill through her midsection at the mere thought of all that he was daring. He must be as aware as she that such an undertaking was as foolhardy as it was dangerous. Black sheep or not, he should have known better than to risk life and limb, not to mention the sort of scandal that would forever ruin him in the eyes of the *Ton*. And yet, she could not quite quash the wholly improper feeling that he must be having a glorious, grand adventure. Quickly, she reminded herself that it was just the sort of adventure, however, that must surely end with the Black Rose swinging from the gibbet.

Flinging herself over onto her back, she clutched a pillow to her riotous breast. Not that she would care one way or the other if the man who had sworn to destroy her father got just what he deserved for his lawless endeavor, for she would not, she told herself firmly.

It was a lie. She knew it immediately. The terrible truth was that she would mind very much if Vere were caught and sent to the gallows. Indeed, no matter how many times she tried to convince herself otherwise, she was very much afraid that she had proven far more vulnerable to the nobleman's devastating charm than she would like to admit—and all because of a kiss that had shaken her to the core and awakened her to emotions that she had never before known that she possessed. Really, it was too bad of him. It was, in fact, inexcusable of him.

A plague take the marquis, she thought, angry at where her musings had taken her. It was bad enough that he invaded her dreams at night, but that he had taken to creeping unbidden into her waking thoughts at all hours of the day was beyond what was acceptable. She was a woman of five-and-twenty, not some silly school-girl given to childish romantic fantasies. Besides, she had other, far more pressing matters to concern her than a man who could only despise her and whom she herself should hold beneath contempt. Enough was enough. She *would* banish him from her thoughts!

Resolutely, she made herself ponder instead the still strange reality of being once more at Landford Park.

After more than a decade of living in London with her maternal Aunt Sophie, she had forgotten what it was like to wake up to the fresh, clean air of the country. Faith, she had become so used to the pall of smoke that hung over the City that she had very nearly ceased to regard it. She had become inured as well to the clatter of carriage wheels over cobblestoned streets, the raucous cries of street mongers, and the bustle of humanity in general. Even after a little more than two months at Landford Park, Constance, listening to the stillness, was still struck by the serenity of northern Somerset's rural environs.

Snuggling more deeply into the warmth of the bed, she luxuriated in the peace of the moment. She knew all too well that it was not like to endure past her descent to the breakfast room if any of the family happened to be in attendance.

Constance breathed a long sigh. Faith, who could have predicted that her Aunt Sophie's sudden marriage to the colonel would cause such an upheaval in Constance's own existence, which until then had been just as she might have wished it to be? She had, after all, grown accustomed to the independence she had enjoyed under Aunt Sophie's liberated tutelage. Of course, it was not as if she could not have continued as she had before. Thanks to the substantial fortune left to her by her mama, she was not dependent upon her father's largesse, or the lack of it, as the case might be, for her existence. She was perfectly free to make of her life whatever she might wish it to be. She might even have stayed on with Aunt Sophie, who was kind enough to assure her that she would always be welcome beneath her roof. Constance, however, had found little to recommend in the notion of foisting herself on newlyweds, and it had been more than fifteen years since last she had seen the place of her birth.

She had chosen to return to Landford Park—why? Certainly, her decision had not stemmed from any fond memories of her early years in the sprawling Elizabethan manor. Her mother's failure to provide the earl an heir had little endeared Constance's father to his only offspring. On the rare occasions that he had deigned to pay heed to the fact that he had a daughter, it was to draw attention to some defect in her appearance, her manners, or her behavior. She had felt little remorse when she departed the only home she had ever known and the father who was as tightfisted with his emotions as he was with his purse. In truth, she had not once in her fifteen-year absence looked back. Certainly, the last thing she had contemplated was ever to step foot across her father's threshold again. And yet, here she was, when she might have been somewhere a deal more pleasant, not to mention amusing. Indeed, almost anywhere would have done. So, why had she agreed to come?

Surely a rather vague curiosity to meet the woman who had taken her mama's place in her father's house had not provided sufficient impetus for her to accept the earl's invitation to return home. Nor had her natural wish to make the acquaintance of her six-year-old half-brother, the heir that Constance's own mother had been unable to provide the earl, brought her here. She had knowingly burned those bridges behind her when she flouted her father's wishes by refusing to wed her Cousin Albert—or any of her numerous other suitors, for that matter. In truth, the only thing that had surprised her more than receiving her father's missive suggesting she return to Landford Park had been her agreeing to do so.

A faint, wry smile touched Constance's lips.

She had been vastly mistaken if she had thought any overtures of friendship to her stepmother, Rosalind, would be received with anything other than a chilly disdain. Despite the fact that the Countess of Blaidsdale was only four years Constance's senior and that they might, as a consequence, have entertained some interests in common, the reality had proven far different. But then, Rosalind, it seemed, *had* no interests other than her husband, her son, and her role as chatelaine of Landford Park.

Lady Blaidsdale was, if nothing else, a conformable wife who would never dream of doing or saying anything that might in any way conflict with the views of the earl, Constance reflected with no little amusement, unlike the previous Lady Blaidsdale. *She*, after eleven years of marriage and a single, bitter quarrel with the earl, had removed herself and her ten-year-old daughter to Wells, set up housekeeping on her own, and, according to popular rumor, taken herself a lover. In truth, Regina, Lady Blaidsdale, had proven a sad trial for the earl, who was of the unshakable opinion that a female's proper role in life was to be subservient to men.

It came to Constance to wonder if there had ever been any real affection between her two exceedingly proud and vastly different parents. Regina, with her red-gold hair and laughing green eyes, had taken London by storm upon her coming-out. As the eldest daughter of the Duke of Westerlake, she had had her pick of the eligible partis who swarmed to her presence like bees drawn to honey. The betting books at White's had not had Blaidsdale in the list of favorites to win Lady Regina's hand. Indeed, the odds had all been in favor of the Earl of Bridholm's youngest son, with Viscount Esterbridge holding a close second and Mr. Royce Pemberton close on his heels. That she had chosen the Earl of Blaidsdale out of all of them must surely have meant that she had felt *something* for him other than the cold contempt in which she had held him while living her life apart from him.

Not once in the long days of the wasting sickness in which that life had ended had she spoken his name.

Nor would she allow word to be sent that she lay ill, not even to Constance, who, at her mother's insistence, was visiting her Aunt Sophie in London. She had allowed only one to attend her during those days, her one and only constant friend, and now he, too, was dead.

Constance writhed in the grip of a familiar, rending pang. She should have been at her mother's side at the end. She should have been the one to offer solace and comfort. Instead she had been sent away on a shopping spree in London while little guessing that her dearest mama lay dying. *Why?* At fifteen had she been thought too callow to know the truth? Faith, she was her mama's daughter. She had been reared according to the tenets of Mary Wollstonecraft to believe that in intelligence and in essence she was the equal of any man. Not only had her mama seen that she was provided the sort of classical education normally reserved for males, but she had also been allowed to follow her natural inclination for athletic pursuits. Thanks to her mama's friend, she had learned to ride and shoot as well as any boy. She had even been allowed to master the manly art of fencing. And yet, in the end her mama had chosen to deny Constance the right to share those final, precious moments with her. It was something Constance had never understood, never really forgiven her mother.

But then, there was so *much* that she had never understood, she reflected soberly. Indeed, even the letter conveying Regina's last words to her daughter, rather than clarifying matters, had served instead to cast a sinister shadow over the entire affair. After all, aside from the assurances of her love, it had hinted at some sort of menace to Constance's future against which she had taken measures to protect Constance through her solicitor, Mr. Malcom Enderhart. She had only to send him her diamond-and-pearl brooch if ever she found herself in dire straits. He would know what to do.

"'Dire straits'?" queried Constance out loud to the

empty room. "What in heaven's name were you trying
to tell me, *Maman?* What trouble did you see before me
as you lay, ill and dying?"

There was some dark secret here, something so terrible that it had led her mama to sever all ties with her
husband and remove to Wells—something that she believed would threaten even her daughter's well-being.
And still she had chosen to leave Constance in ignorance as to what had occasioned the quarrel that had
forever hardened Regina's heart against the man who
was her husband and the father of her child. *Why?*

Perhaps that was the reason she had chosen to brave
the forbidden halls of Landford Park once more,
Constance mused whimsically. To see if she could come
to some sort of understanding of her mama and that
which had turned her against the earl.

If it was indeed that which had brought her here, she
reflected wryly, then she had thus far failed abominably.
She hardly saw her father, let alone engaged in fruitful
conversation with him. He was, as he was constantly re-
minding her, an exceedingly busy man who must spend
his days overseeing his numerous holdings, not to mention his shipping interests, his mills, and his duties as a
member of the House of Lords. And if she had hoped
to learn anything from Lady Blaidsdale, she had soon
discarded the notion.

Her stepmother little hid the fact that she disapproved
of Constance and her reprehensible habit of flouting
the earl's wishes, even to refusing to take a husband. It
was, after all, a woman's duty to wed and bear children.
But then, what was one to expect of the offspring of a
woman who had thought nothing of abandoning her
husband and her wifely responsibilities to live in the utterly scandalous manner of a freethinker? What was more,
Lady Blaidsdale entertained a deep resentment over
the fact that the former countess's fortune had gone to

a wayward daughter rather than into the earl's estate to the future enrichment of the Blaidsdale heir.

To her father's credit, perhaps, the earl had thus far abstained from broaching the subject either of her fortune or her single state. But then, neither had he deigned to inquire as to what she had been doing the last ten years with her aunt, Constance noted with sardonic amusement. What a strange man he was, to be sure. It was as if he refused to acknowledge even to himself that his daughter had by choice lived away from him for the greater part of her life. She was home now, where she belonged, and that was the end of it. And yet Constance could not bring herself to believe that the earl had not had *something* in mind when he extended her an invitation to come home at the very least for a visit.

If she remembered anything about her father, it was his predilection for ordering the lives of all those who came under his sphere of influence. That he had failed to play the tyrant with his first countess, Constance attributed to her mama's extraordinary ability to tactfully outmaneuver him. The truth was, Blaidsdale had never been up to her mama's weight when it came to subtlety of wit. But then, her mama had been possessed of a generosity of heart that Constance suspected was beyond the earl's understanding. Regina Blaidsdale could no more contemplate deliberately hurting anyone than she could countenance cruelty in others. More than that, however, she had been blessed with a keen intelligence that chafed at the limitations imposed on her because of her sex. No doubt it was this latter attribute that led her in her final years on earth to embrace the enlightened philosophies of Olympe de Gouges and Mary Wollstonecraft, not to mention the Frenchmen, Voltaire and Rousseau. Perhaps, then, it was that aspect of her character that had also led her to remove her daughter and herself from her husband's influence.

Instantly, Constance dismissed the idea. Somehow she did not think that could have been the sole motivating force for so sudden and radical a move. Her mama, after all, had remained with the earl for eleven years. Presumably, she had long since reconciled herself to the reality of her marriage to a man who did not share her belief that females were not lesser creatures than men. Surely, she had learned to cope. Besides, such an explanation would hardly have posed a threat to Constance. Her mama's adamant silence concerning the cause of the rift between husband and wife would seem to point to something of a sudden, far more irreconcilable, perhaps even sinister, nature.

Whatever it had been, it was obvious Constance was not going to learn anything by remaining in bed. Besides, it appeared to be a perfectly lovely morning for mid-February. Perhaps she might be allowed to take Viscount Hazelton, her half-brother, for a walk.

Flinging aside the counterpane and sliding out of bed, Constance rang for her abigail.

An hour later, having been made privy to all the latest gossip from belowstairs while she drank her morning cup of chocolate, dressed, then sat to have her hair, the fiery red of autumn leaves, pulled up at the crown and allowed to fall in loose ringlets down the back of her head, Constance made her way downstairs.

If she had thought that at the hour of eleven she would find the breakfast room happily deserted, she was soon to be proven sadly mistaken.

"No doubt she will be down directly," pronounced her stepmother's voice from the other side of the door, "though I am never quite sure what to expect from one who considers herself a liberated woman. The poor dear. I am sure I feel the greatest pity for her. It is hardly her fault, after all, that she was not brought up to know the proper behavior for a female of her station."

Constance hesitated, sorely tempted to forego the morning meal rather than endure Lady Blaidsdale's honeyed barbs over toast and eggs. Then a reply couched in a feminine contralto served not only to pique her curiosity, but also to put her on her mettle.

"I suggest you save your pity, Rosalind dear. She will be brought to a proper understanding of her duties before the day is out. She is the daughter of an earl. You cannot imagine that Blaidsdale intends to let her squander her future, can you?"

Before Lady Blaidsdale could attest to what lay in the realm of her fancy, Constance, who had heard more than enough as to leave little doubt in *her* mind what the earl intended, thrust open the doors and blithely entered.

"Good morning," she lilted, sliding the doors closed behind her before coming about with a bright smile for her stepmother and her guest. "And what a lovely morning it is, too."

Pointedly, she let her gaze come to rest on the second of the two women seated at the breakfast table. "I do beg your pardon," she said, allowing her eyes to widen in feigned surprise. "I had no idea we had company. It is Aunt Clarissa, is it not? It has been many years since last we met, but I daresay I could never forget you or the occasion. I was nine, and you had my little dog put down for nipping at Cousin Albert's coattails, as I recall. How *is* Cousin Albert? Still suffering from a nervous disposition? Or was it dyspepsia? I am afraid I have forgot which it was that we were supposed to be careful not to exacerbate."

Lady Sinclair, to whom these various observations had been directed, grew noticeably chill in her demeanor while Lady Blaidsdale uttered a gasp. A tall, imposing woman who might have been quite attractive had it not been for an habitual hardness about the feminine features and a decided lack of humor in her demeanor, Constance's fraternal aunt calmly reached for her morning cup of coffee.

"Constance," the baroness acknowledged in flat tones that left little doubt as to the esteem in which she held her only niece. "I see you are as impetuous as ever you were. A pity your aunt did not see fit to teach you the demureness proper to a female. In answer to your question, Albert is doing quite well, thank you. He is, in fact, soon to join us here—upon which time you may see for yourself the sort of gentleman into which he has grown."

"A treat no doubt devoutly to be desired," returned Constance, giving no sign that her stomach had just constricted in sudden alarm. "And when may we look forward to seeing my cousin? I had made plans to go into Bridgwater today to purchase a few things. Naturally, I should not wish to be absent upon his arrival."

"No, that would not do at all," piped up Lady Blaidsdale, a plump, blond beauty with a predilection for adorning herself in a profusion of pink. "You will simply have to put off your little shopping spree until tomorrow."

"Nonsense." Lady Sinclair eyed her sister-in-law with chilly disfavor. "As it happens, we do not look for Albert before nightfall."

"Splendid," beamed Constance, who would prefer not to have to see her cousin at all. "Then I daresay I should leave at once if I am to be back in time."

"Yes, no doubt that would be wise," agreed her aunt smoothly. "Before you go, however, I believe your father would like a word with you. Did I not hear him mention something to that effect, Rosalind dear?"

"Oh, indeed, yes," Lady Blaidsdale fairly gushed in her eagerness to provide corroborating testimony. "How silly of me to have forgot."

Lady Sinclair's expressionless blue eyes shifted to Constance. "He is in his study at present with Sinclair. Still, I imagine he will be free to see you directly."

Undaunted, Constance returned her look squarely. She was perfectly aware how little it had cost Lady Sinclair to appear to be amenable to her niece's proposed outing. She knew as well as did the baroness that Constance would never be allowed to leave the grounds.

"You may be sure I am all eagerness to hear what my father has to say to me," Constance returned with a smile that was as cool as was the manner in which she inclined her head to her aunt before turning to the door. "After all," she added, pausing with her hand on the door handle, "I have been trying for two months to have a talk with him. And now I pray you will both excuse me. I have a few matters to which I must attend before I see the earl."

Without waiting for an answer from either of the two women, Constance exited and made her way swiftly back up the stairs and along the corridor to her rooms.

Upon finding her abigail still tidying up her mistress's things in the bedchamber, Constance halted, momentarily undecided. She had experienced an immediate sense of unease the instant she realized her Aunt Clarissa was arrived at Landford Park without warning. To learn that Cousin Albert was soon to follow had left her little doubt as to the purpose of her aunt's visit. It was all to begin again—the cajoling, the threats, the ultimatums. Only this time it would not be done by correspondence and through intermediaries. She was here in her father's house. They would try more forceful means of persuasion to bring her to wed her Cousin Albert.

Faith, what a fool she had been to walk blindly into the snare! And yet she had not come completely unprepared. Some instinct for self-preservation had prompted her to insist on making the journey with her own coach and Will Trask, her driver. And then, too, there was Millie, her abigail. She and Will were loyal to Constance alone. The small advantage they offered would simply have to be enough.

"Millie," she said, her mind racing, as the germ of an idea began to grow and take root. "I believe I may have need to depart Landford Park in something of a hurry. It will mean leaving everything behind, save for the most vital of necessities. It will also require complete secrecy. You must tell no one. Do you understand? No one. Everything depends on it, Millie."

"I can keep a secret, Lady Constance," asserted the abigail, her eyes keen on her mistress's face. "Don't you worry none. You just tell me what you want me to do."

Constance felt a lump rise in her throat. She should have known Millie would never falter in her loyalty. When she, Constance, had arrived at the age to require a lady's maid, she had elevated the girl from the kitchen staff to serve in that position. She had recognized in Millie a bright intelligence that was being wasted belowstairs. Not only had Millie proven quick to learn her new duties, but she had displayed a natural gift for turning out a well-dressed lady. In the seven years that Millie had served as her abigail, Constance had never once had occasion to regret her decision.

"Dearest Millie," Constance said, her eyes shimmering. "I knew I could place my trust in you."

With a sharp sense of urgency, she hurriedly gave the abigail her instructions.

"Here, take this," she finished, handing Millie a plump purse. "Hide it on your person. Do not forget—if anyone asks, your mistress, having decided to remain here in anticipation of her cousin's arrival, has sent you to Bridgwater to purchase a few things."

"Yes, milady," Millie nodded, securing the purse in the bodice of her dress. "I'll remember."

"I am depending on you, Millie," said Constance, giving the maid a bracing smile and a hug. "Now, on your way. I fear we haven't much time."

Hardly had the girl slipped out the door than a servant arrived to summon Constance to the earl's study.

"Pray inform his lordship that I shall be along directly," said Constance, stalling to give Millie time enough to retrieve her hat and cloak from her chamber and make her exit from the house. At last, judging that she dared not linger further, Constance steeled herself for the coming interview with her father.

At fifty-one, Edgar Greyson Lawrence Landford, the seventh Earl of Blaidsdale, was only just beginning to show the first signs of middle age. Still, in spite of the streaks of grey in his brown hair, which was developing a decided widow's peak, and the start of a small bulge around his middle, he was yet a handsome figure of a man. Indeed, Constance, studying him from where she sat on the caffoy-covered settee near the fireplace, could not but see why her mama might initially have been attracted to him. Unfortunately, the austere cast of his face, which was dominated by an aquiline nose, thin lips, and an uncompromising jaw, must soon have put her off. If he had ever in his distant youth been blessed with so much as a smidgen of *joie de vivre*, it must long since have withered from a cruel lack of nourishment, Constance decided. She could only suppose that she was unable to recall the sound of her father's laughter because she had never, to her memory, heard it.

Certainly, he was not laughing now. He was, in fact, regarding her with a singular lack of amusement.

"I believe I have not heard you aright," he said with chilling deliberation. "Or have you forgot that I am your father and that it is your duty to obey me? I have not forgot that it is *my* duty to ensure your future well-being. You are five-and-twenty and clearly at your last prayers. You will not ignore the fact that you are unlikely to receive any further offers of marriage."

"No, how can you say so, my lord," queried Constance with a demureness belied by the sparkle in her eye, "when it has been little more than two months since I attended my maiden aunt's wedding? Though she would adamantly deny it, she is, by my calculations, eight-and-forty if she is a day. Not that age has anything to say to the issue at hand. I should not marry my Cousin Albert if I were nine-and-ninety and on my deathbed. I should, in fact, be pleased not to marry anyone unless I should find someone who would have my love and respect. Albert, you will agree, could not possibly meet either criterion."

"If that is what you think, then you are as foolish as you are impertinent," pronounced the earl in no uncertain terms. "Albert Sinclair has proven a sober young man with a fine sense of familial duty. He shows promise of a brilliant career in the army. You should be pleased that he has agreed to offer for you. It will, in fact, be the saving of you."

"I was not aware that I required 'saving,' my lord," returned Constance, marveling that she had ever thought she might somehow win some small measure of her father's regard. Clearly, he saw her only as a means to an end. The question was to what end? "Nor do I understand why you should be so keen on marrying your only daughter off against her wishes."

"Pray do not play the naïve miss with me," Blaidsdale snapped. "You know as well as I that it is your duty to look to an advantageous marriage for the good of the family. As it happens, it has ever been Lady Sinclair's fondest wish that you and her only son should be joined one day in matrimony."

"You mean that my *fortune* should be wed to his, do you not, my lord?" said Constance, a great deal more enlightened than she had been before. The rumors, after all, were rife that Sinclair had made a number of exceedingly unwise investments. Clearly, Aunt Clarissa looked to Constance to retrieve the family's fortunes. It was equally plain that Sinclair's business with his brother-in-law had been in the nature of a petition for a loan. Constance gave the earl a searching look. "Really, Father, can I truly mean so little to you that you would rather force me into a marriage I cannot want in order that you might be saved from having to dip into your purse?"

If she had thought the plain truth would in some way help to clear the air, she was soon to be proven correct in her assessment.

Blaidsdale's face went livid with rage. Constance was given to see the stern mask of control stripped away to reveal a soul twisted with rancor. And then her father's hand lashed out to strike her a savage backhanded blow against her cheek. Her head snapped to the side, and lights flashed before her eyes. Still, she clung tenaciously to consciousness.

"You ungrateful little baggage," he uttered in scathing accents. "If not for me, your mother would have been branded a whore and you a nameless bastard. And so that that does not happen, you will learn to hold your tongue and do as you are told. And if you have yet to be convinced, ponder this, my sweet. Should you persist in refusing to marry Albert, you may look forward to a short and miserable life in the confines of a mental institution. After all, you would clearly be mad to disobey your loving father, would you not, Constance? You may be sure that all it would take is my word on it. Now, have I made myself perfectly understood?"

Constance, stunned by Blaidsdale's sudden, brutal attack, not to mention his unexpected revelations, willed the bile to recede from her throat. Shaken but undaunted, she lifted her eyes to the man who had declared he was not her father.

"You may be certain that I understand you better than I have ever done before," she said, marveling that her voice should sound steady, when inside she was feeling something of quite a different order. Ignoring the trembling in her limbs, she made herself rise calmly to her feet. "No doubt I should thank you for making it clear why I could never summon even the semblance of a daughterly affection for you. Now I need no longer feel the least compulsion about detesting you." Deliberately, she folded her hands at her waist. "And now if there is nothing more, my lord, I should like to return to my rooms to consider Captain Sinclair's offer."

Blaidsdale raked her with his hard, flat stare. For a single, sickening moment, it appeared that Constance had overplayed her hand. She steeled herself to meet Blaidsdale's fury.

Without warning, the earl's mask slid back in place.

"You have until Albert's arrival to prepare yourself for your nuptials," he pronounced with a steely dispassion. "You will be married by special license before the day is out. Until then, you are confined to your rooms. The sooner you reconcile yourself to a future as Mrs. Albert Sinclair, the sooner you will be allowed a measure of freedom. I daresay once you are wed and bedded, you will have fulfilled whatever obligation Albert will demand of you. He might even agree to allow you to return to your Aunt Sophie."

"How exceedingly generous of him, to be sure," returned Constance, who did not in the least doubt that, once Albert had his hands on her fortune, he would happily be rid of his wife. He, after all, had need of only one woman in his life—his mama, who ruled him with an iron hand. A wife, especially one who loathed and despised him, would prove something of an impediment in that endearing relationship.

But then, she would die before she let Albert or any of his blood kin touch so much as a farthing of her mama's fortune.

Something of her thoughts must have shown in her face. Suddenly, Blaidsdale's eyebrows fairly snapped together over the bridge of his aristocratic nose. He took a menacing step toward her.

Constance, vowing that she would not docilely submit to being beaten, steeled herself to do battle by any means available to her. Mentally, she gauged the distance to the iron poker near the fireplace.

No doubt it was fortunate that at that moment there came a scratch on the door, which heralded the arrival of Vice Admiral Sir Oliver Landford to see the earl.

Blaidsdale came to a halt. Constance, watching him, could not but be struck with the feeling that the earl was less than pleased at the prospect of an interview with his younger brother. Indeed, for a moment it seemed that he had forgotten her, as he appeared to contemplate the purpose of the vice admiral's unexpected visit.

Constance, deeming retreat the better part of valor, took advantage of Blaidsdale's momentary distraction to move to the door.

"As it would seem you have other business to occupy you, Lord Blaidsdale," she said, reaching for the door handle, "I shall not hesitate to leave you to it."

He did not stop her, nor did she wait for him to dismiss her. Opening the door, she exited in time to come face-to-face with Landford.

He did not deign so much as to acknowledge her as he shoved past her into the room.

"He is at it again, Blaidsdale," boomed Landford, his florid face even redder than was usual. "Vere, that scoundrel, has managed to buy up my markers. Where the devil does he come up with the blunt? Not from Albermarle, you may be sure of that. And not from any fortune of his own. He got little enough from his father, thanks to us. It is time the devil's cub was given a lesson like the one we gave his father. Hell and the devil confound it, Blaidsdale. It should be easy enough to arrange."

"Calm yourself, Sir Oliver," said Blaidsdale, staring significantly past the vice admiral's substantial figure to Constance. Deliberately, he closed the door in her face.

Landford's words echoed in her brain. "It should be easy enough to arrange." A lesson like the one they had given Vere's father. The gambling markers, the loss of the *Swallow*, the yachting accident that had taken the lives of the marquis and marchioness—all part of a lesson arranged by Blaisdale and Landford? Constance felt sickened to her soul. Had her mama realized at last the depths of depravity of which the earl was capable? Was that why she took her daughter and left him? Whatever the reason, it had arisen five years before the events that had culminated in the deaths of Vere's parents and the loss of the fortune that should have come to him. And now Blaisdale and Landford might very well be hatching a new plot, this time one meant to ruin Vere.

This time, however, there was someone who knew the truth. She, Constance, would make sure that Vere knew it, too. It was more imperative than ever that she escape Landford Park and Blaisdale's evil machinations.

A low cough jarred her from her thoughts.

"Begging your pardon, m'lady, but I have been instructed to see you to your chambers." It was Higgens, the butler. Obviously, he had been waiting for Constance to make her appearance.

"Yes, of course, Higgens." Constance smiled and turned her steps down the hallway. "And I suppose I am to be locked in my room as well, am I not?"

"I am afraid so, m'lady," agreed the butler, seemingly little pleased with his orders.

"Very well, Higgens, if you must. It will be just like old times, will it not? I spent a great deal of time, as I recall, locked in my room. But then, *Maman* always made it fun by sneaking in Toby, my little dog, along with milk and cakes."

"Yes, m'lady," intoned the butler, opening the door for her, then standing aside to allow her to step past him. "I should be pleased to bring you a tray if you like, m'lady."

"Thank you, Higgens. You are very kind," Constance said, placing her hand on his arm, "but no. I fear I haven't any appetite. Perhaps later. I wonder, however, if you would be so good as to open the window in the guest-room intended for my Cousin Albert's use. I could not but notice that the fireplace was smoking as I passed by. I daresay there is a bird's nest in the chimney. At any rate, it would hardly do to receive Captain Sinclair in its present state."

Higgens, exchanging a long look with Constance, nodded slowly.

"Indeed, m'lady," he said, his face utterly expressionless as befitted a servant of his superior station. "I shall look into the matter at once."

Closing the door and turning the key in the lock, Higgens stood for a moment, his normally impassive features giving way to a somber expression. Lady Constance was a fine lady, kind and generous like her mama before her. Things had come to a sad pass—a sad pass, indeed—if she were to be forced to marry the likes of Albert Sinclair. The gentleman was a mean one, he was—like his mama. Lady Constance deserved better than to be tossed to the wolves, so to speak.

Higgens turned and made his way to the door next to that of Lady Constance's room. Letting himself in, he crossed to the window and, after only a moment's hesitation, unlatched and opened the sash. Lady Constance had ought to have a fighting chance, he told himself, remembering the hoydenish little girl who had used to steal out into the garden and climb the oak tree. She had been as agile as a cat and more daring than was strictly good for her. Somehow the memory was not so comforting as he might have liked, he decided, as he exited the chamber.

Lady Constance, however, taking time only to don her ermine-lined pelisse and carriage bonnet and to snatch up her reticule, was already climbing out the bedroom window onto the narrow ledge that ran along the front of the house. Resolutely refusing to consider the possibility that Higgens had not done as she requested, she pressed her back against the wall and began to grope her way toward the window of the adjoining room.

She could not have been farther than a yard from her goal when, directly below her, a carriage drew up to the front of the house and stopped. Constance froze where she was, her heart pounding beneath her breast, as Blaidsdale and Vice Admiral Sir Oliver Landford emerged from the house. Telling herself that this was no doubt her just reward for having wished for a little adventure to enter her life, she closed her eyes and willed the two men to finish their good-byes and depart. In spite of the sun shining out of a cloudless sky, Constance was numb with cold when at last Landford climbed into the coach and pulled away along the drive. Indeed, it was all she could do to will her feet to move. Then, at last, she was scrambling through the open window.

Some twenty minutes later, having made her escape from the house and across the down to the spinney in which Millie and the coach were, according to their mistress's instructions, waiting for her, Constance was well on her way to Wells. Nevertheless, she was keenly aware that she was far from safe. The earl would waste little time sending men out to find her. No doubt the first place they would look would be her mama's house in Wells. Still, she would seem to have little choice but to risk a brief stop at her old home. She could not but consider it a queer twist of fate that, thinking to take up permanent residence in Wells, she had had all her belongings sent there before she left London. Other than the trunk that she had left behind her at Landford Park, everything she owned was at present in the house her mama had willed to her.

She really must have a few things to tide her over until she could think what to do. First, of course, she must find and speak with Mr. Enderhart. And if he could not help her, then what? she wondered. Where could she possibly go that would place her beyond the earl's reach?

And, barring that, where could she possibly find a safe haven in which to hide? The devil, she thought, even if she were to find such a place, how could she possibly live her life always looking over her shoulder, constantly afraid of the day that someone she knew would see and recognize her?

Every instinct rebelled at the mere thought of such an existence. Indeed, by the time the coach pulled into the posting inn on the outskirts of Wells some two hours later to inquire into Mr. Enderhart's direction, it had become clear to her just how impossible was her situation. Ironically, she saw only two plausible solutions to her dilemma if her mama's solicitor failed to be the savior the countess had promised he would be. Either she must wed someone other than Albert Sinclair posthaste, or she must certainly consider removing herself from England with as much dispatch as was possible—not, however, before she sent a letter to Vere, informing him of everything she had learned.

She was contemplating the less than appealing notion of buying passage on a ship to the New World, when she was brought to note the arrival of a handsome coach drawn by a magnificent team of perfectly matched blacks. Thinking she had never seen a more striking equipage, she was drawn inevitably to glance into the window at the passenger.

She was hardly prepared for the sudden, hot rush of blood to her cheeks or for the riot of emotions that awakened within her breast as the gentleman turned his head and looked at her. Indeed, she could only be exceedingly grateful for the concealing veil over the front of her bonnet, as she found herself staring into the arrogant features of none other than the Marquis of Vere.

Certain that he must surely recognize her despite the veil, Constance could only be exceedingly relieved when the nobleman was distracted by the arrival of a hostler, who begged a word with his lordship. She was equally grateful that Millie, who had been dispatched to make inquiries of the innkeeper, returned just then as well.

"Mr. Enderhart's gone away to his son's house in London," said Millie, settling into the coach across from her mistress. "Mr. Halstead, the landlord, didn't know when he'd be coming back. His lordship must know that you've escaped by now. He'll be coming looking for you. He mustn't find you, Lady Constance. He means you no good. What are we to do, m'lady?"

Constance, who suddenly knew precisely what she meant to do, smiled, her mind already busy making plans.

"You and Will are going to Aunt Sophie in London," she answered, signaling the coachman to drive on. "And I, if I have my way, shall be going to the devil I doubt not."

An hour later, Constance, dressed in a suit of black dittos, which had belonged to her mama's friend and which she had found stored in a trunk in the attic, along with a black cape and loo mask, sat her horse in a thick copse and waited. With her glorious red hair concealed beneath a black scarf and broad-brimmed hat, she might easily have passed for a slender youth. A brace of deadly looking pistols thrust in her belt and a sword slung at her hip lent her a distinctly dangerous air, which was strangely incongruous with the red rosebud she pressed to her nose to inhale its sweetness.

She frowned slightly at the thought that, from all accounts, the rose in question should have been in full blossom. As it was, however, she had been fortunate that the hothouse, which had once been her mama's pride and joy, had contained this single specimen.

At the sound of carriage wheels on the graveled road, she slipped the blossom in the inner pocket of her coat and drew the pistols from her waistband.

It came somewhat whimsically to her, as her stomach gave vent to a rumbling protest, that she might have liked to have had time for more than a plate of day-old raisin biscuits and a glass of milk before she embarked on her career as a captain moonlight. In truth, she was devilishly sharp set.

The next moment, the travel coach swept around the bend into sight. Constance, setting spurs to her mount, bounded out of cover to confront the approaching team. Firing a warning shot into the air, she held the other pistol with unerring accuracy on the driver.

"*Hold to!*" she shouted in a ringing voice.

Chapter 3

Constance thrust the empty pistol in her waistband and kneed her horse to the window of the coach.

"Good evening, my lord," she said, marveling as she met Vere's cold stare over the barrel of her second gun that her aim held rock steady. Faith, her heart, beneath her breast, was pounding wildly. "No doubt I should apologize for causing you this delay. However, I promise I shall require no more of your time than it takes you to hand over your purse and the diamond solitaire you are wearing."

Vere, who had not failed even in the initial onset of confusion to note the seemingly youthful timbre of the voice that assailed his coach, drew suddenly still at that pronouncement from the stripling who had had the temerity to think to rob him. The devil, he had heard those words before or something remarkably close to them. Indeed, if he were not mistaken, he himself had spoken them not more than two months past! It had not, however, been a slender youth to whom he had addressed them, but a spirited young beauty whose pluck in the face of peril had persuaded him to spare her her valuables.

She had, as he recalled, promised that they would meet again, and he had warned her what might happen in such an unlikely eventuality.

"And if I refuse?" he murmured, his eyes appearing suddenly sleepy beneath drooping eyelids.

Constance, who had expected precisely that response from the marquis—indeed, had hoped for it—deliberately thumbed the hammer back on the pistol. And yet, the devil, she thought with reluctant admiration. How dared he call her bluff! "I should have thought it was obvious, my lord," she said, aware of the blood running, light and swift, along her veins. "I should naturally have to shoot you."

"Spoken like a true villain," observed his lordship. Slowly, he unloosed his grip on the gun concealed in the pocket of his many-caped greatcoat. Damn the chit. She had not the smallest notion how close he had come to putting a period to her existence, and now she dared to imagine that she held the upper hand with Vere? The impetuous young beauty was as mettlesome as she was foolhardy. Or could it be that she knew precisely what she was doing? he wondered, struck by the faint gleam of a smile on the lovely lips.

The little rogue, thought Vere. He entertained not the least doubt that the masked rider was indeed the woman who had so sweetly returned his stolen kiss— with the result that he had found himself on more than a few occasions since then speculating on the memory of eyes the dazzling blue of sunlit water and hair the fiery red of an autumn forest. And how not when she was possessed not only of a striking beauty that was not easily forgotten but also a rare courage of which few men could boast? Certainly, it would seem that his warning that a second meeting would prove too great a temptation for him to resist his more primitive masculine urges had failed to daunt her in the least. On the contrary, she had deliberately sought him out!

He could not but wonder what game she was playing, as he contemplated the rather pleasant prospect of teaching her a much-needed lesson in the danger of pitting herself against the notorious Marquis of Vere. Even more intriguing yet, however, was the proposition that she alone out of all of his numerous victims had apparently seen through the disguise of the Black Rose to arrive at his true identity. Patently, she had known him well enough to recognize him in spite of his mask. But who the devil was *she?*

Suddenly, it came to him that he was beginning to enjoy himself.

"I wonder," he said speculatively, "if you have the nerve to shoot an unarmed man."

Opening the door to the coach, Vere coolly stepped down to face the beauty who had had the audacity not only to hold him up but, further, to point a gun at him.

If he had expected to unsettle her by his display of unflinching arrogance, he was soon to be vastly disappointed.

Constance, who had never any intent of putting a bullet in Vere, but, indeed, had something far different in mind for his lordship, awarded him a flashing grin.

"You are quite right, my lord," she said, slinging her right leg in front of her over the pommel and dropping lightly to the ground. With her free hand, she unclasped the cape and slung it over the saddle. "I should derive very little pleasure from shooting you in such a fashion." Easing the hammer down, she thrust the pistol in her waistband. "On the other hand," she added, smoothly drawing her sword from its sheath, "I haven't the smallest qualm in engaging you in a duel. You do not, I believe, carry that walking stick purely for ornamental reasons."

Egad, thought Vere, faced with the prospect of engaging in swordplay with a female. At least it would appear that the lady was not wholly unfamiliar with the proper etiquette, he noted dryly, as his would-be opponent tested the blade with a calm composure before assuming the waiting position with the sword held horizontally before her across the hips.

"My lord?" she queried archly.

Hell and the devil confound it! Vere silently cursed, as he took in the lithe, supple figure, rendered wholly fetching in skintight unmentionables. She was tall for a woman and had a tiny waist no larger than the span of his hands, a firm, flat belly, and long, shapely legs. She was possessed as well of bewitching curves, he noted, observing the delectable contour of wholly feminine hips and the soft swell of well-rounded breasts, which the masculine waistcoat and short-tailed double-breasted coat did little to camouflage. Egad, "fetching" did not begin to describe what she was! She was an exquisite creature who might tempt even a saint to sin. And he was no bloody saint.

His every instinct for self-preservation warned him that she was no common female to be dallied with and then discarded. On the contrary, on the occasion of their first encounter, she had presented every manifestation of a woman of quality. Still, she was an impertinent wench to presume to challenge Vere to a duel. And why *should* he not teach the little baggage a lesson in the finer art of fencing? Flinging off his greatcoat, Vere tossed it inside the coach. He would take care to hurt nothing more than her pride, and afterwards, he would find other things in which to instruct her. If nothing else, the flame-haired beauty promised an evening of uncommon diversion.

With a hiss of steel, Vere unsheathed the blade contained in his walking stick. "This will not take long," he called up to John Vickers, his coachman, who liked leaving his horses standing in the cold as little as he cared for being held up by highwaymen. Vere tossed the walking stick in the coach after his greatcoat. "Pray do not interfere."

"As you wish, my lord," replied the coachman with the air of one who was far too well acquainted with his employer's whims to be surprised by anything Vere might choose to do.

Constance, facing the man who was notorious for his coldblooded nerve and deadly proficiency with the sword, could not but think she might have bitten off a tad more than she could chew. It was not fear that she felt, however, as she watched Vere slash the air with the blade to loosen his wrist. No doubt it was some hitherto unknown perversity in her character that led her to experience a distinct thrill at the prospect of matching wits and skill with a swordsman of Vere's remove. She, after all, had been instructed by one of the finest fencing masters in all of England. Vere would be her first real test of all that she had learned.

And, in truth, she was keenly aware of the cold prickle of excitement beneath her skin as Vere, bringing the haft of the sword to his lips, paid tribute to her in a salute that was deliberately mocking.

Faith, but he was magnificent in his masculine pride, which, she knew from recent experience, was yet tempered with his own peculiar code of honor and an odd sort of generosity that he was careful to conceal behind a façade of cynicism. Nevertheless, she did not doubt that he was every whit as dangerous as his reputation painted him. If she had gauged him wrongly, she might very well pay for it with her life, and still she was not afraid. She had always considered herself an excellent judge of character. And in this particular case, she had the advantage of having had a kiss from which to draw her conclusions.

Lifting the sword over her head, she released the tip and brought it to bear on the marquis.

"*En garde*, my lord," she said, dropping down into the fighting stance, her left arm lifted behind her for balance.

Vere, following suit, smiled ever so gently. "*En garde*, my lady."

"As it turns out, I am *not* a lady," retorted the surprising young beauty with a tinge of bitterness that was not lost on Vere. They were circling, touching sword points, feeling out one another's strengths and weaknesses as each looked for an opening. "Certainly, I am not *your* anything," declared Constance, passing her blade over Vere's with the quickness of a cat. She lunged.

Vere parried with the twist of a wrist. "Then I collect I am mistaken," he said. Content, it would seem, to toy with her for the moment, he did not offer to counter with the riposte. "On the other hand," he observed, holding a straight thrust with his point and deflecting it, "'tis plain that you are no gentleman, but a woman in need of a man's guiding hand."

"And I suppose you, my lord," Constance flung back at him as she caught the end of Vere's blade close to her guard and, spinning her point around full circle, thrust his sword aside for the attack, "think to be that man."

Vere parried her ensuing thrust with a sharp tap. "You flatter yourself, my girl," he said, reading her feint to the right and countering to the left with a neat downward swipe which brought them suddenly chest-to-chest. "I prefer that my lights of love already know the rules of the game. It has been my experience that green girls are a deal more trouble than they are worth."

If he had thought by that to rouse her temper and throw her off her fighting balance, he was soon to discover that he had hit wide of his mark.

Constance, finding herself staring up into Vere's hard, mocking eyes at exceedingly close range, did the unthinkable. Lifting herself up on tiptoe, she kissed him fully on the mouth.

It was hardly what Vere was expecting. More surprising yet, however, than the kiss itself was the sudden, hot leap of blood in his veins. Green girl? Hellfire, she was a bloody temptress with the uncanny power to set him afire with her touch. Wrapping his free arm about her waist, he bent his head, his lips seeking hers with a hunger that must have surprised her almost as much as it did him.

Only then did the unpredictable beauty, pushing against his chest, stop him. Lifting his head, Vere found himself gazing into the mysterious depths of eyes that might make a man forget everything but the desire to possess this tantalizing, unpredictable female. Fascinated, he watched her lips curve slowly upward in a smile that was both whimsical and provocative at the same time.

"I believe, if you came to know me better, my lord," she said, cradling the side of his face with the palm of her free hand, "you would find that I am, if nothing else, a fast learner."

The next instant, the surprising minx disengaged herself from his arm and, standing away from him, brought up her sword.

"And now, my lord," she challenged, "to the matter at hand. Your purse and your other valuables, an' you please."

A singularly satanic smile played gently about Vere's mouth. "I fear you will have to find something else by which to remember me, Lady Moonlight," he said, a gleam in his eyes. "I have no intention of handing over my property to you."

"As you wish, my lord," returned Constance, who was quick to demonstrate that she, no less than Vere, had been holding back. Now she made no pretense of the skill that she possessed.

Light and quick on her feet, she impressed even Vere with the brilliance of her attack and parry. More than that, it soon came curiously to dawn on him that her peculiar style very nearly approached his own in its execution. He found himself watching for the small, distinctive variations on the otherwise characteristic movements of the Angelo school of fencing, variations that his own instructor had taught and perfected. That he saw them performed by this slip of a woman both intrigued and mystified him.

If anyone had ever told him that someday he would encounter a man who knew the intricacies of this particular style of fencing, Vere would have said that that person was mad. Only one man other than Vere had ever wielded the sword in this fashion, and he was long dead. That Vere was now facing a woman who displayed a mastery of it would seem to defy all rationale. It occurred to him with cynical appreciation of the irony of his position that it was rather like dueling with a younger, less experienced version of himself.

At last, narrowly avoiding pinking his opponent, he deemed that matters had gone on long enough. Drawing her on with a deliberate retreat behind a series of parries without any attempt at riposte, he waited, biding his time until, overconfident, she lunged, her body fully extended.

Vere moved with lightning swiftness. Catching her blade with a sudden, sharp twist of the wrist, he simultaneously disarmed her and flung her off balance.

All in an instant, it seemed, Constance, unable to recover, found herself sprawled ignominiously on her back on the ground. The very next, she froze as the point of Vere's blade came to rest at the base of her throat.

"And now, Lady Moonlight," said the marquis with steely-edged softness, "you will tell me who you are and what the devil you think you are doing."

"How very ungallant of you, my lord," declared Constance, awarding Vere a comical moue of displeasure. As if he did not know precisely who she was, she reflected sardonically. "I thought it was obvious. I am the

Black Rose, and I was desirous of robbing you of your valuables."

"The Black Rose, is it?" Smiling ever so gently, he ran the tip of the sword lightly, tantalizingly down the valley between her breasts. "You will no doubt pardon me if I take exception to the word of a lady."

"It would seem that at the moment you can do whatever you please, my lord," Constance returned, making no attempt to hide the irony in her voice. The devil to use her so, she fumed, drawing a sharp breath as the blade point circled the peaked thrust of her nipples beneath her shirt, first one and then the other. He was obviously enjoying himself immensely at her expense. Helplessly, she felt the blood rise, hot, to her cheeks not only at the liberties he was taking in his explorations, but also at the unfamiliar flood of sensations that his manipulations were arousing in her.

"It would, indeed," agreed Vere, noting with interest the unmistakable quickening of his captive's breath. It would seem that the red-haired temptress was a female of strong passions. But then, he was sardonically aware that her lissome beauty was having no less an effect on him!

Hell and the devil confound it. He had meant merely to punish her a little for her impertinence in challenging him to a duel. He had not thought to find himself sorely tempted to cast all caution to the wind and take his pleasures with the girl right here and now. He had a distinct aversion to bedding virgins, who were wont to place far too much significance on the loss of their maidenheads. But then, neither had he been prepared for the stark intensity of his own masculine arousal. Egad, he was all too keenly aware of the painful bulge against the front of his breeches. The devil, it was time to send the chit packing before he was driven beyond the bloody limits of his self-control! "I say indisputably that you are *not* the Black Rose," he declared baldly.

"And, further, that I am very nearly certain it is not my purse that you were after."

"You are right, of course, my lord," replied Constance, growing heartily weary of her less than dignified position, lying flat on her back on the ground, not to mention a helpless prey to Vere's sadistic pleasure. "I am not the Black Rose. We both know that *you* are. And it is not your purse that I am after, but something of far greater importance to me. And now that that much is settled, would you mind very much removing your blade from my person so that I might sit up?"

"Naturally, I am pleased to comply with your wishes," said Vere, flicking the blade aside and extending a hand to help her to her feet. "Nothing, however, has been settled. Or need I point out that you have yet to tell me your name or what the devil you thought you were about?"

Constance, retrieving and sheathing her sword, busied herself with dusting herself off before making any attempt at a reply to his curious insistence that she give him her name. Faith, he *could* not in truth be ignorant of who she was—or could he? She had naturally assumed that he had held up her coach because she was the daughter of his father's greatest enemy and therefore his enemy, too. And yet, his subsequent behavior, now that she thought of it, would seem to put some doubt on that assumption. *Would* he have kissed her and then generously allowed her to keep her valuables if he had known she was Lady Constance Landford? Faith, might he not have stopped her coach merely on a whim and because it had happened to come along as he lay in waiting for a plump-appearing pigeon ready for the plucking?

Suddenly, it came to her with terrible significance that she might very well have acted upon a wholly erroneous line of logic. She had based everything she had done on her belief that Vere had knowingly held up

Blaidsdale's daughter as a small measure of vengeance. His gallantry toward her, she had supposed to be the product of his own peculiar code of honor toward an unprotected female. Indeed, she had been counting on that supposed sense of honor to lead him to treat her with the same sort of generosity that had prompted him to spare her her mama's brooch. Now, all of a sudden, it would seem she had placed herself in a cursedly uncertain position.

Good God, if he did not know who she was, then there was no telling how he would react were he to learn the truth of her identity! And yet, she would seem to have little choice in the matter other than to follow through with what would now appear to be a far less than ideal plan. She required, after all, a safe haven in which to hide until she could decide her future course, and where better than the Marquis of Vere's hunting lodge? Constance had reasoned. Surely that would be the very last place the earl would come looking for her.

It had all seemed to make perfect sense when she had seen Vere at the inn and the idea had come to her. Now she could not but question the wisdom of her thinking. She, after all, was about to place herself at the mercy of a man who, far from being inclined to help her, had every reason to wish ill of her. The prospect, as she steeled herself to face him, was far less than comforting.

Vere, watching her, could not but wonder what clever story the minx was devising in that pretty head of hers. Whatever he had thought to hear from her, however, it was not what was presently to issue from her lips.

"As it happens, I haven't a name," declared Constance, matter-of-factly removing her hat, followed in swift order by the mask. "Oh, I can see that you do not believe me. And how should you, when I, too, am having a deal of difficulty believing it myself. But there it is," she said, shrugging, as she reached up and pulled off the scarf to allow her luxurious mass of curls to cascade down around her shoulders.

"Indubitably," agreed Vere, who, a man of keen discernment, did, in fact, believe her. He had not missed noting, after all, the blur of hurt and anger cross her face just before she turned away to shake out her glorious hair, which even in the moonlight shone a deep coppery red. Inexplicably, he felt the birth of a cold anger in the pit of his stomach at the thought that someone had dared to inflict pain on this exquisite creature. "But then, unless you happened to spring into being fully grown only two months ago, I daresay you have been called something."

He was rewarded for this bit of absurdity with a brittle laugh, which did little to relieve his growing conviction that this intriguing young beauty was about to embroil him in trouble that he could well do without. Indeed, his every instinct for self-preservation cried out to him to climb into his coach with all dispatch and leave her to her own devices before it was too late. That he did not was no doubt due to his own perverse nature, which demanded that at the very least he remain long enough to satisfy his curiosity.

There was a mystery here, which he sensed somehow was not entirely divorced from him. The red-haired temptress had known when he held up her coach that the Black Rose was the Marquis of Vere, and yet she had kept that tidbit to herself. Certainly, she had not acted randomly when she concocted her elaborate and dangerous charade for his benefit. That much was all too obvious. And then, too, there was her singular knowledge of a style of fencing that had been developed and perfected by only one man other than himself. Perhaps that was the most intriguing mystery of all, he thought.

"Perhaps in a sense I *have* only just sprung into being," said the temptress, as though having given the matter its due consideration. "The thing is, you see, all of my life I have been living a lie. No doubt you can imagine the consternation I felt when I was informed by the most reliable of sources that I am not who I thought I was at all."

"A hideous prospect," confirmed Vere, who could make little sense of her cryptic utterances, but who had little difficulty discerning the distress under which she was laboring. "On the other hand, I daresay we are what we make of ourselves. In which case, it can hardly be a lie."

"In this instance, I'm afraid that is," replied Constance, aware that the prospect of facing Vere with a sword had been a deal easier than was that of confronting him with the truth of her dilemma. Turning, she walked a few paces before turning back to him. "I am, in fact, a nameless bastard, which, considering who I thought was my father, is not such a bad thing. The truth is I never really liked him, and now I need not feel the least compunction in betraying him. Oddly enough, however, I do."

Her movements had taken her near the coach so that she now stood in the full circle of light cast by its lamp.

Vere, given to see her clearly for the first time since he had been thrust into his unlooked-for adventure, suddenly frowned. Stepping close, he carefully brushed the hair back from her face to reveal a purplish bruise over her left cheekbone.

"If this is a sample of his fatherly affection," Vere said grimly, "then I daresay it is odd, indeed, if you persist in feeling the least loyalty to him." Clasping her firmly by the arms, he gazed intently into her eyes. "Tell me who the devil he is, and I promise to instruct him in the proper manner to treat a lady."

At the touch of his hands, not to mention his nearness, Constance was prey suddenly to a host of emotions, none of which had anything remotely to do with her infelicitous relationship with the earl. Nevertheless, she felt an alarm go off in her head.

The last thing she could wish was to have Vere confront Blaidsdale on her behalf. Convinced that Blaidsdale was responsible, either directly or indirectly, for the loss of his parents, Vere had stayed his hand and bided his time for ten years. She would not be the one who upset that uneasy balance.

"Pray do not be absurd," she retorted, pulling away. "I told you. I am not a lady. If I were, I should not have done something so improper as to hold up a gentleman's coach at gunpoint, now would I?"

"If you were not a lady, it is hardly likely that you would know what was proper," Vere countered dryly. Hell and the devil confound it. He found himself wishing that she would trust him, though he could not recall that he had ever before been remotely interested in earning the confidence of an innocent, not even for the dubious purpose of enjoying her favors. After all, he was not such a fool as to dally with single females, who were naught but bait for Parson's Mousetrap. Clearly, this one would seem to have the power to arouse in him the primitive male instincts to succor and protect the female of the species. He found the realization as curious as it was cynically amusing. "Pray do not try and tell me that you are not gently born, for I promise I shall not believe you. Your looks, your manner, your speech—all cry out that you are no common-born wench."

"Do they? Then I suppose one might say that I am uncommonly born," said Constance with a wry smile. "And who could deny it? I was born, after all, without a father. And it were better so than to be born of a father who commands neither love nor respect. Still, I daresay I owe him something. He gave me a name, which is something my real father apparently failed to do."

"Which would appear to bring us full circle," observed Vere with cynical appreciation of the mysterious beauty's mastery of circumlocution. The devil, there could be only one reason that she was afraid to reveal

her name to him. It had to be the name of one with
whom he had had past dealings, undoubtedly of an infelicitous nature.

It was the name of one of his enemies. It had to be.
The question was, which one? Hell and the devil confound it. He had enemies too bloody numerous to
count.

"Not quite full circle, my lord," replied Constance,
bracing herself to tell him the truth. "First, you should
know that I have reason to believe that you are in grave
danger from men who would stop at nothing to do you
harm. They are both powerful and exceedingly dangerous."

"And this is why you have attempted this absurd little
stunt?" Vere demanded in tones heavily laced with
irony. "To warn me of my impending danger?"

Constance's head came up, her eyes flashing glorious blue sparks of feminine indignation. "It was that, in
part. No doubt you will say I was foolish to think the
Marquis of Vere might need assistance in guarding his
back against his enemies."

"You, my girl, have been foolish beyond permission,"
Vere did not hesitate to inform her. Clasping her ruthlessly by the arms, he seared her with his gaze. "Have
you the smallest notion how close I came to putting a
pistol ball through that pretty head of yours?" he demanded, sorely tempted to throttle the meddlesome
chit for having brought him to the very brink of killing
a woman. "Did it never once occur to you that a letter
might have sufficed as a warning?"

"Dear me, why, I wonder, did I not think of that?"
Constance bitterly retorted. "Perhaps it is because I have
been a trifle preoccupied of late with trying to escape with
my life. No doubt you will pardon me if, while perched
on a third-story ledge, I failed to conceive of penning
you a missive. I daresay I should not have bothered to
warn you at all. Indeed, had I realized when I saw you at

the post inn that you were a stubborn, pigheaded, over-bearing, disagreeable, arrogant, tyrannical . . ."

Before she could complete the catalogue of Vere's various unsavory attributes, the odious marquis peremptorily silenced her with a hand clamped unchivalrously over her mouth.

"*Softly,*" he hissed, holding her powerless with the piercing intensity of his gaze. "Listen."

"Riders coming, my lord," Vickers called quietly down to his master.

Constance froze, her heart leaping to her throat, as it came to her with chilling certainty who was traveling along the lonely country road at this time of night.

Vere, staring into his lady moonlight's eyes, uttered a low curse. The alarm was clear to read in those mysterious depths. *Who the devil was she,* he wondered, and what in hell's name had she involved him in? Grimly he vowed that he would know the whole of it before this night was finished. Until then, it would seem he had little choice but to serve as her protector. Abruptly he released her.

"I suggest you cover those titian curls of yours," he said tersely. Leaving her, he strode to her mount. "Do the villains know your horse?" he queried curtly, as, taking the reins, he led the animal back to the troublesome beauty.

Constance, who had hesitated only the barest moment as she digested the fact that Vere intended to help her, was busy tying her hair up in her scarf. "No. I purchased him in London and had him delivered straightaway here to Wells." Pulling the hat down low over her forehead, she glanced up at the frowning marquis. "Why?"

"Because, my girl," he replied, slinging the cloak about her shoulders and proceeding to fasten the clasp at the front of her throat, "you are about to become Lord Huntingdon, my young, inebriated second cousin on my mother's side." Drawing a flask from an inner pocket of his greatcoat, he held it out to her. "I fear I cannot offer you ratafia, nor would a woman's drink suffice to do the trick. Brandy is the quaff of gentlemen. Do you think you can play the part?"

Constance awarded him her flashing grin. "Rather better than I played the part of the Black Rose, I doubt not." Taking the flask, she drew a deep breath, threw back her head, and downed a long pull of the stuff.

The fiery, foul-tasting liquid burned her throat and brought tears to her eyes. That she nevertheless managed to swallow it down without succumbing to a fit of coughing occasioned her to feel no little self-satisfaction.

Vere, retrieving the flask, was less than reassured. "It is to be devoutly hoped that you are in the right of it," he grimly replied, flicking a few drops on the front of her coat to add to the aromatic flavor of the role. Tying the horse's reins to the back of the vehicle, he next helped Constance to a seat inside. "I suggest, however, that you keep your head down and let me do the talking."

"As you wish, my lord," said Constance, assaying a flamboyant bow, which inexplicably set her head to spinning. Indeed, she had the curious sensation that her nose and lips had gone quite absurdly numb. "I shall be content to allow you the leading role."

"It is a role in a farce that I daresay I should do better without," declared his lordship in repressive accents. "When it is finished, you, my girl, will have no little explaining to do."

Constance, meeting the hard glitter of Vere's eyes, could not but wish that she had managed to get out all of the truth before she was so rudely interrupted by the imminent threat of recapture.

"Quite so," murmured his lordship, correctly interpreting the swift rise of color to his temptress's cheeks. Leaving her then to issue low-voiced instructions to Vickers, Vere shrugged into his greatcoat. At last, restoring his blade to its sheath in the walking stick, he climbed into the coach beside her.

At his signal, John Vickers set the team in motion.

In moments, the riders, an army captain in crisp regimentals and a corporal with two subalterns, were upon them. For the second time in thirty minutes, the command to hold to brought the coach to a halt.

"You, driver," called out the corporal, who leaned out to take the lead horse's head. "Have you seen a horseman come this way?"

"What I see are four horsemen," spoke up John Vickers, his tone exceedingly dry, "who had ought to think twice before stopping a gentleman's coach."

"The devil you say," the captain exclaimed with no little outrage. "You will keep a civil tongue in your head when you speak to your betters, or I shall have you hauled down from there and horsewhipped."

"Aye, gov'nor," agreed Vickers, who did not doubt the bloody captain would have been as good as his word when it came to venting his spleen on them what couldn't fight back. But then, the captain didn't know what awaited him in the coach. A faint sardonic smile touched Vickers's lips. A pity he was about to find out.

"You in the coach," called the officer, savagely hauling his sidling mount to a standstill. "I would have a word with you."

"Would you, indeed?" came gently from the coach interior. "A word, you say? What word, I wonder. Not a few come to mind at this untimely delay, but none, I daresay, that would make an impression. *Stultus sonum suae vocis amat.*"

As this last observation was offered up in Latin, it did, indeed, fail to make an impression on the officer. *He*, it would seem, had not excelled in a classical education—unlike Constance, who silently translated to herself, *A fool loves the sound of his own voice.* She had perforce to quell a startled burble of laughter as the barb sank home.

"The devil, I am in no mood for games, sir," blustered the officer. "I am Captain Albert Sinclair of His Majesty's Royal Guards, and I demand to know if you have seen a rider."

In the darkness, a slender hand suddenly gripped Vere's arm. If he had entertained the smallest doubt that his mysterious lady moonlight was the rider in question, it was instantly dispelled, along with not a few of the intriguing questions that she had previously left unanswered.

Vere's lips thinned to a grim line.

"To you, sir, it is 'my lord,' " returned Vere with a velvet-edged softness that chilled even Constance. "If it is a rider you seek, I suggest you go in search of him—now, before I cease to be amused."

It was made suddenly and profoundly clear that, if Sinclair had hitherto failed to note the crest on the side of the coach, he saw it now with stark significance.

"*Vere*," he uttered with a mixture of fear and loathing.

"Unsettling, is it not?" sympathized the marquis. "I hear there is a great deal that is unsettling these days for those of your house. Your father's latest financial debacle, for example. How detestable it is to find oneself on the rocks. I am moved to inquire how your uncles fare."

"Well, you may be sure, my lord," Sinclair growled unpleasantly. "Nor is my father's case so desperate as you would like to imagine. A Sinclair can always raise the wind when necessity demands."

"Or cut the wind, as the case may be," mused Vere whimsically. "But to the matter at hand," he added before Sinclair could give vent to the angry retort that so plainly trembled on his white lips. "This rider you seek. Some poor fellow, is it, who has chosen to desert his post?"

"Hardly. Merely a runaway who must be found and returned home, safe from harm. I see that you are not traveling alone, my lord," Sinclair added, bending down in the saddle to peer into the murky interior of the coach.

"Am I to assume it is your companion to whom that rider-less horse belongs?"

Constance, listening from beneath the concealment of her hat pulled down low over her face, felt a clamp close down hard on her vitals. A plague on Albert Sinclair, she thought. She would shoot him herself if it came to that. The last thing she had ever wished was to place Vere in the position of having to risk life and limb to protect Lady Constance Landford from the Earl of Blaidsdale's twisted schemes. Heaven help her. Albert *must* not guess the identity of Vere's companion.

"I daresay you may make whatever assumption you choose," said Vere, little caring for the prospect of ex-changing gunfire with King's men, even if one of them was Blaidsdale's nephew. Bloody hell! He had not spent the past ten years painstakingly crafting the machinery of his revenge only to have it all brought to naught by a deucedly strange quirk of fate. Still, if worse did come to worst, it might be worth something to deprive Lord and Lady Sinclair of their only heir, he mused, adding gently, "I myself make it a rule never to assume any-thing."

Sinclair, clearly distrusting both Vere's words and his possible motives, glanced once more at the animal in question. "It would, however, seem the logical conclusion. He looks to be a prime bit of blood, but hardly up to your weight."

"No, I should say he is better suited to a woman," Vere replied coolly. "Or a stripling, who has yet to learn the measure of his cups. If you are interested in adding him to your stables, Sinclair, I fear you will have to wait. Lord Huntingdon is at present sunk in a stupor."

"Lord Huntingdon, is it?" uttered the captain, patently unconvinced. "Deep in his cups? Still, I shall have a word with him."

Driving his spurs home, he sent his bay around to the other side of the coach and dismounted.

Constance, slumped in her corner during the entirety of the less than genial exchange between the two men, had had for the past several moments her own battle to fight. Never having partaken of hard spirits before, she was becoming thoroughly acquainted with the less than salubrious effects of a gentleman's quaff on a stomach that had, in the past twenty-four hours, been fed only a hurried plate of stale biscuits and a large glass of milk.

Cruelly reminded by the crunch of gravel beneath Sinclair's boot soles that everything now depended on her ability to portray convincingly the part of a drunken lord, she willed her head to cease its odious spinning. Heroically, she struggled to ignore the increasingly delicate condition of her stomach and to remain perfectly lax despite an annoyingly persistent urge to scratch an itch somewhere in the vicinity of her left ankle. Desperately, she tried to dismiss her discomfort from her mind by concentrating instead on breathing in through her nose and exhaling gustily through her lips in what she hoped was a fair approximation of a gentleman asleep in his cups. Nevertheless, despite her best efforts, she could not quell the sickening lurch of her stomach as Sinclair's hand found and started to turn the door handle. Faith, it was become horribly and unavoidably clear to her that she was rapidly losing a grip on herself.

And then Vere's voice, infinitely gentle, sliced through the silence.

"I should not do that if I were you, Sinclair."

Sinclair paused for the barest moment, his eyes leaping with sudden excitement.

"Corporal Hess," he called without taking his gaze off Vere. "To me."

The corporal, trained to obey with alacrity, bounded forward on his horse. Coming to a sliding halt, he vaulted from the saddle to stand at the ready beside his captain.

"Corporal, you will train your pistol on his lordship, the marquis," Sinclair ordered, his handsome face wearing an expression of dark anticipation. "If he so much as moves a muscle, you may feel free to shoot him."

"Yes, *sir*," barked the corporal, drawing his pistol and bringing it to bear on the marquis, who, to all outward appearances, remained unmoved by this new turn of events.

Constance, on the other hand, feeling distinctly ill with suspense, not to mention a churning stomach, was moved to give vent to a most convincing groan.

"Well done, 'Lord Huntingdon,' " crooned Sinclair, wrinkling his nose as the distinct aroma of brandy drifted to him through the open window. "You have spared no attention to detail. You almost have me convinced that you are a callow youth under the influence. However . . ."

Sinclair yanked the handle down.

Corporal Hess froze at attention, his gun held unwaveringly on the marquis.

Vere's hand tightened on the butt of the pistol in his pocket.

Sinclair yanked the door open, one hand reaching for the slumped figure in the coach.

"I know as well as you that not only are you not a gentleman, but you are anything but three sheets to the wind."

It was too much. Constance, having reached the end of her tolerance, thrust her head out the opening and heaved sour milk and biscuits all over the captain's boots.

"Hellfire!" uttered Sinclair, jumping back in disgust.

"I did try and warn you," Vere offered mildly, taking care to haul his temptress back into the coach before she toppled out headfirst on the ground. "And now I suggest you close the door and allow us to continue on our way. Clearly, my young cousin here is in need of his bed."

"Yes, yes," rasped Sinclair with an impatient gesture of the hand. "Let them pass."

"Brava, my dear," Vere commented in dry amusement

some moments later, as the coach lurched into motion. "I had no idea the extent of your theatrical talents. Your performance was perhaps a trifle melodramatic, but no less effective. In fact, I daresay nothing less would have served to avert almost certain calamity."

"Would it be too much to ask if we might postpone this conversation until some later date?" returned Constance, heartily wishing his lordship to the devil. "I fear I am in no case to engage in badinage at the moment. As it happens, I am unaccustomed to disgracing myself in a manner that can only be described as mortifying. Besides, I feel perfectly dreadful."

"Yes, of course you do," said Vere, pressing his white linen handkerchief into her hand. "I assure you it is nothing, however, from which you will not soon recover."

Constance, gratefully blowing her nose, shook her head. "I feel such a dreadful ninny. Even if Sinclair is convinced that Lord Huntington soiled his boots, I shall never be able to forget that *you* knew the truth of the matter. Really, it is the shabbiest thing."

"Quite unforgivable," Vere agreed with a suspicious twitch at the corners of his lips. "On the other hand, *you* had not the pleasure of seeing Sinclair's face at the crucial moment. If you had, that alone must have made up for any embarrassment you were made to suffer."

"That is easy for you to say," observed Constance, stifling a yawn.

"Yes, no doubt," Vere agreed quietly. Pulling the carriage rug up over her, he drew her, unresisting, into the cradle of his arm. "Rest now, knowing that you are safe from further pursuit."

"For the moment, at any rate," Constance answered somewhat thickly. With the imminent threat of danger past and a delicious warmth stealing over her, she felt herself pleasantly adrift. "Is one thing to have shaken Cousin Albert off the track. Has more hair than wit. Dearest Papa another story altogether. Blaidsdale will never give up. Cannot bear the thought of a fortune slipping through his fingers." A small frown of concentration knit her brow. "Not my father. Said so himself. Then who . . . ?"

Breathing a long sigh, she drifted into the waiting arms of sleep.

Consequently, she did not see the hard leap of muscle along the lean line of Vere's jaw. Nor was she aware that he stared with a strange sort of fixity out at the deepening night.

Chapter 4

Constance, turning away from the night-darkened window to stare down at the leap of flames in the study's Gothic fireplace, could not but wonder at the fate that had landed her in her present circumstances. Certainly, when she had made her escape from Landford Park, she had never thought to find herself soon after residing in the Marquis of Vere's hunting lodge. Neither, she wryly reflected, had she thought to be wearing a Turin gauze gown over a deep blue satin underlining, one, moreover that, besides having a low, square-cut neck that must inevitably draw attention to her breasts, had almost certainly once belonged to one of the marquis's former mistresses. As for the exquisite sapphire necklace clasped about her throat and the diamond-and-sapphire earrings dangling from her earlobes, she could only speculate that the marquis preferred his lights of love to present an elegant appearance, even in the wilds of Somerset. The jewels had been laid out, along with the gown, when she returned from her afternoon tramp through the woods. Even the long white gloves and low-heeled satin slippers, dyed to match the dress, had been included. Really, it was all quite extraordinary, she thought, smiling to herself in no little bemusement.

Stranger than the gown, however, and far more intriguing was the fact that the marquis had treated her with the deference due a lady of impeccable reputation. She, after all, had sunk herself beneath reproach with her every word and deed.

What an odd man he was, to be sure, she thought, her brow puckering in a frown of perplexity. In the six days and as many nights that she had lived as a guest in his house, she had, upon orders from his lordship, been given every consideration. Even that first night when she had been rendered wholly vulnerable and at his mercy, he himself had not failed to behave toward her in the manner of a gentleman. This, from a man who was, by all accounts, a conscienceless womanizer, one who had fought three duels over the dubious honor of married women with whom he had enjoyed brief liaisons, was hardly what she had thought to encounter. But then, he was noted for the beautiful women whose company he kept. No doubt Constance Landford did not meet his stringent standards in that regard, she reflected, recalling with wry amusement her thoughts upon awakening her first morning in an unfamiliar bed to discover, despite the teasing relic of her rosebud set in a vase on the table, that she could remember nothing of what had occurred after she disgraced herself all over Cousin Albert's boots.

No doubt she could attribute her peculiar lapse of memory not only to the effects of a gentleman's quaff on a nearly empty stomach, but also to the circumstance that she had unquestionably been suffering from shock in the wake of the earl's savage blow, her harrowing escape, and the aftermath of discovering she was not at all who she had been led to believe she was. She had been ill and listless the first two days after awakening in the marquis's guest bedchamber—she, who was almost never ill. But then, she had had a great deal to think about. Not the least of it was her exceedingly uncertain future, the outcome of which would seem in great part to depend upon the one man who had little reason to wish to help her. Really, her whole life would seem curiously topsy-turvy.

Awakening in strange environs had been unsettling enough, but discovering that she was clad in a sheer, lacy nightdress unlike anything that she had ever worn before had been beyond disturbing with its many embarrassing implications. She was quite certain her cheeks must have flamed as red as her tousled tresses. Fortunately, perhaps, Mrs. Turnbough, the housekeeper, had bustled into the room with a cup of hot chocolate. Fussing over her new charge, she had soon alleviated Constance of any erroneous notions that Vere had had any hand in the undressing of her—or anything else, for that matter. The marquis, it seemed, had carried her in and, laying her "as gently as if she were a babe" on the bed, had instructed Mrs. Turnbough and Fanny, the upstairs maid, to tend to the lady's needs. Upon which, he had left her to their tender ministrations.

Nor, having departed at first light, had his lordship been in attendance to greet her at breakfast, nuncheon, tea, or dinner that day, the devil. Indeed, for the past *six* days, Constance had been left to her own devices. Worse, she had been left to fret over where the odious marquis had gone and what the devil he was up to.

It had little alleviated her anxiety to tell herself that there was no real reason to believe that Vere's absence had anything to do with her. After all, she had never been allowed to finish telling him who she was and why she was on the run. All he really knew was that a King's officer and some of his men had been in pursuit of her. He would naturally be curious, but he would hardly feel moved to do anything so foolhardy as seek out Albert Sinclair for an explanation of that fateful night's events.

Nor, she told herself repeatedly, would he do any of the countless other things that had come to her mind as she paced the floor of her room, pretended to read in Vere's study before the fire, or occupied herself with playing fetch with Sheba, Mr. Turnbough's English setter. Indeed, why should he?

The woman who had held up his coach and whom he had rescued from King's men, after all, meant nothing to him beyond causing him a deal of trouble that he, himself, had declared he could better do without. And yet, Constance could not dispel the uneasy conviction that Vere was capable of anything.

"A plague on the man!" she uttered out loud to the empty room. "I daresay Vere may do whatever he pleases, and the devil be damned. I care not if he gets himself killed. Why the deuce should I?"

"As a matter of fact, I cannot conceive of a single reason why you should," observed a thrillingly masculine voice from the doorway. "On the other hand, it would appear a moot question at best. As it happens, I am very much alive."

Constance came about with a swirl of satin skirts to be met with the sight of Vere, unharmed and as magnificently arrogant as ever. For the barest instant, she could not quell the fierce stab of joy that shot through her at the realization that he was returned at last. Then, almost immediately, she composed herself.

"I do beg your pardon, my lord," she said, dropping into a curtsy as she swiftly collected her thoughts. "I did not mean it, you know," she added, rising to favor him with a rueful grimace. "How dare you choose to reappear just at the moment when my patience had run out. Really, it is too bad of you."

"It would seem I have the happy knack of trying the patience of not a few of the people with whom I am acquainted," murmured Vere, who could hardly have failed to note with keen interest that first swift flash of warmth in his temptress's eyes. Egad, she was even more beautiful than his memory had served him. The gown and the jewels perfectly suited her, just as he had known that they would. "A pity I was unaware with what eagerness you anticipated my return. I should have been tempted to forego leaving you at all. Unfortunately, however, I had an appointment in London that could not wait. You were, I trust, made comfortable in my absence?"

"Exceedingly so, my lord," replied Constance, thinking that he had traveled swiftly indeed to have been to London and back in little over five days. And yet, immaculately clad in a double-breasted coat of blue Superfine and dove-grey unmentionables, he showed little signs of his recent journey. Faith, his compelling presence seemed to fill the room! "Mrs. Turnbough has spared no kindness in making me feel at home," she added, striving for her habitual calm composure. "For which I thank you, my lord. Indeed, I cannot think how I shall ever repay you for—for . . ."

"Repay me?" he interrupted, strolling across the room to reach for the brandy decanter set out on a silver grog tray. "Repay me for what? We are even, surely?"

"Even, my lord?" queried Constance, smiling quizzically.

"I held you up and stole a kiss, and you were quick to follow suit," he pointed out with a shrug. "Would you care for something? Sherry, perhaps?" he asked, glancing over his shoulder at her.

"No," Constance replied, quelling a small shudder of distaste. "Thank you, but I believe I am not cut out for spirits. Nor can I think the scales are at all balanced. You have been everything that is generous, while I have caused you nothing but trouble."

"On the contrary," murmured his lordship, calmly pouring a libation of brandy. Casually, he set the decanter aside and picked up his glass. "You will find if you should come to know me better that I am never generous."

"Of course you would say that, my lord," Constance instantly rejoined. "You have, have you not, a reputation to maintain? Nevertheless, you will admit that, rescuing me from Captain Sinclair, taking me into your home, even dressing me, if not in the style to which I am accustomed, at least in the fashion of a lady, are all evidence of your generosity."

"I am prepared to admit nothing of the sort. As I recall, you saved yourself from the boorish captain in a manner that was as effective as it was original. After which, you were hardly in any case to be left to your own devices. I had little choice but to bring you into my home. And as for your apparel, it occurred to me that, as charming as I might personally find you dressed in a gentleman's unmentionables, you might prefer something rather more feminine. As it happens, my mother left a few of her personal belongings here the night before she embarked on her ill-fated voyage aboard the *Swallow*. The gown and the jewels were hers."

Constance was made suddenly and uncomfortably aware that she had grossly misjudged his lordship based solely on his reputation as a womanizer. Even more unsettling, however, was the realization that she was wearing the personal possessions of the former Marchioness of Vere; indeed, no doubt all of the gowns she had worn the past few days had also been hers. Faith, how greatly Vere must deplore his kindness when he learned that he had lent them to a woman who, until as recently as five days ago, had thought herself to be the Earl of Blaidsdale's daughter!

It came to her that she would be exceedingly grateful if the floor would suddenly open up and swallow her. Barring that highly unlikely eventuality, she could think only that she must tell Vere the truth at once. She owed him that much at the very least. And yet, how difficult to summon the words that must inevitably bring him to despise her!

"From all accounts she was very beautiful," murmured Constance, her hand going unconsciously to the necklace at her throat. "My Aunt Sophie was used to say that the marchioness was as gracious as she was generous of heart. I regret that I never knew your mother."

"I daresay she would have liked you," said Vere, watching the play of emotions over his temptress's lovely face. There was no mistaking the dismay she felt, or the sincerity of her other feelings. She had even let drop the name of her maternal aunt. But then, he had been counting on just such a reaction when, before he left for London, he gave Mrs. Turnbough instructions to lay the gown and other things out for her on the evening of his planned return. "In that dress you remind me of her somewhat. She was perhaps not quite so tall as you, and her hair, of course, was dark. But the way you carry yourself is very like. More than that, she was possessed of a dauntless independence, which was used to test the mettle of my father, the marquis. I believe you would have found her a kindred spirit in that regard."

"Should I, my lord?" queried Constance with a smile that did not quite reach her eyes. "I daresay I should have found her everything to be admired. It is rather more doubtful, however, whether she would have approved of me, let alone your many kindnesses to me. My mere presence in your house places you in the gravest peril. You should send me away, my lord—now, before it is too late."

"Yes, no doubt," agreed Vere. "And if I were to follow your advice and cast you out on the world," he said, testing the bouquet of the brandy in the glass, "where would you go, I wonder."

It was the question that had been plaguing Constance,

night and day, since she had fled Landford Park. After nearly a week, she had yet to come up with an answer.

Turning away from Vere to hide the blur of uncertainty in her eyes, she shrugged. "It would hardly be your concern where I went," she said, trailing her fingertips over the oaken desktop. "Perhaps I should take up a career as a highwayman. I have always yearned for a life of adventure, and I daresay not every gentleman would be so quick to reply as you did."

"No, not everyone," agreed Vere, who did not doubt there would be some who would not hesitate to shoot without bothering to ask questions first. Egad, what a devil of a notion! "Perhaps you might even learn to kill an unarmed man, though I daresay you would not find it salubrious to your conscience."

The devil, thought Constance, hard-put not to choke on an unwitting burble of laughter. It was not as if the drawbacks to the life of a highwayman were not perfectly obvious to anyone of a rational mind, though it had hardly deterred *him* from pursuing so dangerous a pastime. How dared he make fun of her! Really, he needed taking down a peg.

"Perhaps not," she said, assaying an audible sigh. "And yet, no profession is perfect. At least robbing coaches is preferable to the other options available to a single female in need of making her way in the world." Coming about to face him, she favored him with a guileless look. "There is, after all, a certain dignity to taking a man's purse at gunpoint that I daresay would be lacking, for example, in being forced to cater to his whims and pleasures to obtain it. Besides, the life of a highwayman would seem to complement the existence of one who must remain in hiding at any rate."

The devil it would, thought Vere, who could not but note that her words would seem fraught with double entendre. He had the peculiar feeling that it was not the life of a Cyprian to which she was referring, but something else altogether. Bloody hell, it was time that she told him the truth!

"That would depend," observed Vere, gently swirling the amber liquid in his glass, "on why one is hiding and from whom." Taking a sip, he deliberately lifted his eyes to hers. "I cannot but wonder what you could dread so greatly that you would willingly embrace the existence of a fugitive to escape it."

"Marriage, my lord," Constance stated baldly. "Marriage to a man I despise or confinement in a mental institution. Those were the options that were presented to me. Since I found neither in the least appealing, I created a third of my own choosing. I escaped."

"And proceeded immediately to set yourself up as an imitation Black Rose with me as your first victim—is that what you would have me to believe?" demanded Vere. He was aware of a hard fist of anger in the pit of his stomach at thought of the man who had callously sought to use this rare and lovely creature to his own unscrupulous ends. It was all too true that the word of a husband, father, or brother was sufficient to commit a dependent female to Bedlam or other institutions of its kind. Nor would this have been the first time it was used to punish or instruct a rebellious wife, sister, or daughter in the error of her ways. That his beautiful, spirited temptress had so narrowly escaped a similar fate made his blood run cold in his veins.

"It was not precisely that coherent a plan," confessed Constance, recalling with a queasy sensation the seeming eternity that she had spent on the cursed window ledge in the cold. "The notion of assuming the guise of the Black Rose came to me only after I saw you pull into the post inn on the outskirts of Wells. At the time, it seemed a fortuitous encounter. I had been pondering, after all, how I might get word to you."

"Ah, yes, to warn me of my impending danger," said

Vere, suddenly enlightened. The veiled beauty who had been watching him from her travel coach must naturally have been his temptress. Egad, he must have been distracted, indeed, not to make the connection between the two singular events for himself. "And while you sat in your coach observing my arrival, did it never once occur to you that all you needed to do was call me over to you?"

"Perhaps later, when it was too late," Constance admitted ruefully. "But then, I was, you see, operating under the erroneous supposition that you knew who I was when you robbed my coach. In which case, I had every reason to think that you would not have believed a word of what I had to say to you."

"I am to believe you now, however," Vere did not hesitate to point out, even as he ignored for the moment her oblique allusion to her true identity. "Honor among thieves, as it were."

"Devil!" exclaimed Constance, awarding Vere a comical moue of displeasure. "You make it all sound so dreadfully absurd, when it seemed to make perfect sense at the time. Looking back, I confess that I am not at all sure what I thought."

No, mused Vere darkly. She had obviously been feeling rather desperate. And how should she not, when she was a woman alone in the world with no one to help her save for the one man who she must have supposed had the least reason to wish her well? She was, after all, Lady Constance Landford, the daughter of the Earl of Blaidsdale.

Curiously, Vere wondered when she meant to tell him that pertinent little detail. Inexplicably, it came to him that he wished that she could bring herself to trust him. And yet, how unlike the dissolute Marquis of Vere to desire any such thing of an Innocent, especially one who had the distinction of being the daughter of his sworn enemy! No doubt his grandsire would have derived no little amusement from the quandary in which he, Vere, presently found himself.

How ironic it was to think that only a little over five days ago he would have rejoiced to have the Earl of Blaidsdale's daughter at his mercy. A man of the world, Vere entertained few illusions concerning his considerable prowess with members of the opposite sex. How easy it might have been to seduce her to his bed, to rob her of her innocence, and cast her off, a ruined woman. To be in the position to use her against the man who had destroyed his own father must have loomed as a temptation too great to resist. That was before, however, the titian-haired beauty had dropped uninvited into his life.

He could hardly have expected to discover that Blaidsdale's daughter was as fine and good as she was bewitchingly lovely. Even less could he have anticipated that he would find himself drawn to her in a way that he had never been drawn to any other woman before her. Spirited and yet unspoiled, charming but with a quick wit and keen intelligence, Lady Constance Landford was the sort of female who would never pall on him. He had sensed that from their very first encounter, when it had occurred to him that, as much as he would have delighted in intimately exploring every glorious inch of her, he would have derived no less pleasure in waking up in the morning to find her still in the bed beside him. He had known from the very beginning that she was not the kind of woman a man took to his bed and then discarded lightly. If he was a man, he married her. Consequently, the relief with which he had sent her on her way had been no less than the regret with which he had watched her go—and then what must happen, but that she should return to place him in a damnable predicament.

The last thing he could wish, as he stood upon the threshold of seeing all his plans bear fruition, was to become enamored of a woman, especially this woman. How much more complicated it was to discover himself suddenly thrust in the peculiar position of being honor-bound to serve as her protector!

Hellfire! Far from seducing her for the sake of revenge, he was even now forced to call on his considerable willpower not to give in to the nearly overpowering desire to snatch her up in his arms and kiss her. Nor was that all or the worst of his unhappy dilemma, he cynically realized, as Constance turned to look at him with the full force of her beautiful eyes. He was cursedly aware that, if ever he gave in to the temptation to avail himself of her sweet generosity, he would never afterwards be able to convince her that his motive had *not* been one of vengeance!

"No, that is not quite true," said Constance, who had come to the inevitable conclusion that, in all conscience, she could not put off telling Vere the whole truth of what she had involved him in. "I knew precisely what I was thinking. I thought that, if I could show you that I am fully as adept as any man with a sword or a pistol, I could convince you to let me help you prove your father was the victim of an insidious plot. More than that, I hoped you would give me sanctuary from the man you despise most in this world while we work together to bring him to justice."

Vere stared at her from beneath heavily drooping eyelids, his face revealing nothing of his thoughts as he digested *that* interesting tidbit of news. It was not precisely what he had expected to hear from her. But then, he might have known that his unpredictable temptress would come up with an explanation straight out of the realm of the extraordinary.

"I see. We are to be partners, then," he drawled with only the faintest hint of irony.

"I think I prefer to think of us as 'arch-plotters,' my lord," she emended, a wholly fascinating twinkle in her eye. "It is so much more romantic, not to mention appealing to the ear."

"Little baggage," commented his lordship quellingly. "Now you are roasting me. No doubt you will pardon my curiosity. I cannot but wonder what you think to contribute to this joint venture."

"But surely it is obvious, my lord," returned Constance, feeling suddenly somewhat out of her depths. After all, as a fugitive from one who would stop at nothing to have her in his grasp again, she must inevitably be a trifle hampered in her movements. But then, she firmly reminded herself, she had already thought of a solution to that insignificant detail if only his lordship could be brought to agree to it. "First of all," she ventured, unconsciously lifting her chin in unshakable resolve, "you will agree that two heads must always be better than one when seeking to resolve a problem. In this particular case, the problem is an unresolved mystery concerning the tragic loss of the former Marquis and Marchioness of Vere. As it happens, I have the advantage of knowing without a doubt that it was no accident, my lord."

"If that is true, then the advantage is equally mine," said Vere with chilling dispassion. "I, too, know it without a doubt."

"Yes, of course you do," Constance hastened to agree. "You, however, have not heard those responsible admit to having plotted to teach your father a lesson. A lesson which they now intend to teach you, my lord."

"And you did hear it, I must presume," said Vere, knowing now why his temptress had felt compelled to seek him out. She undoubtedly felt that she shared her father's guilt, never mind that Blaidsdale himself had brutally disavowed any such blood kinship. To all the world she was Lady Constance Landford. For her, it was enough to condemn her in her own eyes, and now she thought to make atonement—she, who had never harmed anyone.

It came to him suddenly to wonder precisely what she had in mind to offer in the way of compensation.

"Yes," said Constance, turning away. "I heard them talking. Which is only one more reason why they will never rest until they have me back again. Why *he* will never rest." Instantly, she came back around to face him with searching eyes. "You have not asked whom I heard talking, my lord."

"It is hardly necessary, is it?" said Vere, maddeningly cool. "You said he was the man I despise most in the world."

"Yes," Constance declared bitterly. "And I am his daughter, Lady Constance Landford." She steeled herself for his contempt.

It was not to be forthcoming.

Vere, setting his glass aside, deliberately crossed the room to her. Inexplicably, her heart skipped a beat as she looked up into eyes the mesmerizing blue of lapis lazuli.

"You are mistaken, surely," he said ever so gently. "Call yourself whatever you will, you still are not Blaidsdale's daughter."

Constance stared at Vere in dawning revelation.

"You *knew!*" she exclaimed, grasping the lapels of his coat in her fists and giving them a shake. "All the time I have been dreading this moment, you already knew the terrible truth."

"And how not?" said Vere, placing his hands on her shoulders. "You told me yourself that night in the coach as you drifted off to sleep. And now you will listen to *me.*" Bending his head, he held her with the piercing intensity of his gaze. "Even if he were your father, it would be nothing to signify. None of the events concerning the deaths of my mother and father had anything to do with you. Nor are you to be held accountable for what Blaidsdale did. You owe him nothing, *enfant.* Certainly, you need feel under no obligation to me because of anything that he has done."

"Do I not?" queried Constance, who at that moment was laboring under the impression that she owed him a great deal and would, if she had her way, owe him a great deal more before all was said and done. "I am afraid I cannot agree with you, my lord," she said, marveling at her own brazenness as she gave in to the insurmountable urge to slip her arms up over his chest and around the back of his neck.

A soft thrill coursed through her from head to toe as she felt a small tremor shake Vere's lean, powerful body. It came to her with a sudden glow of warmth that he was not quite so indifferent to her as he would like her to believe.

"Which is why I feel I really must go on to point out that I could be of immeasurable help in your quest for justice if you would but let me," she continued, feeling somehow on surer ground. "As a woman, I could go places you cannot. I am sure to hear things that would not otherwise reach your ears. More than that, I can protect your back. Two Black Roses must surely be better than one, after all."

Two Black Roses! Good God, thought Vere, who could not but envision any number of reasons why such a sudden doubling of highwaymen would not be in the least better than one. The absurd little innocent. She had not the first notion of the danger she would be inviting in such a venture. Far from helping him, she would undoubtedly end by having them both swinging from the gibbet!

"Oh, indubitably," agreed the marquis, as if he were perfectly accustomed to introducing any number of well-bred young beauties to lives of crime. "Indeed, I cannot but wonder why I did not think of it."

"I daresay you would have done in time, my lord," said Constance, no doubt in the way of excusing his shortsightedness. "It is obvious you are a man of powerful intellect. Still, even a strong, intelligent man can benefit from a woman's intuition in such matters." Giving in to an impulse generated, no doubt, by her purely feminine intuition, she brushed a rebellious lock of hair from his forehead. "I am exceedingly adept at seeing through the motives of unscrupulous men, my lord. More importantly, there is not a female alive who could pull the wool over my eyes."

"A talent no doubt greatly to be desired," commented his lordship, who at the moment was having no little difficulty concealing his less than scrupulous desire to give free rein to his primitive masculine instincts and take her right then and there on the Ushak rug in front of the fireplace. Hellfire! She had not the least notion what she was doing to him. Nor was he prepared to let her discover the unprecedented power she possessed to land him squarely in a moral quagmire.

Hell and the devil confound it. He was Gideon Rochelle, the Marquis of Vere, a man who was known to pursue every sort of vice imaginable. How ironic it was that he should have in his arms a beautiful woman who was not only exceedingly desirable, but apparently willing and eager as well, and he, contrary to his own nature, was about to turn his back on her. No doubt he could attribute his newly found conscience to some hitherto unsuspected perversity in his character, which delighted in masochistic self-abnegation. Egad, but it was laughable. Nevertheless, he was demmed if he would add ruining innocent females to his list of ignominies, most in particularly one who was under his protection. At least, he amended with a cynical twist of the lips, he would not do so tonight.

"You would seem to have worked everything out to your satisfaction," he said, noting, in spite of himself, the intriguing manner in which the firelight glinted, like red sparks, in her hair, "save, perhaps, for one minor obstacle. You are already the object of pursuit, by King's men, no less."

"On the contrary, my lord," replied Constance, who, acutely aware of the warmth of Vere's hard, masculine body against hers, could not but wish an end to his Spanish Inquisition. Really, she could not but wonder what, precisely, it took to bring him to kiss her. "There is in truth only one King's man in pursuit of me. The man whom I have been commanded to wed."

"Captain Albert Sinclair," Vere supplied with an air of finality. And, indeed, a great deal had suddenly been made clear, not the least of which was why not even the Prince Regent himself was able to discover a reason for the king's personal guard to be in pursuit of a runaway in the rustic environs of northern Somerset. Clearly, they had not been on any business of the Crown's.

"Cousin Albert, indeed," affirmed Constance, taking the liberty of running her fingertips experimentally along the lean line of Vere's jaw.

She was rewarded for her efforts with a sardonic twist of the marquis's lips.

"Careful, Lady Moonlight," he said, capturing her wrists in his hands and pulling them down to his chest. "I did warn you what might happen if ever you tempted me again."

"You did, indeed, my lord," answered Constance, gazing quite frankly into eyes that remained as impenetrable as the mask of arrogance that Vere habitually affected. Constance assayed a quizzical smile. "And yet, thus far, you have proven remarkably immune to my supposed allure. Am I such an antidote, then, my lord?" she asked, her eyes probing his.

She had the dubious satisfaction of seeing the hard leap of muscle along the uncompromising line of Vere's jaw. *Antidote?* Good God, he thought. Is *that* what she believed? She was a cursed angel of seduction, an untaught beauty the very sight of whom must inspire men to dream of possessing her. Even now he was aware of the painful bulge against the front of his breeches.

"I daresay any number of men have made it patently clear that you are no such thing." Giving in to the temptation to run the back of his hand lightly over the bruise that had only just begun to fade on her cheek, he felt a bleak coldness spread through his veins. "Is that what *he* taught you to believe?"

"No, how could he? The truth is, he had little to do with my instruction," said Constance, sustaining a flutter of queasiness at the sudden hint of steel in his voice. "When I was only nine my mother took me to Wells and set up housekeeping there on her own. Upon her death a few years later, I went to live with my Aunt Sophie in London. I was there until two months ago when I stupidly agreed to come for a visit at Landford Park. No, my lord, I'm afraid I have you to thank for what can only be a reasonable assumption."

"Indeed, Miss Landford?" drawled Vere, who could not but wonder how it was that he had failed to make the titian-haired beauty's acquaintance in Town. Surely, he could never have been in the same room with her without taking note of her. "You intrigue me. How did you arrive at so erroneous a conclusion?"

"It was, in the circumstances, unavoidable, I should think," replied Constance, feeling her heart behaving in a most erratic manner beneath her breast. "You are well known for the beauty of the women with whom you have formed liaisons. *I* apparently do not fall into that category. You, after all, my lord, have been in this room for all of fifteen minutes, and you still have yet to kiss me."

Vere had hardly expected to hear that particular line of reasoning from his surprising lady moonlight. Nor did he react precisely as Constance might have wished. Staring at her with a curiously fixed expression for an interminable second or two, he suddenly threw back his head and laughed.

It was a sound, rich and vibrant with mirth, that took

Constance wholly by surprise. Indeed, she doubted not that it was the sort of thing that few had ever heard from the notorious marquis, who was noted for his cold nerve and cynical arrogance. A pity, she thought bemusedly, having been given to glimpse the free-spirited youth that he once must have been. Blaidsdale had changed all that, Blaidsdale and his brother, the vice-admiral. Why? she wondered. What dark secret had given rise to the enmity between the two houses?

That thought fled as Vere flicked a careless forefinger beneath her delightfully pointed chin.

"It is quite true that you are nothing like my numerous *joies de vivre*," he said, the laughter lingering in his eyes. "You, *enfant*, fall into a category all of your own." The mirth faded, to be replaced by a look of probing bafflement. "A category that I begin to think is more perilous than anything my enemies might devise against me."

Constance, who had gone suddenly quite still beneath his gaze, smiled gravely. "I am not your enemy, my lord. Never that."

"No, I daresay that you are not," he returned, the unreadable mask of the Corinthian slipping once more in place. "If you were, I should bloody well know how to deal with you."

Constance felt her heart sink, as, abruptly releasing her, he was clearly on the point of dismissing her. "But surely there is only one way to deal with me, my lord," she blurted before she could think better of it.

Vere, turning back to her, elevated a sardonic eyebrow. "I'm afraid, no matter how much the idea might appeal to me at the moment, I cannot cast you out on the world. It would hardly be practicable, would it? You, after all, know me by my alias. Of course, I might consider the equally attractive notion of simply doing away with the one person who could reveal to the world the identity of the Black Rose. It would be more in keeping with my reputation for being ruthless."

The devil, thought Constance, little fooled by his seeming harshness. She could not but realize the difficulty the marquis envisioned before him. The truth was, he could no more bring himself to abandon her to her own devices than she could betray him to the King's soldiers, which put him in a devil of a spot. "Pray do not be absurd, my lord. You know perfectly well I should never tell anyone that you are the Black Rose—even if you did send me away, which you have already stated you have no intention of doing. In which case, there would seem but one logical solution. I suggest, my lord, that you marry me. Thus may we kill two birds with one stone."

"But of course we may," agreed Vere, who could not but wonder what sort of conspiracy the fates had contrived to see him wed. *Marry* her. For her, it would be like leaping from the frying pan into the bloody fire! "Which two birds did you have in mind? You, naturally, would be preserved from being forced to wed Cousin Albert, though I daresay, in marrying me, you would be considered an even more likely candidate for Bedlam."

"No, how can you say so, my lord?" smiled Constance, marveling that he had not turned her down outright. "I am, after all, a spinster at her last prayers. To marry the most elusive bachelor in the realm must be thought a *coup* of the first water. You, on the other hand, would have the satisfaction of knowing that you have struck your greatest enemy a telling blow. I am, as it happens, possessed of a not unhandsome fortune, which my erstwhile father intended as a dowry to his sister's son. It was my mother's inheritance, which she left to me. I will do anything to prevent it from falling into the hands of Albert Sinclair and his grasping mama."

It was on her lips to add that, with her as his wife,

Vere would be the benefactor of that wealth. Something, an innate understanding of his masculine pride, perhaps, or a purely feminine desire to have him marry her for reasons other than the plumpness of her purse, kept her from voicing that final, pertinent point, though he must surely have known it for himself. Still, saying it out loud was not quite the same as a tacit understanding, she told herself.

"You would even go so far as to marry a man you know only by his less than sterling reputation. As good a reason for matrimony as any, one must suppose," dryly commented Vere, who could not but be struck by the irony in such a proposal. He wondered what she would say if she knew the duke had ordered him to wed before the summer was out. He could only speculate as to what Albermarle would say to it if his dissolute grandson complied with his demands by marrying the Earl of Blaidsdale's daughter! As for Blaidsdale, he did not doubt that the earl would indeed be moved to a murderous rage when he discovered that the fortune he had intended to enrich his brother-in-law's coffers would go instead to the son of the man he had murdered and robbed of a fortune. Unhappily, upon such an event, that homicidal fury would certainly be aimed at Lady Constance as well as at her unlikely spouse. Egad, it was a convoluted plot, one worthy of treatment by Sheridan, he thought, cynically amused in spite of himself.

And as for himself, he mused, he was to have a marchioness who was everything he might have wished for in a wife if he must have a wife. Only, in marrying her, he must inevitably drag her into an intrigue that was as dangerous as its outcome was uncertain.

Hell and the devil confound it! When he had laid his plans and set into motion the events that must lead to the ruination of his enemies, he had hardly thought to have the protection of a female to complicate his existence. Alone, he had been free to act with the coldblooded arrogance for which the Marquis of Vere was well known. He could not afford the liability of a wife who must inevitably cause him to give pause for thought at a moment when sheer instinct and an utter disregard for his safety—or anyone else's, for that matter—might be all that would carry him through.

"I fear you find yourself in a devil of a coil, my lord," observed Constance, who had been watching Vere with a hollow sensation in the pit of her stomach. "As no less do I. Please believe that I should never have sought to entrap a marquis if I had seen any other way out of my dilemma."

"Am I, then, so easily snared?" queried Vere, who had not till then seen his present circumstances quite in that particular light. "I have had lures set out for me before and have yet to succumb to Parson's Mousetrap."

"You are right, of course, but this would seem a most unusual situation, one that would call for extraordinary measures. Still, it need not be a permanent arrangement," offered Constance, refusing to retreat from the only reasonable solution to their dilemma. "If you find so much that is disagreeable in the notion of having me as your wife, marriages of convenience are not unheard of among our kind. When the danger is past, you could simply have the whole thing annulled."

"A splendid idea," concurred Vere with only the barest hint of irony. No doubt they would both derive no little enjoyment in being made a laughingstock in every salon and gentleman's club in London, which is precisely what would happen were he to do anything quite so lackwitted. But then, perhaps she was not quite so eager to jump into bed with him as she had presented herself to be, he thought suddenly, his eyes narrowing sharply on her face. She had, by her own admission, set herself to entrap a marquis. Perhaps she would be more than happy to do so without having to submit to his unwelcome caresses. If that were the case, then he would prefer to know it now before he bloody well committed himself to anything he might come to regret. "Save for one obstacle that comes instantly to mind," he appended, taking a deliberate step toward her.

"Indeed?" Inexplicably, Constance's heart skipped a beat at something she sensed in Vere's demeanor that had been distinctly lacking before. "What obstacle did you have in mind, my lord?"

"Come, Miss Landford, you may be an innocent, but you are hardly a green girl," Vere replied, looming suddenly over her. "You are a beautiful, desirable woman. You cannot truly believe I should be content to take you as my wife and not avail myself of your feminine charms."

"Should you not?" queried Constance, who, reluctantly, had been trying to reconcile herself to precisely that dismal prospect. *He,* after all, had thus far demonstrated a marked disinclination to take advantage of her less than subtle lures. Folding her hands together at her waist, she gazed limpidly up at him. "Then what would you suggest we do, my lord?"

"Do?" said Vere, presented with a picture of demure feminine loveliness belied by the unconscious tilt of her chin. The minx was *daring* him to behave in the manner that was expected of the notorious Marquis of Vere! And why the devil should he not be himself? If she had thought to entrap a marquis, she might as well learn what she would be getting for her efforts. "It would appear that you have left me little choice in the matter," he murmured in a voice that sent little chills running down Constance's back.

"I am afraid that was my intent," she admitted, sternly quelling the urge to run her tongue over suddenly dry lips. Marveling at her own temerity, she met his look squarely. "No doubt you will pardon my curiosity. I cannot but wonder, however, what *you* intend, my lord."

"Do you?" It was with a singular deliberation that he drew her to him and, bending his head, sampled the exquisitely tender flesh beneath her left ear lobe. "If it is a marquis you want, then you will have him," he whispered in her ear even as he ran his hands tantalizingly down her back until they found and molded themselves to the delectable twin mounds of her derriere. "Unfortunately, I have a distinct aversion to the notion of a marriage of convenience."

If he had thought by that to startle her into betraying her true feelings concerning his amorous advances, he was not to be disappointed.

Constance, caught unawares, gave vent to a gasp of surprise. And how not? The unfamiliarity of a man's hands on her posterior had served to awaken her to a multitude of emotions that she had never hitherto known she possessed, not the least of which was a thrilling pang through her midsection accompanied by the incipience of a melting heat in the vicinity of her nether regions.

"Surely you are mistaken, my lord," she said, acutely aware that his lips were scant inches from her own. "How can it possibly be unfortunate, when I feel no less an aversion to a passionless marriage than do you?"

The devil she did, thought Vere, inhaling the woman's scent of her mingled with lavender and rosemary. Egad, he doubted there was a man alive who could resist the red-haired temptress once he looked into her eyes. Certainly, Vere had never before thought to deny himself such a delectable morsel once his prurient interests had been aroused. And they were most definitely aroused at the moment. Hellfire! He had never entertained the desire to become a reformed character. He was far too set in his ways to change now.

Clasping her ruthlessly to him, he covered her mouth with his.

Chapter 5

Nothing, not even the Black Rose's purloined kiss, could have prepared Constance for Vere, suddenly in the mood to avail himself of her womanly charms. Constance, parting her lips on a startled gasp, was instantly treated to the probing thrust of his tongue between her teeth, which had the curious effect of sending a delirious shock wave coursing through the entire length of her. Then what must he do but trail his hand up her back and down her bare arm until he found with unerring accuracy the soft swell of a breast and cradled it in his palm. A wholly unladylike groan burst from her depths as he rubbed the pad of his thumb over the peaking bud of her nipple, then, as it grew hard, tweaked it through the thin fabric of her dress between his thumb and forefinger.

Good heavens, she had never dreamed that physical passion between a man and a woman could generate so much pleasurable excitement. Faith, her heart pumping and her temperature noticeably rising, she felt on the verge of a conflagration! Nor was that all or the least of it. She was acutely sensible of Vere's manly strength pressed hard against her softer, feminine flesh, not to mention the intimacy of his lips caressing her in a manner to which she had never before been subjected. Awakened to a heady array of sensations that scattered her thoughts and rendered her prey to purely feminine instinct, she molded herself feverishly against Vere's tall frame, her arms reaching about his lean waist and up his powerful back.

It came to her amid a whirlwind of emotions that she had unleashed a tempest the likes of which she had never known before—or perhaps Vere had unleashed it. Whatever the case, it was perhaps fortunate that she had always entertained a particular fondness for storms, she reflected deliriously, as she gave herself up to the riotous prompting of womanly needs now coming fully awake in her.

Indeed, she returned his caresses with a sweet, untutored ardor that ignited a raging fire in Vere's veins. And when at last he lifted his head to look at her, she clung to him, her eyes closed and her face wearing a rapt expression, which left little doubt in his mind that it was not revulsion she felt for him but something on quite a different order.

He was swept at that discovery with a sense of elation that was as powerful as it was unexpected. Egad, but she was magnificent, was his titian-haired temptress. No other woman had ever responded to his lovemaking with quite such wholehearted abandonment. She was all untaught passion and sweet generosity. More intriguing yet, however, was the effect she would seem to have on *him!*

He was ruefully aware that she would seem to possess the singular talent for making him forget who and what he was. More than that, she, like no other woman before her, had the uncanny ability to bestir the softer, human emotions in his breast—emotions which he had not only thought long since dead and buried, but which could only be a bloody hindrance to him now. Egad, with any other woman, he would not have thought twice about taking what he wanted from her and damn the consequences. The redheaded beauty, on the other hand, conjured up unwelcome reminders of the man that the duke expected him to be and that the marquis and marchioness had anticipated their only son to become. But then, that paragon of virtue did not exist—indeed, had no part to play in the drama that fate had chosen for Vere; and, bloody hell, he *wanted* Lady Constance Landford, had wanted her from the first moment that he laid eyes on her.

"My lord?" queried Constance, her eyelids drifting open to reveal eyes dark and vulnerable with yearning. Egad, they took his breath away. She was in truth an enchantress with the power to bewitch him. "What is it? Why have you stopped?"

Indeed, thought Vere, why *was* he vacillating? He, who had never before denied himself of a woman's proffered pleasures. She wanted him as much as he did her. Who the bloody hell was he to disappoint her?

"The devil, Miss Landford," he rasped, "you tempt me too far." Clasping his hands about her willowy waist, he lifted her without warning to the writing table. Spreading her knees apart, he inserted himself between them. "And now I think I must have you."

"An excellent notion, my lord," gasped Constance, who, despite the fact that she could not but think it long past time that he came to precisely that conclusion, was nevertheless more than a trifle startled to find herself perched on the edge of an oak desk with the marquis between her thighs.

It was not quite the way that she had envisioned events when she had imagined herself in the role of Vere's inamorata. But then Vere pressed his lips to the side of her neck as his fingers busied themselves with undoing the tiny pearl buttons at the back of her bodice, one after the other, and suddenly it came to her with a thrill of anticipation that things were precisely the way she should have imagined them. Indeed, when a breathless few seconds later she found herself bared to the waist and her breasts cupped in the marquis's hands, she could not but think that there was a great deal to be said for making love on a writing table. She was even more certain of it when the marquis bent his head to caress the taut buds of her nipples with his tongue, first one and then the other. Faith, she had never felt so stimulated!

Giving vent to a gusty sigh, she leaned against her hands propped on the table behind her and arched her back to give him greater access for his manipulations.

Egad, but she was exquisite, thought Vere, who, had she but known it, was even more stimulated than was she. Hellfire, he was like to bloody expire from it! Reaching down and catching the hems of her skirts, he thrust them up around her waist.

Constance, who had only just been given to digest the novelty of being perched on a desk with her bosom bared above her dress and her unmentionables revealed below, could not but wonder how she came next to be lying on her back, her legs propped on Vere's shoulders.

"My *lord?*" she queried in startled surprise as Vere, slipping his hand through the separation between the legs of her drawers, found and caressed the tiny pearl nestled within the lips of her body.

"Softly, my girl," he uttered thickly. "There is nothing to fear in what I am doing."

"It is not fear that I am feeling," declared Constance, in a growing agony of suspense. "I feel—I feel on the verge of a stu*pendous discovery*!"

"And so you are," rasped Vere on something between a groan and a laugh. He could not but marvel at the readiness of her response to his caresses. Egad, she was already flowing with the sweet nectar of arousal. The petals of her body swollen with need fed his own need, and he delved an exploratory finger inside her.

Constance, who was already in the grips of a mounting conviction that she must soon explode if he did not do something quickly, gave forth with a keening sigh at this unexpected development. Reaching for something just beyond her comprehension, she arched frantically against him.

"Yes, that pleasures you, does it not, *enfant?*" he said, knowing that she was very close to discovering the power of her own body to transport her to a state of ecstasy. How small and tight she was! thought Vere, feeling his blood leap in his veins. Damnation, his loins bloody ached to possess her. Drawing back, he reached hurriedly to undo the fastenings at the front of his breeches.

Constance, left bereft just when she needed him the most, cried out in dismay. "Faith, my lord. *I pray you will not stop now!*"

"Soon, *enfant,*" Vere assured her, beads of perspiration breaking out on his forehead. Then his magnificently erect member was free at last of its constraints. In a fever to plunge himself into her warm woman's flesh, he fitted the head of his swollen shaft to the unguarded lips of her body.

Stop? he thought sardonically. Hellfire! Only God or the devil could stop him now.

No doubt the circumstance of their mutual preoccupation with matters of a most intimate nature prevented them from hearing the approach of rapid hoofbeats on the gravel drive outside the window.

Indeed, Vere, leaning over Constance, was grimly contemplating his flame-haired temptress's unavoidable disillusionment upon the first painful moment of entry.

Constance, in a frenzy of need and anticipation, was thinking she must die if she did not soon find some sort of blessed release.

His muscles standing out in ridges and sweat pouring over his body, Vere molded his hands to Constance's buttocks and readied himself to plunge through her maidenhead. Hellfire. She was ready for him, and the devil knew that he could not wait longer.

The sudden clatter of the door knocker shattered the moment.

"*Open up in the name of His Britannic Majesty!*" followed soon after.

"Good God!" Vere rasped, staring down into Constance's wide, stricken eyes.

"The devil!" groaned Constance.

"Quite so," rumbled Vere and wrenched himself away from her.

Flinging an arm across her heated face, Constance drew in and expelled a long, tremulous breath. Then, as the knocker clamored again, she shoved herself up after Vere.

"Quickly," Vere fiercely uttered, as, painfully, he struggled to put himself to rights again, "upstairs with you. Lock yourself in your chamber and open the door to no one until I come for you. Do you hear? *No one!*"

"Yes, yes, I hear you," answered Constance, slipping her arms through her sleeves and covering her bosom with her dress. "Faith, what do you mean to do? Promise you will not raise arms against king's men. Not for me, Vere. I will not have it."

"You, my girl," said Vere, clasping her ungently by the arm and escorting her to the door, "will do as I say." Giving her a firm shove in the direction of the stairs, he waved off Mrs. Turnbough, who had appeared in mobcap and wrapper at the top of the staircase. The maid, Fanny, white-faced, hovered behind her. "Stay to your chambers, both of you, unless I ring for you."

Cursing the demmed untimely interruption in what

had promised to be an uncommonly enlightening evening, he waited until Constance had vanished up the stairs before, running his fingers through his hair, he turned to the pressing matter at hand.

"For the last time," issued from the other side of the oaken barrier, "open in the name of the King, or we shall be forced to break the door down."

"What a criminal waste of effort that would be," remarked the marquis, upon opening the door to be met with the sight of a by now familiar captain of His Majesty's Royal Guards and his seemingly ever-present minion, Corporal Hess. Behind them in the drive stood John Vickers, an apparent captive, with each of his arms in the grasp of a soldier. "Captain Sinclair," murmured Vere, cocking an inquisitive eyebrow at the officer. "Still on the lookout for runaways? I am moved to inquire what you think to gain by detaining my coachman."

"My men caught him lurking about the grounds," replied Sinclair, who wore the aspect of one inordinately pleased with himself.

"You are mistaken, surely," said Vere ever so gently. "'Lurking' hardly describes one who is here by virtue of being a member of this household."

Vere, who had earlier set Vickers to stand watch at the end of the drive, could only suppose that his servant had become exceedingly clumsy to have fallen into the hands of Sinclair and his men. Stepping indolently past the captain, who was looking rather less certain of himself, Vere called out to the soldiers. "No doubt you may be commended for your vigilance, men, as I shall inform His Highness when next I see him. You have, however, mistakenly apprehended my coachman, whom you will be pleased to release at once."

"And now, Captain," he added, turning back without waiting to see John Vickers yank his arms free of the soldiers' clasp and retreat without preamble to his proper province, the stables. "You will, without further ado, enlighten me as to the real purpose of this untimely visit. I was, as it happens, on the point of retiring."

"No doubt I should apologize for having disturbed your evening, my lord," uttered Sinclair with the air of one who has been forced to swallow something exceedingly distasteful.

"And no doubt I should be moved to accept it," returned Vere with a smile that served to accentuate the cold gleam of his eyes. "It would naturally be what was expected of a gracious host toward welcome guests. You, however, have yet to tell me why you have come. Surely, Sinclair, you do not suspect me of harboring runaways?"

"No, my lord. Not runaways," the captain concurred, the smug look returned to his handsome face. "I daresay you are not unfamiliar with the deeds of a certain highwayman whose practice of robbing ladies of their jewels has earned him the sobriquet of the Black Rose."

The Black Rose, was it? thought Vere, who had been expecting to hear something far different from Captain Sinclair. It occurred to him to wonder what the devil could have brought Blaidsdale's nephew sniffing around the hunting lodge in search of the notorious highwayman. Inevitably, perhaps, his thoughts leaped to the titian-haired beauty waiting upstairs for him. Lady Constance was, after all, the only one who knew the Black Rose's identity for certain, and she had been left alone to her own devices for the past six days.

"On the contrary, I believe his peculiar cognomen derives from the rather somber choice of his attire in combination with his custom of presenting his victims with a rose," emended Vere ever so gently. "On the other hand, I fail to see what any of this has to do with me."

"It has, perhaps, a great deal to do with you, my lord," said the captain, giving every appearance of one beginning to enjoy himself immensely. "It has been brought to my attention that you have the distinction of fitting his physical description."

"Curious," murmured Vere with sardonic amusement. "I should have thought him shorter by several inches, from what I have heard."

"And you are noted for the particularity of your stable," continued Sinclair, pointedly ignoring Vere's interruption. "Only the best, my lord, and only black. You will admit that that alone must give pause for thought."

"Certainly it would seem to have stimulated you to unusual mental activity," observed Vere, "most in particularly your hitherto unsuspected proclivity for the amusing."

"It may not be so far-fetched as you would naturally wish others to believe, my lord marquis," Sinclair snapped.

"As it happens, you could not be further from the truth," shrugged Vere. "I haven't the least interest in what others choose to believe."

Sinclair's expression turned suddenly ugly. "We have orders to search your premises for incriminating evidence."

"Orders, Captain? I have only just returned from Carlton House where the Prince Regent received me most graciously. I cannot recall that he mentioned you or any orders." Vere appeared to ponder. "No, I am quite certain of it. Your name did not come up."

"I daresay it will," growled Sinclair, gripping the haft of his sword till the knuckles showed white, "when I deliver him the Black Rose in manacles."

"That would be a clever trick if you could pull it off," said Vere, stepping pointedly between Sinclair and the door. "What really makes you think you will find evidence of him in my house?"

A look of loathing mingled with what gave every manifestation of a strange, dark, burning triumph twisted across Sinclair's face. "Because," he said, "I know *you* are the Black Rose, my lord marquis. Corporal Hess, prepare to remove his lordship from the doorway. If he resists, you may deal with him as you see fit."

"If I were you, Corporal, I should think very carefully before I did anything quite so unwise," murmured Vere, his eyes never leaving Sinclair's flushed features. "Your captain would seem to be suffering a fit of the megrims. It would be a pity if you were made to pay for his mistake in judgment."

"By the devil, Corporal," uttered Sinclair furiously. "You have your orders! Do your bloody demmed duty."

It was at that instant, as Corporal Hess, apparently galvanized into action, made as if to draw his pistol against Vere, and Sinclair, judging he had the upper hand, started to drag his sword from its sheath, that a single, blood-red rose dropped seemingly from the sky to land on the ground at Sinclair's feet.

In the moment that the eyes of the captain and the corporal fixed on the blossom before lifting to catch sight of the caped figure poised daringly in the open French windows two stories above them, Vere had already surmised what they would see.

Hellfire! To all intents and purposes it was the Black Rose brazenly flaunting his presence before King's men.

Vere's blood turned cold. Far from betraying him to Blaidsdale, Lady Constance had taken it upon herself to demonstrate that Vere could not possibly be the Black Rose. The headstrong little fool! he thought. When he got his hands on her, he would bloody well throttle her for pulling such a harebrained stunt. He would, that was, if Captain Sinclair and his men did not do it for him, he amended grimly, as Sinclair, at last yanking his sword free, gestured wildly to the gaping soldiers.

"It's the Black Rose," he shouted, moving to shove past Vere. "Quick, you fools! After him!"

As one, the officer and his men scrambled for the door. Vere, who was noted for his catlike agility and unparalleled athleticism, appeared to step lightly out of their way. No doubt it was only a fluke that Sinclair's foot happened to catch on the toe of Vere's boot. Stumb-

ling, the captain was sent hurtling headlong through
the doorway. The others, piling in after him, were met
with the unavoidable obstacle of their captain sprawled
on the floor before them. They likewise were sent top-
pling.

"Get the devil *off* me, you bloody idiots!" roared
Sinclair, pinned beneath his corporal and two privates.

Hess was the first to disentangle himself and come to
his captain's aid. "'Ere, sir, let me 'elp you."

"I shall help you to the bloody guardhouse," snarled
Sinclair, striking the corporal's hand away. "Go *after*
him! The Black Rose is getting away."

"That way, men," offered Vere, indicating the main
staircase. The "Black Rose," if she had a lick of sense,
would be making her escape at the moment down the
servants' stairs. "Obviously the blackguard broke into my
house and was in the process of robbing me. I shall give
a reward to the man who brings him to me."

"We'll nab 'im, milord," vowed one of the privates, as
he and his fellows clambered up the stairway with a deal
more enthusiasm than they had hitherto demonstrated.

Vere, who had to exercise considerable willpower not
to follow in pursuit of them, leaned down instead and
leisurely retrieved Sinclair's sword, which, dislodged in
the fall, had slithered across the floor.

"Your blade, Captain," he said, extending the weapon,
haft first, to Sinclair. That worthy, having climbed to his
feet, was in the process of yanking his Regimentals to
rights.

Vere was rewarded for his efforts with a glare from
Sinclair. "It would seem exceedingly fortuitous that the
Black Rose chose to make an appearance here tonight,"
he said, taking the sword and thrusting it without ceremony in its scabbard. "Rather *too* fortuitous, I should
think."

"No, really?" returned Vere with the arch of a single,
arrogant eyebrow. "I, on the other hand, am inclined to

believe it was singularly providential. It would appear, after all, that your unexpected arrival has saved me from being robbed, perhaps even assaulted, on my way up to bed. It would seem I am in your debt, Captain. Ironic, is it not?"

"If that is the case, you may be certain that one day I shall collect on what is coming to me," Sinclair vowed with dark significance.

"Oh, but I *am* certain of it, Captain," smiled Vere, ever so gently, even as he wondered grimly what was transpiring on the floor above him.

Sinclair's eyes narrowed sharply on the nobleman's features, which wore a slightly bored expression. Vere waited for the retort that so plainly trembled on the captain's lips.

He was to wait in vain. A woman's bloodcurdling scream followed in short order by the report of a gunshot from overhead rendered both men momentarily speechless.

Vere, the first to recover, bounded up the stairs, two steps at a time, with Sinclair following behind him.

If, when he reached the top, his heart pounding madly, he had thought to discover Constance, lying limp and bloodied from having been pierced by a pistol ball, Vere was soon to be proven vastly mistaken. What he found was Corporal Hess and his men huddled on either side of Constance's closed bedchamber door, giving every appearance of abject terror.

"What the devil——!"

It was Sinclair, arriving at Vere's shoulder.

"*Softly,* Cap'n, sir," warned Hess, waving his superior back. "She 'as a brace of pistols. Nearly took me 'ead off, she did."

"And little wonder, Corporal," pronounced Vere, grim-faced and piercing of eye. "If you have harmed one hair on her head, I shall see that you and your men are sent to the front line."

"If'n you don't mind me saying so, me lord," returned Hess, "me and the lads'd prefer it if you did. This b'aint no place for the loikes of King's soldiers. We never signed up to be shot at by females."

"*Females?* What in hell's name—?"

"I suggest you watch your tongue, Captain," Vere admonished coldly. "The lady has been made to suffer enough without being subjected to language better suited to the stables."

"'Is lordship's in the right of it, beggin' your pardon, Cap'n, sir," offered Hess, shame-faced. "We never meant no 'arm to 'er. 'Ow was we to know we'd find a woman when we broke in? She 'adn't no clothes on, me lord. Fair knocked the breath out'n us. That scream, and then 'er takin' a shot at us."

"She may take any number of shots at you for all I bloody care, Corporal," growled Sinclair. "It is the Black Rose who concerns us at present. Did you see him? For God's sake, man. Is he holed up in there with the woman?"

"We didn't see 'im, sir. I swear there wasn't nobody in the room but the lady."

"Naturally there was not," Vere confirmed in tones heavily laced with irony. "The villain was in my chamber, next to this one. He has undoubtedly fled down the servants' stairs and is long gone from here by now. I strongly suggest, Captain, that you take your men in pursuit of him and leave me to see to the lady."

"You would like to be rid of us, would you not?" said Sinclair, eyeing the marquis with undisguised suspicion. "As it happens, I mean to question the lady first. She is, after all, a witness to an intended crime."

"On the contrary," murmured Vere with steely-edged softness, "she is a witness only to your gross incompetence. As am I, Sinclair, and so you may inform your uncle when next you see him. Do we understand one another, Captain?"

Sinclair, swallowing, paled ever so slightly.

"Yes," said Vere. "I can see that we do. Now take your men and leave while you still can, Captain. Your welcome, along with my patience, has run thin."

It was, perhaps, to Sinclair's credit that he did not pretend to misapprehend the danger that he had brought upon himself. It was one thing to bluster his way into Vere's house on the pretext of searching for a wanted felon. It was quite another to suddenly find the pretext gone and himself left facing the Marquis of Vere's cold, steely wrath.

Turning abruptly on his heel, he departed, his men falling with alacrity in behind him.

Vere, watching from above, waited until they had gone. Then, "Mrs. Turnbough," he said quietly without turning around, "be so kind as to ring for John Vickers, will you? Tell him I shall join him directly in the study."

The housekeeper emerged sheepishly from behind the Queen Anne oak press cupboard at Vere's back, a brass candlestick still clutched menacingly in one hand. "As you wish, milord," she replied, dipping a curtsy. "Beggin' your pardon, milord, but is the young lady unharmed?"

"You may be sure of it." Vere's hand reached for the handle to Constance's bedchamber door. "And, Mrs. Turnbough," he said, pausing.

"Yes, milord?" queried Mrs. Turnbough, her eyes expectant on the back of her employer's broad, uncompromising shoulders.

"In future, I should be better comforted if I knew my housekeeper was not lurking behind the furniture in preparation of fighting off King's men with brass candlesticks. Is that understood?"

A look of consternation crossed the woman's kindly face, even as she sought clumsily to conceal the candlestick in the folds of her woolen wrapper. "Yes, milord," she said in a small voice.

There was a taut silence as the housekeeper made her way past the marquis to do his bidding. She paused as Vere's voice carried to her.

"Nevertheless," he said, "I thank you for it."

The next moment, giving a light rap on the door with his knuckles, he opened the barrier a crack. "It is all right, my lady," he called. "The soldiers have gone."

Mrs. Turnbough watched as he vanished into the room.

"Vere," she heard, "it was Albert. How I wish it had been he who burst into my room. I swear I should have shot him."

"Yes, no doubt, and brought us all to ruin, you impossible, headstrong girl," Vere said clearly. Then the door was firmly shut, and Mrs. Turnbough heard nothing more.

A bemused smile touched the housekeeper's lips. The lady was a feisty one, she was, and as kind and generous as she was lovely. Belike she would make a fine match for his lordship, if he could be made to come up to scratch. But then, judging from the befuddled way his lordship had looked at her as she lay dead to the world that first night, she had already done more than the other beauties who had caught the master's fancy in the past. She had slipped past his guard and set him off his balance, she had, and with the Marquis of Vere, that was no trifling matter.

It was time *someone* saw through all the arrogance and care-for-naught to the man underneath, Agatha Turnbough thought fiercely, as she turned and made her way down the staircase. He was a deep one, was his lordship, and a body never knew for sure what he was thinking. Yet, for all his gambling and carousing, there was still a spark of good in his lordship. Belike all he needed was a loving wife to settle him down and cure him of his wild ways, and the Lady Constance was just such a one as could do it.

Having determined her master's future to her own satisfaction, Mrs. Turnbough rang for the coachman.

She might not have been quite so certain of a happy outcome, however, if she had been given to witness his lordship face-to-face with the Lady Constance. Her upper regions clad in a mobcap and bedsheet and her nether in a man's black unmentionables and boots, Constance awarded Vere a sparkling look.

"It was a brazen thing to do, I know," she declared, her face suffused with a blush. "It was hardly my fault, however, that there was not time to remove these blasted boots, not to mention the breeches. Besides," she added, deliberately dropping the sheet to the floor, "sitting up in bed in apparent bestartlement with my bosom bared served to distract Hess and the others from taking a good look at my face, which, you will agree, would not have done at all. To all intents and purposes, they saw only that I was a woman with a woman's accoutrements."

Vere, treated to the same singularly distracting view of a particularly fine brace of female accoutrements, could not deny the truth of her assertion. It was, indeed, doubtful that the three soldiers would be able to offer anything other than an exceedingly vague description of the woman who had taken a shot at them. That realization, however, did little to alleviate the pressure in his chest that had had its inception when he first sighted the caped figure flinging her defiance at the King's men and that had grown exponentially at the sound of that nerve-shattering scream, never mind the shot. And now she dared to stand before him in all her woman's glory and pretend that she had not risked her reputation and her life for the sole purpose of saving him from being exposed as the Black Rose. It was bloody demmed time she learned that she could not defy his orders and create havoc and mayhem without so much as a thought as to whether he wished for her interference or not.

"It was a demmed fool stunt, and I shall have your

word you will do nothing remotely similar to it again,"
he uttered, as, grimly, he crossed the room in two long
strides and grasped her ruthlessly by the shoulders with
every intention of shaking some sense into her.

Constance, already on the thin edge of her control,
stared up at him with all the defiance at her command
until his face blurred in her vision, and she was horri-
fied to feel tears welling up in her eyes.

"*Botheration,*" she gasped, averting her face in vexation.
"Now see what you have done. I *detest* tears. They are so
blastedly feminine."

"The devil," cursed Vere, his grip on her gentling, even
as he noted with sardonic appreciation the fact that she
had managed to change the subject. Bloody hell, he
should put her over his knee and beat her for resorting
to feminine wiles. That he did not could no doubt be attributed to his acute awareness that time was growing
short and not to the fact that the little baggage appeared, in her unwonted state of vulnerability, singularly adorable.

"Then I suggest you dry your tears," he said, thrusting his linen handkerchief in her hand. "I never asked
you to obtrude yourself into my existence, but now that
you have, I will not countenance having you place yourself in danger for my sake whenever the notion takes
you. It might surprise you to learn that I am well able to
deal with the likes of Captain Sinclair without your
help."

"I-I never d-doubted it, my lord," asserted Constance,
who could not but wonder what had become of the
marquis notorious for having ice water in his veins, as
she blotted her eyes then vigorously blew her nose. Really,
it was too bad of him to discover his temper at this particularly inopportune moment—when she was only just
beginning to realize the enormity of the things she had
done. Certainly it did not help in the least to know that
a blush had suffused her cheeks at the mere thought of

her unmitigated brazenness. Vere could at least show
some appreciation for her ingenuity, if nothing else. "It
is only that, when I overheard him say that he knew you
were the Black Rose, it came to me that I was in a unique
position to disprove his claim in a most dramatic fashion. After all, I not only happened to be in possession of
a rose, but I was also already dressed for the part."

"Dressed for the part?" echoed Vere in tones heavily
laced with irony. Reaching down to retrieve the discarded sheet, he draped it significantly about her shoulders. "In the circumstances, that would seem something
of an exaggeration."

"I wish you will not be absurd, Vere," Constance retorted, her own temper flaring at his less than sympa-
thetic attitude. "Faced with the distinct possibility that I
might have to resort to sudden flight, I had already discarded the gown in favor of my Black Rose disguise when
I overheard Sinclair's intentions. Surely, you would not
have had me toss such an opportunity away?"

"I would have had you do as you were told," Vere
stated unequivocally, "and thus avoided revealing your
presence here, not to mention precipitating precisely
what I was on the point of averting. Do you really imagine that I should have allowed Sinclair to set foot across
my threshold? He knew as well as I that he had not a leg
to stand on. Perhaps you have forgotten who I am, but
you may be certain that he had not."

"But he had orders," Constance insisted, her cheeks
going suddenly quite pale. "I heard that much at least.
He was going to search the house for evidence." She
paused. Her eyes, huge in the oval of her face, probed
his. "Would he have found anything incriminating, Vere?
You have not been arrogant enough to keep your ill-
gotten gains where someone might find them, have you?"

A wry smile flickered at the corners of Vere's mouth.
"You have a strange notion of my character if you think
I should do anything quite so lackwitted," he said, a queer,

cold gleam in his eyes. "On the other hand, I have no doubt that, given the opportunity to search the house, he would have discovered all the evidence he needed to send me to the gallows."

Constance, no slow top, stared at Vere with dawning comprehension. "He brought it with him," she stated with utter certainty. "He meant to plant it—jewelry or some such thing that belonged to Lady Blaidsdale or Lady Sinclair, perhaps—and then conveniently find it. No doubt one or the other has already claimed to be one of the Black Rose's latest victims. But then, his orders . . ."

"Came from Blaidsdale," Vere finished for her. "There *were* no orders. Corporal Hess and the others, I daresay, were mere dupes in what was intended to be an attempt to frame me. It was, after all, the sort of thing about which you came to warn me."

"The lesson the earl and his brother were going to teach you," breathed Constance, marveling at her own failure to recognize the evening's events for what they were. "Faith, I should have seen it. Instead, my one thought was that Albert had somehow figured out that it was never Lord Huntingdon who soiled his boots."

"As it happens, that was my first thought, too," admitted Vere, marveling at the ease with which his temptress had recovered her equilibrium in the wake of the evening's disturbing events. Other than his sisters, perhaps, he could not think of another woman of his acquaintance who might have dared what she had and still managed to appear as undaunted by the experience as if she were perfectly accustomed to baring herself to any number of King's men in order to throw them off balance. It was time now, however, that he took matters into his own hands. Indeed, he was acutely aware that he had come perilously close to leaving it till it was too late. "What we thought, however, hardly matters," he said, unwontedly annoyed at himself for his own dereliction. "What *is* to the point is that it is time we were leaving here."

"Leaving?" echoed Constance, who was not quite so composed as she let on, though her unsettled state had a deal less to do with her recent confrontation with soldiers than with the turmoil of emotions Vere's unexpected revelations had generated. "But where——?"

"Never mind *where* for the moment," interrupted Vere, unprepared at present to offer lengthy explanations for the plan that had taken shape as he stood watching Sinclair's departure. "Suffice it to say *away from here.* I shall send Mrs. Turnbough up to help you dress and pack a few things. We shall be departing within the hour."

He paused. A hand beneath her chin lifting her head up, he gazed deeply into her eyes. "Trust me, *enfant.* I promise I shall let nothing happen to you. Only, I must have your word there will be no more heroic stunts for my benefit. From now on, there will be only one Black Rose."

"And I daresay that, my lord, is one too many," answered Constance, returning his look steadily. Her heart sank as she watched the bored mask of the Corinthian descend over the nobleman's features.

"Yes, no doubt." Vere let his hand drop. "He, however, serves my purpose for the moment."

As he turned to the door to leave her, Constance took an involuntary step after him. "Vere," she said, her voice sounding a trifle breathless even in her own ears. "I do trust you, as I should hope you trust me. You have my word that in future I shall try to be more circumspect in my behavior."

He paused for the barest instant, his back to her. Then, "Splendid," he said, in tones heavily laced with irony. "Be sure I shall hold you to it."

The next moment he had gone, leaving Constance to stare after him with troubled eyes.

The devil, thought Vere, as he made his way downstairs to the study. He had the peculiar feeling that Lady Constance Landford was a disturbing force that was about to change his life forever. Indeed, if he were not mistaken, she had already diverted him from his original course to the extent that he was about to take himself a wife that he had not wanted and who must inevitably complicate plans that he had been ten years in the making.

The devil, it was a perilous road for a woman, and he would be doing her no favor in making her his marchioness. Lord Sinclair and Vice Admiral Sir Oliver Landford had already been made to feel the first thrusts of Vere's long-awaited vengeance. He had struck where they were the most vulnerable—in their purses. It had been an absurdly simple matter to entice the baron into investing in a smuggling venture that had been doomed from its inception. Once again Caleb Roth, acting as the agent for a mysterious—indeed, mythological—smuggler chieftain, had proven of inestimable value. While Sinclair had yet to discover the source of his sudden reverses, Landford was most certainly fully aware that Vere had acquired the admiral's substantial gambling markers. No doubt that discovery was what had spurred Blaidsdale to action. Having failed in their spurious attempt to frame Vere, Blaidsdale and his brother would not hesitate to implement another "lesson" for Vere's edification. It would not be the bumbling captain of the King's Guards next time. Sinclair's failure to recapture his intended wife followed immediately after by this night's fiasco would insure his uncles' disfavor. But then, Sinclair had accomplished one thing—he had returned Vere to rationality.

The devil, he had known Blaidsdale would try something sooner or later. He had been an arrogant fool to let himself be caught literally with his pants down. Certainly, he had not been thinking with his brains when he came to within a heartbeat of succumbing to his prurient desires. A hard fist closed on his vitals at the thought of how near his arrogance had brought them all to disaster. He should have had his titian-haired temptress well on the road away from Somerset long before this. More than that, he should have made sure to remove her immediately from his own unsavory sphere of influence.

Now there would seem little choice but to keep her with him, at least until he could provide her with the one sure defense against Blaidsdale's determination to marry her off to a man who, clearly, was beneath her. The bile rose to his throat at the mere thought of Lady Constance at Albert Sinclair's mercy. Bloody hell, he *knew* what Sinclair was. He had not spent the past ten years studying his enemies without learning that the captain was as corrupt as he was brutal. But then, he was his mother's son, and Lady Sinclair was a serpent-toothed dragon. Together, Captain Sinclair and his doting mama would have sucked the life out of the spirited young beauty.

To preserve her from that less than felicitous fate, he, Vere, would take Lady Constance Landford as his wife, and it would not be in name only. He knew that now with utter certainty. Before he claimed his rights as a husband, however, he would see to her safety, as he should have done from the very beginning. And then he would take care of his enemies. When and only when he was quit of his obligations to the past would he be free to dedicate himself to learning everything there was to know about his wife, perhaps even to teach her to love him. He did not doubt that it would take him a lifetime.

Egad, but he was become a reformed character, he reflected, cynically amused at himself. He realized that he was not nearly so loath at the prospect of a future of marital domesticity as he might previously have imagined. Indeed, he doubted not that he would be hard put to remain focused on the dangerous business before him just when he needed most to be the Marquis of Vere and all that that name had come to imply.

The devil, he thought, as he entered the study to discover Vickers there before him. It behooved him to get the matter of his marriage behind him and then remove himself as soon as possible from the disturbing source of his distraction. His bride would have to wait. But then, she had set out to entrap a marquis, he sardonically reminded himself. Indeed, no doubt any marquis would have done, so long as it meant she would be saved from being forced to wed her cousin. Once she was assured of her goal, no doubt she would be more than content to take up the threads of her new life without her husband's troublesome presence.

Somehow he did not find that all too plausible prospect in the least comforting.

Chapter 6

"I confess, Vere, that I had come almost to despair that I should ever see this day. Now that it has come, however, I regret only that your grandfather was not here to witness it for himself. He will not soon forgive me for being a part of denying him that pleasure."

"On the contrary," said Vere to the Right Reverend Long, a man in his middle seventies who had the distinction of being the Duke of Albermarle's brother-in-law and Vere's great-uncle. "I daresay the duke will be inordinately pleased that you have clapped the leg shackles on the black sheep at last. And now that it is *un fait accompli*, I fear I must ask one more favor of you."

The two men were alone in the Bishop of Exeter's withdrawing room in which the Right Reverend Long had just performed the ceremony joining Constance and Vere in holy matrimony. The newly elevated marchioness had been whisked away by Mrs. Long to allow the gentlemen to catch up on family news while she regaled Constance with tea and availed herself of the opportunity to become acquainted with her guest.

"You have only to name it, my boy," the bishop rejoined, his blue eyes keen on his grandnephew's face. "In return, I shall remind you that you once promised to tell me the location of your secret pool in which the grandfather of all trout is to be found."

"I fear that venerable patriarch may have long since met his end, Bishop," smiled Vere. "It has been more than ten years since I last visited the place."

"A pity," murmured the bishop, his intelligent features wearing a thoughtful expression. "Even as a boy, you were one of the finest anglers I have ever seen. Perhaps one day you will rediscover your passion for fishing. A lonely stretch of river far from the boisterous crowd, a man alone with his fly rod—it is balm to the soul."

"If I have a soul, it is in need of a far different sort of balm," replied Vere with a cynical twist of the lips. "Which is why I must ask that you tell no one of this marriage for the time being."

"No one, Vere?" queried Bishop Long, clearly taken aback. "But surely the duke . . ."

"The duke will learn of it when the time is right. Pray do not press me for explanations. The less you know, the better for all concerned."

It was obvious Bishop Long was less than comforted by that pronouncement from the marquis. He gave Vere a long look filled with sober understanding. "It is a dark course that you have chosen for yourself, my boy," he said, shaking his head. "Are you sure it is what you would wish for yourself? And your new bride? Have you given proper consideration to what is right for her? I was in hopes that your marriage was an indication that you had at last turned your thoughts away from the past to the future. A future which to me would appear to be bright with new promise. Your lady wife is a charming girl, and it is as plain as the nose on your face that she loves you."

"I fear you are a romantic, Uncle," answered Vere,

who was a deal less convinced of his wife's affections. She, after all, had set out to entrap a marquis. It would remain to be seen whether her seeming ardor would survive past the wedding ceremony. She had what she wanted. Neither she nor her fortune would ever fall into the hands of Albert Sinclair and his mama now. Vere had made certain of that, and he would go on making certain of it. "As fate would have it, I have unfinished business with which I cannot allow anything to interfere, least of all a wife."

"It has been ten years, Vere," the bishop persisted. "Surely, it is time to let go of the ill feelings. I daresay it is what your mother and father would have wanted. In His goodness, the Lord has given you this chance at happiness—a loving wife and children, perhaps, to bring you hope for the future. For your sake and your young wife's, allow Him to mete justice out to those who have wronged your house."

"'Vengeance is mine, saith the Lord'?" quoted Vere with only the barest hint of irony.

"God's vengeance is eternal," the bishop pointed out.

"Yes, no doubt," agreed his lordship. Turning away, he leaned an elbow along the mantelpiece and stared down into the blaze in the Adams fireplace. "Think you my enemies will be willing to let bygones be bygones that I might have the leisure to set up my nursery?" he said after a moment. "If so, then I shall be pleased to leave such tiresome matters in God's capable hands. Unfortunately, I cannot think the Earl of Blaidsdale and his brother would be similarly inclined. Would you have me take that chance, Uncle, and risk Constance's life on it?"

Bishop Long, having no answer to that, stared at Vere's somber figure in helpless silence.

"No, I thought not," murmured Vere, lifting sapient eyes to the older man. "We are beyond turning back, and you must see that to acknowledge Constance publicly as my marchioness would serve only to put her in harm's way. It is just as well that it is not a love match. In truth, that emotion does not enter into it. We have contracted a marriage of convenience. I daresay she will not repine at my absence."

"Perhaps not. And yet, even marriages of convenience may come to be blessed with love," submitted the bishop, staring past Vere with a curiously fixed expression. "I have seen it occur too often not to believe it could happen with you and your lovely wife."

A frisson of warning brought Vere around to be treated to the sight of his new marchioness limned in the open doorway. Behind her, stood his great-aunt, who, some ten years younger than her husband, looked acutely uncomfortable. Indeed, she did not hesitate to award Vere a censorious frown.

"I beg your pardon. Am I interrupting something?" Constance queried with a brightness that was belied somewhat by the heightened color in her cheeks. "It is just that I discovered I had lost my brooch. It was my mother's, you see," she added, her glance darting busily over the Aubusson carpet. "It means a great deal to me."

"But of course it does, my dear," concurred the bishop, adding his efforts to the search. "I understand perfectly."

It was Vere who, after a long, studied glance at his bride's determined efforts not to meet his eye, bent to retrieve an object from the floor near his feet.

"You may rest easy," he said, straightening with supple grace to his considerable height. "I have it."

"There, you see, my dear?" exclaimed Julia Long, fairly beaming in her eagerness to dispel the undercurrent of emotions running rife in the room. "I told you we should find it."

"Thank heavens," murmured Constance, who failed to appear wholly comforted at the recovery of her mama's relic. Lowering her eyes after a single glance up into Vere's face, she reached out her hand, the one on which he had placed the plain gold band less than half an hour earlier. "I should never have forgiven myself if I had failed to recover it."

"No doubt," said Vere, clasping strong fingers about her small, shapely member. "However, I suggest you allow me to keep it a while for you."

"No, really, I—" Constance, her heart leaping wildly in her chest, tried ineffectually to pull her hand free.

She was rewarded for her efforts with a piercing glance from her new husband.

"Softly, child," said Vere, acutely aware that the hand enveloped in his was as cold as ice. Grimly, he wondered just how much she had overheard before the bishop had observed her presence. Obviously it had been more than enough to squelch the glow of happiness she had worn when she departed the room. "If you insist on wearing it, you will only lose it again. The clasp appears to be loose. Trust me to see that it is repaired and then returned to you."

Constance ceased to struggle. "Yes, of course. You are quite right. How perfectly ridiculous of me." At last, she met his look gravely. "Naturally, I must thank you, my lord, for your continued thoughtfulness."

"'My lord'?" queried Vere with the arch of an ebony eyebrow. Egad, it was not her bloody gratitude that he wanted from her, but something of quite a different order. Ruefully, he was aware that she had put a distance between them. "You are my wife now. Surely you can bring yourself to call me by my given name. It is Gideon, you know. Or at the very least you might try 'Vere.' "

"Or no doubt you can come up with any number of appropriate names to call him when you have been married a tad bit longer," offered Julia before Constance was forced to come up with a reply to Vere's pointed query. Patently, the kindhearted matron, having taken an immediate liking to the new marchioness, was troubled by what she had unintentionally overheard. "With Vere, however, they might not always be repeatable in public," she added, leaving little doubt whose side she had taken.

"Now, Julia," admonished the bishop, "you must not be so hard on Gideon. You will have him thinking he has dropped in your estimation when you know perfectly well he has always been your favorite."

"On the contrary, Uncle, she always favored the girls," Vere smoothly interjected, "as well she should. They, at least, are deserving of Aunt Julia's affections."

"Well, it is true, at least, that *they* never introduced frogs into the withdrawing room at afternoon tea or dipped the kitchen feline's tail in the inkwell," observed Julia, shaking her finger at the marquis.

"I protest, Aunt Julia," smiled Vere, who was obviously genuinely fond of his great-aunt and -uncle. "It was Elfrida who misused the cat. I only set the poor creature loose among the guests at your musicale."

"And caused ink to be splattered on Lady Montescue's Viennese white lace. Really, Gideon, it was too dreadful of you," Julia scolded, laughing. "To this day, Lady Montescue has not forgiven me for the ruination of her dress."

"Lady Montescue would not forgive the pope for being Catholic," submitted the bishop. "But then, who am I to judge a woman who donates so lavishly to the Anglican Church?"

"In exchange for a monument to her profligate son who perished at forty from an excess of self-indulgence," Julia did not hesitate to point out. "Still, I suppose that, if we had been blessed with children only to outlive them, I might feel the same as Lady Montescue."

"No, how can you say so," objected Vere, "when you have had a hand in the rearing of two generations of Rochelles? That alone should relegate you to the order of sainthood."

In the laughter that ensued in the wake of that pronouncement from the marquis, Constance could not but stare in something of astonishment at Vere. She had, after all, been given to see a new, wholly unexpected side of the man she had just wed.

While the small glimpses into his childhood, portraying a fun-loving boy full of mischief, had been enchanting, she had found the intriguing sensitivity of the grown man maddeningly fascinating. She had known that he could be devastatingly charming when he chose to be. She had learned that much a little more than five months ago when, in London, their paths had crossed for the very first time. That he was also capable of unaffected warmth was something that he was obviously at great pains to keep hidden from all but a select few of his intimates.

It hardly helped Constance's unsettled frame of mind to realize that she, his wife, was to be excluded from that small circle of people whom the marquis favored with his affections. Love was not to play a part in their marriage. He himself had declared it to be so.

What a fool she had been to allow herself to confuse Vere's physical passion for something deeper! No doubt it was a universal flaw in the feminine psyche that led women to believe that males were actuated by the same instincts for love as motivated females. She had refused to accept that the emotions he aroused in her and which he himself had appeared to manifest were nothing more than purely physical responses to his lovemaking. And yet, Vere had been perfectly honest with her, even going so far as to declare that he preferred his inamoratas to be women of experience. And little wonder! The married women and Paphians with whom he formed his liaisons had already learned the lesson that, with Vere, physical passion had little or nothing to do with love. They expected nothing more from him than he was willing to give. Observing him now, she wondered if they were truly as emotionally detached in the physical act of love as he obviously believed them to be.

Somehow, Constance doubted it. Perhaps with some men, it might be possible, but not with Vere. Vere was a man whom women would find it all too easy to love. Certainly she, Constance, had not proven immune to his allure. Recalling the absurd fantasies in which she had indulged while at Landford Park, she was ruefully aware that he had captured her heart almost from the very beginning, the devil. And then what had she done but let herself be drawn into the sentiment that must inevitably surround a woman pledging her troth to a man in a wedding ceremony? Good heavens, what an idiotish thing to do. He had said nothing to lead her to believe that he viewed their union as anything other than a marriage of convenience. And still she had let herself dream. Really, it was too bad of her; indeed, she would not soon forgive herself. And now she had been delivered a rude awakening. But then, no doubt she had got just what she deserved for abandoning her usual practicality, she told herself, and was not in the least comforted.

Even having been brought to realize that he felt nothing for her, indeed, had married her solely out of his own peculiar code of honor, changed nothing. She knew that she yet loved him, irrevocably and without reservation. She was quite sure that she could not stop herself.

On the other hand, she told herself sternly, as, having bid the bishop and his wife good night, she allowed Vere to lead her to the waiting coach, she could save him the embarrassment of having to deal with a doting wife. He need never know the truth of her feelings for him. It should not be difficult. He, after all, intended to establish her in a safe haven somewhere and then abandon her to her own devices while he went in pursuit of his vengeance. She had surmised that much, at least, from what she had unintentionally overheard.

Really, it was too bad of him. Indeed, it was the shabbiest thing. If nothing else, she had expected to be allowed to play a part in exposing Blaidsdale for what he
was. It was her right. He, after all, had done what no
man had the right to do. He had struck her! Damn his
soul for that. And damn him for thinking he could strip
her of her independence, not to mention her fortune
and her humanity, either by marrying her off to a man
she detested or by confining her to the horrors of a
mental institution and all simply because she was a female. Faith, she no longer wondered why her mama
had left him. She only marveled that she had put it off
for as long as she had. And now, Vere, the man she had
just married, intended to treat her in a similar manner—as an impediment to be disposed of while he went
about the weightier affairs reserved for the masculine
gender.

The devil take him. In truth, she had thought better
of him. But then, there was nothing, really, to keep her
from pursuing her own course. It was not as if she were
dependent upon Vere for anything more than the protection of his name. Faith, perhaps she had not even
need of that, she thought suddenly, recalling her mama's
final words recorded in the letter she had left for
Constance, her daughter.

Good heavens, in all the excitement of the past several days, she had completely forgotten about Mr. Malcom
Enderhart! Suddenly, she found there were a great
many questions that she would like to ask him. Who, for
example, her real father was, and why, of all her suitors,
her mama had chosen Blaidsdale to serve as surrogate
father to her unborn child. Yes, and why she should
have waited nearly ten years to make her escape from
his household. And, finally, Constance would like very
much to know why Blaidsdale had been content to allow
his estranged wife to live in Wells without any further interference in her existence.

It came to Constance with sudden, astounding clarity that the first Lady Blaidsdale must have had something in the way of protection that had served to keep the earl at a safe distance. Furthermore, she had little doubt that, knowing the sheer malevolence of which Blaidsdale was capable, her mama had meant to pass that something on to her daughter to use as an assurance of Constance's safety. Somehow she had to make her way to London and her mama's former solicitor, whom she had been supposed to contact if ever she found herself in dire circumstances. Her mama had been quite specific on that point. Certainly, her sudden turn of circumstances was dire enough to necessitate Mr. Enderhart's services.

Upon having had that particular suddenly recur to her, Constance bolted upright in her seat.

"Vere," she said, turning to stare out the coach window, "this is not the way we came. Indeed, am I not mistaken, we are headed in the opposite direction."

"You are not mistaken," confirmed Vere, who, acutely aware for no little time of his bride's lengthy preoccupation with her own thoughts, had been wondering when she would become aware of that cogent fact. They had left the streets of Exeter behind some twenty minutes before and were presently wending their way along a little-used road running parallel with the river.

"But why?" she demanded, trying to make out his face in the coach's murky interior. "Where are you taking me? Not back to the hunting lodge, it is obvious. But then, surely you do not intend to leave me hidden away here, somewhere, wherever *here* is?"

"No, not in the hills overlooking the River Exe or the hunting lodge," agreed Vere, wondering if he had come to the best decision in the circumstances. "Neither would suit our purposes. On the other hand, it occurred to me that you would prefer to spend your honeymoon in more familiar surrounds."

"London!" pronounced Constance with utter certainty,

even as she marveled at the ease with which she had been delivered a solution to her problem. "Vere, you are taking me home. You really are the most thoughtful of husbands."

"I should not be too sure of that, if I were you," answered the marquis with a wry twist of the lips. "We will be in Town only a day or two, until I can make other arrangements for you. In the meantime, I'm afraid I must insist that you make no attempt to visit your Aunt Sophie or any of your usual haunts. You may be sure that the earl will be expecting you to do that very thing."

"But what can it matter, Vere?" queried Constance, her heart inexplicably sinking. "I am a married woman now. There is nothing Blaidsdale can do to hurt me."

"He can have you abducted and held for ransom—or worse," Vere stated unequivocally. "He has already engineered the death of one Marchioness of Vere. You may be certain he would not hesitate to rid himself of another if it appeared to serve his purposes."

Constance went deathly still, a great deal suddenly made clear to her.

"Faith, you are suggesting that he might see fit to use me against you," she stated flatly.

"I am certain of it, which is why you will remain sequestered in Albermarle's Town House during our stay in London." Slipping an arm around her shoulders, he drew Constance close. "It is not the manner in which I should prefer to begin our marriage together, *enfant.* It is, however, the only way that I can be sure of your safety. Blaidsdale will not think to look for you in the duke's house. Indeed, not even he would go so far as dare to openly incur the duke's enmity. For a time we will be lost to him while he searches the roads out of Somerset. I consider it exceedingly doubtful that it will occur to him that we have not chosen to travel overland."

"And have we not, Vere?" queried Constance, sitting up to peer into the marquis's shadowy features.

"Indeed, we have not," affirmed Vere, as the coach came to a halt. Without waiting for the groom to descend, he opened the coach door and stepped lithely down. "See for yourself." Reaching up, he helped Constance to alight after him.

Constance, drawing her mantle tight against the chill breeze, was no little astonished to find that she was standing at the edge of a pier, which gave the appearance of long disuse. The lap of waves against the stone pilings carried with it the aroma of salt water and rotting timber. In the dark of a moonless night, she could see little beyond the jetty projecting out into the black glimmer of water. Even the stars were little more than pale points of light gleaming coldly in the firmament. Involuntarily, she shuddered.

It was strange to think that she had lived all her life on an island and never once in her life before been on the water. The closest she had ever come to it was a walk along the dockside of the upper Thames. She was not certain what she felt at the prospect of venturing out on the open sea. Certainly, when she had dreamed of having a little adventure impinge upon the even tenor of her life, she could not possibly have imagined she would be swept up in a chain of events that would lead to a hurried elopement with none other than the Marquis of Vere, and now it seemed she was to embark on a sea voyage!

She was only vaguely aware when Vere loomed suddenly out of the darkness.

"The devil, you are shivering."

The sudden warmth of a heavy cloak slung unexpectedly around her shoulders pulled her from her silent musings to the awareness that Vere had sent Vickers and the coach on its way. She was alone with Vere, who was studying her face in the pale light of a dark lantern of the sort used by mariners. Abruptly he set the lamp on one of the pilings.

"I regret that I cannot offer you a more comfortable passage," he said, taking her hands in his. "Had there been time, I should have had the barge waiting for you. As it is, we shall simply have to make do. Fortunately, we have not far to go."

"I am fine, really," Constance hastened to assure him, as he briskly chafed her cold hands in his. Really, he was the most puzzling of creatures, she could not help musing. Indeed, if she did not know better, she might have been fooled into thinking he was not quite so indifferent to her as he took pains to make her believe. But then, no doubt he would have treated any other woman with the same solicitude merely because he was a gentleman in the truest sense of the word. "You need not worry that I am like to perish from a little cold," she added blithely. "I am not such a poor creature, I assure you."

Vere, bending down to peer into her face, was hardly reassured. In the uncertain light, her features appeared pinched from the cold. Silently, he cursed the necessity of exposing her to the elements in the rather less than luxurious means of transportation at his immediate disposal. But then, he could hardly have known ahead of time that he would have need of a vessel suitable to carry his bride.

Angry with himself, he gathered up the trunk of clothes that had belonged to the former marchioness. With the lantern dangling from his other hand, he led Constance out along the jetty.

Constance, staying close to Vere's large, comforting presence, hardly knew what she had been expecting to find at the end of their walk. Certainly, it was not what appeared to be a rather poor excuse for a boat tied to the dock. Possessed of two wooden oars and what she strongly suspected to be bilge water on the bottom, it was hardly the sort of conveyance one would have associated with the Marquis of Vere. It was, consequently, with no little dismay that she beheld Vere deposit the trunk in the bow, then, stepping lightly down in after it, turn to extend a hand up to her to follow. Taking a deep breath, she moved to the edge of the dock and, with as much grace as she could muster hindered by her skirts and the cloak, climbed into the unprepossessing vessel. Only then, as she scrambled to a seat in the bow, did it come to her to wonder what sort of vessel it was upon which she was expected to make her maiden sea voyage.

She no doubt should have been somewhat comforted by the obvious ease with which Vere, releasing the dock lines, shoved off; then fitting the oars in the oarlocks, he began to maneuver the boat away from the dock out to sea. Vere, clearly, was no novice at this sort of thing. Nevertheless, it was no little time before Constance, losing herself in the steady rhythm of Vere's long, powerful strokes and the gentle rise and fall of the sea, felt the hard clench of her muscles slowly relax.

In order to divert her thoughts from the black, watery expanse around her, she turned—inevitably, perhaps—to a contemplation of the man facing her in the stern. Even in the dark, relieved only by the pale light of the stars, she could sense a change in Vere. Indeed, as she watched the easy, supple movements of each stroke, it came to her that he was relaxed, as she had never before seen him. Only gradually did it occur to her that he was at home in his element and further that he was actually enjoying himself.

Inexplicably, Constance experienced a warm glow within at the realization that she had discovered something special and private about the complex man she had married. Vere loved the sea. She supposed he came by that sentiment naturally. His father, after all, had been a sailor of no little renown. More than that, however, the sea afforded him some sort of surcease from the thing that drove him—indeed, from the need to be the Marquis of Vere and all that that name had come to mean. Here, away from the land, he could simply be Gideon Rochelle, the man.

Constance, watching him, could not but speculate what it would be like to know the man behind the façade Vere assumed for the rest of the world. She wondered if he ever let anyone inside—his sisters, perhaps, or his grandfather. Somehow she did not think that he did. It came to her with something resembling a pang that his must be an exceedingly lonely existence. But then, he was the Marquis of Vere. Perhaps he did not need anyone to fill any voids in his life.

Constance found that a sobering thought. As much as she valued her independence, she knew all too well that she was not completely sufficient unto herself. No matter how much she enjoyed losing herself for hours at a time in her beloved books, no matter how greatly she treasured her privacy, she had still the need for human contact, for love and laughter. There had always been someone in her life—her mama and her mama's friend, Aunt Sophie and the colonel, and Millie, too. She could not conceive of a life without someone in whom she could confide the small things and the big, with whom she could share the absurdities of everyday existence—indeed, with whom she could simply be herself. It would be too much to ask of her. She wondered if Vere, in depriving himself of those small human contacts, was asking too much of himself.

Surely, she thought, it must cost him something to maintain that impenetrable aloofness from the world. One could not live on vengeance alone; at least, one could not and retain one's humanity. It came to her that she would like nothing better than to be the one to breach the impregnable barriers he maintained around him. If she could not teach him to love her, perhaps she might at least bring him to laugh on occasion as he had done in the hunting lodge. She wondered if that would be enough to sustain her, that and perhaps the promise of children.

She knew at once that it would not be enough. Her soul must surely wither and die in a loveless marriage, just as her mama's had done before her. The difference was that she loved Vere, and she was willing to fight to have what her mama could never have had with the Earl of Blaidsdale. To do that, she must first right the wrong that she had done when she entrapped a marquis into marrying her. To win him, she must find a way to set him free of his obligation to her. The answer to her dilemma must surely await her in London.

"Constance, the lantern," impeded on her thoughts. "Hold it high and open and close the shutter. Three times, my girl. Careful, now, that you don't drop it overboard. We shall have a devil of a time finding our way without it."

Constance, who could not come close to guessing how he had found his way with or without the measly light of the lantern, dutifully did as she was bidden.

"Good," applauded Vere, endeavoring to hold the boat on a steady course. "Now keep a sharp lookout to the forward."

"I cannot see a thing," said Constance, twisting around to peer out over the bow. "Not that I have the least idea what I should be looking for."

"You will know it when you see it. There!" he uttered, his voice expressive of satisfaction. "Just off the starboard bow. Roth, the young thatch gallows. He must have sailed the sheets off her to make landfall in two days."

Constance, who, too, had glimpsed the three flashes of light in the distance, could only wonder at the meaning of his last words.

"Two days?" she said, peering at Vere through the darkness. "Are you saying you were not certain the boat would be waiting?"

"Ship, my girl," corrected Vere in sardonic amusement. "Or schooner, to be more specific. And I was reasonably certain Roth would not let me down. He entertains a particular dislike of incurring my displeasure."

Vere offered no more on the subject of the thatch gallows, Roth. And Constance, weary and cold, could not summon the strength to question him further. Instead, she contented herself with staring at the full moon rising like a great orange pumpkin on the horizon.

It was, consequently, with no little bestartlement that she was given to behold the silhouette of a ship's stern appear suddenly to loom out of the darkness before her.

"*Ahoy the ship!*"

Vere's stentorian shout was met with a flurry of activity aboard the vessel.

"It's 'is lordship right enough, Cap'n," called one fellow, leaning out over the bulwarks to stare down at the bobbing boat in the water.

"There be some'un with 'im," shouted out another. "By all the saints, it's a lady!"

"Stand aside, Briggs," a voice ordered curtly. "Let me see."

A head atop a broad set of shoulders jutted out over the bulwarks.

"I see you made it, my lord," observed the newcomer, giving a flamboyant salute. "A mite earlier than expected. It would seem you owe me a shilling. I was, fortunately, a tad beforetime myself."

"Fortunately, indeed," replied the marquis in exceedingly dry accents. "It remains to be seen if you have ripped the masts from her in your mad dash to win your wager. I shall have your hide, Roth, if you have damaged so much as a spar out of recklessness."

"You may rest easy, my lord. Your lovely lady is as trim as when last you saw her. Speaking of which," added the young thatch gallows, "I see you have brought a guest. Captain Caleb Roth at your service, ma'am. May I be the first to wish you welcome?"

"What you may do is make ready to lower the bosun's chair, *Captain* Roth," said Vere with stark significance, "for my wife."

Constance, staring at the stern in the strengthening moonlight, hardly noticed the sudden, stark silence following in the wake of that pronouncement from the marquis. She felt a strange quiver in the pit of her stomach as she made out the letters across the transom.

The schooner was the *Swallow,* and the Marquis and Marchioness of Vere had returned to her.

Chapter 7

It was to occur often to Constance during the gentle passage from Lyme Bay east through the English Channel that her maiden voyage was like being caught up in a dream from which she had no wish to be awakened. Where Captain Caleb Roth had let the swift, agile *Swallow* fly before the wind, Vere seemed strangely content to wend his way on a leisurely course roughly following the coastline. It was almost as if he actually were intent on giving her a honeymoon voyage, perhaps to make up for what was to be, in essence, her confinement at Albermarle House in London.

Almost, she thought. Leaning her hands against the taffrail, she stared out to port at the three chalk monoliths rising out of the water, rather in the manner of giant sailing vessels standing out to sea. The Needles, Vere had called them, off the Isle of Wight. She had the queerest sensation that there were eyes on the island, watching the graceful schooner glide effortlessly through the water.

And little wonder, she thought. The meandering *Swallow* presented the appearance of a rich prize ready for the taking. Only, appearances, especially in this case, could be vastly deceiving. The sleek vessel, made of good, sturdy English oak, might look like a wealthy lord's pleasure yacht, but on her deck she bore two carronades, one forward and another aft. That they were at present innocuously concealed beneath canvas seemed vastly significant to Constance. She did not doubt that it was not the normal practice to mount cannon on the decks of yachts. Yet there was the additional presence of seven square portholes on either side of the ship, each one cleverly hidden behind a close-fitting hatch and having a canvas-covered cannon mounted on runners before it. She had the strongest suspicion that they, too, bespoke the presence of armaments more suited to a ship of war than a pleasure craft.

In truth, the *Swallow* would seem provocative of not a few questions in Constance's fertile brain. Not the least of these was how Vere should have come into possession of a ship, let alone one fitted with cannon. All in all, it must have cost him a not insignificant sum. More importantly in her present circumstances, she could not but wonder why he should have gone to all the expense and the trouble. Certainly, it was not for *her* safety. He could not have known when he outfitted the vessel that he would be sailing with the Earl of Blaidsdale's daughter aboard. But then, it had long since occurred to her that the *Swallow*'s unhurried passage was not designed solely as a pleasure cruise for the entertainment of the marquis's new bride. Indeed, she could not escape the feeling that Vere was dangling the schooner in sight of land like bait in a trap, but a trap for whom, if not Blaidsdale, who had never sailed a day in his life?

If her suspicions were correct, it must certainly be someone connected to the death of the former marquis and marchioness. Indeed, she could not be mistaken in that. He had, after all, named his ship *Swallow*.

She supposed she should not begrudge Vere the dangerous game he was playing in the name of vengeance. If it was not, in truth, precisely what it had been made to appear on the surface, he had still, to all outward appearances at least, been everything that one might have looked for in a new husband on a wedding voyage.

Certainly, save for the long, private talks with the curiously likable Caleb Roth, he had been more than regardful of her presence. He had lounged against the rail beside the deck chair, which one of the sailors had fashioned for her, and pointed out the sights to her or patiently explained the workings of the sleek, ninety-foot schooner manned by its sixty seamen. Or at other times, standing behind her, his hands on the wheel pegs, he had helped her to steer the lively vessel while the crew looked on with grinning faces. Indeed, they were like children, taking delight in their master's new status as a married man. And Vere, seeming to take pleasure in showing off his new bride, had humored them.

Truth to tell, she admitted grudgingly to herself, he was no less attentive when she and Vere were alone together. Their meals in the stern cabin had taken on an air of intimacy undisturbed by Pultney, the ship's steward, padding quietly about as he served the various dishes and picked up afterwards.

She had come to look forward with mixed feelings to their quiet exchange of conversation over those evening repasts. Possessed of knowledge on a wide range of subjects, Vere could be amusing, entertaining her with any number of lively anecdotes about his family, his friends, and acquaintances; or he could be serious, discussing art, literature, history, or the current events, which centered to such a great extent on the reality of renewed war with France. More than that, he had the gift for listening and was adept at drawing her to talk at length about herself, her mama, her life with her aunt in London. And through it all, she was aware that he had set aside the arrogant façade, as if, with her, for this time, he was content to allow her intriguing glimpses into the real man behind the mask of the marquis.

In truth, she had the disturbing sense that he was courting her in the manner of a man who was fully aware that he might claim her at any time, but had chosen for reasons of his own not to rush his fences, the devil.

A plague on the man! she thought, glancing over her shoulder at the tall figure standing near the helm in close conversation with Roth. She was ruefully aware that Vere had never appeared more thrillingly masculine than he did now, dressed in buff unmentionables tucked into brown Hessian boots, and a plain white linen shirt, worn open at the throat. His rather worn sea-going coat that had once been dark blue, but was now considerably faded from the sun, seemed curiously to suit him somehow. In truth, she thought he had never been more compellingly handsome—or more maddeningly unattainable.

She could wish that he would try being less patient to make her his wife in more than name only. These halcyon days of sailing ever toward the sunrise could not last forever. Indeed, she was painfully aware that they must soon come to an end either in armed confrontation with an enemy or peacefully at some harbor within striking distance of London.

That first night on board, she had told herself that Vere was only being thoughtful when he left her to climb wearily alone into bed. And, indeed, she had been reeling from exhaustion when she had allowed herself to be hoisted on board in the absurdity called a bosun's chair. A faint, wry smile touched her lips as she recalled that, wet and bedraggled, she had been just a trifle overwhelmed to find herself the cynosure of nearly forty pairs of masculine eyes. Then, while Vere, securing the boat to the chains, had climbed unaided up the tumblehome and through the entry port, the decidedly dashing Captain Roth had stridden forward to help her out of the sling.

No more than two-and-twenty and possessed of thick, unruly hair the color of sun-bleached sand, he had appeared boyishly young to be in command of the schooner. Gimlet grey eyes set in the smooth, tanned face, however, had belied the devil-may-care insouciance of his slouching stance. He was reckless and probably fearless, but he was nobody's fool. More than that, Constance did not doubt that he could be exceedingly dangerous. It was little wonder that Vere had chosen him to serve as one of his confederates.

Constance was to find immediately that Roth was gifted as well with a boyish charm and a flashing grin that must surely have melted many an unsuspecting feminine heart. Certainly, he had done his best to ingratiate himself into Constance's good graces, a circumstance that she had in the succeeding days found touching and rather amusing. Faith, despite the fact that there were only three years between them, she could not but feel as if she were ages older than he was. And how not, when he displayed every evidence of being a young firebrand who might at any moment go off half-cocked at the least little thing?

That first night, however, as, alighting safely on the deck, she had allowed Roth to pull her to her feet, she had been grateful only to find that she was on something rather larger than a rowboat and with a strong arm to help steady her against the unfamiliar cant of a deck. The young sea captain's solicitude, as he bundled her to the hatch and down the companionway to the stern quarters away from the curious stares, had won him her immediate gratitude.

"I shall have Pultney fetch hot coffee, my lady," he said, seeing that she was seated in one of the two blue velvet armchairs ranged about the small but well-apportioned cabin. "And perhaps a bite to eat."

"You are very kind, but all I really wish is my trunk, if you please," had replied Constance, ruefully aware that her borrowed satin slippers were wet and quite beyond salvation. She had not doubted that the hems of her similarly borrowed skirts were in an equally ruinous state. "And perhaps some hot water with which to wash. I am convinced I must look a sorry sight."

"Not so as you'd notice, my lady," commented Roth, only just managing to take his eyes away as Vere came up behind him.

Constance, who could not but see that she had made a distinct impression on the captain, had hidden her smile. Clearly, Roth was not accustomed to receiving ladies aboard his vessel. Indeed, she did not doubt that he was more used to consorting with a different sort of female when he was ashore. Still, it was clear that he had come from a good home, where he had been taught proper manners. He was at pains to hide both his curiosity and his stunned admiration.

"As soon as the boat is stowed aboard, we shall weigh anchor, Caleb," said the marquis, filling the cabin with his presence. "I want to be well away from the bay before the break of dawn. Set a course to weather the headland. If anyone marks our presence from shore, we shall be only a distant sail."

"Aye, milord," Roth was quick to answer. "I'll call the hands up directly." Bending his head beneath the low-lying deck beams, he turned to leave.

"And, Caleb."

The captain came to a halt, his eyes seeking Vere's.

"Send a lookout aloft. Be certain he is a lad with a sharp eye."

It was clear to Constance, watching the two men, that a message passed between them.

Then Roth had gone, and she was alone with Vere, who seemed strangely indecisive, as he stood, legs braced against the gentle rise and fall of the deck beneath his feet.

"You believe there is a chance that Blaidsdale will send

someone after us even out here," she stated flatly. Coming to her feet, she paced a step and came back again. "How could he possibly do any such thing, Vere? You yourself said it was highly unlikely."

"And so it is, *enfant,*" agreed Vere, his gaze contemplative on the view of moonlight and sea framed in the stern windows. "Highly unlikely, indeed."

He turned to look at her. Inexplicably, Constance had felt her heart sink.

He was not staying. She had known it before he gave his excuses. She was tired, and he had a great deal to discuss with Roth. Rather than disturb her, he would be taking over Roth's quarters for the evening. Only, it had not been merely for that evening, but *every* evening! Really, it was too shabby of him, she thought. She was on her honeymoon with the man who had won her heart, and he had yet to do so much as kiss her.

Clearly, he had indeed determined on a marriage of convenience, a marriage without passion, but *why?*

She could not be mistaken in thinking that he had been as eager as she was that night in the hunting lodge to consummate what they had started. She, after all, had had the evidence of her own eyes, not to mention the intoxicating proof of her deliriously aroused senses. What, then, could possibly have happened in the interim to cause him to cool so rapidly in his ardor?

The only answer that came to her was that it must have been the elopement along with the marriage ceremony itself. No doubt, in that wild dash from Wells to Exeter, he had been given more than sufficient time to dwell on her brash avowal that she had set out deliberately to entrap him. Unfortunately, as it had turned out, the inescapable truth was that she had done precisely that. In retrospect, she could not see that she had had any other choice in the matter. She had, after all, been in rather desperate straits. Still, she could wish now that she had kept her tongue between her teeth.

And now what was she to do? she wondered, wishing for the first time in her life that she had devoted herself a little more to learning the basic feminine skills of allurement, beguilement, and cajolery. The art of entrapment, it would appear, had come naturally to her, she reflected with sardonic amusement at where her thoughts were taking her.

She could not but find it ironic in the extreme that she, Constance Hermione Landford, who had always prided herself on her disdain of feminine wiles, was almost envious of her stepmother Rosalind's proficiency at vacuous coquetry. She would almost have sunk to the level of using artifice had she not known that she would have felt utterly ridiculous in such a role. She was far too practical-minded to twitter and flutter her eyelashes. And the mere notion of feigning a sudden feminine frailty was clearly out of the question at this late date. She could be certain that Vere, rather than be taken in by it, would be moved to laugh in her face. No doubt she would do better simply to challenge the odious marquis to a duel for the honor of bedding him. At least she would be far more comfortable wielding a blade than an ivory-sticked folding fan.

Constance lost herself in a frivolous daydream in which she had the distinct pleasure of persuading his lordship to disrobe at the point of a sword. Consequently, she was unaware when Vere, glancing over at her, went suddenly quite still, his gaze curiously arrested.

She could not have known the striking picture of feminine loveliness she presented, limned against the skyline, her skirts billowing about her long, slender legs and her hair, streaming free, a fiery mass in the wind. She took his breath away. But then, she would seem to be having the same effect on the entire crew. He noted with sardonic appreciation the frank stares of men held spellbound by something beautiful and alien to their familiar world of ships and sea. Even Roth, he thought, who had been born the younger son of nobility only to be outcast and disowned by his father. It had been clear from the very beginning that he was as bedazzled as were his men. But then, Roth must have seen the beautiful Constance as an unwelcome reminder of a life from which he had walked away and never once looked back. It could not be easy for him to be brought to remember it now and in such a manner.

Vere could not but sympathize with Roth. He was, after all, ironically aware that the new Lady Vere exercised a similar chastening influence over him as well. How else was he to explain the peculiarity of his behavior since their arrival aboard ship? She was his wife, his bride of three days and as many nights, and he had yet to take her to his bed.

Hell and the devil confound it! He had landed himself in a devil of a coil, the likes of which he could not but find laughable in the extreme. That he, Vere, who had built his reputation for being dangerous on his conquests of married females, should have suddenly developed what he could only suppose was a conscience was beyond ludicrous. And yet it had come to him, as he stood alone with his new bride in the stern cabin, that to take her then in the aftermath of having inadvertently robbed her of her girlish illusions was tantamount to using her in the same unfeeling manner in which he had used his numerous lovebirds. That the notion was distasteful to him had come as no little surprise to him. In satisfying his manly needs, he had never before taken into account the possible feelings of the women whose pleasures he enjoyed. Egad, why should he? They, even knowing the rules of the game, had yet chosen to play.

That it should suddenly loom as an entirely different matter with the woman who was his wife he had attributed to a previously undetected aberration in his character. Incredibly, it seemed that a shred of decency had yet survived the years of deliberate dissolution. Egad, how the duke would have enjoyed the irony in that, he thought with a mirthless smile.

Irony or not, he had nevertheless perceived with singular clarity a distinct aversion to the notion of bedding a bride who had just been given to hear from her groom's own lips that theirs was to be a marriage without sentiment. It had changed nothing to know with utter certainty that he could bring her to love him. The devil knew that he had done it often enough in the past with other women when it served his purposes. It was a gift, or a curse, perhaps, that women came easily to love him. But then, he was a master at the game of passion.

Vere took no pride in the fact that he had seemingly been born with an innate ability to see into the hearts of those with whom he came in contact. It was, after all, merely an integral part of who and what he was, like his natural athleticism or his taste for fine wine and beautiful women. His singular ability to read men's souls might have been likened to that of a skilled artist capable of capturing the essence of a subject on canvas. He knew men, but, more than that, he knew women.

Unlike his less perspicacious masculine contemporaries, Vere was neither so cynical nor so naive as to think that all women were alike. That would have been as absurd as declaring that all houses were alike because they had ceilings and walls. But then, he had ever possessed the ability to see past the feminine mystique to the unique woman underneath.

Cynically, he knew that his peculiar insight into the emotional depths of others gave him a distinct advantage in manipulating them to his purpose. In the past, he had not scrupled to use it to his benefit, which had served to earn him his reputation not only for an uncanny penchant for winning at cards, but also for his dangerous capacity for luring females to his bed. But not this time, nor this female.

With Constance, it was not a game of passion. With Constance he was keenly aware that he was in deadly earnest. Now, watching her turn her head into the wind, he felt the searing leap of desire. He wanted her as he had never wanted anything else in his life before; but, more than that, he wanted her in a way that he had never wanted any other woman—wholly, unreservedly, and irrevocably. When she gave herself to him, it would not be because he had woven his web of seduction about her. It would be because she wanted him for himself. She had, after all, deliberately set out to entrap him. It would be worth the wait to discover if her ardor would survive the *fait accompli*.

In the meantime, he reflected, made suddenly aware of the freshening of the wind before a gathering mass of clouds, he had other matters to concern him.

Jago Green, the smuggler, ranged these waters between the Isle of Wight and the Downs.

When Vere had conceived the notion of using the *Swallow* as bait to lure the Cornishman out, he had hardly expected to have a woman aboard, let alone a woman who was his wife. It had seemed a simple enough plan at the time. The schooner, which had until recently served as a courier ship with the blockade fleet off the coast of France, had come into his possession some months ago, still, through a strange quirk of fate, fully fitted out with guns and powder. It had not been his original purpose to employ her in the pursuit of free traders. She had captured his eye because of her broad beam and stout oak sides, which were designed to withstand the broadsides of the six-pounders normally employed by coastal marauders. He had had need of a fleet and sturdy vessel if he sailed into French waters. Those qualities had loomed as equally desirable when it became suddenly clear that he had a distinct interest in hunting down one particular privateer.

"He will show himself, milord," Caleb Roth said quietly. "Do not doubt it. He could never resist a prize such as this one appears to be."

"And if he should present himself," speculated the marquis, his eyes following Constance, as, giving the coast one last look, she retreated below to escape the strengthening wind. He turned his gaze on Roth. "Shall we be able to persuade him to accept a flag of truce? And if we fail in that, Caleb, will the men *fight?*"

"You may depend on it, milord," Roth replied without hesitation. "Look at them—experienced seamen all. And every one of them cast ashore because of the Peace of Amiens. With the disbanding of the fleet, we might have had our pick out of forty thousand of them. As it is, we could have found none better. They will fight, milord, because you gave them a ship and a decent wage to go with it. That's something the navy wouldn't give them. They'll fight for that if for nothing else."

Vere looked at Roth, his thoughts on the woman below decks. "I could wish it might be later rather than sooner. *After* we have delivered the marchioness to a safe harbor."

He did not wait to hear what Roth might have replied to that observation. Curtly, he said, "Keep a sharp watch. I am going below."

As Vere made his way down the companionway and along the short, narrow corridor, he cursed himself for having voiced his doubts aloud to Roth. Hell and damnation, he had learned long ago never to confide his private thoughts to anyone. To do so must inevitably reveal a chink in his armor, a weakness that could be used against him. Worse, each lapse of a similar nature only served to make further confidences more difficult to avoid. Next, if he did not guard himself, he would be swapping stories of his youth with the young thatch-gallows—egad. Clearly, the flame-haired beauty had him bewitched, he thought, as he came to a halt before the stern cabin.

He was ruefully conscious of an unwonted quickening of his pulse as he announced his presence with a soft rap on the door.

"It is Vere, *enfant*. May I come in?"

The silence, like his unanswered question, seemed to hang in the air. Vere's eyebrows drew together over the bridge of his nose. Now, what the devil?

"Yes, do come in," sounded then from the other side of the barrier.

Schooling his features to their habitual impassivity, Vere reached for the door handle.

She had not lit the lantern, and the clouds gathering overhead muted the sunlight filtering in through the stern windows. Nevertheless, after the gloom of the corridor, he had to wait for his eyes to adjust to the sudden change. At first he saw her only as a silhouette against the backdrop of sea and sky. She was perched on the padded seat beneath the windows, her chin propped on her knees drawn up to her chest.

"It really is quite beautiful," she said, her voice sounding strangely wistful, as if she had been lost in dreamy contemplation of the Isle of Wight receding in the schooner's wake. "It is little wonder that you love it so. I think I should be content to go on like this forever."

"Even a ship must come to port sometime, *enfant*," replied Vere, turning to close the door behind him.

"Yes, I suppose that it must," Constance agreed. "Indeed, I have been thinking a great deal about that inevitability."

It had been on Vere's mind to add that they needed to talk. There were certain things, after all, of which she should be made aware.

The words froze, unuttered, on his lips, as, coming around to see his bride clearly for the first time, he jerked suddenly upright. He gasped as his head rammed into a deckbeam.

"The devil!" he cursed, his eyes watering as he focused on the vision of loveliness gazing back at him in sudden consternation.

"Vere, you have hurt yourself," she declared, quite unnecessarily, a hand to her lips, no doubt in an expression of shared sympathy—egad, he thought.

"Pray do not concern yourself," he rumbled, tempted to throttle the little wretch for having sprung her little surprise on him. "I have suffered worse and lived to tell of it."

She had risen from the windowseat to stand, facing him, her head held high in unconscious pride and no little defiance. It was not her stance, however, that had served to rob him of his speech. It was her garb, or perhaps the startling lack of it, since it consisted of nothing more than a sheet draped loosely about her slender person.

"Yes, well, it is your own fault for leaving me hanging," she declared, clearly struggling, he noted grimly, not to laugh. "You have left me little choice. I had to do something to gain your attention, Vere."

"Congratulations, you have it," said Vere, eyeing her dangerously. "And now what do you intend?"

"Only this."

Drawing a breath, she turned loose of the folds of linen clasped at her bosom and let the sheet fall.

Had Constance rammed a fist unexpectedly into his solar plexus, she could no more effectively have taken the breath from him. Having spent the past three days and nights grappling with the lascivious side of his nature, he was hardly prepared to have the object of his desire suddenly presented to him in all of her womanly attributes. Good God!

Tall for a woman and slender, with high, well-rounded breasts, a firm, flat belly and small waist that drew particular attention to the seductive curve of her hips, she was even more magnificent than memory and imagination had painted her. She was a veritable goddess of perfection. More than that, however, she faced him unabashedly, her head held high and her beautiful eyes dark and shimmering with her womanly power to make a man forget everything but the need to possess her. Christ knew, *he* needed her. He had been driven nearly to distraction with the desire to plunge himself into her warm woman's flesh. But, no more. His sweet, clever Constance had taken matters into her own capable hands. And by the devil, he had waited long enough to make her his.

Deliberately, he took a step toward her.

It was perhaps unfortunate that Pultney, having been informed by Roth that the marquis had gone below, chose just then to ascertain if his lordship and his lady wife were in the way of needing his services.

At his scratch on the door, Vere halted, his head turning with stark impatience to demand, "*Yes?* Who the devil is it?"

"I-it's only me, your lordship," supplied the steward, his voice distinctly quavery. "I . . ."

"*Go away, Pultney,*" Vere commanded in no uncertain terms.

"Really, Vere," Constance objected, her blue eyes utterly guileless. "Shame on you. I daresay you have frightened the poor man half out of his wits."

"The devil take Pultney," growled Vere, in no mood to discuss his summary treatment of his steward. Ducking his head beneath the deck beams, he reached Constance in two long strides. "Little fool, you will catch your death of cold."

"I shall, indeed, my lord," said Constance, who could not but marvel at her own brazenness, "if you continue to treat me as if I were the vicar's daughter come to call."

"Little baggage," pronounced Vere in dire tones. "You may be sure that I should not treat the vicar's daughter with the civility with which I have treated you."

"No, I daresay you would long since have lured her to your bed and the devil with the consequences," observed Constance, who, indeed sensible of the chill air, was not averse to clasping her arms about the back of Vere's neck and leaning provocatively against him. "Unlike your wife, whom you keep at a safe distance."

"At least she *is* safe, which was, if you recall, the purpose of our present circumstances," Vere did not hesitate to point out. "If nothing else, you will admit that I have kept my part of the bargain."

"Devil," declared Constance, as close as she had ever been to losing her patience with him.

"Jade," he said, returning the compliment. Bending down, he swept her up in his arms. "And now, I think, you must be made to keep yours."

Without further preamble, he carried her into the sleeping quarters, separate from the main cabin.

Laying her on the cot, he left her and, with hard, swift hands, divested himself of his coat and his shirt. His boots, stockings, and unmentionables were quick to follow suit. Then at last, revealed in all his masculine pride, he returned to her.

Constance, greeted with the sight of Vere as nature had intended, could not but marvel that she had waited so long to break through his formidable defenses. She had found Vere, dressed in a Corinthian's style of subdued elegance, as compellingly attractive as he was obviously dangerous, and Vere in the guise of the Black Rose as fascinating as he was outrageously charming. The unexpected Vere, garbed in his worn sea-going coat, had proven curiously devastating to her heart. None of these, however, had prepared her for Vere *in puris naturalibis!*

It was not only that his shoulders were almost indecently broad, but his chest must also be exquisitely sculpted to a masculine perfection and then bedecked with a thick mat of black, bristly hair, which had the curious effect of making her wish to run her fingers through it. And as if that were not all or enough, he had been blessed, too, with a long, tapering torso that narrowed most pleasingly to a hard, flat belly, all of which appeared to ripple with muscle at his every supple movement. No less enthralling were his thighs, which gave every impression of masculine grace coupled with a sinewy strength. Faith, nothing, however, could have prepared her for the reality of Vere in all of his crowning masculine glory!

That consummate touch was enough to cause her breath to catch audibly in her throat.

Coming about to be met with a maidenly gasp, Vere was brought precipitously to a halt. In no little bemusement, he discovered that his Titian-haired temptress was staring at him with eyes wide, her lips parted in an expression of frank bestartlement. Now what the devil, he thought, constraining with extreme effort his savage need to sink his shaft into her.

"My dearest girl," he said, lowering himself onto the cot beside her. "No doubt you will pardon me if I observe that you appear peculiarly discomfited." Gently, he brushed a stray curl from her forehead. "If you are having second thoughts, I suggest now would be the time to air them."

"Second thoughts?" Constance's gaze fairly flew to his. "Good heavens, no, Vere. I have never been more certain of anything in my life before. I do beg your pardon if I seemed to be staring. It is just that I have never—well, actually seen a man in his natural state before."

Egad, thought Vere, torn between startled amusement and something on the order of an unwonted sense of humility. In light of their earlier excursion into the heady delights of an almost-consummated passion, the last thing he had thought to encounter was a Constance disconcerted at the sight of the unadorned male anatomy.

"No, of course you have not," he said, thinking that no doubt he should at the very least have foreseen the possibility of it. "And now that you are faced with the reality," he added, lightly trailing his index finger along the contour of her cheek, "there is no need for you to feel either frightened or embarrassed."

"Pray do not be absurd, Vere," declared his surprising Constance, in all earnestness. "I assure you I am neither. You must be aware that you are a magnificent specimen of the male gender. I'm afraid I was not entirely prepared for what I can only describe as the moment of—of monumental enlightenment."

Vere, caught by surprise, gave vent to a startled chuckle that had more the sound of a groan. He was forcibly reminded that with his new, young bride, he was delving into uncharted waters. A virgin—egad! And yet a woman of generosity and undeniably strong passions. He suffered an unexpected surge of what he cynically suspected to be tenderness at the thought that his sweet, spirited, maddeningly independent, and exquisitely beautiful Constance had chosen to entrust him with the gift of her maidenhead. Clearly, he was in danger of becoming maudlin with sentiment.

"And you, my girl," he murmured, leaning over Constance, "are an unending delight." His hands braced on the bed on either side of her shoulders, he lowered his head to press a kiss into the curve of her neck. "We are about to begin an exquisite journey to learn each other's most intimate secrets."

Constance, experiencing ripples of pleasure, as, with his lips, he began his exploration at the base of her throat and worked slowly down the valley between her breasts, could not but think Vere was already in possession of her most intimate secrets. Indeed, as he paused in his journey to run his tongue over the peaking buds of her nipples, first one and then the other, she was moved to writhe beneath him in a torment of discovery. Faith, he seemed to know precisely where to find delectably sensitive places that she had never dreamed she possessed. More than that, he knew exactly how to manipulate them to arouse her to a feverish pitch of emotions the likes of which she could never have possibly imagined. And still, it seemed he had saved the best for last, she realized deliriously. Working his way down her belly with his tongue and his lips, he came at last to the secret, most intimate place between her thighs. Parting her legs, he found with unerring accuracy the tiny bud nestled within the swollen petals of her body. Constance, uttering a groan, writhed beneath his touch.

Egad, he thought, discovering that his red-haired temptress was already flowing with the honey of arousal. How readily she responded to his caresses! Sweet, generous, and utterly unpredictable, she would never bore him. Indeed, he had the distinct feeling that she was to become an unsettling influence in his existence. Somehow he did not find the notion quite so disagreeable as he might have done before Lady Constance Landford dropped uninvited into his life. In Constance he had found someone with whom he sensed he might in time be able to let his guard down. With Constance, he might look forward to a future in which he need no longer lead a solitary existence. With her he need not walk alone.

Egad, it was a novel concept, one that might never have occurred to him had not his indomitable Constance set herself to break through his formidable defenses. She in all her sweet, untutored generosity had unleashed powerful forces which he had long since learned to keep rigidly in control. She was ready to receive him, and by the devil he could not wait any longer. Spreading wide her thighs, he inserted himself between them.

"Vere?" breathed Constance, finding herself suddenly staring up into eyes that were no longer maddeningly cool, but instead were smoldering with barely controlled passion.

"Softly, *ma mie*," uttered Vere, hurriedly fitting the head of his swollen member against the lips of her body. Then, poised over her, his weight propped on his hands on either side of her shoulders, he lowered his head to kiss her sensuously on the lips. "We find ourselves once more at the threshold of the ultimate discovery," he said thickly, lifting his head to look into her eyes. "I regret, my beautiful Constance, that it will undoubtedly be a painful experience for you at first. Tell me that you want it, Constance."

"*Faith, Vere!*" gasped Constance, frantically clutching her fingers in the pillow. "*Want* it? I am like to perish from it. I pray you will *do* something!"

Vere, in no case to put it off any longer, covered her mouth with his. Slowly, inexorably, he drove himself into her.

His mouth over hers stifled her cry of pain and surprise. In an agony to finish what he had started, Vere went still. Feeling the sweat pour over his body, he lifted his head to look into his temptress's face.

Constance, her legs clenched about Vere's lean waist, stared back at him, her eyes wide with startled surprise.

"My poor Constance," he uttered, his voice hoarse with the effort it was costing him to maintain his precarious equilibrium. "How you must loathe me just now. Believe me when I say that the worst is over, and now all you need do is trust me to carry us both through."

Constance, who was grappling with the marvel of being filled with him when she had not been at all certain that she would be equal to the task, blinked. "Pray do not be absurd, Vere," she blurted before she could think. "How could I possibly loathe you? I have loved you hopelessly with all of my heart ever since you rescued me from that horrid old dragon."

It was not what she had meant to say. Indeed, later she could only suppose that she had been overcome by an irresistible impulse triggered by the peculiar circumstances in which she found herself—with Vere clasped between her legs and buried to the hilt inside her. Still, she could hardly regret it in light of what came after.

Vere, who could not recall any incidents of dragon-slaying in his past, immediate or otherwise, could make little sense of that sudden, unexpected outburst. It came to him briefly that her seeming incoherence could no doubt be attributed to a bride's case of nerves at what was understandably an emotionally charged moment. At any rate, he was in no bloody case at the moment to demand any lengthy explanations. *Constance had said that she loved him.* It was the one thing that stood out in his mind as he began to move carefully inside her.

Wooing her with his lips and his slow, rhythmical forays, he awakened her once more to the pleasurable sensations that had preceded his plunge through her maiden-head.

Never had she felt anything to compare to the burning need that swept over and through her then. With bittersweet certainty, it came to her that Vere and only Vere had the power to unleash the storm within her. She felt a rending pang at the realization that though she would give herself to him with her whole heart and soul, he would take her out of need only. Then even that thought was swept away as she felt herself borne on a swelling tide of arousal. A long, keening sigh breathed through her lips, and frantically she arched.

Vere, sensing she was reaching for the thing that was just beyond her comprehension, drew up and back. Then thrusting hard, he spilled his seed inside her, even as Constance erupted in a rapturous explosion of release that a few blissful moments later left her trembling and weak.

Together, they collapsed in a tangled heap of arms and legs.

Vere, drawing her against him, could only marvel at his bride's boundless generosity. Egad, she had given herself to him with a sweet, untutored abandon unlike any of his numerous mistresses before her. She was everything he might have looked for in a wife, and thanks to some incredible chance she was his.

Damn the fate that had chosen this time and this place to present her to him. With Constance, he was made to envision happiness of the sort that he had long since ceased to dream could be his someday. He was Vere, and he had but a single mission in life—to avenge the deaths of his mother and father. His beautiful Constance should never have been made a part of that.

That she was a part of it now by her mere presence aboard this ship seemed a mockery of everything for which he had striven since he had been forced to leave his carefree youth behind. In all the years of planning and painstakingly laying the foundation for his revenge, he had never looked beyond the day that Blaidsdale and his accomplices would be brought to justice. Why should he have, when there was every possibility that he would not make it through alive? Now, with Constance clasped in his arms, he felt the first cold touch of fear. The future, his future, resided in this slender girl who had broken through his defenses and wormed her way irrevocably into his heart. He was made ruefully aware that, were he to lose her now, vengeance or no vengeance, his life would not be worth the living.

"Vere?" murmured Constance, who had been lying with her eyes open, her senses keenly attuned to the man at her back. "You seem singularly pensive. It is not because you regret what we have done, is it?"

"What am I to regret, *enfant*?" replied Vere, smiling in sardonic amusement. "Having been trapped into marrying a beautiful, redheaded minx who then had the temerity to seduce her unsuspecting husband? Think of my reputation. This is not the sort of thing I should wish to get around, *ma mie*."

Constance's cheeks flamed red. His was not precisely

the response for which she had been hoping. How dared he take offense because she had found it necessary to act in order to be made a wife in every sense of the word! Really, it was too bad of him. "And now I suppose you have formed a disgust for me because I have injured your manly pride. I daresay I should have thought better of you, Vere, if you had admitted to having enjoyed our lovemaking every bit as much as I did."

"But I do admit it," said Vere, raising himself on one elbow in order to press his lips to her bare shoulder.

"And another thing," submitted Constance, flipping over on her back to find herself staring straightly into eyes which besides being a mesmerizing blue were lit just then with an unholy gleam of amusement.

Whatever it was to which she had been about to take exception instantly and quite thoroughly slipped her mind, as, suddenly, his reply sank home. "You do?" she queried, her voice softening to a caress.

"Freely and wholeheartedly." He dropped a kiss on the tip of her nose. "I daresay, in fact, that I have never enjoyed lovemaking quite so much as I enjoyed it just now with you."

"You do not mind, then, that I behaved in a manner that was wholly brazen?" she said, lifting her arms about his neck. "I warn you it was either that or challenge you to a duel for the pleasure of bedding you. For if you must know, I have never been in the least good at employing feminine wiles to woo a man's favor."

"You may be sure that I found your method of wooing wholly enchanting, my sweet Constance," replied Vere, who, just thinking about it, was tempted to initiate a repeat performance right then and there. "I am eagerly looking forward to any further clever schemes you may devise for our mutual pleasure. Unfortunately, at the moment I must turn to the more serious subject, which was the purpose of my coming to see you."

"We are about to be set upon by pirates. I knew it!"

exclaimed his ever-surprising Constance, her eyes light-
ing up. "That is why we have been flaunting the *Swallow*
in sight of shore like a plum ripe for the plucking. I
knew it could not be for my amusement. Roth had to
have some other purpose in mind when he raced to
Lyme Bay in time to rendezvous with you. Vere, you
must tell me now. Who is it, and why are you after him?"

Vere stared at her in no little perplexity. The devil,
he might have known his enterprising Constance would
put all the pieces of the puzzle together. And now he
must tell her their quarry was none other than Jago
Green, the mad Cornishman, who was infamous all along
the southern coast of England for his smuggling and
plundering of coastal traders. He would that he could
put it off, he thought, then went suddenly quite still as
the shout from the masthead rang out.

"Sail on the larboard bow!"

Chapter 8

Vere, dressed in breeches and boots, hastily pulled his shirt on over his head. "I want you to stay below, *enfant*," he said, tucking his shirttails in the waistband of his breeches. "Whatever happens, do not leave this cabin. Do you understand me?"

"I assure you there is nothing wrong with my understanding, Vere," declared Constance, who could not but think that pirates would seem to possess an extraordinarily poor sense of timing.

Vere, experiencing a decided feeling of *déjà vu*, paused in his dressing, his eyes going sharply to Constance. She was sitting up in the cot, the counterpane pulled up over her knees, tucked to her chest, in an attitude of one deep in thought. The devil, he cursed silently to himself.

Settling on the edge of the cot, he pulled Constance to him. "This is not the way I should have planned our first time together, *enfant*."

"No, I daresay it is not," agreed Constance, thinking that there likely would not have *been* a first time if the planning had been left to Vere. "But then, ours has hardly been what one might call a conventional courtship.

Why should this part of it be any different? I ask only that it will not be our last time together, Vere."

"You may be sure that this is only the beginning of what promises to be an exceedingly long and passionate journey of discovery," replied Vere, pressing his lips to the silken mass of her hair. "I must go now, *enfant*. No need to tell you to stand buff. With any luck, this will all soon be over without incident, and we shall be on our way again."

"Yes, of course we shall," said Constance, summoning a smile that did not quite reach her eyes. "Now, I think you had better go before Roth does something heroic and lands us all in a bumblebroth."

Vere dropped a kiss on her forehead and rose. Constance gazed up at him, her expression grave but unwavering. It came to him that just looking at her, one would never have supposed that a confrontation with a pirate ship loomed on the horizon. She was in all ways a worthy successor to the previous marchioness, was his beautiful Constance.

It was up to him now to make certain that his dauntless bride was brought to no harm in the coming hours. It was up to him to make sure that everything went according to plan. The fates grant that Jago Green had received Roth's message, he thought grimly.

Moments later, fully dressed and a sword strapped to his side, he emerged from the companionway and joined Roth at the taffrail.

"It's the *Falcon*, all right, my lord. A sloop of eighteen guns," said Roth, gazing through a telescope off the port bow. "Damme, he's a bold one, is the Preacher. Yonder lie Spithead and the fleet. He sailed her out right under the noses of half the King's navy."

"You forget, he was granted immunity under the Royal Proclamation," observed Vere, peering into the grey cast of thunderclouds at the single-masted ship bearing down on them. "So long as he refrains from piracy and smuggling."

"It looks as if his immunity is about to be revoked," said Roth, snapping the telescope shut. "He just ran his larboard guns out."

"Waller," he called out to the first mate. "Be pleased to have the galley fires put out. And call all hands on deck."

"Aye, aye, sir."

Amid the shrill of the pipes and the scramble from belowdecks, Vere turned his gaze on the steady approach of the other ship some five miles off the port bow. She was bigger than *Swallow* and gave every appearance of having a disciplined crew. She would have the advantage of a captain who was experienced in running down vulnerable coastal craft and intimidating them with her gunnery. *Swallow*, however, had surprise on her side, and she had Caleb Roth. Perhaps it would be enough.

It was soon made apparent that *Swallow*'s captain had not been idle the past six months. Having recruited his men from the cream of the seamen cast ashore during the peace, he had forged them into a fighting crew that would have been worthy of a King's ship of war. But then, he had had a powerful motivation, Vere reflected, watching with grim satisfaction the controlled chaos on the schooner's deck. Roth had been *Swallow*'s commander when she was commissioned with the navy. More than that, he had a score to settle.

All in all, Vere could have found no better weapon to employ against his enemies. And in truth, Roth had proven far more valuable than Vere could have imagined when he sought out the disgraced former commander in the sordid environs of a gin house in London's Wapping High Street.

He had been singularly struck by the familiarity of the scene with which he had been met upon entering to find Roth squared off before three ruffians intent on cutting his stick for him. Egad, how many times had he been in a similar case himself! Curious to observe how the young firebrand would handle himself, Vere had not scrupled to allow events to run their course. Roth laid out one of the brutes with a crushing blow to the chin and was making swift work of sending another to join his fellow on the floor. Only then did Vere, observing the remaining bruiser coming at Roth's back with a dagger, choose to intervene. A single, well-aimed blow with his walking stick had served to bring things to a swift and summary halt.

The young firebrand, far from being grateful, had had the temerity to size Vere up with a single, assessing glance. "No doubt . . . you expect me to . . . thank you . . . for what you believe to be your timely interference," he said, panting a little from his recent exertions. "As it happens, however . . . I did not require your help. And now, if you will excuse me, my lord . . . I have some important drinking to do."

"No doubt," observed Vere, as Roth made as if to turn away. The former navy commander was not lacking in gall, he had noted, a faint smile twitching at the corners of his lips. "I am moved to ask, however, if you know who I am."

"I do not care who you are," Roth replied with flat deliberation. Swaying a little on his feet, he favored Vere with an insolent look from eyes that were little wider than slits. "It is enough that I know your sort."

"But of course you do," Vere agreed, swinging his walking stick idly between thumb and forefinger. "We are, after all, cut of the same cloth, you and I. As it happens, I am acquainted with your father. And, no, you may rest assured Lord Manville did not send me to find you. I came on my own to offer you a proposition. I am about to purchase a ship, and I need a man of courage to command her."

The smooth, tanned features hardened to a cold impenetrability, but not before Vere glimpsed a fleeting blur of pain darken the younger man's eyes.

"Then why come to me?" Roth demanded bitterly. "If

you know anything about me, you are aware that I have only recently been court-martialed for failure to engage the enemy. I was dismissed from my ship."

"And now I am offering it back to you," Vere replied steadily. "Along with the chance to uncover the truth behind the events that led to an unjust verdict. I know as well as you that you were ordered to sail your ship into certain destruction. More than that, I can tell you *who* wanted you dead and why."

Roth's interest had obviously quickened. Still, he had been nobody's fool. "You would seem to possess a deal of information about me," he observed suspiciously. "I am moved to wonder why you should care one way or the other what happened. Who the devil are you?"

"I am Vere," replied the marquis, ushering Roth through the curious onlookers toward the door. "Someone with whom you share a common enemy," he added, upon stepping outside into the hardly more appealing aspect of a refuse-infested street. "As fate would have it, I entertain a keen interest in seeing you restored to honor and your enemies brought to justice. In the meantime, if we are successful in an endeavor I have to set before you, you may have the satisfaction of commanding your own ship again. I daresay you will find your *Aurora* much as you left her, save for her name, which I intend to change."

"*Aurora!*"

It had given Vere a strange satisfaction to observe the sudden break in Roth's composure. He had liked Roth the better for it. Indeed, it had served to reinforce his belief in the man's innocence. Later, Vere was to marvel at the fate that had brought Caleb Roth his way. The young firebrand was as resourceful as he was determined. More than that, he had proven as adept at subterfuge as he was at commanding his ship. He had played his part as one of the "Gentlemen" to perfection.

Certainly, Lord Sinclair, Blaisdale's profligate brother-in-law, even now did not doubt that the disgraced naval officer with whom he had aligned himself was a member of that nefarious band of Gentlemen who indulged in "fair trading." He had fallen for the ruse—hook, line, and sinker—just as Vere had known that he would.

It had taken very little to persuade Sinclair to venture a significant sum on a smuggling enterprise that had promised to double his investment. Indeed, it had required only that Albert Sinclair catch Roth in the process of secreting a cache of tobacco, linens, and tea in one of the baron's outlying farms.

"I know you," had said the captain of the King's Guards, tapping his quirt against his thigh as Roth stood, considerably roughened up, between two grinning soldiers. "Commander Roth, is it not? I must say you have a penchant for disaster. First, your father disowns you for behavior unbecoming a gentleman and then the navy casts you out for cowardice. And now it appears you will end up on the gibbet for running contraband goods. It would seem that things can only go from bad to worse for you."

"You can't blame a man for trying," Roth replied, sending a spittle of blood to the floor at the toes of Sinclair's shiny boots. "It was a lucrative enterprise until you showed up to put a snag in it. One more haul, and I should have retired on a pension of three thousand a year. I daresay that's more than you have to look forward to, especially now that you'll likely be heading for the war on the Continent before all is said and done, eh, Captain?"

Sinclair stood quite still, his eyes boring into Roth's bruised features. Then, with a sharp gesture of the head, "You," he said to the soldiers, "get out."

It was soon made apparent that Roth had acquired a partner in his lucrative trade. Not the captain, who, given to bet on the horses, was habitually pockets to let, but the baron, his father, who was always on the lookout for a profitable investment. Roth vociferously bemoaned the fate that had deemed he forfeit the goods in the barn in addition to seventy-five percent of all future profits. In reality, however, he had been more than content to allow Captain Sinclair to use his powers of persuasion to bring his father to venture a tidy sum toward the purchase of an alleged shipload of goods.

Only, the enterprise was a sham effectuated by Vere through Roth with the result that Lord Sinclair had been made to forfeit the entirety of his investment to what he supposed was an unlikely raid by revenuers.

Vere not only had the satisfaction of retrieving at Sinclair's expense a goodly portion of the fortune that had been stolen from him by means of a forged gambling marker, but he also had the wherewithal to purchase the ship he required for an even more lucrative venture. That the elaborate scheme should have led him to Jago Green, however, had been as unexpected as it was fortuitous.

Who could have foreseen that the raid staged by Vere's men dressed as revenuers and the confiscation of what was meant to appear as a smuggler's crop of goods would arouse the hostility of the close-knit brotherhood of free traders? Certainly, Roth had not expected a band of rough-garbed men to liberate him from his supposed confinement. Nor could he have known that he would be taken to a rocky cove, where he would be regaled with rum and tales of the exploits of some of the more infamous local "Gentlemen" before being released.

One of these tales had concerned Jago Green, better known as the Preacher for his conversion to Methodism and his regular practice of holding Sunday service for his crew of felons. Ten years ago, however, the Preacher had been plain Jago Green, a youth of eighteen kidnapped by the then-notorious smuggler chieftain, John Cutler, and forced into a career in the illicit practices of piracy and running contraband. It was in those early days that he had been made a party to a deed that had forever soured him on John Cutler's bloody practices.

Biding his time, he had gradually won the loyalty of his fellow sailors until at last, according to popular accounts, he had overthrown his captain and brought Cutler's reign of terror to an end. The coup had left him master of the *Falcon* and one of the numerous bands of privateers who plied their trade between England and France.

That particular tale had intrigued Vere. Suddenly, he had had a decided interest in meeting Jago Green. Unfortunately, the Preacher had proven most damnably elusive.

It was Roth who, on his own initiative, had sent out the message by word of mouth to the effect that the Marquis of Vere would like a private meeting with the smuggler. When that had seemed to fail, Vere determined on their present course. The *Swallow*, after all, having recently returned from an exceedingly successful passage to France, was still fitted out and ready to sail. If the Preacher were the man Vere hoped he was, he would find the namesake of an older, ill-fated schooner far too curious to resist.

The question that occupied Vere as he watched the other ship's slow approach was whether the Preacher had come to fight or talk. Either way, the *Swallow* was ready for him, Vere decided, his glance sweeping over the gun crews at their cannons, shot and slow match held ready for Roth's command to load and roll out, should the need arise.

His thoughts turned to Constance in the stern cabin. It was not the safest place if the ship were fired upon. He recalled his Uncle Richard's account of the devastation of a thirty-two-pound shot fired into the stern of a man-of-war. Sweeping through from stern to stem, it mowed down men and wreaked utter havoc as it went. The little *Swallow*, similarly struck by an eighteen-pounder, would fare just as badly. Hell and the devil confound it! If it came to a battle, it was unlikely that any place on the bloody ship would be safe.

But then, Roth would know the danger to his ship better than anyone, thought Vere, his eyes going to the captain.

"She will have the weather-gauge," Vere observed, as the *Falcon*, little more than a mile away, jibed.

"Aye," Roth agreed. "If it's a parley she wants, she's not taking any chances. Mr. Waller, load the starboard guns, but do not run out. See that the carronades, fore and aft, are made ready. Prepare to come about on my order. And tell those men at the guns to remain out of sight, do you hear?"

"Aye, aye, Cap'n." Waller, leaning over the rail, relayed Roth's orders in a booming voice.

Roth waited, gauging the wind. "Now! Put the helm down."

With men hauling on the braces and others letting go the headsail sheets, *Swallow* heeled across the eye of the wind like a charger. As she shot forward, the sails hardening on the new tack, Roth leaned his hands on the taffrail. "When we were assigned to the blockade fleet off the coast of France, the one thing that I came to appreciate most about this little lady, my lord, is her agility. There was a time or two when it was all that kept us from being blown out of the water. We shall continue to present the image of a yacht on a pleasure outing. It's only what Green would expect of us, after all, if he has received our message." He turned to look directly at Vere. "Just in case he has something different in mind, however, I intend to bring her about once more at the very last minute, when it is too late for him to follow us about."

"And thus engage him on his starboard," supplied Vere, picturing it in his mind's eye. "With his larboard guns run out, he will be thrown into confusion while he attempts to correct his error in judgment. You will have him momentarily at your mercy. Long enough, perhaps, to persuade him to listen to what I have to say."

"It is a small advantage, my lord," confirmed Roth, a glint in his eye. "But, save for showing him our heels now in the hopes we can outrun his bow chaser, it is all that we have."

"Then it will have to be enough, will it not?" said Vere, ever so gently.

Roth exchanged a long look with his employer before nodding. "Aye, my lord."

He turned away, his glance going to the streaming pennant. The wind was holding steady, he noted with no little satisfaction. *Falcon*, sailing close to the wind, would jibe soon, bringing her on a course to intercept *Swallow*. It would be a close thing. Worse, any number of elements could go wrong. *Falcon* might choose to disable *Swallow* with a shot from her bow chaser. The wind might alter course or fail altogether. Roth had seen it happen before. Thinking of the woman below decks, he wondered if Vere understood the chance that he was taking.

Recalling the look in the other man's eyes as they had met his, Roth thought he knew the answer to that question. Vere understood, all right. He placed his reliance in his captain. The realization brought a hard knot to Roth's belly. Six months ago, he had not thought any man would ever trust in him again. Vere had done more than give him a ship. He had given him back his pride. That knowledge and Roth's unshakable belief that Vere offered him far more than he ever could have imagined— the chance to regain his honor—served to harden his resolve as nothing else could have done. He would have sailed into the jaws of hell to justify Vere's faith in him.

That thought had hardly crossed his mind when an all-too-familiar whirr sounded overhead, followed by the distant bark of an explosion. The white puff of smoke from *Falcon*'s bow and the sullen splash of a cannonball striking water off *Swallow*'s starboard told it all.

"They've fired a shot across our bow!" came the shout from the gun deck.

Constance, left staring at the closed door through which Vere had vanished, slipped her feet to the deck and padded immediately across the sleeping cabin to her trunk. Throwing back the lid, she snatched up one of the gowns that Mrs. Turnbough had packed for her from her previous mistress's wardrobe and hurried to gather up her discarded unmentionables.

Consequently, she failed to note the small purse of red silk slide from the folds of the dress to the deck.

Quickly slipping into her underthings, she pulled the dress over her head. She could not but wish for Millie as she struggled to fasten the tiny pearl buttons at the back of the bodice, but finally the thing was done. She wished for the abigail even more when, moments later, having slid her stockinged feet into French heels, she turned to the task of taming her tousled tresses.

In truth, there was a great deal to be said for the latest fashion of cutting one's hair in short curls that, parted in the middle, were allowed to cluster about the head, she decided, as she tried ineffectually to gather the mass at the crown in a semblance of an acceptable coiffure. Certainly it did not help that the ship, tossed in the strengthening swells, seemed intent on flinging her off her feet. At last, defeated, she confined the riot of curls in a knot at the nape of her neck and covered her head with a lace-edged cap that tied under her chin. She was humorously aware that it, like her *robe à l'Anglaise* of white and rose over a green satin petticoat, had been all the rage something over a decade ago. Still, it would just have to do, she told herself, as, anxious to know what was happening above decks, she turned away from the mirror.

It was only then that she noticed the purse lying irresistibly on the deck beside the open trunk.

Her curiosity piqued, she stooped to retrieve it. After only a moment's hesitation, she opened the strings. A low gasp burst from her lips as a necklace and earrings of diamonds and emeralds spilled out into the palm of her hand. For a moment she stood, staring in disbelief at the exquisitely wrought pieces. Really, she could not imagine what had possessed Mrs. Turnbough to pack jewels along with the other things. Borrowing the former marchioness's gowns was one thing. Her jewels were altogether quite another.

Then suddenly her head came up, her eyes sparkling dangerously.

The devil, if she were to face marauding pirates, she would do it properly dressed. She was, after all, the marchioness. Fastening the earrings to her earlobes and the necklace about her throat, she paused for a moment to examine her reflection in the looking glass.

She was visited with the strangest, queasy sensation at sight of the image in the glass. Faith, she hardly recognized herself. In truth, she had the queerest feeling that it was her mama staring back at her.

But then, it would have been strange indeed if the image in the looking glass had not reminded her of her mother, she told herself firmly. Besides the family resemblance, her last memories of the countess had been of a woman similarly dressed.

With a whirl of satin skirts, she turned away and exited the sleeping quarters, only to come to a precipitous halt in the center of the stern cabin, her legs braced against the pitch and roll of the schooner as it plunged through the waves.

Vere had been no little amazed at the ease with which his new marchioness had gained her sea legs; and, in truth, she had adapted to her unfamiliar environment as if she had been born to it. But then, they had been favored with a steady easterly breeze. Now Constance was become acutely aware that a squall had borne down upon them. The schooner, sailing close to the wind, seemed suddenly to lurch with a groan of timbers to one side even as the bow climbed, borne on a cresting wave, then lunged, sliding down into the trough. Constance, flung off balance, caught herself against the table.

As the schooner crossed the eye of the wind and settled into the opposite tack, Constance fought her way to the stern seat. Unaccountably, she felt fear claw at her vitals as the schooner suddenly vibrated to an unfamiliar squeal and rumble. Then it came to her with terrifying certainty. Good God, Roth had ordered the guns rolled out!

It was strange that she had not really thought it would come to an armed confrontation with the pirate, or whatever he was. Somehow from the little that Vere had said, she was given the impression that it was not a fight that he anticipated. Or perhaps that had been wishful thinking on his part, she reflected soberly, thinking of Vere standing, unprotected, on the quarterdeck beside the daredevil Roth while she was confined to her quarters where she could see nothing of what was happening topside. Really, it was too bad of Vere to order her to remain below where she could only wear herself out with worry. Indeed, it was a deal too much to ask.

No sooner had that thought crossed her mind than a single, deafening boom thundered from overhead.

Constance, driven to her feet, stood, waiting in stricken horror for what was to happen next.

"The devil with Vere's orders," she said when the silence continued to stretch unbearably. Snatching up her cloak, she stumbled to the door.

"He will be in range directly, my lord," Roth shouted above the roar of the wind and the sails. "He knows he cannot follow us around. Not in this gale. It would tear the bloody masts off her. We have the weather-gauge for now and time enough for a single broadside. After that, he'll try to beat around in the hopes of smashing our stern."

"Perhaps," said Vere, who, like Roth, was drenched to the skin from the spray. "On the other hand, the warning shot has told him that we are armed and prepared to defend ourselves—not the sort of thing that he normally encounters. It is time to offer him a more palatable solution. Caleb, send up the signal."

"Aye, my lord." Roth turned and gave the order. Even as the signal flags broke from the mast, spelling out the invitation to engage in a parley, he leaned out over the taffrail. "When I give the order, fire as you bear, lads. And make each shot count. Let's show the buggers. What do you say?"

The gun deck erupted in wild cheering. Roth, gazing ahead at the approaching ship, drew his sword and fastened the lanyard about his wrist. It was not the silver-plated sword that he had purchased in Portsmouth when he was given his promotion and assigned this ship to command—the sword whose blade had been pointing at him in the final judgment at his court martial. That one he had broken and flung overboard. This was the sword that Vere had given him "to herald a new beginning," he had said. A beautiful blade, perfectly balanced, it seemed to have been made to fit his hand. Thinking that he had not long now before he might be brought to test its strength, he raised it above his head.

Vere, staring through the telescope at *Falcon*'s quarter-deck, had little difficulty picking out the figure of the captain. Thick-limbed, barrel-chested, and powerful, a glass trained to his eye, the Preacher was staring back at him.

The devil, thought Vere, his lips thinning to a grim line. It would appear that he had misjudged his man.

Or the stories about the smuggler chieftain were considerably romanticized. Far from demonstrating a reluctance to engage in bloodshed, the Preacher gave every evidence of a man prepared to sail his ship into the teeth of battle. He pictured the mad scramble aboard the other ship's decks to reel in the larboard guns, then shift to the other side. Already, he could see the ragged thrust of cannon through the starboard ports, as *Falcon* made a desperate attempt to be ready for the oncoming *Swallow*.

Even as the thought formulated that he had led Roth and the others to their probable deaths, he saw the pirate captain's glass shift, then hold suddenly steady on some new object.

"On my signal, lads. Fire on the upward roll," shouted Roth as *Swallow* bore down on the converging ship, little more than two cable lengths away.

Roth's sword quivered, ready to descend. Steady, he thought, his eyes on the thrust of *Falcon's* bowsprit. Steady. *Now!* he thought.

"*Wait!*" Vere's hand clamped on Roth's arm. "*Look!* The signal. He is standing off."

"*Stand down! Disengage!*"

"Hellfire," growled Roth, ramming his sword into the scabbard. "It would seem the Preacher has a taste for the suspenseful. He left it till it was almost too bloody damned late. I should have sworn he was set on blowing us out of the water. What the devil changed his mind?"

"He saw something." Vere, turning to look behind him, froze. "It would seem the Preacher is a gentleman," he said grimly, his eyes on the slender figure standing on the weather deck where she had no business to be. "He has an aversion to firing on females."

"Then he's a man after my own heart, my lord," grinned Roth, as Lady Vere, made suddenly aware of two pairs of masculine eyes on her, turned and fled down the companionway.

* * *

"Sailors are a superstitious lot," observed Vere gravely no little time later in the stern cabin. "When the Preacher saw you appear on deck looking like the ghost of my mother, the woman whose murder he witnessed a decade ago, he must have thought God's judgment was come upon him."

"You might say it was the determining moment, my lady," Roth added from where he stood with one broad shoulder propped against the bulkhead. "Until then, he was firmly convinced that Vere's message, combined with the sudden appearance of *Swallow*, was meant to lure him into a trap. He intended to blow us out of the water rather than be pursued by the man he must have supposed would most want him dead."

"Yes, I suppose you are right," murmured Constance, who had just been privileged to preside over a meal at which Jago Green had been the guest of honor. "It would seem to have preyed greatly on his conscience— having been forced to be a part of something so dreadful and to be powerless to do anything to stop it. He could hardly take his eyes off me through the entire meal. Can we be certain, however, it was not these that drew his interest?" she asked, fingering the jewels at her neck. "He has, after all, carried on in the tradition of his previous master, this John Cutler who raided the coasts of both England and France. He has continued to pursue the dubious trade of smuggling."

"And pirating, too, no doubt." Vere turned away from staring out the stern windows at the moonlit water, nearly calm with the passing of the storm clouds. "The Preacher is hardly a saint. I daresay, however, that he would not have that particular necklace if you offered it to him, even if it were not merely paste. The last time he saw the real one, it undoubtedly graced my mother's throat—just before Cutler took it off her."

"Dear God," breathed Constance, her cheeks going pale. He had meant for her to find the jewels. Good God, he had wanted to see them on Blaidsdale's daughter. Reaching up to unfasten the necklace, she held it out to Vere, her eyes probing his. "It was you who put them in my trunk. Vere, why? What in heaven's name did you hope to gain?"

"No doubt precisely what I did gain from it," he said, taking the thing and tossing it carelessly on the table. "Though, in truth, I never meant to ask you to wear them for the Preacher's benefit." A humorless smile flickered over Vere's stern lips as he looked into Constance's eyes. "As fate would have it, however, you could not have been better dressed for the part. By your mere appearance, you brought Green to confirm what we already knew. It was never a yachting accident that killed my parents. I shall always be indebted to you for giving me that, my beautiful Constance."

Constance, feeling her heart give a leap, gave Vere a long, searching look. He meant it, she thought. Indeed, she could not be mistaken in that. All in an instant, Constance felt the hurt melt away.

"It was unfortunate that he could not say who was responsible for setting Cutler on the scent," Roth mused aloud, drawing attention to himself. "He never once mentioned Blaidsdale or Landford."

"And the gold," said Constance, remembering. "If he was telling the truth, they never found it aboard the yacht."

"No, how could they?" murmured Vere. "The gold was still in France where my grandfather, le Comte du Maureaux, hid it."

"In France? Vere, how can you be so certain?" Constance demanded, sitting bolt upright on her seat in one of the blue velvet chairs.

"But how not?" replied Vere, settling on the edge of

the table, his legs stretched out before him. "It was still there in the cemetery at Maison Bellefleur—when Roth and I dug it up three months ago."

Constance stared from one to the other of the two men with dawning comprehension. "Then you have it, and Blaidsdale failed to profit from his venture into piracy."

"He was not made any the richer by it," agreed Vere with chilling detachment. And, thanks to a fortuitous meeting at sea with an East Indiaman, he mused to himself, Blaidsdale had already let another small fortune slip through his greedy fingers. "Patently, Cutler attacked the yacht before it had reached its destination in Normandy. But then, I daresay it was never about the gold where Blaidsdale was concerned. To him, the gold was only a convenient means of persuading Cutler to dispose of his enemies for him with no one the wiser. He, at least, got what he was after."

"Then it would seem we are little better off than we were before," observed Constance, who could not but wonder why Vere had married her. Certainly, it had not been for her fortune! "There is still no proof that the earl had anything to do with it."

"Her ladyship is right, my lord," said Roth, a curious glint in his eye. "Save for one thing. As it happens, I have seen Lady Vere's necklace before, or rather the original, I should think, and under most peculiar circumstances."

Vere felt a cold chill touch his spine. "You may be certain that you have my complete and undivided attention. Under what circumstances and where did you see it?"

Little relishing the tale that he had to relate, Roth went noticeably still. "I suggest, my lord," he said, his eyes going pointedly to Vere's, "that perhaps it would be better to postpone the telling for a more propitious occasion."

"You mean when I am not present, do you not?" interpreted Constance with indignant disfavor. "How dare you, Caleb Roth! I assure you I am not a hothouse flower that must be coddled. I will not be left out simply because I am a woman."

"I think you must tell us," Vere said in exceedingly dry tones. "You have said too much to be let off now."

"Very well, if you insist, my lord," Roth agreed reluctantly, his gaze shifting to Constance. "Never say, however, that I did not warn you."

"You may be sure that I should never be moved to do anything quite so childish," Constance retorted with sparkling eyes. "Now, pray do not be afraid to open the budget."

"I suppose, then, that I should begin at the beginning," offered Roth, fixing his gaze on the stern windows. "It was well over a year ago, before the peace was signed. *Aurora* was assigned to blockade duty in the Bay of Biscay. My duties, when I was not running dispatches, were to scout along the coast of France in search of the French fleet, which was rumored to be gathering for an invasion of England. It was during this time that Landford was sent to relieve Admiral Sir Marcus Llewellyn, who was taken ill with the fever, and *Aurora* was placed under his command. It seems that *Aurora* took his immediate fancy. In fact, as it turned out, he enjoyed nothing better than to employ her as a pleasure craft for his own personal amusement."

"Faith, are you suggesting that Sir Oliver entertained women on this ship and in this very cabin?" demanded Constance in no little incredulity.

"No, not exactly," answered Roth, a ruddy tinge of color invading his tanned cheeks. "This is, however, where I saw the bloody necklace. I came in to report that we had sighted three French ships of the line. Sir Oliver was in the sleeping cabin, and the necklace was lying there, on the table."

"No doubt he was pleased to have been interrupted in his pleasurable pursuits to learn that the French fleet was on the move?" queried Vere in exceedingly dry accents, a curiously hard glitter in the look he bent on Roth.

"He ordered his flag moved immediately to *Neptune*, a three-decker of eighty-one guns," replied Roth in cynical tones. "As he prepared to transfer to the other ship, he handed me written orders to keep the enemy in sight until the squadron could be gathered to give chase." Roth's lip curled in bitter self-mockery. "*Written* orders," he said as if that fact alone stood out most in his mind.

"Only, a storm scattered the squadron and delayed the chase," ventured the marquis. "And you were left alone with the French ships and your orders."

The muscle leaped along Roth's jawline. "We followed them until we lost them in the storm somewhere in the Golfe du Lion," he said. His eyes were distant with the memory of the fight against the fury of the storm as they struggled to remain in sight and yet out of firing range of the massive ships of the line. And then had come the discovery that the French had slipped away under cover of darkness. "The next morning, we searched all along the coast until we found where they had weathered the gale in a harbor protected by a narrow inlet."

"Upon which you turned back in search of the squadron and were immediately placed under arrest for failure to engage the enemy."

"I should have sunk my ship if necessary to block the bloody inlet," said Roth, his eyes dark and tormented in the chiseled hardness of his face. "The French ships were lost to us. Landford accused me of deliberately disobeying my orders."

"The devil, he did," exclaimed Constance in no little indignation.

"He would, of course, since he intentionally set Caleb up to be discredited if the French did not sink him," observed Vere dispassionately. "And how not, when Roth had seen something he was never supposed to see."

"Faith," Constance breathed, her eyes wide with sudden understanding. "The necklace."

"So that was it," said Roth, his look equally expressive of sudden, grim enlightenment. "But the necklace meant nothing to me. Indeed, how could it?"

"Landford could not take that chance," speculated Constance.

"Any more than he could risk the possibility that whoever else might have seen it would not discover its significance," Vere expanded. "I daresay Sir Oliver was more than a little disconcerted to see your ship put in her appearance. He was counting on your reputation for brashness to lead you to your destruction."

"No doubt I should have fulfilled his expectations," said Roth with a sardonic grimace, "if I had not deemed the information I carried was more important than my own glory. We could not sail into the harbor after the French ships and hope to sail out again, but I could lead a landing party in to see what the French were about. What we found was Napoleon's flotilla of small boats which were to be used for the invasion of England. Egad, there were hundreds of them."

"Thank heavens you were able to put Sir Oliver in his place," declared Constance with no little satisfaction. "I daresay the admiralty wasted little time in dismissing his ridiculous charges."

"Not precisely," demurred Vere with only the barest hint of irony. "As a matter of fact, they found Roth guilty and relieved him of his command."

"You cannot be serious, Vere," said Constance, considerably taken aback. "Surely they were pleased to have finally found the flotilla for which everyone has been looking for simply ages?"

"No doubt the admiralty would have been pleased, my lady," Roth said, smiling at her unwavering championship of his cause, "had not the Peace of Amiens intervened. Even so, I daresay that the judgment would not have been against me if my second lieutenant had not upheld Landford's allegations. He accused me of cowardice in the face of the enemy."

"And thus no doubt saved his own career, perhaps even his life," postulated Vere. Then, he added gently, his gaze unwavering on Roth, "It was your second lieutenant, after all, whom Landford would wish most in particularly to eliminate, was it not?"

Roth flushed ever so slightly. Then a hard mask descended over his face.

"It hardly matters now," he said in flat tones. "My former second lieutenant is beyond Landford's reach. He died six months ago, by his own hand. And I daresay he was neither the first nor the last of Landford's victims. Christ, he was all of nineteen when he died."

"He was only a boy," said Constance no little time later, as she lay sated in Vere's arms. "Naturally he was afraid of a man like Landford. He was his admiral, and he ordered him to lie for him. But to kill himself. Really, Vere, sometimes I think we ask too much of the young men we send out to fight for us. I daresay he was brave enough when it came to fighting the French. But to be forced to choose between disobeying a superior officer of Landford's exalted rank and telling the truth—clearly, it was too much for him."

"Clearly," murmured Vere, who was occupied at the moment with running the palm of his hand over the silken curve of his bride's hip. Possibly the last thing he wished to contemplate at the moment was Roth's erstwhile second lieutenant. With Roth's departure to see to the running of the ship, he had desired one thing only—to drive away the images that the day's revelations had brought.

It had been harder than he had anticipated, hearing the truth at last from the lips of one who had witnessed the events of his parents' deaths. The gory details had sickened him to the core. There had never been any doubt from the moment Cutler disabled the yacht and boarded her that he meant to kill everyone. The discovery that the promised fortune in gold was not to be found had only served to whet his appetite for savagery. They had died, all of them, in a manner that was too horrendous to contemplate. And yet, the images, as Jago Green had related them in chilling detachment, seemed as vividly etched in Vere's mind as if he had lived them.

He had felt the black mood descending over him along with the need to drink himself into oblivion. Only, suddenly Constance, a vision of womanly compassion, had taken his hand and without a word led him into the sleeping cabin.

She had been like sweet balm to his embittered soul. And yet it had been a frenzied, burning thing with lips hungrily seeking lips, while hands worked feverishly to be rid of the clothing that kept them from the blissful communication of touching. And when at last he had laid her down against the pillows, she had pulled him to her and ministered to his hurts with an unfettered sweetness beyond anything that he, in all his masterful skill, had ever known from a woman. She had broken through his reserve and breached the barriers built up through all the years of dedication to a single goal. And when it was all over, their passion consummated in an ecstasy of mutual release, he had felt strangely cleansed of the horror.

"Vere?" queried Constance, rolling over on her back to look up at him with troubled eyes. "Did you mean it in the hunting lodge when you said I was not to blame for Blaidsdale's crimes? That even if I were his daughter, which apparently I am not, you did not hold me responsible for any of the terrible things that he might have done?"

"Yes, I meant it," said Vere, wondering what should

suddenly have brought her to doubt it. "How not? You are not Blaidsdale's daughter, after all. You are my wife."

"Yes, my dearest, darling Vere, I am," agreed Constance, smiling a trifle mistily. "Still, you are the heir to a dukedom, Vere. Does it not bother you in the least that you do not know who I really am?"

"Since I trust you do not mean that in a philosophical sense, I shall not answer that no one can ever really know another," replied Vere, dropping a kiss on the corner of her lips. Lifting his head, he looked straightly in her eyes. "The truth is, my darling girl, I could not care less who your father is. That is the question that you meant to ask, is it not?"

"Yes, Vere, it is," said Constance, drawing him down to her. Even as he proceeded to arouse her as only he knew how, however, it came to Constance that it mattered to her to know who her father was. Indeed, for the sake of their future children, if for nothing else, it mattered a great deal.

Chapter 9

The duke's Town House, a rambling Tudor mansion set on a wooded knoll in the Campden Hill District, fairly exuded an aura of stately grace, decided Constance, viewing it from the crest of the descending gravel drive. Four stories and three wings of ivy-covered brown brick gave little doubt that it belonged to a personage of great position and wealth. But then, the Campden Hill District was not called "the Dukeries" for nothing, she reflected, as, stepping down from the carriage, she allowed Vere to escort her to the front door. This was opened immediately to reveal the august presence of a proper English butler.

"Ah, Collings," pronounced Vere, stepping past that most superior of all servants into the foyer.

"My lord," intoned Collings, bowing at the waist. "May I say that it is good to have you home again?"

"Yours, I fear, is not a sentiment that is universally shared. It would seem the duke has yet to inform you that I am once again *persona non grata*. Are you about to rescind my welcome, Collings, and send me packing?"

The butler, obviously a retainer of long standing,

showed not so much as a crack in his composure at being given that interesting tidbit of information.

"I daresay I should never do that, my lord, unless the duke himself gave me the order, and we both know . . ."

"That the duke entertains a decided aversion to setting foot outside of Albermarle Castle," Vere supplied with his gentle smile. "In which case, it gives me great pleasure to make known to you Constance, Lady Vere, my wife. No doubt you will be glad to learn that she will be staying with you for a few days."

It would seem that, while the tidings that Albermarle had cast off his heir made little impression on Collings, the news of Vere's marriage was something of an altogether different order. Indeed, Constance, watching the austere features when Vere made his announcement, was certain she detected an infinitesimal twitch of the man's left eyebrow, followed by the distinct bob of the Adam's apple.

"*Ahem!*" he declared.

"Well said, Collings," applauded Constance, extending her hand. "Indeed, I could not agree with you more. It is all just a trifle unsettling, is it not?"

"Not at all, your ladyship," managed Collings, recovering sufficiently to take her hand with great aplomb. "I am honored to make your acquaintance, my lady, and may I say that I wish you both happiness?"

"Thank you, Collings," said Vere, removing his gloves and dropping them in his curly-brimmed beaver before handing it to the butler with his greatcoat soon to follow. "Her ladyship, however, is to remain incognito while she is here. To everyone else in the household, she is Mrs. Allenby, the daughter of a dear friend of the duke's. She is in seclusion while she recovers from the loss of her dearest husband at sea, is that not so, my dove?"

"Oh, quite," agreed Constance, awarding Vere a darkling glance. "I daresay I shall spend every waking moment thinking of my dearly departed spouse."

"I shall depend on it, my love," Vere said, a gleam of laughter in his eyes. "No doubt it will help you to pass the time while I am gone."

"Devil," said Constance, who had exerted every effort, including lowering herself to feign a shed of tears, to dissuade Vere from confining her in the duke's Town House while he went off on his own to implement his plans for bringing Landford and Blaidsdale to justice. Really, it was too bad of him.

"Quite so, my dear," agreed Vere, who liked leaving his titian-haired temptress to her own devices even less than did she. He had been made all too well aware that she was perfectly capable of doing any number of things certain to land her in a coil of her own making. Indeed, the notion of locking his bride in the cellar until his return had never been more appealing than it was at this very moment. "I shall show Mrs. Allenby up to the Primrose Room, Collings. Be pleased to have her trunk sent up."

"As you wish, my lord," intoned Collings, who, if he had entertained any doubts as to the truth of his lordship's claim of marriage, had had them instantly dispelled by that little demonstration of affection. The two bickered like a pair of lovebirds, behavior that he had never thought to see in the marquis. It was a pity the duke had not been here to witness it, he thought, allowing himself the faintest of smiles as he went to do his lordship's bidding.

"Brava, my girl. It appears you have made a conquest," observed Vere, taking Constance's arm and ushering her up the graceful sweep of stairs to the picture gallery that overlooked the foyer below. "With the exception of my mother, I believe I have never seen Collings quite so taken with anyone before."

"He is obviously quite fond of you, Vere," asserted Constance, glancing at the imposing array of Rochelles displayed in gilt frames along the way. "I daresay he is relieved to learn that you have succumbed to Parson's Mousetrap. There is, in general, nothing like marriage for curbing a gentleman's propensity for sowing wild oats."

"Impudent little baggage," exclaimed Vere, coming to a precipitous halt. "Is that what you think you have done?"

"No, of course not, Vere," replied Constance, her eyes utterly guileless. "Indeed, how could I, when ours is but a marriage of convenience? I daresay you will continue to sow any number of wild oats, and, indeed, I should not dream of trying to stop you. Faith, how very tedious that would be."

"Tedious, indeed," uttered Vere, who, strangely, found this new turn of Constance's to play the part of a conformable wife most demmed unsettling. The urge to punish her just a little for her impertinence was too overwhelming to resist. "No doubt I am comforted to learn that I shall not find it necessary to keep you in the dark concerning my various mistresses."

"No, why should you?" returned Constance, giving every appearance of one engrossed in the portrait of an earlier Rochelle, who, despite the cartwheel ruff about the neck and the swallow's tail beard and moustache adorning his face, bore a striking resemblance to his present-day descendant. Indeed, it would seem that coal-black hair and gimlet blue eyes had run in the family for countless generations. "As a freethinker and an admirer of Mary Wollestonecraft, I should consider myself an exceedingly poor character if I could not freely and openly accept my husband's *joies de vivre*. Besides, it would seem the height of absurdity to try and change the man I fell in love with, would it not? I daresay I should in the end wake up one morning to find I was married to someone I did not even like. And then where should I be?"

"A hideous prospect," agreed Vere, apparently much struck at what would seem an exceedingly enlightened point of view. The little minx, he thought. If she were deliberately trying to distract him from the business before him, she could have chosen no surer way to achieve her purposes. He was at the moment sorely tempted to put Roth off for as long as it took to instruct his impertinent bride in the folly of thinking she could manipulate Vere to her own ends. "No doubt I am sorry to disappoint you, my dove. As it happens, however, I am at present without a mistress."

He was about to add that he entertained no immediate plans of filling the vacancy, when Constance interrupted him with a low-voiced exclamation.

"Good God," she said, staring fixedly at one of the portraits, which, while bearing a marked resemblance to Vere himself, was yet in one respect significantly different from all the rest. "What is *he* doing here?"

"I beg your pardon?" murmured Vere, who could not but note his bride would seem uncommonly agitated where, before, she had been assuming a demeanor that was as charmingly blasé as it was unrealistic.

"*Him*," repeated Constance, pointing to the likeness of a gentleman of perhaps five-and-thirty, with eyes the clear blue intensity of lapis lazuli and hair the shocking red of a forest in autumn. "Why is his picture hanging there?"

"I cannot think where else it would be hanging," replied Vere, his eyes narrowing sharply on the pallor of Constance's face. The devil, he thought, what was this? "It is, after all, a portrait of the previous Marquis of Vere. That is James Rochelle, my . . ."

"Father," Constance finished for him in stunned accents. "But his hair!"

"Was bequeathed to him by my grandmother, Genevieve, Lady Albermarle, who was likewise redheaded. He is, I believe, the only Rochelle to break the mold exemplified by my grandsire, the duke. Constance, why do you ask?"

Constance, who gave every impression of one who had had the breath knocked from her, vehemently shook her head. "I—it is nothing," she said, turning away from the painting as if she could no longer bear the sight of it. She drew a painful breath and let it out again. "It is the silliest thing, but I feel a headache coming on. Indeed, I think I must lie down for a while."

Vere's eyebrows fairly shot together over the bridge of his nose as he observed Constance, his dauntless bride who had faced pirates without a tremor, sway ever so slightly on her feet. The devil, he cursed, a fist closing like a vise on his vitals. Grim-faced, he swept her up in his arms.

Aware of a taut pressure in his chest, Vere had yet to say a word when, moments later, he carried her into the Primrose Room and lowered her to her feet. Nor did he speak as he left her to give a sharp tug on the bellpull. Coming back to her, he wordlessly helped her out of her pelisse.

Constance, who did not doubt from the stern cast of his face that he fully intended to help her out of her gown and her other things as well, then, tucking her into bed, make her drink a bitter tisane, assayed to stop him with a smile. "Vere, I am all right. Pray do not look at me that way. It is only a headache, I promise you. I shall be fine after I have rested."

"You will no doubt pardon me if I say that you had not the look just now of one taken with a sudden headache," Vere said in tones heavily laced with irony.

Constance, turning away from him, occupied herself with untying the ribbons of her bonnet. "Did I not? How very odd, for I was, Vere." Pulling her bonnet off, she carefully set it on a lowboy. "How did I look, then?"

"Like someone who has seen a ghost," Vere answered bluntly. "Constance, I am neither blind nor a fool. You went as white as a sheet out there. You knew my father somewhere before."

"No! I once knew someone very like him. The uncanny likeness startled me, is all." Coming around at last, she faced him with a determined brightness. "What a silly fool you must think me. That is all it was—surprise, and then this stupid headache."

Vere, looming suddenly over her, caught her hand as it fluttered to her forehead. "I should think you are foolish beyond permission, my dear," he said, drawing her shapely member to his lips. Grimly, he noted that it was icy cold to the touch. His eyes holding hers, he placed a kiss in the palm. "*If* you are not telling me the truth. You are my wife, Constance. I should like to think you would feel free to trust me if ever there were something bothering you."

With something that sounded suspiciously like a sob, Constance pulled away. "But of course I trust you, Vere," she said, her back to him held rigidly straight. "It is the headache. I have had them before, I assure you. They always come without warning. I daresay it is just one of those silly feminine things. Now, if you will excuse me, I am convinced you must be anxious to be on your way. And I, as it happens, really am in no case at the moment for a Spanish Inquisition."

Vere's eyes hardened to cold, steely points.

Even if he had not come to know his unpredictable bride exceedingly well in the past few days, Vere could not have been mistaken in thinking that there was a deal more wrong with her than the distress of a female on the point of suffering her feminine cycle. She had just given a very good demonstration of a woman who could not abide to have him touch her!

Deliberately, he took a step toward her. It was time he had the truth from her.

He was brought up short by a discreet scratch on the door. Hell and the devil confound it!

Instantly, Constance came around.

"Yes, who is it?" she called, her eyes going past Vere's formidable presence to focus on the oak barrier.

"It's Alice, mum, the upstairs maid. You rang for me?"

"Yes, you may come in. His lordship was just leaving." Her eyes went to Vere's. "Were you not, my lord?" she said meaningfully.

"The devil, Constance, if this is some ploy of yours to . . ."

"It is no ploy, my lord. I . . ." She stopped and looked away. "I wish you Godspeed," she said dully. "Only, please—go."

She was still standing, staring rather blindly at a point beyond him, when Vere, curtly bowing his head, turned and departed in as close to a cold, blistering rage as he had ever been before in his life.

Reaching the foyer, he flung on his greatcoat and hat and fairly snatched his walking stick from the hand of a noticeably stone-faced Collings. Then, on the point of stalking out of the house in a grand peeve, he stopped, his head dropping to his chest.

For a moment he stood thus, while Collings, frozen in an attitude of stolid impassivity, waited at attention.

At last Vere's head came up. His lip curled in sardonic amusement at himself. Drawing a breath, he said, "Keep a close watch over her, will you, Collings?"

He waited for Collings to say, "I will, indeed, my lord." Then, without a backward glance, he strode out the door.

And, indeed, by the time he climbed into the hackney awaiting him in the drive, he had regained sufficient command of his temper to think a deal more clearly than when he had stalked away from Constance—just as she had wished him to do. And still, it made no sense to him.

Bloody hell! For the first time for as far back as he

could remember, he found himself in a complete and utter quandary in a matter concerning a woman. That it should be his wife who evaded his normally acute understanding of females, he found more than merely ironic. The devil, he was gripped with the demmed uncomfortable feeling that the entirety of his future happiness depended upon his solving the puzzle of this particular female.

Vere was far too astute an observer not to have noted that his normally forthright Constance had throughout the painful interview been studiously avoiding his eyes. Indeed, he would have had to be blind not to see it. He had known, of course, that she was lying to him—Constance, who never lied about anything. Nor was he such a fool as not to realize that it was something concerning the likeness of his father that had upset her and precipitated the resulting scene in the bedchamber. Hellfire, *upset* was hardly the word to describe what she was. *Shaken to the core* was more like it. *Why?* Clearly, she had recognized the face in the portrait. Having done so, how had she failed to know that she was looking at the likeness of the former marquis? More than that, he thought, why should learning the subject's identity have caused the blood to drain from her face? Egad, she had had the look in her eyes of a deer wounded to the heart!

The devil, he cursed. There was a mystery here that boded ill for more than his peace of mind. If he were not mistaken, his failure to resolve it would result in the loss of the one thing that had suddenly seemed to make sense in his life. Worse, if he understood anything about his unpredictable bride, it was that in her own mind she had already determined that there was some insurmountable impediment to their happiness. Constance had withdrawn from him as certainly as if she had announced her intent to leave him.

But then, that was precisely what she had been doing!

Good God, he thought, suddenly sitting up. Rapping the head of his walking stick hard against the roof of the cab, he ordered the driver to turn back. What a *fool* he had been to allow emotion to get the better part of reason! And how utterly unlike him it was to get emotional at all over something so obvious as a woman's determination to sacrifice everything for the sake of love. Clearly, his adorable bride had befuddled his brain and addled his instincts far more than he could ever have imagined.

The hackney, caught up in the traffic entering and departing Kensington Gardens and Hyde Park, made slow work of reversing its direction. Indeed, Vere, cursing himself for his colossal failure to see immediately what had been going on in Constance's mind, was agonizingly aware of the passage of time. At least thirty minutes had elapsed since his departure when the cab pulled up once again before the sprawling mansion.

Vere was out of the cab and through the front door almost before the cab pulled to a complete stop. Ignoring Collings, who had just arrived in the foyer, he took the stairs two at a time and strode grimly along the gallery past two curtsying upstairs maids and an underfootman engaged in refilling the oil lamps.

Coming at last to the room he had departed little more than half an hour earlier, he reached for the door handle and, without bothering to announce his presence, flung open the door.

The chamber's gay primrose wall hangings and rose satin upholstered settee and chairs greeted him in silent mockery, even as the solitary wooden trunk set in the middle of the floor struck him with its air of finality.

Constance, his marchioness, had gone.

A thick fog was rolling in off the Thames when Colonel Jack Ingram, promising he would not be out late, kissed his wife Sophie on the cheek and departed for an evening with the officers of his former regiment. Sophie had herself been looking forward to enjoying a stimulating evening with her Ladies' Literary Society in a discussion of *Thaddeus of Warsaw*, the first published work by the budding novelist Jane Porter. Unfortunately, Mrs. Eugenie Farnwell, who was to have hosted the weekly gathering, had come down with a cold at the last moment, and, as there had not been time to make different arrangements, the meeting had been called off.

It was times like these that she missed Constance the most, Sophie decided, as she stood in the middle of the downstairs parlor feeling rather like a lost lamb. It was not that she was unhappy in her relatively new state of marriage, for she most certainly was not. She had lived forty-nine years as a spinster in perfect harmony with her existence until Mrs. Delaney's dinner party almost a year and a half ago had served to open her eyes to delightful new possibilities. She had known her life had just taken a turn for the better almost from the first moment that she had looked up into humorous brown eyes set in a rugged face that, while not handsome in the strictest sense, had possessed character and intelligence, which, to Sophie's way of thinking, were far more appealing than mere good looks. Colonel Jack Ingram, winning an immediate place in her affections, had filled empty spaces in her life that she had not even known that she possessed. Nevertheless, she could not but realize that when Constance, stubbornly independent as ever, had insisted on moving out of the house, she had created a hole in Sophie's heart that not even Jack could completely mend.

She did not notice it often or even recognize that it was there unless something happened to upset the normal pattern of her life. Like tonight, she thought, annoyed out of all reason with Eugenie for having caught the sniffles and spoiled an evening to which she had

been looking forward with no little pleasurable anticipation. She was left, after all, with far too much time on
her hands and nothing to do to distract her from the
unhappy contemplation of Constance's precipitous flight
from Landford Park and the odious Earl of Blaidsdale.

Good God, she thought, would that man never cease
to be a blight on her life! He had come all too close to
destroying Regina, and now it seemed he would not be
satisfied until he had ruined any chance Constance might
have had at happiness as well. At least Regina, bless her
soul, was beyond ever being hurt by him again.

Even now, after all the years, Sophie could not understand why her sister had settled on marrying Blaidsdale
when she not only had already turned him down once,
but she might also have had her choice of practically
anyone else and been better off. It had seemed at the
time as if Regina had not cared whom she wed; indeed,
as if she had suddenly accepted the first offer that presented itself on that particular day and then, resigned
to the inevitable, had simply followed through with her
pledged troth. Sophie had understood perfectly, however, why Regina chose eleven years later to leave her
husband. She had only marveled that it had taken her
so long to arrive at the decision.

Landford was every whit as miserly in his affections
as he was parsimonious with his purse. He was and always had been, to put it mildly, mean-spirited. It was
perhaps fortunate that Sophie and Regina's father had
vehemently disapproved of the match. His grace had
made sure that Blaidsdale could never gain possession
of the fortune that he intended for his daughter, and
that, in turn, had gone to Constance with the same safe-
guards. And yet, Sophie, worried that Blaidsdale was
not above discovering other means of coercing Constance
to his will, had done her best to dissuade her niece from
accepting Blaidsdale's invitation to come for a visit.

It had been to no avail, of course. And then Millie and Will Trask had shown up at the house on Plover Street with the tale of Constance's harrowing escape. Sophie had been beside herself with worry ever since. It had been all Jack could do to restrain his wife from setting out at once to Somerset for a confrontation with her erstwhile brother-in-law. Indeed, had it not been for Constance's hurriedly scribbled note warning Sophie against doing any such thing, Sophie did not doubt that nothing could have stopped her. *That*, she amended, and her niece's expressed desire that Sophie should be waiting to receive her when Constance felt it was safe to come home.

No doubt it was that single most important word, "home," that had gone farthest in persuading Sophie to wait. It had now been a sennight since Millie and Will's return, however, and Sophie, with the exception of the servants, whom she had already dismissed for the night, was left at home alone with naught to do but conjure up any number of scenarios for disaster in which her impetuous niece might presently be involved.

Weary at last of her unrewarding thoughts and realizing she was like to wear out the Aubusson carpet in the sitting room from pacing back and forth, Sophie snatched up a candle and marched to the kitchen with the intention of fixing herself a libation of warm milk, which she thoroughly detested. Indeed, she would much have preferred a glass of sherry, but she had never taken up the habit of drinking alone, and she was darned if she would start now.

She set her candle on the table and took a glass down from one of the cupboards. She was reaching for the milk when she was visited with a wholly unexpected tingling of nerve-endings at the nape of her neck.

"Pray tell me you do not intend that glass of milk for yourself, Sophie Ingram," demanded a voice from the doorway behind her. "I refuse to believe that marriage could change one so thoroughly in so short a time. You loathe milk, Sophie. You know very well that you do."

Sophie froze, her hand pressed to her throat. "Not so much perhaps as drinking sherry alone." Then, "Constance," she breathed, turning around. "What the devil took you so long?"

"I fear that I have made a terrible mull of everything," Constance said, no little time later. Emerging from her bath wrapped in a bathsheet, she sank miserably down on the rug before the fire in the fireplace to allow her hair to dry. "I daresay it would be better for everyone involved if I simply vanished off the face of the earth forever."

"I pray you will not be melodramatic, Constance," Sophie chided sternly, her heart lurching with concern nonetheless. She had never seen the normally straightforward Constance so elusive. Fidgety with nervous energy one moment and staring off into space with tragic, haunted eyes the next, the girl was proving a sad trial for Sophie's peace of mind. "Tell me what is troubling you. Whatever it is, we shall face it together, just as we have always done."

"Not this, dearest Sophie." Constance, dropping her forehead on her knees, pulled to her chest, appeared to contract. "Good God," she gasped, "I cannot face it myself, much less ask you to share this terrible thing." Then, just as suddenly, her head came up and her eyes blurred with pain and anger. "*Damn my mother for dying! Damn her for keeping secrets from me. How dared she not tell me Blaidsdale is not my father!*"

Sophie, already reeling from the shock of Constance's bitter condemnation of her mama, was hardly prepared for that final utterance from the tormented girl.

"Not your father?" she echoed blankly. "But of course he is, Constance. Faith, what nonsense is this?"

"It is hardly nonsense when Blaidsdale himself told me he is not my father. Sophie, you were closer to my mother than anyone, save for . . ." She stopped, shaking her head as she caught herself. She drew a breath, as if it hurt her to breathe. "You must have known something."

"No, Constance. How could I? I was sixteen when your mama had her come-out. I was at home at Briarcroft with my governess."

She knew as soon as the words were out that she was wrong. She had sensed something all those years ago, and now she knew. Blaidsdale had spoken the truth.

Abruptly, she got up from her seat on the settee. Clasping and unclasping her hands in front of her waist, she took a step, then turned back again. "It would explain a great deal that was puzzling. Why Regina should have married Blaidsdale when she had turned him down once before. And when her letters had all extolled the virtues of another. Why the joy seemed suddenly to go out of her. She was never the same after . . ."

"After what?" Constance shoved herself to her feet.

"After Father caught her one night stealing into the Town House, when she was supposed to have been in bed all evening with a headache." Sophie gave a helpless gesture of the hand. "Regina wrote me all about it. There was a dreadful row. Father was furious. He accused her of terrible things. Regina swore she would run away to be with the only man whom she could ever love. She said it did not matter that Father had forbidden her ever to see him again. She would have him, or she would have no one. And then she never wrote about him again. I thought she had come to her senses. And then, a few weeks later, she accepted Blaidsdale's offer."

Slowly, Sophie sank down on the edge of the sofa.

"My poor, dear Regina," she said. "All those years with Blaidsdale, she never told me. At home, the incident was never once mentioned, and then you came. Regina seemed to blossom again. Her happiness was all in you. You must know, Constance, that she loved you better than life itself. The years passed, and I forgot all about what happened. I cannot even recall that she ever told me his name."

"But she must have done," Constance exclaimed, clasping her aunt's hands in something very like desperation. Indeed, so intent was she on wringing the name from her aunt that neither she nor Sophie heard the step in the hallway come to a halt at the bedchamber door.

"Sophie, *think*," Constance pleaded. "You must remember. Who was the man Mama stole out to meet that night? She said that she loved him. She must have told you his name. Was it—could it have been Albermarle's heir, Sophie? Tell me. Could it have been James Rochelle?"

Without warning, the door was thrust open.

"You may be quite certain that it could not," declared a voice with awful calm from the doorway. "You may be equally certain that you have not committed the cardinal sin of marrying your brother. Good God, Constance. Is *that* what all this was about?"

Startled, both women turned to regard the tall figure limned in the doorway with varying degrees of consternation.

"*Vere!*" exclaimed Constance, going as white as the bathsheet she was wearing.

"*Married!*" gasped Sophie, her eyes flying in astonishment from the gentleman to Constance. "To your *brother*? Constance, what the devil have you done?"

"Nothing which will not soon be remedied by a swift and merciless beating," the gentleman assured her, as he advanced purposefully toward Constance. "I see, my dear, that you are dressed in your usual fetching style. Since you made certain to leave behind every item of clothing that I provided you, am I to assume this is the manner in which you made your way from the Dukeries halfway across London?"

"You know very well that it is not," declared Constance, turning as red as she was previously white. Deeming retreat at the moment the better part of valor, she backed warily before his determined advance. "I wore my own things."

"Splendid," pronounced Vere, little resembling the man noted for having ice water in his veins. "No doubt I am to be comforted that my marchioness fled my protection garbed as a boy. If you are planning to make a habit of it, remind me in future to introduce you to my tailor."

"I wish you will not be absurd, Vere," said Constance, hard put not to choke on a startled burble of laughter that must soon turn to tears if she did not get a grip on herself. "I have no need of your tailor. On the other hand, I am reminded that I have yet to introduce you to my aunt. Aunt Sophie, I have the dubious honor of presenting to you his lordship, the Marquis of Vere. Vere, Mrs. Sophie Ingram, my aunt."

"My lord," said Sophie, dipping a curtsy.

"A pleasure, ma'am," returned Vere without pausing in his pursuit of Constance around the impediment of an occasional table. "I beg your pardon for intruding. I did knock. A servant by the name of Millie let me in. I told her I should find my own way."

"No, it is quite all right," Sophie hastened to assure him. "And now, if you will excuse me, my lord, I have the feeling that I am decidedly *de trop*. I shall just leave you to carry on as you see fit."

"*Sophie*, don't you dare go!" squealed Constance, thrusting an oversized Oriental cushion between her and the ominous figure of the advancing marquis.

"Forgive me, dearest," caroled Sophie, smiling and waving her hands as she made her way to the exit. "I am sure there are any number of things that need my attention elsewhere, and you, it would appear, will be occupied for some little time to come."

With a swirl of silk skirts, Sophie vanished into the hallway and pulled the door to behind her.

"Obviously a woman of uncommon good sense, your aunt," pronounced Vere, flinging the oversized tasseled cushion aside. "Unlike her addlebrained niece."

Constance, coming up hard against the Louis Quinze armoire, stared helplessly up at him. "Enough, Vere," she gasped, clutching the folds of the bath sheet at her breast with nerveless hands. "What are you doing here? You did what you promised to do. You brought me safely to London. And I, by my actions, have relieved you of any further responsibility for my well-being. There was no reason for you to come after me."

"Very generous of you, to be sure," replied the marquis, firmly planting a hand against the armoire on either side of her head. "But you appear to have forgotten two important details. You are my wife."

"Yes," said Constance, nodding through a shimmer of tears. "I am."

"And I promised to return this." Vere, reaching in his coat pocket, drew out his hand and opened his fist.

A sob broke spasmodically from Constance's lips. "Vere, my brooch," she said, the tears spilling forth at last. "Really, it is t-too b-bad of you."

"Yes, no doubt," agreed Vere, the austere hardness of his features slowly relenting. At last, pulling Constance to him, he folded her in his arms and held her.

During the past several hours spent in tracking down the house on Plover Street in which Constance's aunt resided, he had had plenty of time to experience the full gamut of emotions to which his bride's disappearance could subject him. The all too real possibility that she had fallen into the hands of his enemies had been only slightly less tormenting than the fear that, in the grips of whatever had driven her from him, she had contrived to flee England altogether—egad! It was, consequently, with no little sense of relief that, having shoved past the servant girl and barged upstairs, he was rewarded with the sound of Constance's voice issuing from beyond the closed door. It was only with the profoundest sense of *disbelief* that he comprehended the gist of those impassioned words.

Egad, it was little wonder that his bride had recoiled in horror from his touch! She believed that James Rochelle was her father!

It was a pity that she had not been able to bring herself to confide in him, he thought grimly as, holding her against him, he slowly stroked her hair. She would have saved them both a deal of unnecessary anguish. She was, after all, the victim of false assumptions. There was not the smallest chance that James Rochelle had fathered her.

Nevertheless, something had led her to a conclusion that was as erroneous as it was absurd, and it had to be something more than the peculiarity of the color of James Rochelle's hair. She had recognized the man in the portrait. That much was certain. More than that, he was someone she had known exceedingly well and in circumstances that must have convinced her there could have been an intimate relationship between her mother and the then Marquis of Vere. That much he could discern for himself. What he wished to know now was when she had known his father and how.

"Vere?"

Vere's hand stilled on Constance's hair.

"Can you be certain that . . ." She stopped, unable to utter it.

"I am unequivocally certain. There is not the slightest chance that we are siblings. Twenty-six years ago, my father was sent as an ambassador to the East Indies. He was there for two years. So you see, he cannot possibly be your father."

That indisputable evidence was met with a telling silence.

"Constance," Vere said at last. Pulling back, he tilted her head up to look at him. "You do believe me, do you not?"

A rueful smile trembled on her lips, and she nodded gravely.

"Faith, what a fool I have been. When I saw his portrait, I thought that the stories must have all been true. That he was her lover. But he never was, Vere, I know that now. He was her dear friend—even when she was dying."

"He must have been. He taught her daughter how to fence. He is the only one who could have done. I should have realized it that night when you demonstrated his style to perfection. Constance, where did you know my father?"

"In Wells, when I was a little girl," she said simply. "He used to come to see my mother." She pulled away and crossed to the fire. For a long moment, she stared, unseeing, down at the flames. And when at last she spoke, her voice sounded distant, as if she were a long way away from the bedchamber in her aunt's house.

"When my mother took me with her to live in Wells, it was the most wonderful time of my life. Just to wake up in the morning and know that I should never have to return to Landford Park again was like having been set free from a hateful prison. I did not realize for a very long time how lonely it must have been for my mother. There was talk, of course. Everyone said that she had taken a lover, but there was no one. My mother never went out, never saw anyone. I suppose she was protecting me from the gossipmongers. And then your father came one day, and everything seemed to change. Mama was not alone anymore. At long last she had a friend, someone with whom she could relax and be herself again."

Constance smiled, remembering. The house had seemed to come suddenly alive, as it did whenever he came to call after that first time. He had the gift for making her mother laugh, and she, Constance, had adored him.

"She called him 'Pinky,'" she said, glancing quizzically up at Vere. "I never knew him by any other name. To me he was Uncle Pinky, and he was my dearest—indeed, my only—friend."

"When he was twelve," said Vere, his eyes intent on Constance's face, "he broke his finger playing cricket. It never healed properly."

"It was his pinky finger. Yes, I remember. It was crooked."

"Your mother must have known him for a very long time if she called him that," remarked Vere carefully. "No one else ever did, save for Lord Bridholm. I daresay no one else would have dared even if it were commonly known, and I am certain it was not."

"Bridholm?" echoed Constance, strangely vibrating to that name. Then it came to her. The Earl of Bridholm's youngest son had once been thought the favorite to win her mama's hand in marriage. "Why he and no other?"

"He was my father's closest friend even before they attended Eton together. The story of the cricket match was a private thing between them. I suspect Bridholm was somehow responsible for my father's injury. Which would seem to make it all the more remarkable that your mama should also have been familiar with it."

"You think they knew one another as children," Constance said, feeling her heart inexplicably skip a beat.

"It is possible, is it not? When Mama was a girl, the family used to remove to their house in Weymouth for the summer months."

"As the king was particularly fond of Weymouth in those years, it is hardly surprising," commented Vere, who had little difficulty following her line of reasoning. "Albermarle maintained a cottage there for his Genevieve and the boys. As did Bridholm and many another of the most prominent families of the realm. It is not inconceivable that the children of those families were often thrown together. Nevertheless . . ."

He paused, a frown darkening his eyes.

"Constance, perhaps you should not allow yourself to hope for too much. Bridholm had already married and set up his nursery before you were ever conceived. His heir is of an age with me. I cannot think that he . . ."

"No, not the earl," broke in Constance, her eyes sparkling with excitement. "His brother. It was in all the betting books, Vere. Everyone thought that Bridholm's youngest son would win my mother's hand in marriage. Only something must have happened, and she ended up marrying Blaidsdale instead."

"Something did happen," said Vere, suddenly grim.

Constance, turning to pace a step and come back again, seemed not to have heard. "If I could only see the earl's brother, if I could just talk to him."

"Constance," Vere repeated, catching her by the arms to stop her pacing.

"But how silly of me." She laid her hand on Vere's chest and gazed earnestly up at him. "You could arrange it. You could, could you not? Vere, you will do this one thing for me?"

"Constance, he is dead." Silently, he cursed, as she went suddenly quite still. Hell and the devil confound it! He had been brutal out of necessity. Obviously, it was not what she had expected to hear.

She stared at him, her eyes stricken. "Dead?"

Vere steeled himself to further quash her brief, scintillating lift of spirits. "He was killed by footpads, *enfant*," he said, "all those many years ago. If Charles Seton was the man your mother stole out to meet that night, he was killed before he had a chance to make her his wife."

"But then, that was it, was it not?" demanded Constance, as if that explained everything. As perhaps it did, thought Vere, watching her take the blame upon herself. "My mother was going to run away with him. She told Sophie as much in a letter. When he was killed, she must have found out she was increasing. She had no choice but to accept the first offer that . . ."

"The devil, Constance," rasped Vere, shaking her a little. "It is not your fault that your mother married Blaidsdale. Any more than it is your fault that she is dead. It is time you ceased to think like a child."

"Yes, you are quite right," said Constance, her eyes unwavering on his. "It is not *my* fault. I daresay it is not my mother's, either. I find it rather too coincidental that Charles Seton should have died when he did and in such a manner. Vere, he was deliberately murdered. I should wager my life on it. If there is one thing I have learned about the man my mother did in the end marry, it is that he will stop at nothing to have what he wants."

"And if I am not disposed to argue with you, *enfant*," said Vere, who had also long since come to a similar conclusion concerning his old enemy, the Earl of Blaidsdale, "what would you have me do about it?"

"Nothing that *I* do not intend doing, my lord," replied Constance with an ominous jut of her delightfully pointed chin. "With or without your help." Smiling a cat's smile, she set about unfastening the buttons of his coat, one after the other, followed in swift order by the buttons of his waistcoat underneath. "I, after all, have a vested interest in seeing that Blaidsdale's unsavory influence is brought to a quick and summary end."

Vere, sustaining a decided frisson of warning, cocked a wary eyebrow. "No doubt you will pardon my curiosity, *ma mie*," he said, as, pulling his shirt from the waistband of his unmentionables, she provocatively slid her hand up over his delectably hard, masculine chest. "I cannot but wonder what vested interest you had most particularly in mind."

"But I should have thought that was obvious, my dearest, best-loved marquis." Holding Vere with her eyes, she lifted her arms about his neck and let the bathsheet drop to the floor. "I will not have him remain as a constant threat to our future progeny."

Vere, who could not find fault with her reasoning, who, indeed, was already painfully primed and ready to propagate any number of future progeny, uttered something very closely resembling a growl. Ruthlessly, he crushed her to his chest, his lips hungrily devouring her eyes, her cheeks, her lips. At last, in a torment of desire, he swept her up in his arms and, laying her on the bed, he bent over her. His eyes moved over her face in a silent, achingly tender caress. Then, at last, he lowered his head to her.

Constance, his sweet, maddeningly unpredictable bride was come back to him.

Chapter 10

"Mama had *something* that protected her from Blaidsdale," said Constance, accepting a dish of tea from her aunt and setting it on the sofa table in front of her. "Further, I believe that she must have entrusted it to Mr. Malcom Enderhart, her solicitor. Why else would she have insisted in her letter that I contact him should I ever find myself in difficulty?"

Sophie, who had often wondered at her brother-in-law's uncharacteristic forbearance in the matter of his first wife's decampment and subsequent separation, nevertheless shook her head doubtfully. "Perhaps she meant only that you might be in need of a good solicitor, Constance. I daresay Mr. Enderhart would be quite good at his trade."

"I should think he would be exceedingly good," replied Constance with only a hint of dryness. "He was, after all, Westerlake's private solicitor for a number of years until the duke passed away, leaving the title to Cousin Horace."

"Yes, you may be sure my father would not retain someone for long who did not perform his duties satisfactorily," agreed Sophie. "But if one cannot even locate the man, I cannot see what good he is to anyone."

"You are right, of course," smiled Constance, who could not but appreciate her aunt's propensity for going straight to the heart of a matter. "He is of no benefit to me at all in such an event. Which is why I am relying on the colonel's advertisement in the *Gazette* to find him for me."

"You may be sure that, if anything can fetch him, that will," submitted Colonel Jack Ingram, leaning down to knock the ashes from his Meerschaum pipe into the fireplace. Rising to his considerable height, he reached for the humidor on the mantel. "He is a man of letters. Naturally, he will read the *Gazette*. If he is still in London, I daresay we may expect to hear from him no later than tomorrow."

"In the meantime, we may hope that Vere returns soon with news of his own quest for his Mr. Phineas Ambrose," Sophie said, nibbling at a saffron biscuit. "Where did you say he went?"

"I did not say," submitted Constance, who had not been at all pleased to bid Vere good-bye two mornings ago before the sun even had had time to come up, ending the momentous night of their reunion. Indeed, she could not but think it was the shabbiest thing to be left behind when they had come to an agreement. She and Vere were henceforth to be arch plotters in the effort to bring Blaidsdale and his brother to justice. Only, it seemed she was expected to do all her part of the plotting from the safety of her aunt's sitting room, the devil! "How could I when Vere refused categorically to share that pertinent information with me? Naturally, he claimed he did not know yet where his search would take him."

"Then very likely he did not," rejoined Sophie, who could only be relieved that Vere had had the good sense not to take Constance with him on what she did not doubt was a dangerous enterprise. "You must not blame Vere for wishing to be assured of your safety while he looks for a man who very likely betrayed his employers to their deaths."

"Sophie is right, Constance, my dear," said the colonel, gesturing with a pipe-filled hand. "I know it is not the easiest thing to be the one left behind to fret and worry. Naturally, one would rather be on the front lines. Still, if you don't mind my saying so, you are doing your part by holding down the home fort."

"I fear it does not feel like it," Constance replied with a grimace. "Still, I suppose I should be grateful Vere did not insist on my returning to Albermarle House. I should rather be here with you than there, staring at four unfamiliar walls."

"And I could not be happier that you are finally home," said Sophie, well aware that, beneath her calm exterior, Constance was chafing at the bit. Indeed, it had lately occurred to Sophie that perhaps Regina and she might have done better not to encourage the girl's streak of stubborn independence quite so much as they had. Mary Wollestonecraft's notions of feminine equality were fine until one was faced with the reality of a young woman ready to dash off into peril at the drop of a hat. Really, there were times when she was almost glad that she was past the age of bearing children.

As soon as that thought crossed her mind, she knew it was a lie. She would not have traded her years helping to rear her sister's daughter for anything in the world. Nor could she quite quell a sense of regret that she and her Jack would never have children of their own. Still, she could comfort herself with the thought that Constance was not to follow in her footsteps. In spite of Vere's unsavory reputation, Sophie could not but think that, in the marquis, Constance had more than found her match.

Certainly, he had demonstrated that he was more than capable of dealing with her sudden starts, not to mention her dauntless spirit, which was apt to lead her more often than not to a fearless disregard of her own safety. More than that, however, he had managed to capture her wayward heart, which had remained untouched despite the amorous attentions of not a few suitors through the seven years since the girl's come-out.

It had been Sophie's regret that it seemed her dearest Constance was set on remaining a spinster. She was married now, however, and with any luck she would soon have the sobering effects of motherhood to curb her high spirits. In the meantime, Sophie could only hope that Vere would settle the troublesome matter of Blaidsdale in short order, indeed, before Constance was moved to take it upon herself to do something about it.

Hardly had that thought crossed her mind when the peace and quiet was shattered by the clatter of the front-door knocker.

"Now, who can that be?" rumbled the colonel, who had been happily occupied with regaling Constance with a tale of the battle at Seringapatum in which the Sultan of Mysore had finally met with defeat. "You did tell Mrs. Gayle that we are not at home to callers?"

"Oh, but you cannot have done," exclaimed Constance, bolting to her feet to stand listening for the housekeeper to admit the unknown caller. "What if it is Mr. Enderhart in answer to our advertisement? Or someone with word from Vere?"

"If it is, we shall know soon enough," said Sophie, prey to a sudden uncomfortable sense of foreboding. "Pray do sit down, my dear, and finish your tea before it grows cold."

"Oh, but I couldn't," insisted Constance, already heading for the parlor door. "Not until I know for certain. I pray you will excuse me. I shall only be a moment."

She was already out in the hall before Sophie could offer another word in protest. Hurrying to the head of the stairs, she peered out over the banister at the parquetry-tiled foyer below in time to hear Mrs. Gayle insist that the gentleman must be satisfied with leaving his calling card.

"No, wait, Gladys!" called Constance, descending the steps in a flurry of silk skirts. "Who is it?"

"A gentleman, my lady, that says he's come to see the colonel about an advertisement."

"You may let the gentleman in, Gladys," said Constance, coming to a halt near the bottom of the stairs. "You may be sure that the colonel is anxious to see him."

"As you wish, my lady," replied the housekeeper, albeit with obvious reservations. "You may come in, sir. The colonel will see you after all."

The figure that stepped through the door was hardly what Constance might have expected of a solicitor who had once served the Duke of Westerlake. She did not make that judgment from the choice of his attire, which was exact in its cut, if rather austere in its unrelieved black. Nor was it the brown, pomaded hair parted precisely in the middle. He had the unmistakable look of a solicitor, but a solicitor who could not have been above the age of thirty.

"Mr.—er—Enderhart?" queried Constance, examining the calling card that Mrs. Gayle held out to her on a silver salver.

"Mr. Josiah Enderhart, my lady," expanded the gentleman, as Mrs. Gayle relieved him of his greatcoat, gloves, and hat. "At your service, ma'am."

"I fear there has been some mistake, Mr. Enderhart," Constance said, her earlier high hopes plummeting. "The advertisement was for a Mr. *Malcom* Enderhart."

"My father, ma'am," supplied the gentleman. "Who, I am sorry to report, is on his way home to Wells at this very moment and, consequently, never saw the colonel's advertisement. I thought perhaps there might be some way that *I* might be of service to the colonel. Since my father's retirement, I have assumed the responsibilities of many of his former patrons."

"Yes, of course. I suppose it would not hurt to talk," ventured Constance, who, having invited the gentleman into the house, could not feel quite right asking him immediately to depart the premises. "The colonel is upstairs in the withdrawing if you would care to follow me," she added, picking up her skirts and retracing her steps up the staircase.

Mr. Josiah Enderhart, tucking a brown leather pouch under his arm, obediently proceeded up the stairs in his hostess's wake.

Sophie and the colonel, who, like Constance, had been expecting a much older gentleman, listened attentively as Constance clarified the discrepancy.

"Well, Mr. Enderhart, it is no doubt a pleasure to meet you even if you are not precisely what we were looking for," said Sophie, waving him toward the caffoy-covered wing chair near the marble fireplace. "We were just having tea. Would you care to join us?"

"I would, indeed. Thank you, Mrs. Ingram," replied the solicitor, perching on the edge of the chair, the pouch propped on his knees. He went on to supply, in answer to Sophie's queries, that he took cream and two lumps of sugar and that, yes, he would be pleased to sample a saffron biscuit, thank you very much.

It was at that point that, the topics for conversation having seemingly been exhausted, a small silence fell over the company while Mr. Enderhart sipped his tea, carefully ate a bite of biscuit, then set his cup and saucer with exact precision on the sofa table.

"And now," he said, glancing from one to the other, "I assume that you did not send for my father to no purpose. And while my appearance here today is undoubtedly something of a disappointment, I shall endeavor in some measure to make up for it. Your advertisement, Colonel Ingram, mentioned a family heirloom—a brooch, to be more precise—which is adorned with seven diamonds interspersed with an equal number of pearls.

If Mr. M. Enderhart were interested in the purchase of this item, he was to contact Colonel J. I. at Number 23 South Plover Street. May I be permitted to see the brooch, sir?"

"Well, I . . ." began the colonel, glancing uncertainly from one to the other of the two women. "I don't actually have . . ."

"Here it is, Mr. Enderhart," spoke up Constance, reaching up to unpin the relic from the bodice of her dress. "It belonged to my mother, Regina, Lady Blaidsdale. But then, I think you knew that, did you not, sir?"

"I sincerely beg your pardon, my lady. However, before I can answer that, I am afraid I must examine the heirloom in question." Enderhart extended his hand, palm up. "If you will permit me?"

Constance, placing the relic in the gentleman's palm, watched in rapt fascination as Enderhart, removing a jeweler's loupe from the leather pouch, carefully examined the jewels on the front, then, turning the brooch over, as closely studied the back as well.

At last, with a distinct air of satisfaction, Enderhart looked up—directly at Constance. "The brooch is obviously authentic. I have the honor, I believe, of addressing Lady Constance Landford."

"I prefer my mother's maiden name," Constance replied flatly.

"Lowell, am I not mistaken. If you dislike Landford, on the other hand, you are legally entitled to your father's name," pronounced the solicitor. Withdrawing a packet of papers from the leather pouch, he set the pouch aside. "I have here a marriage license, dated the tenth of May in the year of our Lord, 1778. If you examine it, you will see that it was signed by Lady Regina Lowell and Charles William Seton. Further, it was witnessed by the Right Reverend Langtree, Bishop of London, his wife, Mrs. Elzbeth Langtree, and a Mr. Robert Haskins. There is with the document a letter testifying that the single, female offspring of Mrs. Regina Seton is the true daughter of Charles Seton."

"May I see them, Mr. Enderhart?" asked Constance, as gradually it bore in on her that the solicitor was offering her proof of everything that she had only previously surmised.

"No doubt you will pardon my curiosity, sir," the colonel interjected. "I cannot but wonder, however, why my wife's niece was kept in the dark about her parentage all these years. Surely, these are things of which she should have been apprised at the very least upon reaching her majority."

"I'm afraid, Colonel, that it is not my place to speculate on the motivations of those who engage my services, or, in this case, my father's," Enderhart replied. "I know only that my father received instructions to release these documents, along with a sealed letter, upon being presented with a brooch fitting a certain description. He, in turn, entrusted them into my care when he began to fear that his health might fail him. If you examine the brooch closely, you will discover the initials 'C. W. S.' stamped on the back. That was the defining feature for which he was to look."

"The brooch was from *him*," said Constance, marveling that she had never really looked at it before, at least not to see that there were minuscule initials on the back. She had known only that it was special to her mama, who had worn it always. "It was the only thing that she had left of his."

"You are mistaken, surely, my dear," Sophie observed, smiling a trifle mistily. "She had you, after all."

"Yes, I suppose she did," agreed Constance, thinking that she herself would not even have that if anything should happen to Vere. Really, it would be too bad of him to do something so foolish as to have someone put a period to his existence just when she had begun to hope that one day he might actually come to love her, if only a little.

"There is one thing more, Miss Seton," said Mr. Enderhart, extracting a rather plump packet from the pouch. "This was sealed and addressed to you." He handed the packet to Constance.

Constance, recognizing her mama's handwriting at a glance, sustained an unwitting pang through her midsection.

"Constance, dear," said Sophie, concerned, "what is it? You have gone suddenly quite pale."

"I beg your pardon. I am afraid I must ask you to excuse me. Sophie, would you and the colonel please look after Mr. Enderhart?" Constance asked, turning to the door. "I require a few moments to myself. If you would not mind waiting, sir? I shall not be long, I promise."

"Not at all, Miss Seton," replied Mr. Enderhart, who, like the colonel, had risen to his feet. "Please feel free to take all the time that you need."

Constance, fleeing to the privacy of her room, shut the door behind her and crossed to the late afternoon sunlight streaming through the oriel. With trembling fingers, she broke the seal on the packet.

Inside, she found a letter and a second document sealed in wax with a signet that she had only recently come to recognize. She felt a flutter of excitement in the vicinity of her stomach. Setting the document aside, she opened the letter. Slowly, she sank down on the windowseat as she began to read.

It was to occur to her that it was exceedingly strange to read words that her mama had written more than ten years before for a grown daughter she would never know. Reading them now, Constance realized just how little she had really known her mother. Indeed, her memories were tangled wisps of impressions. Sometimes, if she sat very still, she could summon up the sound of her mama singing, as Regina had been wont to do while working in her beloved garden. If Constance closed her eyes, she could see her mama tugging the needle and thread through the fabric as she sat in her tapestry-covered chair by the fire doing needlepoint. The mingled scents of lavender and rosewater never failed to conjure up visions of her mama. Sometimes she could almost feel the warmth of her mama's arm around her shoulders as it had felt when they tramped through the woods together. Her mama had been a calm, loving presence that Constance had taken for granted until she was taken away from her.

Now, reading the story of a young Regina, who had experienced all the same sweet tumult of love that had been given to Constance to know with Vere, was like discovering her mama all over again; indeed, it was like coming to know herself. Smiling through her tears, she could not but think she would have liked the dashing naval lieutenant, who, at one-and-twenty, had dared to woo the Duke of Westerlake's eldest daughter against her father's wishes and, further, had gone so far as to win both her hand and her heart. Charles Seton must have been so very much like Caleb Roth, she thought. Perhaps it was little wonder that she, Constance, had taken to the sea as if she had been born to it. It was, after all, in her blood. But then, she was no less like her mama, she reflected soberly.

Regina had given her heart to Charles Seton, and, after losing him, she had never given it to anyone again. With a pang, Constance realized that she very likely would be no different. She loved Vere with her whole heart and being. She could not see how there could possibly ever be anyone else. Indeed, she did not see how her mama had borne it, losing her love before she even had a chance to win her father's blessing, something that she had felt sure would be forthcoming once the duke learned he was to become a grandfather. The disgrace of wedding in secret would undoubtedly have been wrapped in clean linen had Seton lived. With Seton dead and Regina in a decidedly delicate condition, she had seen only scandal ahead for her father's house, her unborn child, and for herself. Blaidsdale had seen it, too. She must naturally have been in a state of shock and mourning over her loss when Blaidsdale so conveniently offered for her hand—for the second time. And afterwards, when she was his wife, he had not hesitated to remind her that in the eyes of the world Constance was his daughter. Were Regina to do anything so foolish as to try to return to her father's protection, he would make certain she never saw Constance again. It was little wonder that she had tried to make the best of what had turned out to be a bad bargain.

And then, after eleven years of living as a virtual prisoner to her husband's whims, she had gone out for her daily ride through the deer park. Certainly, it was no mere coincidence that James Rochelle, the Marquis of Vere, should have encountered her on the track winding through the forest. He must have been waiting to accost her. He had had in his possession, after all, the signed confessions of two felons attesting that Blaidsdale had engaged their services to waylay Charles Seton and put a period to his existence!

Faith, how she must have loathed the earl when she found out the truth of his deception! She had not hesitated to leave him. Only the need to protect Constance from scandal had induced her to use the confessions as assurance that Blaidsdale would never bother either one of them again. Otherwise, she would undoubtedly have turned them over to the King himself, and the devil fly away with Blaidsdale.

Blaidsdale, mused Constance, must have decided to put his fate to the touch when he concocted his scheme to marry her off to his nephew. Perhaps he had thought the confessions were lost when Regina succumbed to the wasting sickness. Obviously, Constance had not known of their existence, else she would hardly have come to Landford Park. Still, Blaidsdale had waited, biding his time, until he had felt sure of her. With Sinclair pressing him for funds to make up for his losses in his miscarried smuggling enterprise and Landford on the brink of ruin because of his gambling debts, he must have seen Constance as a means of ridding himself of at least one of his petitioners.

He could not have foreseen, however, that Constance would take it upon herself to make her escape. Nor could he have known that she would find her way into the arms of the one man whom he might least wish her to have as an ally. And now he must be wondering where Constance was and whether she had discovered the confessions that could send him to the gibbet.

Constance, picking up the packet, broke the seal. Inside, she discovered several sheets of paper covered in writing. Faith, it would seem that the two felons had had a deal to confess. But then, beginning to read, she soon realized that there was a deal more contained in the pages than the confessions of two hired assassins.

Several minutes later, she let her hands, still clutching the sheets of paper, drop to her lap. A great deal had been made suddenly exceedingly plain to her. Certainly, Vere would be more than interested in what the papers contained. His father had compiled them and given them into the safekeeping of Constance's mother. The signet with which they had been sealed was his.

The devil, she thought, *where was Vere?*

Kent Street, the main highway to the southeast of England, hardly offered a prepossessing welcome to visitors coming into what had long been touted as the greatest city in the civilized world. Long, dingy, and narrow, the street boasted dark, filthy houses into which were crowded the meanest dregs of London society. Near the crossing of Kent Street into Borough High Street stood a particularly disreputable gin house over which were located the lodgings of the proprietor, who had the distinction of occupying two rooms reserved to him alone. This, in an area of the city in which people were wont to live in squalor with as many as fifty to a room, distinguished him as a man of no little means.

But then, in addition to the proceeds from the gin house, he conducted a lucrative business lending money at exorbitant rates of interest.

While this latter enterprise would account for the peculiar nocturnal comings and goings on the back stairs of the sort of people one would not normally associate with Kent Street, it did little to explain why a gentleman of no little means should choose to live in his unwholesome environs. Clearly, he had the wherewithal to take up residence in a more genteel part of town. That he did not was due to his unasked-for affiliation with the Queen's Bench Prison on the west side of Borough High Street to which he had been sentenced as a debtor some four years previously.

While he had lacked adequate means to pay his creditors, he had possessed sufficient assets to purchase "the rules," an agreement by which he was allowed to live outside the walls in an establishment within a three-mile radius of the prison. In that respect, he was fortunate that he had not been assigned to nearby Marshalsea Prison, which offered no such liberties and lacked, moreover, the many pleasant amenities, such as wells with pure spring water, a coffeehouse, and various shops in which to purchase necessities that were provided in its more popular counterpart. The Marshalsea Prison Cemetery was a grim reminder of the many souls who had not been so fortunate as he.

Having descended in status, however, from a free man—one, moreover, who had once held a high position of trust with a family of wealth and nobility—he was wont to view his present condition in light of an unkind trick of fate. It was clear to Vere, viewing the bent and withered creature scuttling up the outside stairs at the back of the house, that Mr. Phineas Ambrose had degenerated to a physical and mental state equivalent with his surroundings. But then, morally, Ambrose had never been on an elevated plane. Having been caught abusing his position of trust, he had not hesitated to play the part of Judas.

Watching his father's former estate agent disappear into the rat hole that had become his proper milieu, Vere settled back into the shadows to await further developments. He was not kept long in a state of anticipation. Little more than ten minutes had passed before a gentleman, wrapped in a cloak and wearing a hat pulled down low over his forehead, made his appearance at the head of the alley. Making his way directly up the back stairs, he was soon admitted into Mr. Phineas Ambrose's lair.

A cold smile touched Vere's lips. It would seem Blaidsdale had at last closed his purse to his profligate younger brother, just as Vere had known that he would. With the uprising of Holkar of Indore against the East India Company, the earl's unwise speculation in the opium trade had cost him a pretty penny. Vice Admiral Sir Oliver Landford had turned to the only other source of funds available to him. No doubt he counted on his former henchman to allow him, out of purely sentimental reasons, a generous cut in interest rates.

It hardly mattered, however, since Landford would never be allowed to pay it back in any case.

His thoughts were interrupted by Landford's emergence on the landing above. Pulling the pistol from his belt, he waited for Sir Oliver to descend the stairs. Noiselessly, Vere stepped out of the shadows and followed Landford into the alley.

The arrival of the Earl of Blaidsdale at his Town House on Portland Square in early March was as unheard-of as it was unexpected. That he had come unaccompanied by his wife and his young heir was, to those of his household who scrambled to make the house habitable for their employer, unsettling to say the least. His lordship, it was clear, was in a devil of a mood, a state that was not alleviated by the convergence on the scene of his brother and brother-in-law almost before the earl had time to alleviate himself of all his dirt.

"Egad, the two of you have the look of whipped dogs," he observed with scant humor upon joining the two men in his study. "What the devil has happened now?"

"Nothing, save that I have been held up and most infamously robbed by that scoundrel, the Black Rose," declared Landford, mopping his flushed face with a linen handkerchief. "And now I shall not be able to buy back my gambling markers, let alone pay off Ambrose, the ungrateful wretch. He is charging me an exorbitant sum daily compounded."

"I daresay it is only what you deserve for going to a cent-per-cent," observed Sinclair, helping himself to a glass of his brother-in-law's brandy. "Especially one who holds a personal grudge against you. He blames you, after all, for his present circumstances. And how not when it was your miscalculation that prevented us all from profiting from Vere's gold? I daresay none of us would be pockets to let if you had got your information right."

"If *I* had got it right!" Landford uttered in wheezing accents. "It was Ambrose who informed me of it. The fourteenth of April off Alderney, he said. How was I to know the blasted yacht would run afoul of Llewellyn's squadron and be forced to take cover in a blasted cove until it was safe to come out?"

"Need I point out that you were a rear admiral at the time, old boy?" queried Sinclair, sniffing the liquid in his glass before taking a sip. "You were supposed to know that Llewellyn's squadron had been ordered home for repairs. That was your part in the plan, if you recall. To keep us all apprised of the movements of the navy's vessels. What was it? Too absorbed at the time with playing with one of your little poppets to take notice of the change in orders?"

"Why, you insufferable little popinjay," blustered Landford, turning purple in the face, "I shall cut out your bloody tongue and . . ."

"You will sit *down*, Oliver," uttered Blaidsdale with chilling deliberation. "Now."

Landford, going as white as he had been ruddy before, swallowed the bile in his throat. "Oh, very well," he said with a sniff. Sinking down on the sofa, he blotted his face. "Only, I beg you will do something about this Black Rose, Blaidsdale. You must see that I am in dire straits. Ambrose may be a sniveling weasel, but he has means of collecting his pound of flesh. You know that he has."

"Then let him collect it, for all I care," said Blaidsdale, patently unmoved at his brother's dilemma. "I have spent the past thirty-five years cleaning up after you, Oliver. Ever since Eton, when you committed the supreme folly of forcing yourself on young Whitney. You fool. Did you truly think Vere would not discover what you had done? Or Seton, for that matter? If Vere had not beaten you to within an inch of your life that summer at Weymouth, I should have done it for him."

"You needn't make it sound as if I did not give him back some of his own," blustered Landford.

"You broke his finger for him," the earl said scathingly. "You went after him with a cricket bat and the best you could do was break his bloody finger. And you could not wait to make a fool of yourself when there was no one around. You had to do it in front of the Duke of Westerlake's daughter."

"Regina, you mean," Landford sneered. "You cannot even say her name, dearest brother. She made a fool of you with Vere, and you cannot say her name."

Blaidsdale went very still.

"You forget yourself, Oliver," he murmured with a chilling lack of passion.

Landford noticeably fidgeted in his seat. "I beg your pardon, Edgar," he said, licking suddenly dry lips. "I spoke without thinking. It is just that I have been in such a state, what with Vere buying up my demmed markers, and then having to beg Ambrose for the blunt to pay them off, only to have that abominable Black Rose take it all from me. I swear I have not had a moment's rest, Edgar. I pray you will do something before it is too late."

Apparently satisfied, Blaidsdale released the squirming Landford from his protracted stare. "Very well, tell me about this Black Rose," he said, turning to stare out the bay window onto the square below. "When you exited Ambrose's filthy den, he must have been waiting for you, of course."

"But he wasn't, Edgar, I am sure of it," Landford demurred. "I went directly to the hackney cab without incident. It was not until I reached my lodgings. The cur appeared out of nowhere and accosted me as bold as you please right on St. James's Street, if you can believe it. 'Hand over your purse and your other valuables,' he says, 'and then you may be pleased to go on your way.' I swear he would have been happy to see me resist. He was that keen to cut my stick for me."

"And you, naturally, complied with his demands," surmised Sinclair, obviously vastly entertained at the thought. "Our intrepid vice admiral hastened to unburden himself of his valuables without so much as a whimper."

"And I suppose you would have done it differently," snarled Landford, turning on Sinclair. "*You* did not see his eyes. He wanted to kill me, I tell you."

"And yet he restrained himself," observed Blaidsdale, coming around. "I think we must ask ourselves why he should have done."

"I gave him what he wanted," insisted Landford. "Anyone would have done the same."

"And because he is a gentleman, he kept his word not to put a period to your existence?" queried Blaidsdale. "Curious, is it not?"

"I believe it is in keeping with the rumors going the rounds," Sinclair offered, his eyes watchful on the earl. "From all accounts, he is noted for his gallantry."

"And how are we to be sure that he was the Black Rose?" Blaidsdale asked, looking at Landford, who stared from one to the other of the two men rather in the manner of a rodent caught between two cats. "Did he announce himself as such?"

"No, of course he didn't. He gave me a bloody rose. And he was dressed all in black. It is perfectly obvious who he was."

"Yes, I shouldn't be at all surprised," said Blaidsdale strangely. "I daresay he is someone who is quite familiar to us. Someone, in fact, who knew you were in need of funds. Further, he must have been aware that you would not go to just any cent-per-cent. He knew you would go to Ambrose."

"Who, other than the three of us and Ambrose, would know that?" demanded Landford, clearly in a state of nonplus.

"He means Vere," Sinclair stated positively. "Vere has your markers in his possession, after all. Further, he has always suspected that Ambrose was somehow involved, along with us, in the loss of his parents. Still, it would seem far-fetched, Blaidsdale. Albert said he was looking directly at Vere when the Black Rose made his appearance at the hunting lodge."

"I should not draw renewed attention to Albert's fiasco, if I were you," Blaidsdale suggested coldly. "On the other hand, since you have, I might point out that the young fool also said Vere's cousin, Lord Huntingdon, was with him. If one wished to throw dust in the eyes of one's pursuers, what better way to do it than to present a decoy?"

"You mean Lord Huntingdon was dressed up in Vere's Black Rose disguise," said Landford, sitting up. "And who, I wonder, was the woman in the boudoir?"

"Who knows?" shrugged Blaidsdale. "One of Vere's numerous conquests. It hardly matters. What is important is the identity of the Black Rose. If it is Vere, you may be certain he is not through with us yet. I think it is time we set our minds to devising a little surprise for the Black Rose."

"I daresay you are right," agreed Sinclair. "In the meantime, however, there is the small matter of the missing heiress whom you promised to my son as a means of recouping my recent setbacks."

"You may thank Albert that she has apparently found a way to vanish off the face of the earth," declared Blaidsdale, ignoring the fact that she had originally slipped through his grasping fingers. "In his usual inept fashion, he has managed to lose her."

"Not altogether, my lord," Sinclair said, smiling conspiratorially. "As soon as it became clear to me that she had fled Somerset, I arranged to have someone keep a watch on her aunt's house. My man got a glimpse of her in one of the windows. Lady Constance, it would seem, has gone straight home to her Aunt Sophie. And that is not all."

"Well?" demanded Blaidsdale, when it seemed Sinclair meant to keep him in suspense. "I presume you mean to share your findings with us."

"Four days ago, a gentleman arrived at the house. He seemed in something of a pet. He went in, but he did not come out until early the following morning. My man gave a very detailed description, my lord. It was Vere. I have no doubt of it."

* * *

The mood that prevailed in the house on Plover Street was not one conducive to good spirits. It had been five days since Vere departed Constance's bed with the promise that he would return for her as soon as he found Ambrose. Left to fret over Vere's continued absence, not to mention the disturbing contents of the packet bearing Vere's seal, Constance was wearing herself thin with pacing. Nor did it help that she had lost her normally robust appetite. She picked at her food until Sophie was at last moved to threaten her with a strong dose of cod liver oil if she did not soon mend her ways. Indeed, restless and prone to sudden fits of temper, she knew all too well that she was poor company for Sophie and the colonel. Still, she could not help herself.

And how not? she thought irritably. It was not enough that she was worried to distraction about Vere, but she must also be shut indoors when she was used to going out in all sorts of weather. Faith, how she missed her early morning gallops in Hyde Park! Then, too, always before there had been afternoon calls to make to her numerous acquaintances and the occasional shopping sprees in Bond Street with her Aunt Sophie. In the evenings, there was nearly always dinner with friends, followed by cards or the theatre. Egad, how she chafed at being confined. Indeed, she was sure she would go quite mad if she were not soon allowed at the very least to stroll in the small garden at the rear of the house.

The devil, she thought, tossing aside the book that she had been unsuccessfully trying to read for the better part of an hour. Across the sitting room from her, Sophie was studiously occupied with her embroidery frame. A rueful smile twitched at the corners of Constance's lips. Things were come to a sad pass, indeed, if her aunt had been reduced to taking up needlepoint. Sophie detested handwork, which she was wont to claim had been designed for the express purpose of dulling the female brain.

"Embroidery, dearest aunt?" murmured Constance,

swept with an unwonted sense of shame for her less than exemplary behavior the past several days. "I have been a sad trial to you, have I not?"

Constance suffered an unwitting pang as Sophie's eyes met hers with a wariness that was not usually there. "You have been under a deal of strain, Constance," said her aunt carefully, "which, in the circumstances, is perfectly understandable. I daresay we shall all be relieved when his lordship returns."

"Nevertheless, it is unconscionable for me to cut up your peace and drive you to embroidery, best of all aunts." Taking the embroidery frame from her aunt and laying it aside, she pulled Sophie to her feet. "Come, dearest, to the kitchens. I find I have a sudden craving for chocolate. We shall indulge ourselves to excess on hot chocolate and whatever else we can find that is deliciously sinful until the colonel returns with the latest news from the outside world."

She was rewarded for her efforts at gaiety with a return of her aunt's ready affection. "You cannot know how glad I am to see you smile again, Constance. I pray you will forgive me for being a nagging female, but you really must try not to worry so. Vere will be back any time now. I know it."

"Yes, of course he will," agreed Constance, leading the older woman to the sitting room door. "And when he does, you may be certain that I shall . . ."

Whatever it was that she was certain to do upon Vere's return, Constance was not allowed to say. As she stepped out into the hall, powerful arms clasped her in a savage embrace. A cry of alarm leaped to her throat, never to be uttered as ruthless lips covered hers in a demanding kiss.

With a groan, she melted against her assailant's lean, hard strength, her arms reaching about his waist.

"Vere," she breathed when, no little time later, she was allowed to come up for air.

"Even so," murmured Vere, a smile playing about the corners of his lips as, lifting his head, he gazed down into Constance's face. Her passion had not cooled in his absence. She had responded to his kiss with the same fiery sweetness that had ever the power to make the blood leap in his veins. Egad, but she was even more beautiful than he remembered, was his titian-haired wife. Still, a frown darkened his brow as it came to him that her face was thinner than before and that her complexion had taken on an ivory pallor quite unlike the Constance who had stood on the decks of the *Swallow* with her face to the wind. Clearly, she had not taken well to being shut up in the house. But then, she was Constance. He should not have expected that she would. No doubt she would be pleased, however, to learn that her confinement was over, never mind that it meant she would be fleeing into danger.

"The devil, Vere," said Constance, reeling still from the heady rush of emotions that had swept over her to leave her knees trembling and weak. "What in heaven's name kept you so long? There is so much that I have to tell you."

"I am eagerly looking forward to hearing everything, *enfant*," replied Vere, dropping a kiss on her forehead. "Unfortunately, we shall have to postpone it for a while. You and your aunt are about to have visitors, whom you would do better to avoid at present. My carriage is waiting in back. There is only enough time for you to throw a few things together. Mrs. Ingram—"

"Sophie, if you please," calmly insisted that worthy. "You are, after all, my nephew now."

She was rewarded with one of Vere's rare, flashing smiles. "Sophie," he said, "when do you expect the colonel to return?"

"Any moment, I should think," Sophie answered a trifle doubtfully. "He was going to his club, he said. I suspect, however, he was intent on doing some reconnoitering. He has been convinced that the house is being watched."

"And so it is," confirmed Vere, ushering both women up the stairs. "Or was, in any case. I was careless in coming here before. An error I have since taken steps to rectify. Not before, however, Sinclair's spy was able to report to his employer. Quickly, now. Only enough for your immediate needs, my girl."

"But I am quite ready, Vere," declared Constance, pointing to her travel trunk and bandbox. "I have spent no little time the past several days thinking about any number of exigencies that might arise with your return. You may be certain that I did not fail to consider the distinct possibility that we might be forced to depart in haste."

"No, of course you did not," said Vere, properly humbled. "No doubt you have thought to prepare your abigail as well for a swift departure."

"How well you have come to know me, my dearest lord marquis," Constance said, smiling sweetly. Throwing on her ermine-lined pelisse, laid out in readiness on the sofa back, and donning her Gypsy hat with the veil and blue ribbons, she crossed to the bellpull and gave it three sharp tugs. "I really could not leave Millie behind, now could I?"

Vere, who had indeed come to know his bride better than she imagined, was hardly surprised to discover Millie, wearing her cloak and hat and clutching a straw valise in one hand, waiting at the foot of the servants' stairs.

"Beggin' your pardon, m'lady," said the girl, clearly frightened. "It's the earl and that other one. They're at the front door. Mrs. Gayle was just going to let them in."

It was only then that Constance, faced with leaving her aunt behind, was suddenly given to falter. "Vere, we cannot go—not yet. Not until the colonel returns."

"But of course you can," Sophie promptly insisted, ushering Constance through the kitchens to the servants' entrance. "I am quite looking forward to seeing my former brother-in-law. Besides, I have Will to protect me. And the colonel will be back at any moment. This is Plover Street in London, not the wilds of Somerset. Blaidsdale will not dare to raise a hand against me. So you see, I shall be perfectly all right."

"Nevertheless, I cannot like to leave you like this. Sophie, you do not know what Blaidsdale might be capable of."

At the sudden, importunate clatter of the door knocker, Constance went quite pale.

"Sophie—"

"Will be fine, my love," said Vere, taking her by the arm and urging her through the door. "You have a fine notion of my character if you think I have not provided for your aunt's protection." Handing her up into the carriage, followed in short order by the abigail, he stepped lithely in after them. "No doubt your aunt will be surprised to discover that her weekly meeting of the Ladies' Literary Society is about to converge on her." Pulling his pocket watch out, he checked the time. "Three o'clock. The ladies are, if nothing, punctual."

As the carriage swept out of the mews and into the street, Constance was given to see Blaidsdale and his brother-in-law in the midst of half a dozen ladies, waiting to gain admittance to her aunt's house.

"Vere, however did you manage it?" demanded Constance, settling happily back into the cradle of her dearest marquis's arm.

"Since we forced Sinclair's spy to talk, the colonel and Captain Roth have been busy delivering invitations. It seemed a better solution to the problem than setting men to guard the house. After all, this is Plover Street in the heart of London. An armed melee would not have been in the least *comme il faut*, you will agree. And now, my love, it seems we have some arch plotting to do. It occurs to me it is time I presented my marchioness to the world, do not you?"

Chapter 11

To say the appearance of a notice in the *Gazette* announcing the marriage of Miss Constance Hermione Seton and Gideon Edmond James Rochelle, Marquis of Vere, was one to cause a deal of speculation would have been to put the matter mildly. The very fact that Vere had fallen to Parson's Mousetrap would by itself have been sufficient grounds for tongues to wag in every salon and gentlemen's club. That he had fallen to the lures of one who had been supposed to be the only daughter of the Earl of Blaidsdale was enough to generate a bumblebroth of prattle. The added spice of the new marchioness's biographical claims, however, was to create a veritable feast for the scandalmongers.

All the old *on dits* from the Season of Lady Regina Lowell's come-out were brought out for airing, along with the speculations concerning the untimely demise of Charles Seton. Blaidsdale could hardly have been pleased to learn that he was variously cast as the cuckold, the dupe, or the opportunistic villain in the piece. The mere fact that everyone dismissed out of hand the notion that his motives for marrying Lady Regina might have been noble or benevolent served as incontrovertible evidence of the esteem in which Blaidsdale was generally held.

Blaidsdale never did anything for purely altruistic reasons. But then neither did Vere, it was noted with keen interest. It was generally held that the marquis had married Constance Seton out of motives of revenge and that the young beauty had been fool enough to fall for his deadly charm. The bad blood between Vere's house and Blaidsdale's was hardly a secret, after all. Speculation on Blaidsdale's expected reaction to the news that his stepdaughter had wed the son of his old enemy was only slightly more titillating than that regarding Albermarle's probable sentiments concerning the matter.

There was, in short, a taut air of expectancy surrounding the event of Vere's marriage that promised fair to occupy the gabblemongers for no little time to come. As well there should be, Vere reflected grimly, in light of most recent developments.

The papers that Mr. Josiah Enderhart had given to Constance had shed a deal of light on the affairs that must surely have led up to the premature deaths of his father and mother. That his father had chosen to leave them in Enderhart's keeping instead of Albermarle's left little doubt as to their dangerous nature. Obviously, he had known what Albermarle would do with them in the event of his son's death. A mirthless smile played about Vere's lips at the thought of an Albermarle moved to unleash the full extent of his wrath on the likes of Blaidsdale and his brother. It was doubtful that either house would have survived the repercussions of such an eventuality.

No doubt his father had known, as well, that to entrust his only son and heir with the proof would have been just as devastating to Gideon himself. It was one thing to know in his heart that Blaidsdale and Landford were guilty of his parents' loss. It would have been quite another to have had evidence of it when he was twenty. He would have had little choice but to act then, before he was fully prepared to do so with a cool head. His father must have realized that. He had chosen instead, after all, that Constance should be the one to discover them.

Clearly, Vere's father had believed Constance would not be brought to read the papers before she reached her majority. No doubt even as a child, she had demonstrated the same clear-headed thinking and shining courage that she possessed now as a woman. James Rochelle had trusted her to know how best to use the information contained in his carefully documented evidence of Landford's corruption and cowardice, evidence that should have convicted the then rear admiral of behavior unbecoming a King's officer. Instead, James Rochelle and his marchioness had died at sea with the evidence left in concealment until the day that Constance should grow to womanhood and discover it. In the meantime, Blaidsdale's wealth and influence at court had won Landford exoneration from all charges, along with a promotion to vice admiral.

Not for much longer, however, mused Vere. He had not waited to see the proof of their guilt before setting into motion events that would bring Blaidsdale and the others to retribution. As luck would have it, the announcement in the *Gazette* and the public reaction to it had become an unavoidable part of it.

Indeed, Vere, who had known what would result from it—indeed, had counted on it—was also depending upon Albermarle's *not* hearing about it for at least the week it would take for the *Gazette* to be delivered to Devon. The last thing Vere could wish was to have his grandsire find out about his nuptials from such a source. Ever unpredictable, the duke was perfectly capable of undertaking the arduous journey to London for the sole purpose of demanding an explanation from his heir. Which was why Vere had taken the added precaution of sending word of his marriage to Elfrida and Violet with a somewhat abbreviated explanation of who Constance was and why he had undertaken to make her his wife. His sisters would know how best to deal with Albermarle.

In the meantime, Vere could take some satisfaction from knowing he had made certain that Blaidsdale realized the futility of making any further efforts to force Constance into marriage with Albert Sinclair. In addition, Blaidsdale would be aware now that Constance had proof of her parentage and that, further, she was removed from his aegis, not only by her marriage, but also by virtue of her blood ties to Bridholm. In short, even if she were made a widow, she would still be under Albermarle's powerful protection, or Bridholm's, if she preferred. Blaidsdale no longer had any legal claim on her.

"Nevertheless, you are not safe from Blaidsdale's spite," said Vere, drawing Constance to him in his bed in his house on Berkeley Square. "In removing you from one threat, I have quite possibly made you the object of an even greater peril, *enfant.*"

"There is no threat so great that we cannot overcome it together, my dearest Gideon," returned Constance, who, only a little more than an hour earlier, had been borne across Vere's threshold and carried up the stairs to the master suite. There the enchanting aspect of a bridal repast laid out with champagne, red roses, and candlelight had greeted her. More delectable than dining on *potage crème de champignons, crêpes fruits de mer, asperges à la Gruyère,* and *carottes glacées* followed by strawberries covered in *crème frâiche,* however, had been Vere's hunger for Constance herself.

It was not that Vere had not made love to her during the five days since he had removed her from her Aunt Sophie's to Albermarle's Town House, for, in truth, he had come to her bed every night to transport her to delirious new heights of passion. It was only that he was different somehow in this, his own house.

She had felt it in the way he kissed her as he carried her across the threshold into the bedchamber—slowly, deeply, seeming to savor her and the uniqueness of the moment. Then, holding her as he let her legs slide sensuously down his muscular length until he set her on her feet, he had kissed her again, lingeringly, as if she were a delectable morsel of which he could not quite get enough. She had been acutely aware of his gaze on her as, banishing the silence with banter and small talk, they dined on the exquisite cuisine his newly acquired French chef had prepared especially for her. Faith, the smoldering caress of his look as, dipping a strawberry into thick cream, he had held it up for her to eat, had had a more intoxicating effect on her already aroused senses than did the champagne with which she washed the morsel down! Nor was that to be all or the most delicious part of this magical evening, which he had taken care to create for her and her alone.

At last, seemingly unable to pretend an interest in the food on the table, he had risen and, taking her hands in his, pulled her to her feet. In the candlelight his eyes were no longer remotely cool, but possessed of a light, piercing flame. They had held her, as he undressed her with slow deliberation, until at last she stood before him, the blood hot in her cheeks, but her head held high. With a groan, he bent his head to kiss her, as if she were some exquisite creature, when she was only Constance, who by chance had entrapped him into marrying her. Then, lifting her in his arms, he carried her to his bed before divesting himself of his own clothing.

His lips caressing her, his hands moving over her, he had made love to her with an aching tenderness and a fierce possessiveness in his touch that had never been there before. Now, lying deliciously sated in his arms, she could not but wonder if, in her delirium of bliss, she had only imagined it. He was Vere, after all, a man noted for his amorous conquests. And he, in the full sway of his masculine pride and passion, had never said that he loved her, only that he wanted her.

Still, she told herself, *she* loved *him* with every fiber of her being. Surely, it would be enough to sustain her. Indeed, it might have to be. Certainly, it was all that she had any right to expect. She, after all, had trapped him into marrying her, she reminded herself, as, reluctantly, she allowed Vere to turn her thoughts to contemplation of the ramifications of his most recent actions in placing the announcement in the *Gazette.*

"Now that Blaidsdale has begun to feel the walls closing in on him, he will move to strike back," said Vere, running his hand over the silken mass of Constance's hair.

"I should not be at all surprised, Vere," agreed Constance, snuggling closer to his lean strength. "Blaidsdale will not be in the least pleased that you have foiled his plans to replenish his brother-in-law's coffers with my fortune. And now he is perfectly aware that you are the source of Landford's difficulties, as well. You, after all, hold Landford's gambling markers."

"And how, my dove, have you garnered that singular tidbit of information?" queried Vere, his hand going still in her hair. The devil, he had intentionally allowed Landford to learn who the purchaser was, but not another soul had possessed the information. Not even the intermediary he used had known Vere's identity. And now his unpredictable bride had announced it as casually as if it were not a carefully guarded secret—egad! His beautiful Constance was proving a veritable fountainhead of information. He could not but wonder what she would spring on him next.

"How do you think I should have known it?" demanded Constance, looking like a contented kitten with her chin resting on the back of her hand placed on his chest. "The day that I escaped from Landford Park, I overheard Landford tell the earl. Blaidsdale was not in the least pleased, I can tell you. Just when he thought he could rid himself of Sinclair's problems, who should arrive but Landford, with problems of his own. I should think you would demand payment. Surely, Landford is close to his wit's end by now. What, precisely, are you waiting for, Vere?"

"For Blaidsdale to begin to feel the pinch in his own pocket," replied Vere, thinking that it could not be soon enough for him. With Constance in his arms in the wake of his lovemaking, he was aware of a growing impatience to have done with it. "As fate would have it, the earl has just suffered significant losses on the Exchange. He has, in fact, just learned that the market in opium has suffered a dramatic drop due to Holkar's uprising in Indore. He will soon begin to wonder at the source of his unexpected ill luck and then he will undoubtedly look to me."

"But why should he?" asked Constance, sitting up to look at him with incredulous eyes. "He can hardly blame you for the uprising in Indore. Not even your influence extends that far, Vere."

"No, you are quite right," agreed Vere, feeling his loins stir all over again at the mere sight of Constance in all of her womanly glory. "It does, however, extend to a particular broker in the Royal Exchange."

"A broker." Constance, pausing to consider the possibilities in that admission, was unaware of the effect she was having on Vere's powers of self-control. Vere, however, was acutely conscious of it. Indeed, he did not doubt that it would be wholly evident in little more than a matter of seconds. "Do you mean you persuaded Blaidsdale's broker to mislead his client into speculating on the Exchange? Vere, he could be banished from the Exchange for perpetuity for such a thing."

"He not only could, but would," agreed Vere, who was close to wishing Blaidsdale's unfortunate broker straight to the devil. "It was not quite so direct as that, however. On *Swallow*'s return voyage from France, we had the good fortune to meet an East India trading vessel on her way home to Bristol. Fortuitously, the captain was bursting with the news of Indore's rebellion. Armed with that intriguing tidbit four days before it was made public in London's papers, I did not hesitate to use it to my advantage."

"But of course you did not," Constance said with a conspiratorial smile. "You convinced Blaidsdale's broker—"

"Mr. Franklin Teasdale," supplied Vere with perfect gravity, and waited to see what his unpredictable bride would come up with to say about the business of stock trading.

"Mr. Teasdale," Constance repeated, nodding her head, "to—to do what, Vere? What does Indore have that the rest of the world would want?"

"Poppies, my never-ending delight. Fields and fields of poppies."

"Opium," extrapolated Constance, experiencing a warm wash of blood from head to toe at Vere's term of endearment. "Vere, you persuaded Mr. Teasdale to advise Blaidsdale to invest in the opium trade."

"It was a relatively simple matter," concurred Vere, thinking that, if he lived to be a hundred, he would never grow bored with Constance, his wife. "It required, in fact, only that I engage Mr. Franklin Teasdale in an anonymous purchase of a substantial block of shares in the commodity."

"Naturally, Mr. Franklin Teasdale did not hesitate to inform his biggest patron of something so significant."

"He did more than that. He took special pains to discover the identity of his anonymous patron. An East India nabob, as it turns out, who had made a fortune in speculating."

A frown darkened Constance's brow, only to dissipate almost immediately. "You made him up," she declared, giving a small bounce on the bed. "How very clever of you, Vere. Whom did you persuade to play the part? Not Caleb. He is much too young to pass for a nabob."

"I daresay you would not believe me if I told you, my sweet," said Vere, fast losing all interest in Teasdale and the opium trade and yet fully aware that he would fail abominably in trying to woo Constance off the subject before she had had her fill of it.

"It would have to be someone of substantial age, middle forties to late fifties, I should think," speculated Constance, unconsciously pressing the tip of her right index finger to pursed lips in a manner that Vere could not but find provocative in the extreme. "A gentleman or at least someone capable of portraying cultured manners and speech." She stopped, her eyes widening on Vere's. "Oh, good heavens," she exclaimed, "you used Collings! But, no, that cannot be right. Collings could never convince anyone that he was anything other than a butler, could he?"

"You might be surprised at the hidden talents that Collings possesses," said Vere, who was ruefully aware that he could not humor Constance's curiosity much longer. He was fast approaching a state of personal crisis. "It is true, however, that it was not Collings. I persuaded my man, Gresham, to play the part for me."

"Gresham," echoed Constance, clearly disappointed. On the other hand, she obviously could not deny that Gresham was no doubt the better choice. He was all of forty-five and possessed of distinguished-looking grey hair besides, not to mention a slender, upright build and, for a gentleman's gentleman, a spirit of adventure. The last was undoubtedly the one thing that had enabled him to tolerate his master's sudden starts with what amounted to a great aplomb. Besides, having been with Vere since the marquis first had need of a personal servant, he entertained a stolid loyalty, perhaps even a fondness, for his employer. "I suspect he did a perfectly famous job," granted Constance, sliding down once more so that she lay partially across Vere's chest. "Still, I should like to have gone on imagining Collings in the part."

"No doubt I am sorry to disappoint you, my love," said Vere, moved to plant a kiss in the palm of her hand. "If ever I am in the position to require a repeat performance, you may be sure I shall be moved to ask Collings first."

"Devil," said Constance, wrinkling her nose at him. "You will do no such thing. You know very well Collings would only turn you down. At any rate, Teasdale, convinced that Gresham was an East India nabob, went to Blaidsdale with what amounted to a tip. And Blaidsdale, as a result, invested a sizeable sum of money in poppies."

"Opium, my sweet," Vere corrected, taking advantage of her recumbent position to trail his fingers along the exquisitely sensitive curve of her back. "Actually he made a speculative transaction based on his belief that the shares were on the point of rising sharply. If he had been correct in his assessment, he most assuredly would have doubled, perhaps even tripled, his investment since a speculator is paid the difference between the fixed price and the price that he gave when the bargain was struck."

"But we know that the Indore uprising caused a sharp drop in the price," ventured Constance, following Vere's line of reason.

"Precisely," applauded Vere, who could only marvel at the quickness with which she arrived at the logical conclusion. "Blaidsdale was forced to pay the difference, which amounted to a pretty penny. I daresay he will feel more than a trifle disinclined to throw good money after bad."

"You mean he will be even less willing to help either Sinclair or Landford out of their difficulties." Immediately, Constance frowned. "But does that not mean that you have suffered a similar loss? I mean, you did make the same investment, Vere, did you not?"

"You need not worry that I have lost the family fortune, my sweet Constance. I paid the full asking price with the intention of staying in until the market recovers. I daresay Holkar will be put down in short order, upon which the shares will more than double in price. Would you be disappointed to learn that I expect to realize a tidy sum, my love?"

"I shall use it to refurbish Vere House, my dearest lord marquis," retorted Constance, smiling mischievously at Vere. Immediately, she sobered, however, as she added, "I should like it above all things to see it once more the way it must used to have been—full of laughter and gaiety. For Pinky and your mama, Vere. But money from opium," she added with a small, troubled frown. "Somehow it does not feel quite right, does it?"

"Those whose pain it is used to ease would hardly agree with you," observed Vere with only a hint of irony. Egad, he thought. He was, indeed, fast becoming a reformed character. "Still, if it bothers you, *enfant*, we shall find some other use for the profits. A charity, perhaps."

"A charity," agreed Constance, gazing down at Vere with eyes that shimmered in the candlelight. "Yes, I think that would be splendid. The house can wait for a later time."

Vere, awarded a dazzling smile, could only marvel at the fate that had placed his red-haired bride in his way. She could not know the striking picture of feminine loveliness she presented. Egad, she took his breath away, did his sweet Constance. More than that, she had breached his defenses and touched his heart in a way that he had long since ceased to believe was possible. With Constance, he could for the first time envision an end in sight to the dark, bitter task he had set for himself. With Constance, he could see beyond the years of brooding obsession to a return to life as he had once known it, a life in which he need no longer work alone and in secret toward a goal that seemed forever just beyond his reach. With sweet, generous Constance, he could foresee the sort of future that he had once taken for granted would be his and that he had thought forever taken from him.

It came to him that the duke would have found no little enjoyment in knowing Vere's thoughts at that moment. But then, Albermarle had ever a way of seeing to the heart of a matter, Vere reflected with a sardonic appreciation of his own unwonted plunge into sentimentality. He undoubtedly owed that chink in his armor to his spirited bride as well.

Then, without warning, he clasped strong arms about his sweet, incomparable wife. Rolling over on his side, he pulled Constance over with him and leaned over her, one hand propped on the pillow beside her.

Constance, startled at finding herself suddenly pinned beneath Vere's lean, hard strength, went suddenly still at the look in his eyes.

"You may do whatever you wish to refurbish Vere House, *enfant*," he murmured, lowering his head to press his lips to her neck where it met the soft curve of her shoulder. "*You* are all that is required to make it come to life again, as it once was."

Constance, rendered speechless by that unexpected pronouncement from Vere, experienced a sharp, melting pang in the vicinity of her breastbone. Faith, had her dearest lord marquis with the ice water in his veins truly just come very close to declaring that she was in some way necessary to his existence? Surely, she could not deny the blaze of warmth in his eyes. Nor could she dismiss the urgency of his hands moving over her, once more awakening, as only he knew how, the delirious flames of passion. She knew only one thing for certain, and that was that he needed her, fiercely, urgently.

With all of her strength she reached out to him. And when at last he took her, driving her and himself to a rapturous explosion of release that left them sated in one another's arms, she thought that she had never felt so close to any human being as she did at that moment to Vere.

During the days following that first night at Vere house, Constance was kept busy with preparing both the house and herself for the coming Season. When she was not meeting with decorators, painters, and drapers, she was occupied with modistes whom she had contracted to create a new wardrobe more in keeping with her new station. Then, too, there had been the necessity of hiring new servants to add to the skeleton staff Vere had kept during the lean years.

The entire third floor, along with the servants' quarters, had required drastic measures. New wall hangings, carpets, drapes, even linens had been necessary for those rooms that had remained vacant and unused since the passing of the previous marquis and marchioness. Fortunately, the kitchens had been completely refurbished only weeks before *Swallow's* ill-fated voyage. Henri Baptiste, Vere's recently acquired French chef, had not been discontent with his new domain, especially when he was provided with two additional downstairs maids, an assistant, and two kitchen girls to scrub the pots and pans.

The arrival of Mr. John Wilkers to fill the position of butler, however, was to mark a turning point in the chaos that had reigned for nearly a fortnight. Magically, order was restored. Workmen requiring instructions now went to Wilkers for their orders. The hiring of servants was left to his capable hands as well, along with the establishment of a hierarchy of duties among the staff. Suddenly, Constance was left with spare time to wonder what Vere was about during the daylight hours and oftentimes well into the night.

It was to come to her that perhaps it had been better when she was too occupied to think. It was only after Wilkers worked his magic, after all, that she began to sense a renewed air of secrecy about Vere. The devil!

She had thought all that sort of thing had been banished after that first night in the house. And, in truth, the change was so subtle that she could find nothing with which to take Vere to task. When he was with her, he was as attentive as ever before, even seeming to take a sincere interest in hearing her prattle on about the house, the servants, and the small daily domestic crises. At first, she had been gratified by his willingness to listen and even laugh with her over the little frustrations inevitable in so large an undertaking. Now, suddenly, she had begun to suspect that he was only too glad to have something to distract her from questioning him too closely about his own affairs!

And how not, when he was so damnably elusive, parrying her inquiries about how he had spent his day or whom he had seen or where he had gone with the adroitness of the fencing master that he was? Really, it was too bad of him.

It did not help in the least that, with the publication of the marriage announcement, callers had begun to drop by the house on an almost daily basis. Despite her Aunt Sophie's insistence that it would be perfectly understandable if she removed the front door knocker and informed Wilkers that she was not at home to callers until after the house was made presentable, Constance, conscious of her new position, felt that to do so would be thought exceedingly ungracious. She received them, with the result that she opened herself up to all the intentionally snide remarks, not to mention the gossip going the rounds.

It was soon made apparent to her that, while some thought her a sly puss for having lured the heir to a dukedom to the altar, the prevalent feeling was that she was the one who had been duped. Clearly, it was only a matter of time before Vere, having set out to embarrass Blaidsdale, would grow bored with the game and seek his pleasures elsewhere. A leopard, after all, did not change its spots.

Really, she could not but wish that she had listened to her Aunt Sophie. Having opened her door to the quizzes and tittle-tattlers, she could hardly close it now. To do so would serve only to give credence to the wretched rumors. Besides, she was demmed if she would show craven before a bunch of tongue-clucking hens! It simply was not in her nature to do so.

Nevertheless, despite the fact that she refused to be baited, she could not quite dismiss the distinct possibility that there was a grain of truth in all the rumors and speculations. Like a maw worm gnawing at her insides, she began to wonder if Vere had taken himself a lover. It little helped to remind herself that theirs had begun as a marriage of convenience and that, as such, he had every right to look for his pleasures elsewhere. Indeed, he had her assurances that she was perfectly willing to accept that he would in all probability continue to have kept women on the side. The truth was that she had been foolish enough to allow herself to believe that he might come to care for her one day. Worse, she had all but convinced herself that he *did* care for her a deal more than she had previously let herself ever hope that he might.

She had, after all, the endless wonder of the nights spent in his arms.

And, indeed, there was not a single night that he had

not come to her, sometimes to make love to her with a hard, driving urgency or at others with a slow, tender intensity that left her feeling all trembly inside with emotion. Faith, how she loved him! Or sometimes he came merely to hold her.

It was those times that, strangely enough, she felt the closest to him. Lying in the darkness relieved only by the firelight, after all, they were led quite naturally to talk. For the very first time, she was given to hear the story of how the red-haired adventuress, Genevieve Hayden, had stolen the Albermarle betrothal ring and, in so doing, forever won the heart of Edmond Rochelle, the Duke of Albermarle. Hardly less enthralling, however, had been the tale of the vision in a shew stone, which had led Elfrida Rochelle to win the heart of her astrologically predetermined mate, the unsuspecting Earl of Shields.

Clearly, the family into which she had married was not of the common order. They were, however, Vere's family, and despite the sardonic wit with which he described them, she could not but be brought to a sense of how much they all meant to him. Especially the duke, she realized with a growing sense of the significant role Albermarle had played in all of their lives and Vere's most in particularly.

She was brought to strongly suspect that it was Albermarle who, despite his own grief at the loss of his son, had kept the youthful Vere from wreaking immediate retribution upon those whom he presumed to be his father's enemies and therefore his own. It had been Albermarle, too, she did not doubt, who had instilled in Vere his strong sense of family pride, not to mention his own peculiar notions of what it meant to be a man and a gentleman bound to a gentleman's code of honor. Inescapably, it came to her to wonder how the duke would greet the news of Vere's marriage to Blaidsdale's stepdaughter.

Constance felt a queasy sensation in the pit of her stomach at the thought that the duke would hardly view it in a favorable light. Indeed, it came to her with dreadful clarity that he must surely see it as a calculated act on her part to entrap the heir to his dukedom in marriage. It was, after all, what many were already saying. More than that, it was far too close to the truth than was good for her own peace of mind. Nor did it help that she was all too keenly aware that Albermarle must naturally assume that she had done it for Blaidsdale, his sworn enemy. Really, it would seem a dreadful coil that she had made for herself.

The last thing she could ever wish was to become a bone of contention between Vere and his grandsire. She had seen what that sort of thing had done to her mama. Regina had felt the alienation from her family most sorely, as would Vere, if ever it came to that. Constance did not doubt that in the end he must surely come to resent her for it. He would never say it, but he must inevitably feel it. Indeed, perhaps he was already having second thoughts. He had yet, after all, to inform his grandsire of the marriage, and, furthermore, there was something that he was keeping from her. She was sure of it.

But then, there was something she was keeping from him, as well, she reminded herself, as she smoothed her blue satin gown over the flat surface of her belly. It was a secret that, afraid that she might yet be mistaken, she had been hugging to herself for the past two weeks. And, in truth, she was not prepared to put her fate to the touch before she knew beyond the smallest doubt that she could not be in error. Nevertheless, she could not quell the suspicion that she carried, growing within her, the seed of the next Albermarle heir.

And therein lay the crux of her dilemma, she thought, turning away from the ormolu looking glass in her bedchamber and flinging on her pelisse. If she were increasing, she would indeed have entrapped Vere in marriage. Faith, what a silly fool she had been ever to think that there was the smallest possibility she could simply give him his freedom if things did not work out as she had hoped that they might. For what had supposed to be a marriage of convenience, it would seem that matters were becoming absurdly complicated, she reflected, as, picking up her reticule, she exited the chamber and made her way downstairs to the foyer.

Weary of being cooped up in the house with her unrewarding thoughts, she had ordered the carriage brought around to the front. Sophie had invited her yesterday to go on a shopping spree in Bond Street. Feeling just a trifle rebellious, she had accepted, never mind that she was quite sure Vere would not have approved, which was why she had not bothered to tell him about it. She would have Mr. Finney with her, after all. The former pugilist whom Vere had engaged to accompany her if ever she went out should serve to discourage anyone from approaching her. And she would have Will Trask at the reins, not to mention Colonel Ingram's pocket pistol in the placket pocket of her dress.

Seeing Wilkers waiting at the door, she straightened her shoulders in an unconscious air of defiance.

"Wilkers, I am going shopping in Bond Street with Mrs. Ingram, and afterwards, I may join my aunt for dinner. If his lordship should inquire, you may tell him that I should be home no later than eleven tonight."

"Very well, my lady," responded the butler, opening the door for her and standing back at stiff attention. "Er—I beg your pardon, my lady," he added carefully. "Shall I just have the drapers come back tomorrow then?"

Constance, thus gently reminded that she had been supposed to pick out the drapery fabric for the formal dining room that afternoon, quelled the urge to stamp her foot in an unseemly display of vexation. Instead, she summoned a rueful smile.

"Dear, you are quite right, Wilkers," she said with disarming frankness. "I had indeed forgot. Pray tell Mr. Hodges that I have decided on the floral design, will you? I should not like him to have come all this way to no purpose."

"As you wish, my lady," replied Wilkers, never revealing by so much as the blink of an eye what he thought of that sort of condescension from one of his mistress's exalted station. It was hardly the common practice among the gentility to think of the inconvenience that might be caused a tradesman. Clearly, her ladyship was not cut of the usual mode. But then, he had seen that from the very first. The marchioness was a lady in the truest sense of the word.

Constance, unaware that she had just made a conquest of her butler, placed her hand in the ham-like fist of Mr. Finney, who, with his large frame and the distinguishing marks of a broken nose and cauliflower ears, resembled a hulking brute. She could not but wonder how Vere had come to know the former pugilist, as she allowed the giant to help her mount into the carriage, then, thanking him, settled gratefully back against the squabs. Despite his unprepossessing first impression, Finney, she had come to suspect, was a gentle giant who simply because of his size had fallen by happenstance into the uncertain career of a prizefighter.

Still pondering Finney's probable history and Vere's part in it, she failed to note the curricle and pair pull out from the curb three houses back and follow after her. But then, neither did she see a slender figure leave the house by way of the mews and, hailing a hackney coach, depart in the opposite direction.

"You are creating a tempest in a teacup, Constance," declared Sophie no little time later, as the carriage turned into Bond Street and came to a halt in front of Madame

Laverne's Millinery Shop. "I daresay every newly wed-
ded couple has these little misunderstandings. Why, even
I was foolish enough to think that our marriage had
palled on the colonel. And all because he would make
excuses to leave the house at the oddest times. You cannot imagine my consternation when at last I confronted
him only to learn that he had been afraid to smoke his
cigars in my house. *My* house, Constance. As if it were
not our home and just as much his to do in it whatever
he might wish. He has his own private study now where
he can feel perfectly comfortable with his nasty cigars."

"I fear it is not a matter of cigars with Vere, Sophie,"
observed Constance, smiling in spite of herself. "Indeed,
I do wish that were all it was."

"And how do you know it is not if you do not ask
him?" Sophie persisted with all the assurance of a married woman of vast experience. "You must simply talk to
Vere, my dear. Tell him about all the mean and spiteful
things that people have said to you. Then ask him if
there is something he is not telling you. Let him know
that you are troubled. You will find that that is the best
way to iron out these little difficulties. It always works
for the colonel and me."

"Yes, but you did not trap the colonel into marrying
you against his will, Sophie," insisted Constance, ab-
sently tugging at the strings of her reticule.

"And neither, I daresay, did you," retorted Sophie, as
close as she had ever been to losing all patience with
her niece. "It is as clear as the nose on your face that
Vere loves you, Constance. You cannot tell me that he
would go to such extreme lengths to marry you, not to
mention provide for your protection, merely out of some
absurd gentleman's code of honor. You really must stop
thinking that he is some sort of a saint, child. He is the
Marquis of Vere, and from all that I have ever heard of
him, that means he is every bit a man of flesh and blood."

Constance, who could not deny that final statement—

indeed, was all too aware of its truth, yet could not convince herself that love was the motivating force behind his actions. Sophie, after all, did not know him the way that she did. Constance did not doubt in the least that his gentleman's code of honor would indeed have led him to do all that he had done. It was precisely what made him who he was.

"No doubt you are in the right of it, dearest Aunt," she said nonetheless. "Forgive me. I should never have made you the brunt of my absurd misgivings. I pray you will forget everything I have told you."

"Now you *are* being absurd," scolded Sophie, allowing Mr. Finney to help her out of the carriage and waiting for Constance to join her on the walk. "I should be terribly upset with you if ever I thought you did not feel free to confide in me. You are, after all, the closest I shall ever come to having a child of my own."

Having spoken with the intent of comforting Constance, Sophie was hardly prepared to see tears suddenly well up in Constance's eyes.

"You cannot know how much you mean to me, dearest Aunt," said Constance, hastily turning away. "I shall always be grateful that you took me in when Mama . . ."

"Constance, for pity's sake," exclaimed Sophie, drawing the younger woman into the milliner's shop away from prying eyes. "What is it? In all the years that I have known you I have never seen you like this."

"It is absurd, is it not?" sniffed Constance, with a watery laugh. "Truly I don't know what has come over me. No doubt it is only a cold coming on. I shall be fine, I promise you. I daresay a hat and a new pair of shoes will serve to fix everything."

As there just happened to be, directly in front of the two women, the most fetching straw bonnet done up with green ribbons and bedecked with a feather dyed to match the silk trimmings, the cure was put into immediate effect. In fact, by the time Constance and Sophie departed the shop of an exceedingly happy Madame Laverne, they had purchased between them two bonnets and three pairs of shoes with a blue beaded reticule to go with one of the pairs. Nor was that the end of the spree, which was to take them next to Mr. Zachariah Sedgewick's Haberdashery to look at ribbons and some particularly lovely combs to be worn in the hair.

They were, in fact, so thoroughly wrapped up in trying to choose between the cloisonné and the pearl combs that they utterly failed to notice when the door opened to admit a tall figure draped in a black many-caped greatcoat and wearing a curly-brimmed beaver beneath which glittered a pair of hard, gimlet eyes.

"I really cannot make up my mind," declared Sophie to Constance, who was equally in a quandary. "The pearl would perfectly complement my ivory jaconet chemise robe with the pearl embroidery and the mother-of-pearl buttons. The cloisonné, on the other hand, is just what I need for my new Spanish frock in Valenciennes lace."

"Then naturally you must have them both," said Constance, who did not doubt her aunt would never forgive herself if she chose one at the expense of the other. "You purchase the ivory, and I shall make you a gift of the other. That way I shall not feel in the least guilty when I wish to borrow one or the other from you."

"Oh, but I would not dream of letting you do that, Constance," Sophie protested, setting down the cloisonné with every manifestation of reluctance. "You know very well that you would never ask to borrow either one of them, and then I should be the one to feel guilty."

"Better you than I, dearest Sophie," laughed Constance, picking up the cloisonné and reaching to open her reticule. She turned with the intention of summoning the proprietor to inquire as to the price—and came up hard against a rather large, immovable object draped in black Superfine.

"I beg your pardon," she exclaimed, glancing up. "I

was just . . ." She stopped, a sudden, peculiarly queasy sensation in the pit of her stomach.

"On the point of purchasing a comb for your aunt," a thrillingly masculine voice finished for her. "An excellent choice, by the way. Only, I shall be pleased to purchase it for you. It occurs to me, after all, that I have yet to thank Sophie for putting up my wife."

"But you must know it was my pleasure," said Sophie. "Indeed, I am always happy to have Constance come for a visit."

"Vere!" interjected Constance, recovering both her voice and her equilibrium. "Where in heaven's name did you come from?"

"Originally from the south of Devon," replied his lordship whimsically, extracting the comb in question from Constance's nerveless grasp and handing the proprietor coins enough for both folderols. "More recently, however, from Tattersall's, where I was in the process of purchasing a sweet goer when I was rudely interrupted by a message from Wilkers to the effect that her ladyship had disobeyed my orders."

"What a cawker," declared Constance, awarding Vere a comical moue of displeasure. "Wilkers would never be so coming as to write any such thing."

"No," Vere readily conceded, escorting both ladies out of the haberdashery, "but he did send a messenger. No doubt young Thompkins got the wording wrong, but not, you will agree, the essence. You are here, after all."

"Yes, and why should I not be?" demanded Constance, her eyes flashing blue sparks of anger. "I cannot remain cooped up forever, Vere. You know very well that I cannot. You may be sure that I took every precaution, including bringing Mr. Finney with me. And if he is not enough, I have my pocket pistol with me," she added, extracting the weapon from her pocket to show it to him. "You are well aware, Vere, that I know perfectly well how to use it."

"Constance, for heaven's sake," gasped Sophie, clearly aghast at her niece's temerity in carrying a loaded weapon in her skirts about Town. "Pray do be careful. You might shoot someone."

Hardly had those words left her mouth than the nerve-splitting crack of a gunshot rent the air.

Sophie uttered a scream. Vere, grabbing at his arm, spun halfway around. Constance, coming about, lifted her gun and fired.

Chapter 12

It was all over in a matter of a few seconds. At Constance's snap shot at his retreating back, the would-be assassin appeared to lurch forward. Then, catching himself, he fled, stumbling, away down the street to vanish around the corner occupied by the house of Blackwell & Son, Ltd. Constance, stuffing the pistol back into her pocket, reached for Vere even as Finney, burdened with parcels, lumbered toward them.

"The devil, Vere," said Constance, spotting the well of blood between the fingers clutched to his arm. "You're hurt!"

"Softly, my girl," Vere said with a grimace. "It is nothing to signify. The ball creased me. I am not like to die of it. Unfortunately, the same cannot be said for my greatcoat, not to mention my coat. I shudder to think what Gresham will have to say to it."

"Idiot!" declared Constance, glancing sharply up to see the wry gleam of humor in his eyes.

"Yes, no doubt," Vere agreed philosophically. He was, indeed, cursing himself for what would seem a singularly witless lack of vigilance as Constance set herself to

try and rid him of his aforementioned apparel in order
to see the extent of the wound in his arm. The devil, he
thought, keenly aware of the targets they made even now
on the street. "Finney, rid yourself of those demmed
parcels and get the ladies into the carriage."

"Yes, milord," rumbled Finney, turning to look up
the street for Will Trask, who, weaving through the maze
of horses and vehicles, pulled up with a flourish at the
curb beside them. With a quickness rare for one of his
size, Finney gained the carriage and thrust the parcels
inside.

"Beggin' your pardon, milady," he said, reaching next
for Constance, who was in the process of easing Vere's
arm out of the sleeve of his outer garment.

"I shall be only a moment, Finney," said Constance,
as she reached next to undo the buttons of Vere's coat.
It was on her lips to add that she could reach the carriage perfectly well by herself when Finney forcibly interrupted her by clamping huge hands about her waist.

"*Vere?*" gasped Constance, her eyes wide with bestartlement. Vere could only watch in something resembling
stunned amusement as Finney, picking her up off her
feet, lifted her bodily toward the carriage. "Vere, you
devil!" she cried.

Next, Finney, turning to Sophie with singular determination, took a purposeful step forward.

"That will be quite enough, Finney," Aunt Sophie hastened to say, stepping with alacrity up to the carriage.

"It is all right, Finney," Vere intervened quietly. He
handed Sophie up, then turned to Finney. "My curricle
is waiting down the block. Be so good as to tell Vickers
to meet me at the Town House. You will ride with him."

"If you are sure, milord." The big man shuffled his
feet. "Beggin' your pardon, milord," he said. "I never seen
the bugger till it was too late. Belike you'll be wanting
some'un else to look after her ladyship."

"Pray tell, who would that be?" Vere closed a hand on

Finney's arm. "I am depending on you, Finney. Now go and do as I told you."

"That was kind of you," said Constance, as Vere stepped into the carriage and sank down on the seat beside her. "It was hardly Finney's fault. It happened far too quickly. I daresay there was nothing that anyone could have done to stop it."

"Perhaps," murmured Vere, less than satisfied with the recent unfolding of events. Then, "Did you see him, Constance?"

Constance did not pretend not to understand to whom Vere was referring. "I not only saw him," she replied, reaching once more to undo Vere's coat, "I am reasonably certain that I shot him."

Vere's hand clamped around Constance's wrist. "Then perhaps, my love," he said ever so gently, "you can tell me who the devil it was."

"It was Lord Sinclair, Vere," she said, looking him straightly in the eyes. "I could not be mistaken in that."

Releasing her, Vere settled back against the blue velvet squabs. "So, at last he has come out of hiding." He turned his head to Constance. "And you say that you hit him."

"I seldom, if ever, miss what I aim at," Constance calmly assured him. Helping him to pull his arm from the sleeve of his coat, she ripped the blood-soaked shirt-sleeve from wrist to shoulder. "Fortunately, the same cannot be said for Lord Sinclair," she said, the vise grip on her heart easing at sight of the deep, angry furrow, high up on the outside of Vere's left arm. Thank heavens. It would be painful for a number of days, she thought, but there would seem little danger of his losing his arm.

"Sophie," she said, "I shall have need of Vere's neck cloth."

No little time later, after the departure of the doctor who had redressed Vere's wound, Constance turned to look at Vere. Dressed in a magnificent example of the *dishabillé*, which, bound at the waist, served perfectly to accentuate his broad-shouldered, narrow-hipped frame, he was staring broodingly down at the leap of flames in the fireplace. He was, she knew, blaming himself for their narrow escape from a would-be assassin when, really, she supposed it was her fault for having selfishly thought only of herself and her wish to escape the house for a while. And yet, it had never occurred to her that Sinclair would go so far as to stalk her with the intent of cutting her stick for her. Indeed, how could it? It was one thing to wish to marry one's son to an heiress by force. It was quite another to shoot the golden goose because she had wed another. And yet that is what Vere believed Sinclair had intended, until he had seen the opportunity to make her a widow instead.

Nevertheless, she could not but feel there were still things about the afternoon's events to which she had not been made privy. And then she recalled Vere's earlier words. Even then, in the coach, they had struck her strangely.

"My dearest lord marquis," she said suddenly. "It is time, I think, we had a talk." Deliberately crossing to him, Constance put her hands on Vere's chest. "Tell me about Sinclair. You said that he had come out of hiding. What did you mean by that?"

Vere made no attempt to evade her question. Drawing her to the overstuffed chair before the fireplace, he sat down and pulled her across his lap. "Sinclair," he began, "is a desperate man. No doubt you have guessed that he was in greater need of your fortune than you realized."

"From some of the things that Mama was used to say, I am hardly surprised," replied Constance, wondering where Vere was leading. "He apparently was never very good at staying beforehand with the world. Blaidsdale was constantly having to bail him out."

"He would seem no longer to have that option. Blaidsdale, it appears, has closed his purse strings for good." Thinking that, indeed, the fate that had dropped Constance into his life would seem to work in mysterious ways, Vere ran his hand over the silken mass of her hair. "Would it surprise you to learn that I have known for some little time that Sinclair's estate was heavily mortgaged? That it was, in fact, the contributing factor that led me to induce Sinclair to participate in my little smuggling venture when I did?"

"I daresay that nothing would surprise me where you are concerned, Gideon," said Constance, leaning her head against his shoulder, seemingly conveniently placed there for that very purpose.

A faint, wry smile touched Vere's handsome lips. "No doubt I should take that as a compliment," he said with only the barest hint of irony.

"I am sure that is how I meant it, Gideon," Constance replied dulcetly. "You were, however, telling me about Sinclair."

"And you, I am convinced, would not rather engage in something a deal more interesting than discussion of a cowardly wretch," speculated Vere, feeling, with Constance so sweetly on his lap, the distinct stirrings of primitive male passions. "No, I did not think you would," he added with a sigh that was only partly feigned. "Very well, since there is no dissuading you. Sinclair has been unable to raise the wind to the extent that he now finds himself on the rocks. I have it from a reliable source that not only has Lady Clarissa removed herself to Landford Park, but Sinclair's estate is about to go under the gavel. As for Sinclair, he reportedly availed himself of his wife's jewels and walked out on the day that our wedding announcement appeared in the *Gazette*. He had not been seen since, until today. Now perhaps you understand why I have been so insistent on your remaining in the safety of the house."

If he had thought by that concise summary of events

to turn Constance's thoughts at last to more pleasurable pursuits, he was soon to be proven vastly mistaken.

"The devil, Vere." Constance bolted upright to stare at him with eyes of dire enlightenment. "*That* is what you have been doing these past two weeks!" she exclaimed, thinking suddenly that, indeed, a great deal would seem to make sense. "You have been trying to find Sinclair." She clapped the palms of her hands against his chest. "Why the deuce did you not tell me?"

The devil, thought Vere, arching a single, arrogant eyebrow sharply toward his hairline, what in hell's name was this? "There seemed little point in worrying you with it," he said, and indeed, having taken a lesson from Shields, his brother-in-law, he had been more than happy to have his headstrong young wife occupied with domestic pursuits for a while. "Caleb and I were sufficient to the task."

"Were you?" Constance pushed herself to her feet to stand facing her infuriatingly arrogant husband, her hands ominously on her hips.

He stared back at her, his eyes narrowed in sudden intense concentration on his wife's animated visage.

"No doubt you will pardon me if I take exception to that assertion," said Constance, who, in the wake of recent events, suddenly could not stop herself from giving vent to all the things that had been building up inside her—indeed, she had no wish to have done. "You did not find him, and you left me at home to fret over what you were doing the past fortnight. And if that were not all or enough, you abandoned me to face the insinuations and speculations of the tittle-tattlers and gossipmongers over afternoon tea." Falling into pacing about the room, she gave an eloquent gesture of the hand. "I have put up with the Mrs. Smythes and the Lady Fortescues who feel that, for my own good, they must warn me about the profligate nature of my husband, who will undoubtedly keep a whole *string* of high-steppers, if not his own bagnio, to relieve himself of the boredom of having a wife. Still, I am to be congratulated on having had the brass to lure him to the altar. Having failed, after all, to secure a husband before I was at my last prayers, I am clearly lacking in both countenance and polish, a fact which his grace will undoubtedly consider to be evidence enough that I am at heart a cold, calculating adventuress. And all the time *you* were out combing the streets for Sinclair, *I* was left to wonder what the devil it was that you were keeping from me!"

Vere, who had risen grimly to his feet at the very beginning of what had become a full-fledged tirade, took this opportunity to step in front of his distraught wife, a maneuver that effectively brought a halt to her agitated pacing. She stood stiffly erect, her face white and her eyes staring at him with a curiously stricken expression. Then wordlessly, Vere drew her into the circle of his uninjured arm and held her.

"It would seem," he said quietly after a long moment, "that we have both erred in keeping secrets that were better brought out in the open. I sincerely beg your pardon, Constance, for failing to realize that you were putting on a front for my benefit. If I have any excuse for my behavior, it is that I wished to spare you unnecessary worry. Obviously, however, I only added to your distress. I regret that more than you can possibly imagine."

He was rewarded for that forthright, not to mention unwonted, apology with what gave every evidence of being a watery burble of laughter.

"Faith, what a peagoose you must think me," gasped Constance, lifting rueful eyes to look at him. "You cannot know the terrible things that came to mind after those horrid women planted their seeds of doubt. In truth, I cannot think what came over me. I am normally accounted to be a female of no little common sense."

Vere, folding her to him, pressed his lips to the top of her head. "I think, my impossible girl, you refine too much on it. It hardly matters what others think of us. You are the Marchioness of Vere, Constance. They will all be looking to you to know how to go on."

"That is easy for *you* to say," retorted Constance, leaning her cheek against his hard, masculine chest, bare beneath the fabric of his robe. "You were born to the position. I have only recently gone from being a no-man's child to finding myself married to the heir to a dukedom. You will admit it takes some getting used to."

"Now you are being absurd, my poor, misguided Constance," said Vere, thinking that his dearest delight had indeed been having a bad time of it to entertain such doubts in herself.

A bleak look darkened his eyes at the thought of how near he had brought her to danger that day. He doubted not that Sinclair had been stalking her with the intent of abducting her for ransom. Only, Wilkers had remarked the carriage a short way down the street and, suspicious, had not hesitated to send word to Vere, as he had been instructed to do in the event of an emergency. It had been that close, and all because he had been neglecting her of late. It was time he made it up to her.

"You are the granddaughter of a duke on one side and of an earl on the other. I fail to see how you can think you were not *born* to it. On the other hand, it does occur to me that you are worn out from working yourself too hard. I daresay what you need is a good night's rest followed in the morning by a gallop in Hyde Park."

"Really? I should like that above all things, Vere." Constance lifted her head to favor him with the full force of her eyes in which, Vere did not fail to note, was contained a gleam of mischief. He felt his loins leap at the sight of her. "Does that mean you will let me ride Dark Reverie? My own mount, after all, is still at the hunting lodge in Somerset."

"It does not mean that at all, Lady Malapert," said Vere, who did not doubt his dauntless Constance would not have hesitated to take him up on it if he were fool enough to make such an offer. "Dark Reverie, I am convinced, would take exception to being ridden with a sidesaddle. And, no, my irrepressible marchioness, you will not appear in Hyde Park wearing breeches and riding astraddle."

"Pooh," retorted Constance with an unladylike grimace, which made him wish to take her right then and there on the Oriental rug on the floor if necessary. "Really, it is the shabbiest thing." Lightly running her index finger from his lips down over the slight cleft in his chin to the strong column of his neck, she said, "I am, if you must know, a bruising rider."

The little minx, thought Vere, his blood leaping hot in his veins. How dared she use feminine foils against him! It was time she was taught a lesson in what it meant to arouse his masculine ardor.

"I should be surprised only if you were not," he growled, silencing any further protest by covering her mouth with his.

Really, it was not in the least fair, thought Constance, feeling herself melting irresistibly against Vere's tall frame. He had ever the power to scatter her thoughts and tumble her defenses. On the other hand, there was a deal to be said for postponing an argument until a later date, she decided, as Vere released her lips to kiss the exquisitely tender place beneath her left earlobe, then farther down, to the soft swell of her bosom above the square décolletage of her gown. And he had, after all, promised her a ride on the morrow in Hyde Park.

Giving herself up to the inevitable, Constance turned her energies to the more profitable business of unfastening the sash at Vere's waist, a task that revealed Vere, bare to the tops of his breeches beneath the anklelength robe. Reminded with a rending pang of the fear she had felt at sight of his bloodied coat sleeve, she slid her arms hard about him. And still it was not enough.

Pressing her lips to his chest, she reached to undo the fastenings at the front of his unmentionables.

Vere, who was equally occupied with working to release the plethora of tiny pearl buttons at the back of Constance's bodice, could only be exceedingly grateful that Sinclair's bullet had spared his right arm. He wanted Constance, even if it meant ripping the bloody dress off her to do it. And in truth, hampered by the cursed wound, he was sorely tempted to take her with all of her blasted clothes on.

It seemed that Constance was of a similar mind. Having released Vere's already magnificently erect male member and in no mood to address herself to the problem of removing his boots, she shoved him backward into the chair that he had only recently vacated.

"No doubt you will pardon me, my dearest lord marquis," she said to her considerably startled husband. Lifting her skirts, she yanked the bow loose at the waist of her drawers. "I fear I am a shameless wanton. It seems I have a particular desire to ride astraddle, and this," she added, stepping out of her shoes and letting her drawers slide down her legs, "would seem the quickest way to go about it."

"As it happens, I have always entertained a singular fondness for shameless wantons," confessed Vere, who could only applaud his wife's originality. "And this, after all, is not Hyde Park."

"Devil," said Constance, as, holding her skirts up, she mounted with a knee planted on either side of Vere's hips. There was, she decided, something deliciously wicked about being astride her dearest marquis. The only thing was, she was not sure what to do next.

Vere, who *was* certain, slipped his hand between her thighs. She was magnificent, was his sweet, wanton marchioness, he thought, finding her already slick with the dew of arousal. Experimentally, he slipped a finger inside her.

Constance, grasping the back of the chair, instinctively lifted herself, a keening sigh breathing through her lips. Quickly, Vere fitted the head of his swollen shaft against the vulnerable lips of her body. "It would seem, my beautiful Constance, that we are poised and ready. Now it is all up to you to take us where you will."

Constance, who was never a slow learner, was quick to grasp the unique possibilities in her present position. Casting all caution to the wind, she lowered herself onto Vere's waiting blade. Vere's groan of anguish only served to whet her appetite for more. She lifted herself again, then with agonizing slowness, filled herself once more with him.

"Jade," rasped Vere, his eyes smoldering points of flame.

And, indeed, her dearest lord's face wore a wooden expression. His breath came harsh in his throat. And the sweat stood out in beads on his forehead. Clearly, he was at her mercy.

Running her hands over his chest, she felt his nipples hard with need and marveled that she had never before realized that she, no less than he, possessed the power to drive them both to the delirious heights of ecstasy. Always before she had relied on Vere to take her there. Now she discovered that she was possessed of a cruel streak that she had never before known that she had. And in truth, she could never have dreamed that she would derive such sweet pleasure from unmercifully teasing and tantalizing her beloved marquis.

"Witch," groaned Vere, in a bloody agony of suspense. Egad, she was like to drive him mad with it.

Upon which, it came to Constance on a wave of tenderness that she had never known anyone quite so generous as Vere. He, after all, had surrendered himself to her.

"Faith, Gideon," she gasped, "I do love you so. So much so that I think I should die if ever I lost you."

A blazing light flashed in Vere's eyes. Before he could summon an answer, however, Constance, lowering her head, kissed him fully on the mouth. Then, at last no longer able to contain her own mounting need, she gave herself up to a frenzied rhythm that carried them both to a rapturous release.

In the days that followed Sinclair's thwarted attempt to cut Gideon's stick for him, Constance was to notice a decided change in Vere's demeanor toward her. Before, he had been wont to leave immediately after breakfast to return long after the sun had gone down. Now it had become his practice not only to take her riding each morning in the early hours of dawn, but also to appear without warning at her side at odd times during the day.

Certainly, she was never to forget the morning of her first gallop in Hyde Park with Vere at her side.

She had awakened at first light to Vere's lips brushing feather-light against her brow and the admonishment to hurry and dress if she wished to indulge in a gallop in the park before the fashionables were wont to arrive. Sensing something in his manner, she had made short work of donning her riding habit and allowing Millie to pin up her hair. Then, descending the stairs, she had been made to feel as silly as a schoolgirl as Vere, maddeningly inscrutable, had mysteriously covered her eyes before leading her out into the mews.

For once, it seemed that Vere had been telling her nothing but the truth when he claimed that he had been engaged at Tattersall's the day before in the purchase of a sweet goer. The stallion, white as the driven snow and with the unmistakable signs of the Godolphin Arabian in his wide-placed eyes and scooped face, was a dainty stepper. Small, but clean-limbed and showing speed and endurance in his every line, he was a magnificent creature. His name was Shaheen, the White Falcon. And he was Vere's wedding present to her.

Faith, how she loved him—and Vere, for giving him to her! And how she gloried in their rides, wholly abandoned and thrillingly improper, through the genteel environs of Hyde Park.

Her much-treasured morning outings with Vere were not the only manifestations of change in him, however. There was also the memorable occasion of his first appearance at afternoon tea.

How very like the arrogant marquis to drop in unannounced!

Constance, fortifying herself behind a façade of Olympian detachment against the poison-tipped remarks allowed to drift her way above the clink of cups and saucers, was not the first to detect his presence. The sudden stultifying absence of any sound at all was her initial clue that something momentous was in the offing. Made additionally aware of an instantaneous tingling of nerve-endings at the nape of her neck at sight of Lady Smythington's peculiarly frozen expression, she instinctively turned her head in the direction of her guest's fixed stare.

Vere, looking devilishly handsome and commanding instant attention as only he knew how to do, stood poised in the doorway, his heavy-lidded glance roaming the assembled ladies with calculated arrogance until it came at last and inevitably to rest on her. The effect was galvanic, not to mention provocative, just as he had known that it would be. And, indeed, she was hard put not to give way to a helpless choke of laughter as he made his inimitable way through the sea of ostrich plumes and straw hats directly to her.

"My lord," she uttered, her eyes brimful of mirth as she allowed him to pull her to her feet. "How good of you to join us."

It was on her tongue to inquire if he cared for tea, when he made speech impossible by drawing her near and kissing her full on the lips for God and the entire assembled tea party to see! Nor was that all or the least of it. Releasing her lips at last, he continued to keep her close in his arms while, with his head bent, he held her with the mesmeric blue blaze of his eyes—until at length Aunt Sophie, left to feel the brunt of the roomful of bosoms heaving in scandalized reproach (or envy, as the case might be), was moved to give vent to a cough.

Only then did Vere release Constance to greet her aunt with unfeigned warmth.

"Sophie," he said with his infinitely gentle smile. "It is, as always, a pleasure to see you."

"Likewise, you may be sure, my lord," murmured Sophie with only the barest hint of dryness. "No doubt you are acquainted with most of your guests?"

"No, am I?" Raising the quizzing glass that was suspended on a black riband about his neck, Vere made a languid survey of the feminine faces turned expectantly toward him. "No," he drawled at last, "it would seem that I am not." Deliberately, he let the quizzing glass drop.

If Constance had been harboring the thirst for revenge in her breast, Vere's response to her aunt's query was to lay it firmly to rest.

He was to lay to rest, as well, the maw worm of discontent that had gnawed at her over his seeming disaffection. Determined, it seemed, not to make the same mistakes with his new, young bride that he had committed in the past, he kept nothing from her.

Roth, whom she had not seen since she left *Swallow,* became a frequent caller, bearing reports of the continuing search for Sinclair. For the first time she was made to realize the extent of Vere's careful planning over the years. It seemed there was not a corner of London in which he did not have someone with eyes and ears. "The fruits of a long and disreputable career, my love," he replied with his sardonic smile when she quizzed him about it. Even in the enemy camp, he had planted or cultivated spies in the various households. It was little wonder that he knew so much about the activities of Blaidsdale, Landford, and Sinclair.

Sinclair, nevertheless, was proving most demmed elusive.

"I fear we shall have to face the distinct possibility, my lord," said Roth one day, "that Sinclair has managed somehow to slip out of the country. Perhaps north into Scotland or across the Irish Sea into Ireland. I daresay there is even the possibility that he has bought passage for foreign parts."

"Perhaps," said Vere, who was staring out the study window, his back to the room.

"But you do not think so," offered Roth, studying the set of his employer's shoulders.

"I think," said Vere, coming around to face the younger man, "that he is holed up somewhere, licking his wounds. He is undoubtedly aware that we are searching the City for him. He will wait until he thinks it is safe to come out again."

"Where the devil could he go where he would not be remarked?" posed Roth, running his fingers through already tousled hair. "He would be far too conspicuous to remain unnoticed in the seamy parts of London. And in the fashionable quarters to which he is accustomed, he would most certainly run the risk of being recognized."

"That would seem to leave the decent, if unfashionable, neighborhoods, would it not?" Vere observed with the sardonic arch of an aristocratic eyebrow. "I daresay he could contrive with little difficulty to go unnoticed among the bourgeoisie. A rooming house, perhaps, or a hotel."

"No," said Constance, who until then had been sitting, listening, by the fire. "I daresay he has barricaded himself in the home of a lady friend."

A momentary silence fell over the room, as both men turned to regard Constance with varying expressions.

"That was, I confess, my first thought," admitted Vere, his gaze speculative on his redheaded wife. "I was brought reluctantly, however, to dismiss the possibility. Lady Clarissa, after all, is hardly the sort to tolerate that sort of indiscretion. If Sinclair has a mistress, he has taken great care to keep it a secret."

"He would, of course," agreed Constance, looking very much like the cat that ate the canary. "Unfortunately, he was not quite careful enough. He made the error one day of riding out with her in her carriage. No doubt he thought it was highly unlikely that he would be noticed in the less than exalted neighborhood of South Plover Street. To this day, I daresay he is unaware that my aunt and I caught a glimpse of him as he drove by. Nor could he have dreamed that his companion, a frequent visitor to the lending library, would be a chance acquaintance of my Aunt Sophie."

"Naturally, we find all of this enormously intriguing," submitted Vere with only the smallest tinge of irony. "I cannot help but wonder, however, my dearest, if you intend to tell us the lady's name."

"Mrs. Amelia Lawrence," Constance supplied promptly. "She is, I believe, a widow. Her late husband, if I am not mistaken, died of the fever in the East Indies. She lives on a modest jointure, which would not begin to bail Sinclair out of his difficulties. Other than that, she is, according to Sophie, a woman of charm and countenance."

"Splendid," smiled Vere, keenly aware of Constance's studied look of demureness. "No doubt I shall take inordinate pleasure in meeting the widow. Have you by any chance her direction?"

"Twenty-three South Hedley Street," retorted Constance, wrinkling her nose at him. "And I feel sure you and the widow will deal famously."

"No doubt," agreed Vere with his maddeningly gentle smile. "More importantly, however, is how Wilkers will deal with her."

Wilkers, it was soon to develop, while reticent at first to test his untapped potential for extemporaneous utterance, was not averse to doing his humble part in apprehending the villain who had shot his employer by foul means from the back. Being an avid reader of botanical treatises, moreover, he was not displeased with the prospect of staging an "accidental" encounter with the widow in the lending library. He was, after all, comfortably familiar with that particular milieu and, consequently, must surely find some topic with which to begin a conversation with a stranger, he speculated ponderously.

"I have every confidence in your ability to perform to perfection," Constance assured her butler, who, despite his customary stoic façade, was, she did not doubt, a trifle nervous at the immediate prospect of deliberately attracting the attention of a stranger of the feminine persuasion. "Remember, his lordship and I will be nearby to lend you moral support, if nothing else."

"Thank you, my lady. You may be certain that I shall do my best," replied Wilkers, stepping down from the carriage and strolling with apparent confidence down the street and in the door of the lending library.

It was all Constance could do to remain in the carriage with Vere as the moments ticked endlessly by. Still, it was in actuality little more than a quarter of an hour before Wilkers reappeared. Under one arm he carried numerous books. Under the other, he sported the gloved hand of a female in a wholly fetching straw bonnet, her trim figure smartly decked out in a Spanish vest of green velvet worn over a cambric frock of canary yellow sarcenet. She was an attractive woman who could not have been above her middle thirties.

"Mrs. Amelia Lawrence," pronounced Wilkers, bringing his companion straightly to the carriage door, "I should like to present to you Lord and Lady Vere. My lord, my lady, Mrs. Lawrence has a great deal that she would like to tell you."

It soon transpired that it had not been sufficient for Sinclair to abscond with his wife's jewels. He had thought to deprive his lady friend as well of the small nest egg which she had been used to keep in a stocking in her drawer of ladies' unmentionables. And that, after she had taken him in practically off the streets and dressed a wound for him that had been on a most delicate, indeed altogether mortifying, part of his anatomy. Really, he was not the gentleman that she had been led to believe he was. Neither, however, was he quite so clever as he would like to be. Having made deep indentures in a second bottle of gin, he let slip that he had booked passage on the *Esterbrook,* an East Indiaman bound for the Orient. She had doubted not that if they hurried, they might yet catch him. He had departed the house less than half an hour ago to make his way to Billingsgate and the boat that would carry him to his ship.

The cloaked figure descending from the hackney coach glanced furtively up and down the quay lined with boats. Then, clutching the grip of a tapestry bag, he turned to limp his way through the maze of barrels, crates, and bales waiting to be loaded and hauled away to the warehouses that abounded in the area of the dockyards. At last, with apparent relief, he spotted two seamen garbed in striped trousers and faded sea coats loitering on the jetty near a small rowboat tied to the dock.

"You," he said, approaching the pair. "I have need of a boat to carry me to the *Esterbrook.* Do you know the ship?"

"Aye, we know 'er," replied one, a handsome youth of perhaps two-and-twenty with a shock of fair hair the striking hue of bleached sand. "For a shilling, we'll take you to 'er."

The gentleman, apparently in no mood to haggle, tossed the fellow a coin. Without further preamble, he climbed gingerly down into the boat and settled his derriere with infinite care on one of the seats.

It was probable that the fog rolling in off the Channel played some small part in addling the gentleman's senses. Certainly, it would explain in some small measure why, some little time later, the gentleman, suffering the indignities of a boatswain's chair, failed to note that the ship onto whose deck he was dropped bore little resemblance to an East Indiaman bound for the Orient. But then, it was not the captain of the *Esterbrook* who strode forward to help him out of the sling.

No doubt it was bewildering enough to find himself face-to-face with a caped figure dressed all in black and wearing a mask. To find himself confronted by *two* such figures, one considerably taller than the other, must certainly have been doubly disorienting.

"What is the meaning of this?" he demanded, clutching his tapestry bag to his chest. "Who the devil are you?"

"The Black Rose, my lord," replied the two caped figures in unison, bowing.

"And now," said the taller of the two, "you will hand over all of your valuables, beginning with your valise."

A full moon shone pale in a sky mottled by drifting clouds. A crisp breeze, sweet with the scent of promised rain, riffled through the trees of an apple orchard on the grounds of an old abbey that had fallen to ruins centuries before. From somewhere close by came the chuckle of a stream and in the distance the muffled pound of horses' hooves in company with the creak and rattle of a coach approaching along the narrow, winding road.

In the shadow of the abbey wall, a black-garbed rider mounted on a coal-black steed waited.

The travel coach swept around the bend into sight. The rider spurred his mount into the road at the rear of the enclosed conveyance. Swift-paced, the horse easily overtook the coach. Upon which, the rider, kicking free of the stirrups, lifted himself to his feet on the saddle seat and launched himself to the roof of the vehicle. His hand reached for one of a brace of pistols thrust through the belt at his waist, as, his cape billowing, he made his way to the front of the coach.

Unregarded, he knelt behind the two unsuspecting figures on the bench.

"Softly, my good fellow," said the rider, pressing the pistol between the shoulder blades of the man riding guard. "I suggest you drop your weapon over the side. *Now*, if you value your life."

A single startled glance into the eyes framed in the holes of the mask covering the upper portion of the man's face was sufficient to convince the driver of the peril of resisting.

"Fer Christ's sake, Tom," growled the coachman to the guard. "Do as the gen'leman says."

Muttering a curse, the guard flung the blunderbuss wide of the coach.

"Very wise of you," commended the masked man. "And now, you," he said to the driver. "Bring the coach to a halt."

"You'll not get away with this," declared the guard, a sizeable fellow draped in a box coat. "This is Lady Sinclair's coach. Lord Blaidsdale will have your bloody heart on a platter if you harm a single hair on his sister's head."

"No, will he?" murmured the highwayman with the

faintest gleam of a smile which not only failed to reach his eyes, but also had the peculiar effect of sending a chill down the guard's spine. "No doubt he is welcome to try. On the other hand, you may be sure I have no intention of harming the lady. Stop the coach, driver—*now*. You and your companion, I am afraid, have no such assurance of your continued well-being."

Grumbling to himself, the man pulled the team to a halt.

"Coachman, what is it?" called an imperious feminine voice from the interior of the coach. "Why have we stopped?"

"It's a bloomin' highwayman, m'lady," answered the coachman. "The Black Rose, from the looks of him. We've been held up, we have."

"The Black Rose, indeed. Well, he will get nothing from me, and so you may tell him," declared the lady in no uncertain terms.

"No doubt that is fortunate, then," observed the Black Rose, as, motioning both men to disembark before him, he dropped lightly to the ground behind them. "As it happens, you have nothing I want."

"Nothing you want?" demanded the lady in offended tones. "Then what is the meaning of this effrontery in stopping my coach?"

"To give you back something you had lost," came the answer, followed in swift order by a shrill whistle.

Immediately, the sound of horses' hooves heralded the arrival of two riders, one masked and dressed all in black, and the other, his hands bound before him and his head thrust in a sack.

The Black Rose, reaching up, dragged the bound man from the saddle ignominiously to the ground. Then, in a single supple movement, he swung up into the empty saddle.

"Faith, what is this?" demanded Lady Clarissa, eyeing these proceedings with no little astonishment.

The Black Rose kneed his horse near the coach.

"Your husband, my lady." Leaning down, he proffered a single, perfect red rose. "With my compliments, ma'am."

As the two Black Roses turned their mounts and spurred away to collect the riderless black stallion grazing a short distance away, Lady Clarissa's shrill voice carried to them above the pound of the hooves.

"*Ridgley, you fool! So, I have you back again—and without my jewels, I do not hesitate to add! I trust you have some explanation for where you have been. You may be sure my brother, the earl, will not be pleased to hear of your stupid indiscretion. I daresay he will have your head served up on a platter for it.*"

"By God," said one Black Rose to the other, "one could almost be moved to pity the man for such a wife. I daresay before all is said and done, Sinclair will not be thanking us for sparing him his life."

"Precisely so, my dove," replied the other Black Rose. "Which is why we have done it."

"There is something sweet about revenge," reflected the Marchioness of Vere one night nearly a week following the peculiar events on the road to Landford Park. Getting up from her dressing table, she turned to regard the Marquis of Vere, watching her from the comfort of her bed. "Do you think Sinclair realizes yet how he came to be abducted by the Black Rose at the very moment that he was set to embark on the East Indiaman for the Orient?"

"I think," said Vere, lying with one arm folded beneath his head on the pillow, "that Sinclair is exceedingly fortunate if he is not even now chained to a damp wall in Blaidsdale's cellar and living off a diet of foul bread and water. Even that would be better, however, than being forced to listen to Lady Sinclair's vituperative tongue for what is left of his life. In short, my love, I believe that you may rest easy on Mrs. Lawrence's account. Lady Sinclair will never again let her erring husband out of her sight, let alone allow him the freedom to return to Town."

"And now that that is settled . . ." Lifting the bedcovers, Vere gave the sheet-covered mattress a meaningful pat.

"You are right, of course." Constance kicked off her slippers and slid into the bed beside Vere. Settling with her head in the curve of his shoulder and an arm across his chest, she could not but think that Sinclair had got just what he deserved. "But then, it is not settled, not really," she said, struck by a new, troubling thought. "There is yet the matter of Landford's gambling markers, not to mention your father's documents." Lifting herself up on one elbow, she gazed earnestly into Vere's face. "You will be careful tomorrow, Vere, will you not? I should not be at all pleased to be made a widow just when I am becoming used to being a wife."

Vere, pulling her down to him, held her close. "You may be sure that it will never come to that, my sweet Constance." Reaching up, he turned down the wick of the bed lamp. "It will all be over soon, I promise. And then we shall have a lifetime to put this all behind us."

Constance, staring into the darkness relieved only by the glow of the firelight, was not comforted. In truth, she would have been better pleased had there been some way to end it now, this minute, without going a single step farther. Barring that, she would have at least felt better if she could be with Vere when he confronted Landford. Unfortunately, she could hardly expect to be welcomed into a gentlemen's private gambling club, especially one on the order of White's. She might sooner aspire to be allowed to vote in the next parliamentary election as hope for that.

Still, she supposed she could comfort herself with the

knowledge that armed confrontation in the confines of one of the hallowed establishments reserved to gentlemen was not only heavily frowned upon, but firmly disallowed. It would not be in White's that Vere would have to guard himself. It would be out in the streets. In that regard, too, at least, she could be grateful that it was Vice Admiral Sir Oliver Landford whom Vere was to confront. Had it been anyone else, there would have been the distinct possibility that Vere would find himself facing his opponent on the field of honor. The utter certainty that Vere would win in such a confrontation made the mere notion of a duel abhorrent in the extreme. She could hardly relish the notion, after all, of living the rest of their lives in exile. Indeed, it was not to be thought of.

It was inconceivable, after all, that the future Albermarle heir should be born on foreign soil.

It came to her, not for the first time, that she should have told Vere days ago of the very real possibility that she was already breeding. Indeed, she should tell him now. And yet, how could she? Far from deterring him from the course to which he had committed himself ten years ago, it must surely serve only to distract him when now, most especially, that was quite possibly the very last thing that he needed.

Nevertheless, knowing that he would be ill-disposed to forgive her for keeping a secret of this magnitude at the very time that they had agreed not to hide anything from one another was troubling to say the least. Indeed, she was acutely aware of a distinctly queasy sensation in the pit of her stomach which she knew could not be attributed solely to the salmon croquettes that she had ingested for dinner. She did not doubt that it was due to an uneasy conscience. The possibility that she was breeding, after all, was not the only secret that she was keeping from him.

It came to her that she had created a devil of a coil

for herself just when things had been beginning to look
so promising, a conviction that Vere's hand beginning to
move in slow, steady strokes over her hair served only to
strengthen. Catching her bottom lip between her teeth,
she quelled the almost overwhelming urge to blurt everything out and have done with it, as Vere chose at last to
break the lengthening silence.

"You are singularly quiet, *enfant*."

"Am I? I suppose I was thinking," said Constance. "I
seem prone to do that a lot lately, and at present I am
excessively weary of it. Would you mind terribly making
love to me?"

She was no doubt gratified to feel his hand still in
her hair as he contemplated an answer to what could
only be construed as a curiously worded request preg-
nant with possibilities. Abruptly, Vere shifted in the bed.
Raising himself on one elbow, he leaned over her to
peer down at the white blur of her face against the pillow.

"A hideous prospect, indeed," he confessed and lowered his head to hers.

Chapter 13

Vere disembarked from his carriage and strolled leisurely up to the door to White's private gambling club on the east side of St. James's Street. He was not displeased to note Beau Brummell and Lord Sefton along with two other gentlemen occupied with ogling passersby. In truth, it served his purposes admirably to have the Arbiters of Fashion present tonight, he thought. Carelessly, touching his walking stick to the brim of his hat in salute to them, he entered.

The club had already begun to fill in anticipation of an evening spent in gambling. But then, Vere had purposely timed his arrival to coincide with the end of supper, laid at six and paid for at nine. Landford made a habit of fortifying himself with food and wine before indulging himself at the gaming tables.

Checking his greatcoat and hat at the cloakroom, Vere found a certain irony in the discovery that he felt little of anticipation in the game that lay before him, but only a wish to be done with it. Hell and the devil confound it. He was become a strange character, one that he hardly recognized anymore. He had worked teyears for this night, and now that it had come, he found that he had been tempted to put it off rather than leave Constance to herself—good God. Further, it had come to him lately that he had not missed the gaming, drinking, and evening debaucheries that had been his wont before he met Constance. Rather, more and more, he had come to find that he looked forward to the hours spent with his undeniably fascinating wife. He did not doubt that he would come eventually to embrace the notion of setting up his nursery with the same relish as that which he had witnessed in his brothers-in-law. Strangely, he did not find that thought so displeasing as he once might have done. No doubt it was poetic justice that he should have fallen victim to the spell of a titian-haired beauty with the power to transform Vere into a model subject—egad!

But then, this was hardly the time to indulge in an analysis of his new state of circumstances, he reminded himself, as he nodded to Chester Windholm of the Sussex Windholms and moved on to the stairway that led to the gaming rooms on the floor above. Most in particularly, it was not the time to dwell on the nagging suspicion that all was not quite as it should be at home with his wife. The devil! Something had been troubling Constance last night. He could not be mistaken in that.

It was not that he had not been more than happy to oblige her in her request to make love to her. Good God, he was far from advocating abstinence, especially with his delightfully passionate Constance. Nor was it the fact that she had asked him, when it was patently unnecessary to have done. He had had every intention of tasting her sweet delights. It was her unwonted silence as she lay in his arms, followed by the driving sense of urgency with which she had made love to him.

The devil take him if every aspect of her behavior did not point to some affliction of the conscience!

Vere's eyes narrowed to cold, steely points at the

thought, a circumstance that could not but occasion young Lord Hadley, who had just been on the point of accosting Vere, to blanch and shrink away. Hell and the devil confound it! What could Constance possibly have done that was so terrible that she could not bring her self to tell him of it? He could think of nothing, short of cuckolding, that he could not have forgiven her. And surely, it was inconceivable that she had taken herself a lover. She could not have so misled him when she had blurted in the heat of passion that she could not bear a life without him.

But enough! His troublesome wife was proving a far greater distraction than he could ever have previously imagined, and he had other, more pressing matters that required his full attention. Nevertheless, even as he banished her from his thoughts with a cold deliberation well known to his intimates, he was aware of an over weening impatience to be done with the business of re venge that he might devote all his energies to unraveling the mystery that was Constance.

Pausing at the head of the stairs, he deliberately sum moned up the old, dark feelings that had made Vere what he was—indeed, what he had need to be to finish what he had started. *What Landford had started*, he cor rected himself, and what Blaidsdale had perpetuated to the length of plotting the cold-blooded murders of the former Marquis and Marchioness of Vere. And then, at last, Charles Seton as well had been made to pay the price of Blaidsdale's thwarted pride.

To forget that James Rochelle and the gentle, loving Clarice were dead because of Oliver Landford's corrupt and unseemly appetites and Blaidsdale's ruthless arro gance would be to deny who and what he was. He was Vere, the heir to Albermarle. He had only to summon up the gory images evoked by the Preacher's tale of sav agery to feel a cold, steely calm descend over him.

The silver-headed walking stick propped negligently

on one fashionably clad shoulder, he strolled leisurely into the smoky environs of the gaming room, aptly named "Hell" by its patrons. To those noting his arrival, he appeared elegant, arrogantly cool, and infinitely dangerous.

He was in all respects the Marquis of Vere.

Nodding in answer to the greetings of acquaintances and pausing here and there to exchange pleasantries with those with whom he enjoyed a greater intimacy, he came at length to a faro table remarkable for the number of gentlemen crowded around it and for the wealth of chips flowing in and out of the bank. Landford, already red in the face from the effects of the wine he was steadily imbibing, was seated at the forefront, his attention fixed on the banker in the act of drawing a seven of hearts from the shoe. This, the loser, the banker set beside the shoe. The winner revealed on top of the deck was a four of diamonds. Landford had lost.

It was not Landford, however, running his tongue over dry lips and watching the banker rake in the chips, who caught and held Vere's immediate attention. A faint smile, distinctly ironic, touched the corners of Vere's lips as the banker deliberately met his eye. The devil, he thought. The last thing he might have expected was to find the Earl of Shields in Town, let alone ensconced at White's, dealing faro. On a sudden premonition, Vere let his gaze stray over the roomful of gentlemen. He was hardly surprised to espy the Earl of Blackthorn, observing him from where he stood with one broad shoulder propped negligently against the wall.

It seemed that his meddling sisters had determined after all how best to deal with the news of his marriage to Blaidsdale's stepdaughter. Putting their heads together, they had decided to send Vere reinforcements while they, no doubt, had converged on Albermarle ensconced in his castle. Only Constance, however, could have told his two brothers-in-law where he would be tonight.

Egad, it was little wonder that his normally forthright Constance had been demonstrating all the signs of one suffering from a guilty conscience. Grimly, he vowed that the little baggage would be suffering from something a deal more painful when next he got his hands on her!

Still, he told himself, gesturing to a serving man for a glass of wine as he settled negligently into a chair, the presence of his kinsmen changed nothing. He would allow no one, not even Blackthorn and Shields, to interfere with his plans now. The patience with which he had plotted the engine of his revenge had come to an end. Tonight, he would see Landford's debts paid in full. And then at last he would turn his attention to Blaidsdale.

As Landford lost again on the next turn, followed in the third by a triple win, Vere once again put all else from his mind but the matter at hand. And indeed, sprawled in the chair, his legs crossed at the ankles and stretched out before him with the silver-headed walking stick swinging idly between his thumb and forefinger, he presented to the casual observer a magnificent appearance of languor. And yet, with the apparent exception of Landford, there was not a soul present who was not singularly aware of Vere's presence in the significant proximity of the man for whom he was known to entertain a long-standing animus.

If Sir Oliver took the least note of Vere's lounging figure, he little showed it as he placed his winnings on the ten to win. He lost. Then won again. Calling for a drink, he bet on the five to lose and won yet again.

It did not, however, go unremarked by the rest of the gentlemen present. Beau Brummell himself was heard to comment to Lord Sefton on the necessity of immediately bringing up one of the gentlemen from the Young Club to fill the vacancy in the Old Club. Vice Admiral Sir Oliver Landford, after all, had just been blackballed. He simply had yet to know it.

Unbeknownst to Sir Oliver, who had, by now, begun to lose rather more often than not, the odds in the betting book were running heavily in favor of a duel with pistols on Finchley Common no later than dawn of the following morning, though there were some who held out that there was a greater chance that pigs would fly than that Landford would ever agree to meet Vere in a duel. Either way, there was no doubt in anyone's mind at all that Landford, to all intents and purposes, was finished in London.

It was not until the hall clock struck the hour of eleven, however, that Landford began to get a glimmering of it. Having lost the entirety of his chips, but eternally convinced that his luck must inevitably change with the next turn of the card, he demanded to be allowed to run a tab on the bank.

"No doubt I should be happy to oblige you," said Shields, raking in the chips and paying out to the winners. "Unfortunately, your credit is not sufficient to carry you." The earl rose to his considerable height. "I am sorry, gentlemen, this bank is closed for the night."

"The devil it is." Landford, slamming his hand down on the table, heaved himself out of his chair. "You cannot close the cursed bank now. These gentlemen and I demand the opportunity to recover our losses. It is our right, I tell you."

"These gentlemen are welcome to move to another table. You, however, Sir Oliver, have been cut off. If you doubt my word, I suggest you consult the ruling committee. Afterwards, if you require further convincing, I shall be happy to oblige you—at twenty paces or with swords, if you prefer."

It was the general opinion that the sudden cold glint of eyes the steel blue of rapiers should have been sufficient to give Landford pause for thought. That it did not must have been due either to a brain befogged with drink or to simple gross stupidity. But then, everyone there knew that it was not Shields whom Landford had to fear this night.

"Yes, you would like that, would you not?" rasped Sir Oliver, running his fingers around the inside of his neck cloth as if it were a slowly tightening noose. "My credit is good, damn you. Ask anyone."

It was perhaps the wrong thing to say at that particular juncture, as was patently clear to everyone who saw Vere's elegantly clad figure at that instant leisurely unfold itself from the chair.

"Indeed, my lord, you may ask *me*."

Vice Admiral Sir Oliver Landford, it was later to be reported in every fashionable salon and gaming club in London, went, at those gently uttered words, fully as white as a sheet.

"*You!*" he said in a voice that had the sound of a rasping croak. "All along this is what you have been waiting for."

"It has, in fact, been ten years in the waiting," confirmed the marquis with his inimitably gentle smile, which had the effect of causing a film of moisture to break out on the vice admiral's forehead. "A pity, do you not think, that Lord Sinclair was not possessed of a truer aim. You might have been spared the final accounting." He drew forth a sizeable wallet fairly stuffed with promissory notes and laid it on the table. "However, as fate would have it, my lord vice admiral, I am now in the position to demand payment in full—for all that you owe me and my house."

As the full significance of Vere's words sank home, Landford, turning a most peculiar shade of purple, uttered a strangled gasp, as if he could not quite find his breath. Slowly, he began to fall back before Vere's awful presence like a man who had just had his feet cut out from under him.

"Splendid—I see that you do begin to understand," observed Vere, propping the silver head of his walking stick on one elegantly clad shoulder. "Perhaps, then, you would care to tell me when I may expect satisfaction?"

It was only then that Landford, apparently robbed of the power of speech, turned his head from side to side, as if searching the crowded room for a friendly face. Finding he was met with a singular lack of sympathy, he turned at last on his heel. Shoving his way past the circle of onlookers, who parted to let him pass, he fled.

"The devil, Vere," remarked Shields, staring after the retreating figure, "I suppose now we shall have to go after him."

"I daresay it is only what you both deserve for thinking to meddle in my private affairs," replied Vere, as Blackthorn added his presence to theirs. He felt a cold, hard anger explore his vitals. This was to have been his task to perform alone. Not even Roth was to have a part in it. If anything should fail to go as he had planned it, there would have been no one but himself to pay the price. "I should be better pleased if you would take yourselves home and leave Landford to me."

"You forget, my friend," said Blackthorn with a queer, cold gleam in his eye. "It was Landford who branded me a traitor to king and country and ruined my naval career. I believe you could say that that gives me some small stake in him."

"I suppose you might say that I have no claim on him," submitted Shields, who, being the oldest of the three, might have been expected to help the others to keep level heads. "Save for the fact," he appended in soft, chilling accents, "that he was instrumental in depriving my wife of both her mother and father. Something, I might add, for which she has blamed herself all these years. Perhaps you understand, then, why I might feel some obligation to see Sir Oliver brought to justice."

"And if I grant you that," returned Vere, who was perfectly aware that their real purpose in coming was to stop him from cutting Landford's stick for him, "it does not alter the fact that my claims on him anticipate either of yours by several years. He is hardly worth the efforts of all three of us."

"He is not worth the efforts of a single one of us," Blackthorn observed, a hand coming to rest on Vere's shoulder. "I suggest, therefore, that we put a swift and speedy end to the business. At this rate, the wretch is like to run all the way to Landford Park before he stops."

"On the contrary," Vere stated with unnerving certainty, "Sir Oliver will run no farther than his lodgings in the Ridler Hotel." Abruptly, he smiled. "I suggest, therefore, that since you have come all this way to look after my best interests, we stay and enjoy a drink together. You can bring me up to date on the progress of my various nephews and nieces. I daresay I shall be enormously impressed. And in the meantime, Sir Oliver will have opportunity to ponder the error of his ways." Turning with a fine condescension to lead them toward an unoccupied corner table, he queried lightly, "How is my namesake, by the way?"

Shields, all too well acquainted with the vagaries of his brother-in-law's moods, exchanged a long look with Blackthorn, who shrugged. Vere, it would seem, was disposed to be at his most maddeningly elusive. Prepared to play out the game with him, they joined him at the table. No doubt the marquis would in due time see fit to tell them what he intended.

Vere was brilliantly charming, as only he knew how to be when the mood suited them. A superb conversationalist, he led them to speak on any number of subjects, none of which remotely touched on the matters that were uppermost in all their minds, but instead served effectively not only to fill the time, but also to deflect the discussion away from himself. Shields and Blackthorn, who had seen him like this before, were not fooled by it. Vere knew something that they did not. That much at least was abundantly clear. He was waiting, letting the clock play out, but for what?

The evening, consequently, was well advanced when Vere, setting his glass with a strange sort of finality on the table, shoved back his chair and rose.

"White's begins to pall, I think," he said quietly. His eyes beneath heavily drooping eyelids held a queer, glittery intensity. "I suggest that it is time for a change of scenery."

Where before, Vere had been talkative, using his wit like a rapier to parry the questions that he obviously was in no mood to answer, in the carriage he seemed wrapped in an impenetrable cloak of silence.

His brothers-in-law, sensing the temper of his mood, grimly contented themselves with settling back to wait. They knew Vere of old. He had not welcomed their obvious intent to intrude into his affairs, even as they had been aware that he would not. It was a dangerous business, forcing themselves on Vere. And still they had come. Whether he liked it or not was of little significance. They had not come, after all, to protect Vere from his enemies. They had come to protect Vere from himself.

Neither doubted in Vere's unique ability to deal his enemies a swift and summary justice. His reputation for being dangerous had not been lightly earned. He had killed before. Neither doubted that he would do so again without compunction and with little regard for either the consequences or his life. Neither was prepared to stand idly by and do nothing to prevent him from flinging his life away. There were Elfrida and Violet to consider, after all, not to mention the duke, who, in spite of everything, had never ceased to place his hopes for the future in the black sheep. And now there was Constance, his marchioness, too. They deserved better than to see Vere swing from the bloody gibbet.

The carriage, entering Holborn Street, came at last to the Ridler Hotel, a four-story Georgian house of brown brick. Vere, stepping down onto the walk, had shed any pretense of indolence. Without waiting for the others, he entered the hotel and crossed the foyer in long, swift strides, then went on to take the stairs to the upper floor two at a time. Arriving on the upper story, he made straightaway to Landford's door and, reaching for the handle, thrust the barrier wide.

He halted on the threshold, his hand going to the pocket gun in his greatcoat. Drawing the weapon out, he took a long stride forward.

"I should hold very still, if I were you," he said. The very next instant, he lifted his arm and fired.

The explosion of the gun, along with the crash of a heavy object, shattered the silence.

Blackthorn and Shields arrived only a split second later. They came to a standstill, their faces grim at the scene before them.

Landford lay lifeless on the floor, his face contorted in fear, terrible to behold. Only, it was a Landford they had never seen before. Garbed in a woman's dress, a blond wig covering his hair and his face a painted caricature of femininity, he presented a grotesque and grisly picture. About his bleeding throat he wore a necklace of diamonds and emeralds, a necklace that had once graced the gentle Clarice's neck.

Nearby, still clutching a bloodied knife and writhing amid the shattered debris of a brass chandelier, was a filthy, moaning creature with bony limbs and lank, grizzled hair.

As Blackthorn crossed to relieve the wretch on the floor of his knife, Shields favored Vere with a long, speculative look. "Who the devil is he?"

"More to the point," said Blackthorn, glancing sharply up, "how did you know what we should find?"

"Perhaps," replied Vere with a smile that was as chillingly divorced from all feeling as it was deliberately enigmatic, "I saw it in a crystal ball. Allow me to present to you Mr. Phineas Ambrose, my father's former estate agent, who is now employed in the dubious occupation of a cent-per-cent. It would appear that he has just finished instructing Sir Oliver in the penalties of failing to discharge his debts."

"A leech," said Blackthorn in no little revulsion. "I might have guessed. Egad, he has the look of one."

"Ironic, is it not?" Vere agreed, his thoughts already turning to the final task that lay before him. His eyes, as bleak and cold as winter, went back to the thing at Landford's throat. "Mr. Ambrose is at present consigned to the Queen's Bench Prison for the very thing to which he took exception in his own unfortunate client."

Kneeling, he unclasped the necklace from around Landford's neck and wrapped it in his linen handkerchief before thrusting it hard in his pocket. Vere, starting to rise, suddenly froze. His eyes fixed on the hideous aspect of Landford's face. On the left cheek was a bruise that would seem curiously in the shape of a man's signet ring. The devil, he had seen another bruise that had borne a marked resemblance to this one. He had seen it on Constance. He was aware of the sudden, hard clamp of a fist on his vitals as it came to him with stark significance that Blaidsdale had been here before them. He stood to find Blackthorn watching him with a curiously intent expression.

Unreasonably annoyed, he reached down to haul Ambrose to his feet. "I should be in your debt, old man, if you would see to this for me," he said, thrusting Ambrose at Shields.

"The devil, man, what is it? Where are you going?" It was Blackthorn, taking a step toward him.

"Home," said Vere, feeling the seconds pressing upon him. "I haven't time to explain, save to say that I believe Constance is in danger."

"You will not go without us," said Shields, searching for something with which to bind Ambrose.

It soon proved that the drapery cord suited admirably to the task. In short order Phineas Ambrose was trussed up like a parcel awaiting delivery to Newgate Prison.

The house was dark when the carriage pulled up in front of it. But then, that in itself should not be alarming, Vere told himself, as he stepped down and walked with apparent unconcern to the front door. It was little more than an hour before dawn. The household would naturally be abed. Nevertheless, as he let himself in with his key, he was singularly conscious of the fact that the pistol in his pocket was empty. He was made even more keenly aware of it when he discovered that the lamp, normally left burning in the foyer for his return, was missing from its customary place on the sideboard.

He paused, listening to the silence, as he weighed the risk in alerting the household to the presence of an intruder in their midst. The chilling image of Constance somewhere in the house with a knife to her throat was enough for him to discard the notion instantly.

On the carriage ride to the Town House, they had already gone over their options and come up with what would seem their most logical course. It was to be supposed that Blaidsdale had dropped in on his brother for one reason or another to find Landford in the guise that presumably he preferred when he was in privacy. A quarrel had obviously ensued in which Blaidsdale, enraged to discover the full extent of his brother's scandalous ruin, had rendered Landford unconscious. Little knowing the wretched fate that had waited, lurking in the shadows, Blaidsdale had left his brother an easy prey for Ambrose's murderous blade. He had come here, to Vere's house, unaware that Vere would find Landford and, seeing the telltale mark of the signet ring on the dead vice admiral's face, would know where Blaidsdale had gone and to what malicious purpose. He would be unaware, too, that Vere was not alone.

Shields and Blackthorn should already be entering at the back of the house. With any luck, however, Vere would find Blaidsdale first.

Bitterly, he cursed his own bloody arrogance in having failed to foresee the advisability of posting armed guards about the house in his absence. He had been worse than a fool to leave Constance here, alone and unprotected. Bloody hell, he should have *known* that Blaidsdale would come!

At last casting all caution to the wind, he ascended the staircase and strode down the corridor that led to Constance's chambers. If Blaidsdale was, indeed, within, waiting for him, Vere had no intention of disappointing him. And by the saints, if Blaidsdale had harmed a single hair on Constance's head, neither God nor the devil could save him.

Coming to Constance's room, he reached for the door handle.

Vere could not be sure what he expected to find when he thrust the door open and stepped inside the room. Certainly, it was not to find Constance, garbed in a black coat and breeches and waiting with a pistol, cocked and ready to fire, aimed at his chest!

In the split second before mutual recognition, Vere was given the dubious satisfaction of seeing his life flash before his eyes.

Then, "The devil, Vere," Constance exclaimed, lowering the gun. "What the deuce took you so long?" With extreme care, she let the hammer down.

"I shall no doubt be happy to oblige you with an explanation," said Vere, pulling the door to behind him, "as soon as you tell me why you were standing behind the door waiting to shoot anyone who stepped across the threshold."

"I fear there is not time for either tale at the moment,"

replied Constance. "Blaidsdale is here, and I cannot think that he has come for the purpose of exchanging pleasantries over an early morning breakfast. If I had not been up roaming the house all night, I daresay I should even now be on my way to Somerset with a bag thrust over my head. I have been staying just out of his sight until I could steal in here to slip into something a little more appropriate to the occasion than my silk night dress."

"Somehow 'appropriate' is not quite the word that comes to mind," returned Vere, his tone exceedingly dry. "On the other hand," he added, availing himself of one of the brace of pistols with which she had seen fit to adorn herself, "I cannot take exception to your accessories. Where is Blaidsdale now?"

"In the study. I am very nearly certain he is helping himself to your brandy, not to mention the contents of your writing desk. I am sure I heard him rifling through your papers."

"Then if you are finished making yourself presentable," said Vere, reaching to open the door, "I suggest, my lady, that we go and see to our uninvited guest."

Constance, who had hardly thought to hear that condescension from Vere—indeed, had expected him rather to order her to stay out of sight in her room—awarded him a flashing grin, designed, he did not doubt, to take his breath away. "After you, my dearest lord marquis."

Blaidsdale was, in fact, so preoccupied with ransacking Vere's private study that he failed even to note when Vere, followed closely by Constance, stepped into the room.

The earl, who had his back to them and was in the process of raking the books off of the shelves to the floor, went suddenly quite deathly still at the sound of Vere's voice.

"You will not find the documents here, Blaidsdale. They are already in the hands of the admiralty."

"*Vere.*"

That single-word utterance, pronounced with unmistakable loathing, seemed to hang in the sudden, stultifying silence. Deliberately, Vere put Constance away from him.

"It is over, Blaidsdale," he said. "Landford is dead."

The earl's head came up. Still, he remained with his back to them, his head tilted slightly to one side, as if listening for the distant approach of a step. "It is a lie," he said. "I was with him less than an hour ago."

Vere slipped his hand into his pocket and pulled out the thing wrapped in the linen handkerchief. "So was I." Vere spilled the thing out on the desktop. "He is where I left him, Blaidsdale—on the floor, with his throat slit open."

Constance stared, sickened, at the necklace of diamonds and emeralds covered in blood.

Blaidsdale jerked as if he had been struck. At last he came around to impale Vere with terrible eyes. "You took your vengeance out on him in such a manner. Like a pig for the slaughter."

"It was no less than you had done to my mother when this necklace was ripped from her throat. Oh, yes. I have been privileged to hear the tale from the Preacher's own lips. Nevertheless, it was not I who killed Landford. But then, I did not have to. If you valued his life, Blaidsdale, you should have settled his debts for him. Ambrose, as it happens, was not so merciful as I. No doubt you will be pleased to learn that he is even now in the hands of the Bow Street Runners. I daresay he will prove an invaluable witness at your trial—should it come to that."

"Ambrose." The name was a curse on Blaidsdale's lips. "You have left no one out. First Sinclair and now Sir Oliver. I confess I underestimated you, Vere. You even stole Constance from me, just as your father did her mother before you."

"You are mistaken, surely, my lord," said Constance, recalling the feel of his heavy hand against her face. "I was never yours. Your claim on my mother was as false as your black heart. You had my father killed because she refused you. For that alone, I should gladly see you hanged."

Only, it would never come to that, thought Vere, watching Blaidsdale. It was in his eyes. Blaidsdale was finished, and he knew it. The devil of it was, he meant to take someone with him. It was only as Blaidsdale moved, flinging himself hard to one side, that Vere saw the gun, smaller than a man's fist, aimed at Constance. Vere shot. Blaidsdale's gun went off, and out of the corner of his eye, Vere saw Constance flung to the floor.

A searing stab of pain lanced through Vere's chest as it came to him that, in the end, Blaidsdale had won. He had killed Constance! Vere flung the pistol aside. The silver-headed walking stick clamped in his hand, he crossed the room to Blaidsdale, unaware that, behind him, Shields and Blackthorn came through the door and stopped. Tearing his eyes away from Vere, Blackthorn knelt beside Constance.

Vere stared down at the earl's gloating look of triumph. With a hiss of steel, he unsheathed the blade in the walking stick. He had but one task left for him to do. He waited to feel something. Ten years. Ambrose, Sinclair, Landford, and now Blaidsdale. They had all been made to pay, each in his own way. How ironic, really, he thought, feeling the weight of the sword in his hand. The duke had been right, after all. Revenge left naught but the bitter taste of ashes in one's mouth.

Deliberately, he lowered the point of the blade to Blaidsdale.

Blaidsdale, clutching at the gunshot wound high up on his chest, felt the icy touch of fear as he looked up into eyes as cold as death. The smile of triumph faded. With his eyes, he pleaded.

"*Gideon, no!*"

Shields clamped a hand on Vere's wrist.

"Vere. It is over," he said. "Listen to me. Blaidsdale missed."

Vere's blue eyes lifted to regard him with a cold, piercing intensity.

Grimly wondering if he would find himself facing Vere at twenty paces for this day's work, Shields tried again. "Constance is unhurt. Finney shoved her out of the way."

The resistance went out of the arm beneath Shields's hand. Vere stepped back, the sword dropping to his side.

His eyes went to Blackthorn, helping Constance to her feet. And behind them, Finney, who had saved her.

He felt the cold grip of winter unloose its hold on his heart as Constance, smiling uncertainly, started toward him.

At last, flinging the sword aside, he caught her in his arms.

"It was Landford, all those years ago," said Constance a good deal later, lying with her cheek against Vere's chest. "They were all children together when it happened. How dreadful that so many lives were ruined because of it. So much hatred. So many of them died. And Landford—I could almost pity him so ignoble a death."

"He was Landford," said Vere, who had no pity in his heart for the man who had been as corrupted as was Blaidsdale, his brother. Whatever nature had made of him, he had yet chosen to use his position to manipulate others to his own insatiable pleasure. In that, he was no different from Blaidsdale, who had done the same to serve a dark and overweening pride. "And now he is dead. I should wish that to be an end to it."

"No less than should I," replied Constance, who could not be more grateful that at last they could put the past behind them. "There is, after all, the future to consider now."

Vere, who had been thinking of little else since, carrying her to his bed, he had driven out the last bitter remnants of despair that had gripped him when he believed Constance was forever lost to him, was inexplicably made to feel a sudden frisson of warning. That feeling was not in the least alleviated when Constance, lifting her head, propped her chin on the back of her hand for the apparent purpose of studying his face.

"I have been thinking," she said.

"A sobering prospect, indeed," murmured Vere, thinking himself that his flame-haired bride had never looked more alluring than she did at that moment with her curls gloriously disheveled and her lips delightfully pursed in contemplation.

"Beast," retorted Constance, awarding him a censorious frown.

"No doubt," agreed Vere, feeling the renewed stirring of primitive animal urges.

"I have been thinking," firmly repeated Constance, who, choosing to ignore his unfortunate sally, instead adopted a new tactic, designed, no doubt, to capture her troublesome lord's undivided attention. Touching the tip of her index finger to the middle of his aristocratic forehead, she began a slow, titillating journey down over his nose, his handsomely formed lips, the slight cleft in his chin, and further. "I am not yet completely satisfied with the house."

"Ah," said Vere, inclined in the circumstances to grant her carte blanche to refurbish the blasted house to her heart's content, "the choice of the flower design for the draperies. You now feel that perhaps your decision was made in haste."

Constance, who had not at all had in mind the drapes for the formal dining room, and who, indeed, had been inordinately pleased with the effect of a profusion of lavender and blue delphiniums adorning those otherwise austere environs, abruptly jerked her head up. "I do not feel that in the least, Vere," she declared, nar-

rowing her eyes at him in a manner that left little doubt
that he had made a strategic error in mentioning them.
"What is wrong with the draperies in the dining room?"

"Nothing, my dearest delight," he made haste to rectify. "You may be sure that I have come recently to view
them as indispensable to my happiness. If not the dining room," he added, no doubt in the hopes of divert-
ing her to safer grounds, "then what did you have in
mind? The downstairs withdrawing room, the third-story
guestrooms, and, indeed, even the water closets and the
ballroom—all would seem to defy the notion that one
can improve upon perfection."

Constance frowned, not at all certain that Vere was
not roasting her. Judiciously, however, she decided to ignore his seeming ambiguity in favor of moving on to
the real purpose of her having introduced the subject
in the first place. "No, you are quite right, my dearest
lord marquis. It is not the ballroom or any of my other
endeavors at interior design. As it happens, I had the
nursery and the schoolroom most particularly in mind."

If she had wished to punish him for what she suspected to be a reprehensible levity in his demeanor, she
was no doubt gratified by her dearest lord's reaction to
that casually worded declaration.

Vere, no slow top at logical deduction, went suddenly
still, his eyes, the mesmerizing blue of lapis lazuli, narrowing to penetrating pinpoints on Constance's serene
countenance. Certainly, he did not waste any time in a
pointless exercise in roundaboutation.

"The devil, Constance," he exclaimed, framing her face
between strong, shapely hands. "A child? Are you sure?"

"I believe I have never been more certain of anything
in my life before, Gideon," answered Constance, her
beautiful eyes shimmering with happiness, "save that I
was meant to fall in love with you almost from the very
first moment I saw you."

In spite of the fact that he was in the grip of powerful

emotions engendered by the unexpected news of his impending fatherhood, that latter assertion from his unpredictable wife yet served to strike a chord of memory in Vere. "No doubt you will pardon my lamentable lapse of memory, Constance," he said, marveling at the fate that had given him his sweet, incomparable love. "I cannot but wonder, however, when that memorable occasion was. In truth, I cannot recall ever having seen you before I robbed your coach. I am moved to ask how the devil you knew the identity of the Black Rose when no one else seemed able to penetrate his disguise."

"But how could I not, Vere?" queried Constance, laughter dancing in the look she bent upon him. "When you had already held me up once before, even going so far as to save me the mortification of being mauled by Lord Clairborne, who, besides being more than twice my age, was ridiculously made up at the time in the guise of a man-eating dragon."

"Good God," said Vere, staring at her with dawning recollection. "Lord Ravenleigh's masquerade ball. You were Queen Mab."

"And you were Robin Hood," Constance finished for him. "You were masked the first and only time I met you. You introduced yourself that night as Vere. It is hardly marvelous, then, that I should have recognized you when the Black Rose held me up and gallantly stole a kiss from me."

"Unfortunately," replied Vere, rolling over so that Constance lay pinned beneath him, "I was not so clever as you, my sweet. I failed utterly to recognize in the beautiful Lady Black Rose the woman who stole my heart." Lowering his head, he kissed her with an aching tenderness that left little doubt that what had begun as a marriage of convenience had become something else altogether. Then lifting his head, he whispered in her ear, "I do love you, Constance. And that is something I thought I should never say to anyone."

Epilogue

It was the twenty-third of November, a most significant date to those gathered in the Queen's Salon at Albermarle Castle, because it heralded the arrival of the newest Albermarle heir. Measuring twenty-one inches in length and weighing in at six pounds, twelve ounces, James Charles Gideon Rochelle gave fair promise of having broken the Albermarle mold. It was true enough that he possessed blue eyes that might in time have the mesmerizing quality of lapis lazuli, and there was no doubting that he already demonstrated an uncanny ability to capture unsuspecting feminine hearts, as was demonstrated just then by the number of Albermarle females gathered, oohing and ahing about his cradle. The bright curl of hair peeping out from beneath his lace cap, however, was unmistakably the color of leaves in autumn.

It was also a singular gathering because it included, besides a duke, a marquis, two earls, and a rear admiral, a newly promoted commander in His Majesty's navy. And, indeed, Commander Caleb Roth presented a strikingly handsome figure in his blue coat with its single gold epaulet, as could be testified to by the lovely Miss Alexandra Rochelle, who, at eighteen, could not keep from glancing at him from beneath the luxurious veil of her eyelashes. As for the new commander of the frigate *Ajax*, he, at first sight of the rear admiral's elder daughter, had experienced the queer sensation of having been stricken by an unfamiliar affliction of the heart.

The duke, who gave every appearance of enjoying unusual robustness for a man looking forward to his eighty-third birthday, stood to give the toast for good health and long life to the new scion of his house. And it was to be noted by those present that there seemed not to be a single fly in the ointment of his contentedness.